BULL MOON RISING

RUBY DIXON

✳

BULL MOON RISING

ACE

New York

ACE
Published by Berkley
An imprint of Penguin Random House LLC
penguinrandomhouse.com

Copyright © 2024 by Ruby Dixon
Excerpt from *Ice Planet Barbarians* copyright © 2015, 2021 by Ruby Dixon
Penguin Random House supports copyright. Copyright fuels creativity, encourages
diverse voices, promotes free speech, and creates a vibrant culture. Thank you for
buying an authorized edition of this book and for complying with copyright laws
by not reproducing, scanning, or distributing any part of it in any form without
permission. You are supporting writers and allowing Penguin Random House to
continue to publish books for every reader.

ACE is a registered trademark and the A colophon is a trademark of
Penguin Random House LLC.

Library of Congress Cataloging-in-Publication Data
Names: Dixon, Ruby, 1976– author.
Title: Bull moon rising / Ruby Dixon.
Description: New York: Ace, 2024. | Series: Royal Artifactual Guild; 1
Identifiers: LCCN 2024004968 (print) | LCCN 2024004969 (ebook) |
ISBN 9780593817025 (hardcover) | ISBN 9780593817032 (ebook)
Subjects: LCGFT: Fantasy fiction. | Romance fiction. | Novels.
Classification: LCC PS3604.I965 B85 2024 (print) |
LCC PS3604.I965 (ebook) | DDC 813/.6—dc23/eng/20240206
LC record available at https://lccn.loc.gov/2024004968
LC ebook record available at https://lccn.loc.gov/2024004969

Printed in China
1   3   5   7   9   10   8   6   4   2

BOOK DESIGN BY KATY RIEGEL

For my husband.

Just 'cause.

CONTENT WARNING

ALTHOUGH THIS BOOK takes place in a fantasy setting, it deals with emotionally difficult topics, including claustrophobia, cave-ins, spiders, corpses, rats, grave robbing, parental neglect, financial insecurity, gambling addiction, alcoholism, unprotected sex, and rampant misogyny. Any readers who believe that such content may upset them or trigger traumatic memories are encouraged to consider their emotional well-being when deciding whether to read this book.

—*Ruby Dixon*

BULL MOON RISING

ONE

ASPETH

27 Days Before the Conquest Moon

THE COACH TAKING us to Vastwarren City is creaky, the seating is uncomfortable, and I paid far too much for the ride. But it's also very obviously an artifact, which is why I wanted to take it. The exterior looks the same as every other coach that was waiting on the street in front of the inn, but this one had no horse harnessed to the front, nor a yoke for it. Instead, there was a symbol carved into the wood that I recognized as Old Prellian.

The coachman charged a pretty penny but I didn't care. I wanted to ride in that damned artifact coach.

And now here we are, and it's a dreadful, bouncy ride. I can't help but eye the coach covetously anyhow. It speeds along the cobbled roads without a horse to draw it, heading for the city in the distance. The driver is a cheerful sort, too, and seated inside with us instead of riding on a bench atop the coach. He faces the windows and holds reins as if he's steering a horse, yet there's nothing pulling us along. More symbols in Old Prellian crawl over the front of the coach and I'm absolutely dying to lean forward and read them, but I'd have to shove my face into his lap to do so because my vision is so dreadful. I have to content myself with the knowledge that the coach is indeed magical and the merrily chatting coachman won't sell it. No one sells an artifact.

Well, no one except my foolish father.

I bite my cuticles, squinting out the window as the magic coach barrels past a field with a great deal of people standing in it. They dig at the dirt with shovels, and it looks as if there's a booth at the far end of the muddy land. A sign next to the booth reads in bright, colorful letters, DIG FOR ARTIFACTS! YOU FIND YOU KEEP!

"Does that work?" I blurt out to our driver as we pass by. "Does anyone truly find an artifact in the fields?"

The driver chuckles. "Oh, no, that's purely for the tourists. Everyone shows up with a few pennies and their spades, ready to turn their luck around. They all think they'll find the next automaton or Pitcher of Endless Wine. No one does, but they leave at the end of the day happy. I heard some of the more unscrupulous sorts take broken artifacts and bury them in the fields so people can find something." He shakes his head. "You're better off avoiding that sort of thing."

"But your coach is an artifact," I point out, ignoring the stomp of Gwenna's foot on mine. "How did you acquire it?"

He reaches out and pats the coach like it's a person. It might as well be. Any working artifact is more prized than gold. "A gift to an ancestor from the king. It's been in the family for generations. I'm lucky to have her."

"It's quite rare," I agree. "No one's tried to steal it from you?"

This time Gwenna pinches me.

"It'd be useless if they did," he tells me cheerfully, oblivious to my line of thought. "It dies at sunset and there's a magic word to make it activate at sunrise. That word is a carefully guarded secret in my family and we wouldn't share it, even upon pain of death."

I think perhaps this man just hasn't been pressed enough yet. Surely someone could coax a magic word out of him with the right sort of convincing. Then I'm disgusted at my own thoughts, because I'm imagining someone torturing a coach driver (who's been quite lovely, honestly) over his artifact.

It's just that the Honori family needs artifacts dreadfully. I debate how to approach my next question in a delicate manner, and all the while Gwenna stares at me with narrowed eyes. "I don't suppose you'd sell it?" I ask. "I'd make you a very wealthy man."

I'm lying, of course.

If I had two pennies to rub together, I wouldn't be fleeing Honori Hold. If I had two pennies to rub together, I would have married Barnabus Chatworth despite the fact that he's a title hunter. As it is, I am quite, *quite* broke . . . but that doesn't mean I can't try. If I could get the driver to sell this carriage to me, it wouldn't solve my problems, but it'd be a step in the right direction.

It'd be *something*.

"Oh, I can't do that," the coachman says, and I'm not surprised. "I inherited this girl from my father, and she'll be going to my son after me." He caresses the front of the coach again, like a lover. "I can't sell my family out for money when the money will come in simply because of the artifact."

"I understand." I still think someone could torture the word of power out of him, but I understand.

He glances at the back seat of the coach, where Gwenna huddles next to me, holding my cat's carrying sack. "Some things aren't for sale."

If they *were*, then my problems would be solved . . . or would they? Considering I have no money as well as no artifacts, I wouldn't know. "Indeed."

"So you ladies are heading into Vastwarren? This your first time in the city?"

"First time," I agree, glancing back at the dirt field as it disappears from view. I'm tempted to grab a spade and try my luck with all the others, just to see if one can truly find an artifact in all that mud. If there's even a chance, it's worth trying, isn't it? For a moment, I dream about shoveling a few spadefuls of dirt, just enough to put in a bit of effort, and then striking down upon metal. I'd pull it up and uncover a gilded, gleaming artifact. Not just any artifact, either. One with endless charges, just like the coach we're in right now. Or perhaps one of the ones that recharge in sunlight.

And it'd have to be something useful, too. Nothing like the glass candle that creates an endless wisp of rose-scented smoke. Something like one of the shielding crystals that are used in the capital would be perfect. Or something that creates a sought-after item from thin air, like the decanter that pours serpent venom. An artifact of war from Old Prell, that's what Honori Hold needs. Several of them, actually. We need defense, and a way to fund our hold.

And we need those artifacts to actually *work*. The ones currently filling our vault are all dead. A dead artifact is as useless as . . . well, as a holder heiress with no funds and no artifacts to defend her family's holdings. I bite back a sigh and lean my head against the window of the coach, watching as another family hurries toward the field with buckets and spades in tow, chattering excitedly.

Gwenna nudges me, and I realize the coach driver was talking to me.

"Mmm?" I inquire, straightening.

"You didn't say who you are and why you're heading to Vastwarren City. Attending a party of some kind?" The way he says it sounds hesitant, as if he doesn't understand why anyone would host a party in Vastwarren. The king avoids the place because it's said to be rough-and-tumble. That makes me a little nervous. When I envision "rough-and-tumble," I think of some of my father's stableboys and how they get loud after they've had a few drinks. But that's only a few stableboys. I cannot imagine an entire city of that. Leaning forward, I peer out the windows of the coach to the city in the distance. It looks like a great big stain spread over a hill, with the smog of a thousand chimneys polluting the air overhead. All of it looks dirty, but that doesn't mean it's unsafe . . .

Does it?

I've read a heap of books about Vastwarren City, but mostly in a historical context. I know all about how this spot on the plains between two rivers was once the hub of a large ancient city called Prell, and Prell was full of magic. The gods grew angry at the people of Prell and had it swallowed up by the ground, where it was forgotten for hundreds of years. Then, three hundred years ago, the Mancer Wars broke out. At the end of the conflict, magic was outlawed, and a new industry was started—artifact retrieval. Vastwarren City was built atop the bones of Old Prell.

Vastwarren is truly the only city that's not under holder rule. The rest of Mithas is divvied up into great estates lorded over by holders like my father, and all of the holders are ruled by the king. But Vastwarren? It's a place unto itself, and the Royal Artifactual Guild holds sway over it.

I don't know what the city looks like inside. I know Old Prell had grand plazas with magical fountains, and the inhabitants imbued everything they used with magic, from cups to horse carts to weapons. It sparkled with energy and the people there were rich and glorious . . . but the dirty stain on the horizon tells me that Vastwarren City is an entirely different sort of place, and so are its people.

The coach driver wants to know if we're attending a party, but he's just making conversation. Everyone knows that the nobility avoid Vastwarren and its hardscrabble, rough people. We stick to our isolated holds and to court.

But the driver doesn't know I'm noble, and he wants an answer. Might as well give him the truth. The *new* truth.

"My name is Sparrow," I tell him, and just saying the name fills me with pride. I straighten, squaring my shoulders. "And I'm heading to the city to join the Royal Artifactual Guild."

I expect him to make the appropriate awed noises that such a pronouncement deserves. Guild artificers are exciting, dangerous individuals, the ones stories are written about. They're respected everywhere they go, and every holder employs the best artificer teams to hunt for them. Everyone reveres an artificer.

Not our coach driver. Instead, he looks back at the two of us again and bursts into laughter.

Rude.

ONCE WE'RE DEPOSITED onto the outskirts of Vastwarren City with our baggage, Gwenna glares at me with anger before I can even take a good look at our surroundings. She pinches my arm, scowling the moment the coach lumbers away. "You absolute fibber! Why did you tell that man your name was Sparrow?"

Squeaker howls for attention in her carrier, the sound loud enough to make people pause in the busy street. I open the specialized satchel and heft the large orange cat into my arms. It's like hugging a sack of flour that sheds, but my pet is mollified once she's held in my arms like a baby. I run my fingers over her white chest fur while she purrs. Poor sweetheart. It's been a terrible ride from home. Bad enough that I had to spend the last three days in various coaches bouncing across the countryside. My poor Squeaker had to spend them in a bag. I couldn't leave her behind, though. She's all I've got.

Well, her and Gwenna.

I frown at my maid. "I'm not a fibber. I told you before. Everyone who joins the Royal Artifactual Guild takes on a bird name. It's to honor the first artificer, who was turned into a swan by a cursed artifact. Everyone in the guild is a bird, and the applicants are called fledglings. I've decided that I like the name Sparrow." I pause and then add, "I know this isn't your dream. It's not too late for you to go home. We can say you were kidnapped. Better yet, I can write you a lovely letter of recommendation that would get you hired at any hold. Just say the word."

Gwenna gives me a narrow-eyed stare. "Why are you chasing me off?"

I resist the urge to raise my fingers to my mouth so I can bite my cuticles. Grandmama thinks it's a disgusting habit—and it is—but I can't help myself. When I get anxious, I nip away. I scratch at them with my thumbnail instead. "I just . . . I appreciate your companionship, Gwenna. Truly I do. But this place isn't for proper ladies, and I don't want you to feel trapped into a fate not of your choosing."

She stares ahead at the bustling street in front of us. People of all kinds crowd the cobblestone ways, and all of them look like they come from the rougher parts of the city. Then again, perhaps *all* of Vastwarren is rough.

"Do you remember when I was nine and you were fourteen? We were girls and my mother had just been hired into your father's kitchens. We played in the garden together before your tutor came and found us. Remember what you said to him?" Gwenna asks.

I squint at her, because I don't recall this day at all. Most of my days as a child were spent sitting alone in Honori Hold with a tutor, because Father would be away at court. Sometimes it would be a mathematics tutor, sometimes an etiquette tutor. The best tutor was the one who encouraged my interests in Old Prell, and the worst was the one hired by Grandmama who wanted me to sew and "work on my laugh" so I could catch a husband. "I'm sorry, I don't recall. What did I say?"

She looks at the buildings around us, holding a hand to her eyes to shield them from the late-day sunlight. "You asked if I could take lessons with you. That you wanted a friend at your side and you liked me."

I smile softly, because I still don't remember, but it sounds like something I would have done. I was so lonely as a child that I was desperate for any sort of attention. "I don't recall. Did we take lessons together, then?"

"No." Her voice goes flat. "Your tutor said that I was a servant, and there was no point in educating someone destined for a kitchen. That educating me would be a waste." Her jaw hardens and she meets my eyes. "I remember that, and I remember the next day that a position was found for me in the scullery, and I had no choice but to say yes, because my mother needed the coin. I think about that all the time."

My mouth goes dry. "I'm sorry, Gwenna—"

"I'm not. His words made me angry." She sets her shoulders back. "It made me realize I wanted more than just a job. I want to learn. I want to be something. Someone. And I'm going to make my own path if it mucking kills me."

Her determined words send a thrill down my spine. "I love that. I'm so happy you're here."

She reaches for my hand and gives it a squeeze, and I hug her. Or at least, I try to hug her. But I'm juggling Squeaker, and she's got our bags, and it all turns into a mess. She pulls away with a puzzled frown and I pretend to pick lint off her sleeve instead. It's a shame, though. I do so love a good hug and they're so very rare. No one likes to hug a holder's daughter. "It's settled, then. I shall be 'Sparrow,' and you shall be 'Chickadee.'"

"By Hannai's tits I will," Gwenna declares, indignant. "That's a terrible name."

"Then you choose." I shrug. "We're assuming new identities starting today. I can't very well go around declaring myself as Lady Aspeth Honori, heiress to Honori Hold. That's just asking to get kidnapped and held for ransom."

And my father can't pay the ransom. At all. He can't even pay for his knights. I can only imagine the chaos that would ensue if our neighboring holds knew just how stretched thin Honori Hold truly is. A hold is considered only as strong as the land it protects, and Honori is the oldest holder family. We're thought to be strong with artifacts—undefeatable. If the truth came out, my family's hold would be overtaken by our enemies, our lands annexed to theirs, and our entire family would be executed. And while I'm beyond frustrated with Father for gambling away our last working artifacts, the people who live on Honori lands are blameless. They don't deserve whatever terrible fate is on its way for the hold.

It's the lord holder's responsibility to protect their people, and since my father cannot, it falls to me.

So no, I have to do this. When Father left for court to visit his mistress, the courtesan Liatta, I knew I had to act. I slunk out of the hold in the middle of the night, carrying a few bags with my possessions, and left a note to the staff explaining that I would be visiting my grandmother in the eastern hills.

In the meantime, I'll become an artificer myself, find an absolute hoard of artifacts, and replenish the Honori holdings.

Aspeth Honori was left behind on the dusty roads to Vastwarren City. Sparrow is who I am now.

Gwenna rents a luggage cart with a penny, dragging it after her. We load up the cart—or rather, she does while I juggle my cat. Then all of our gear is loaded and there's no reason to wait any longer.

"Come along, Chickadee," I say brightly. "The guild recruitment meeting isn't until the morning. Shall we find lodgings?"

"Not 'Chickadee,'" Gwenna protests, her hands going to her hips. "That sounds incredibly dumb."

"Then pick a bird. What's your favorite bird?"

"To eat? Turkey."

"Mmm, I don't think calling yourself 'Turkey' is a good idea, though I doubt it's taken." I purse my lips, thinking, and adjust my heavy cat in my arms. Good gods, she's shedding like a dandelion all over my dark traveling dress. I try to put Squeaker back into her satchel but she howls with anger and digs her nails into my arm, so I sigh and heft her onto my hip like a fat orange baby. "What about 'Blue Jay'? 'Robin'? 'Wren'?"

"How about I stay Gwenna for now?" She gives me an irritated look and picks up the handle to the luggage cart. "Guild first, bird name later. Lead the way, Lady Sparrow."

"Just Sparrow," I tell her brightly, and then breathe deep.

It's a mistake. Vastwarren City has a peculiar *smell* to it. It's a smell like a compost pile, along with unwashed bodies and a variety of other undelicious stinks. There's a cloud of smog hanging over the city, no doubt due to several thousand hearths working all at once. I cough, juggling my heavy cat, and then wish I hadn't laced my corset so tight this morning. "By the Lady. There's a real stench to this place."

"Smells like I rubbed the back of my ear," Gwenna agrees.

"That's disgusting." I pinch my nose shut with one hand, juggling Squeaker with the other. She's not *wrong*, though. There's a distinct, unwashed scent to everything that I've never experienced before. Honori Hold is austere and lightly populated and above all else, *clean*. Vastwarren City looked a little run-down from afar, but I had resolved to withhold judgment until I stood in its streets.

Now I'm standing there and, well . . . it's bad.

It's crowded. That's one of the first things I notice. Gwenna wrestles with the luggage cart while people flow around us in the street, giving us dirty looks for not moving with the foot traffic. I hug Squeaker a little closer, because if she runs away, I'll never find her again in this crowd. Not that this is a problem—the only thing Squeaker runs to is her food bowl. Vastwarren City is dirty, too. There's a layer of grime in the cobbled streets and there are potholes everywhere. The buildings—two and three stories tall—all look as if they're sagging and weather-beaten, and I don't see a single bit of greenery. Everything is gray and brown and drab and dirty and crowded. Rising above the clutter of buildings is a large wall around the heart of the city. Behind it, I see spires and tall, arching roofs.

That's where the guild will be. I just have to get through the rest of Vastwarren first.

I eye my surroundings with distaste. There are so many people—people of all kinds. There are the pale northerners from the mountains like myself, and the sun-kissed southerners from the coast. There are Taurians marching through the crowds, their sweeping horns threatening to take out the nearest awning if they walk too close to a building, and their hooves clop on the cobblestones. I even see a slitherskin darting amongst the crowd, small and quick, his portable home perched on his back. I want to stare but it doesn't seem polite. Honori Hold is high in the mountains, isolated by the landscape and our name. Honori is the oldest of holds, and we're expected to hold ourselves to a higher standard than the newer holds. We only consort with other families nearly as old, and even though I've traveled to many other holds while attending court and visiting allies, I've always been left with the women, supervised and stuck in a parlor somewhere, pretending to embroider. Most of the time I can't even bring a book, because Grandmama thinks no one will wish to marry a bookish woman and that's why I've remained unattached for so long despite the Honori name.

(Then again, Grandmama would have wanted me to marry Barnabus regardless of the fact that he was a title hunter. I would be fine with that if the title wasn't bankrupt. I'm just afraid of what would happen when he found out it is, and we've got no artifacts to boot.)

I once read a pamphlet that compared Vastwarren to an anthill built atop a graveyard, and now I can't unsee it. The houses perching up the slope that elevates Vastwarren City above the surrounding lands are all clustered together, sharing walls and overhanging roofs, and I get the impression that if one house were to fall, the entire city would crumble. The streets seem to wind around the city in a spiral, lined with more run-down buildings every step of the way. Everything seems to be made of wood and patchwork remnants of other old houses. Overhead, laundry lines hang between houses on opposite sides of the street, dripping water on passersby below.

Something wet drips on my face and I swipe at it in horror. I certainly *hope* that was from laundry.

"Where to now?" Gwenna hisses at me, her expression expectant. "Do you need to consult your pamphlets about the guild?"

No need—I have them memorized. For years, I've gathered every book I could find on the Royal Artifactual Guild. I have the memoirs of Sparkanos the Swan. I have three books written about Guild Master Magpie and her adventures. And every time the guild releases an informational pamphlet, I have one sent to me so I can pore over it. I know precisely the location of the guild headquarters. "The annual meeting is tomorrow. At that time, the doors will be opened for newcomers to find a master to apprentice to. Until then, I suppose we find a nearby inn for the night and bide our time." I smile brightly at her. "All according to plan."

"Is it?" Gwenna asks. "Is it *really*?"

"Do you have a better idea?"

She thinks for a moment and then sighs heavily. "I do not."

"Me, either. So come on." Squeaker howls at me and I adjust her on my hip once more. "Let's find ourselves a nice clean inn and tidy up."

"Oh, a *clean* inn?" she grumbles at me. "Are we leaving the city, then?"

"Very funny."

But I suspect she's correct, which is a little alarming. Vastwarren City *is* a dump.

Still, I knew that this place would be a little sketchy. No one comes to Vastwarren for the scenery. They're here because this is where all the great risk-takers live, after all. Men daring enough to brave the deep tunnels of the ruins of the Everbelow, seeking out the artifacts of the ancients and fighting off thieves and monsters. Teams of artifact hunters delving the ruins of Old Prell and then celebrating their discoveries in the legendary guild hall. Fighters forcing back hordes of ratlings. Of course the city's going to be a little frayed around the edges.

Quite, *quite* frayed, actually.

"Hey!" Gwenna's indignant screech interrupts my thoughts. "That's not yours!"

Turning around, I see Gwenna in a wrestling match with a strange man over one of my bags. The man snarls at my maid with a mouth full of yellowed teeth, and to my surprise, she snarls right back. He rips the case from her grip and then races away down the busy street, Gwenna chasing after him.

It's like when Cook feeds the fish in the moat the scraps after dinner, I realize. Several others turn to look at the cart, adrift in the middle of the street.

They're about to swarm in a feeding frenzy.

Too late I realize that the rich brocade dress I'm wearing is a terrible idea when one is trying to lie low. As another man in worn clothes surges toward the cart, I do the only thing I can think of—I fling myself on it and promptly sit on the pile.

Squeaker howls with indignation as she's jostled about, but the moment my rump hits the stack of suitcases, the onlookers seem to pause. The newcomer heading to steal another of my bags scowls and waves me off, heading in the opposite direction. My skirts (and let's be frank, my arse) are big enough to cover the smaller bags and I recline slightly, doing my best to cover my luggage with as much of my person as possible and snarl fiercely at anyone who comes near.

Maybe it's the sight of the enormous orange cat on my chest or the fact that a woman is sprawling atop a mountain of luggage, but no one else tries to steal one of my bags. Gwenna returns a short time later, panting and sweaty. She puts a hand to her bodice and gasps for air. "Bastard got away with it."

"Which bag was it?" I ask, worried. If I'm here without my sensible boots . . .

"Your jewelry." Her mouth is set in an angry line.

Oh. Well, that's all right, I suppose. Anything valuable was sold off the moment Father started to have gambling issues, and the thieves made off with a bunch of paste jewels and fakes, nothing more. Still, a well-made fake can bring in coin, and I had been hoping to sell them when we arrived. It limits what we can use for funds, but there are worse things that could have been stolen, like my books, or the outfit I've prepared for when I meet the Royal Artifactual Guild. Or Squeaker's favorite kibble, because she's a rather particular cat. "I managed to save the rest," I offer when she continues panting. "Thank you for trying."

She waves a hand in the air. "Didn't realize there were that many thieves here."

I didn't, either. Indeed, the entire city seems as if it's full of crooks and brigands now. Every man who passes looks like a potential thief, and whenever someone sidles too near to the cart, I stiffen in alarm. Gwenna grabs the handle of the cart and groans as she gives it a tug, with me still atop the baggage. "Milus's bones, Aspeth, what have you got under that dress? Rocks?"

"Think frocks, not rocks," I joke, keeping a bright smile on my face so Gwenna doesn't panic. I know she hates this trip already. I know she's afraid of how vulnerable we are now that we've left Father's hold. I could be kidnapped by another holder family for ransom. I could be set upon by thieves. I could be compromised in any number of ways a noble-woman is compromised. I could find myself dumped in the woods to the east and lost there forever. All of these things she's brought up multiple times during our journey here to Vastwarren City.

I've considered them all. I'm not stupid. I'm just completely out of options.

Gwenna's right that this place is unsavory and dangerous, but coming here is worth the risk. If anyone finds out that Honori Hold has nothing but a few dead artifacts and that my father's gambled the rest away? We'll be tossed out by rivals before a fortnight passes . . . and that's the best-case scenario. This is something I have to do.

As another passerby eyes the cart, I scowl at him and clutch Squeaker harder. The cat is squirming dreadfully, but I keep her tightly in hand. I know I'm heavier than Gwenna. My upbringing as a holder's daughter has been full of sweets and books and very little physical work, and it shows in the size of my derriere. "If you want to sit while I pull, we can switch."

"Don't be ridiculous," Gwenna says, jerking on the handle of the cart. "You're the lady and I'm the maid."

That makes me frown, because I've left the hold. I'm no longer a lady. I'm supposed to be Sparrow and she's supposed to be my equal and friend, Wren. We've *discussed* this. But the middle of a crowded street is not the time to argue, so I just hold my squirming cat harder. "Let's find an inn and get settled, shall we?"

We fight our way down two more streets (or rather, Gwenna does) before we come to an inn. There's a wooden sign hanging over the entrance with a mug of beer and a bed on the shingle. The smell of hot food wafts out the open door, along with laughter. Gwenna points at it, raising her eyebrows, and I nod. The moment we're over the threshold and out of the street, I leap off the cart, hand Squeaker to Gwenna, and then approach the bar.

"One room, please." I beam my most winning smile at the woman barkeep, who wipes the wood down with a rag that could quite possibly be filthier than the bar itself.

She pauses, eyeing Gwenna with my luggage. "For a lady and her maid?"

"For two friends," I say brightly. "We are bosom companions."

She blinks at me, then at Gwenna, and shrugs. "Whatever. Price is the same. Costs extra for the animal, though."

The innkeeper assures me that food will be sent up later, along with a basin of water for washing. She doesn't ask our names, but I offer that mine is Sparrow, which earns another bark of laughter. I'm starting to grow offended at how many people think that it's funny. Is Sparrow a common name for guild artificers? I should think "Raven" or "Peregrine" or even "Hawk" would be far more usual. But then we're settled (on the first floor, thank the five gods), and we've eaten. There's even some cooked chicken in a bowl for Squeaker, who makes greedy noises as she eats as if we've been starving her in a cruel and unjust manner.

We sit on the edge of the bed and, bowls in hand, eat our meal. I nibble on a small bite of stew, too exhausted to eat much. This is the first time I've traveled so far from home, and after days of anxiety and worry, we're finally here. I feel like collapsing into a heap, but I know the real work has only just begun. Tomorrow I must introduce myself to the Royal Artifactual Guild as a student of the arts and see where they assign me for schooling. Imagine. Schooling, and me at the ripe old spinster age of thirty.

Briefly, I think of Barnabus and his perfect red hair and gorgeous smile and my heart hurts. But only briefly. It's an improvement. He doesn't deserve any of my thoughts.

"So," Gwenna says at my side.

"Yes?"

"Am I sleeping on the floor?"

I put my spoon down in my bowl and give my head a shake, focusing on her. Gwenna has been at my side for three days now, traveling through the holder lands by night, taking coach after jostling coach through the mountains and back through the forests again, all without complaint.

Well, no more complaint than usual.

I'm *grateful* for her presence. She's slightly younger than me, twenty-five years to my thirty, and I like that she's bold about telling me what she thinks. She's been my maid ever since she was twelve, and I think of her as a friend. Come to think of it, she might be my *only* friend.

It makes the fact that she's here with me that much more meaningful. "You'll sleep in the bed, of course. We're in this together, and I'm determined that we consider ourselves equals, Gwenna. You're the only one I can trust, and it means everything to me that you're at my side. I know Vastwarren City isn't a dream of yours—"

She snorts, then takes a heaping bite of her stew.

"—but I appreciate that you're here, just the same."

"I'm here because you needed someone at your side," Gwenna grumbles. She stirs her food briskly with her utensil, staring at it and not at me. "And I can't very well be a lady's maid if there's no lady to serve, right?"

"You know I'd write you a very effusive letter of recommendation," I say gently. "Being in the Royal Artifactual Guild isn't for everyone. I know it's dirty, difficult work, and guild members spend much of their time in tunnels, digging through the dirt. I'm told that the training is difficult and long, and many don't make it through to the two-part test. I'll understand if you wish to leave. I'm sure I can sell something and you can take a coach back to Honori Hold. I bet we could find that nice man with the artifact coach, too. His wasn't too bad."

"I'm staying," Gwenna says, a stubborn look on her round face. Gwenna might be the only person more obstinate than I am, and I adore her for it. "But don't call me 'Chickadee.' It sounds ridiculous and . . ." She flaps a hand. "Too fussy. Too dainty."

"Fussy" and "dainty" suit neither of us. I'm tall and broad, with thick legs and a waistline that shows my enduring love for nibbles. I bite my cuticles and read books and wear spectacles. I'm not pretty. I'm bland. Gwenna is pretty, though. She's got a round, sweet face and thick black hair. She comes up to my shoulder, on the short side of things, but she's stout and strong and busty and could never be mistaken for a delicate creature. I like the name "Sparrow" because it suits me to blend in. A sparrow is a creature that strikes me as unfussed by the need for flashy feathers or intricate birdsong. A sparrow just does its job. That appeals to me.

"Not 'Chickadee,' then," I offer, though Gwenna really does look like a cute, plump chickadee to me. Even her no-nonsense bun of black hair looks like a chickadee's cap. "You decide on a name. Did you like the idea of being called 'Wren'?"

"Humph. Only wrens I know of nest in the hayloft and shit all over the barn."

"Well, then, it's the perfect name," I say brightly. "I come up with plans and you shit all over them."

We blink at each other, Gwenna staring at me in surprise. Then we both burst into laughter.

"'Wren' will do," Gwenna tells me, chuckling. "I won't remember it, just like I won't remember to call you 'Sparrow,' but it'll do."

I grin at her and take another bite of my food, glad that, whatever route this journey of mine will take, I'll have a friend at my side.

It isn't until much, much later, as I'm lying in bed and staring up at the ceiling as Gwenna snores next to me, that I think of my father. Has he returned from court yet? Or is he still in his mistress's bed? When he returns, will he even notice that I'm gone? That I haven't come down to dinner for many nights in a row? Will he inquire with the staff about my absence?

No, probably not.

The thought's a depressing one. I told everyone that I was visiting Grandmama at her Celen Hills manor, which will work until Grandmama sends one of her letters wanting to know why I haven't married yet and enumerating all the ways I've grown up into an unmarriageable spinster instead of the in-demand heiress I should be. She sends those sorts of letters about once a fortnight (Grandmama is nothing if not determined), and once one arrives, they'll realize I'm gone, but I figure it'll take a while, and by the time my disappearance is noted, I'll be enrolled as a guild fledgling and safe in Vastwarren City.

I picture the scene. Father will return home from court after being away for months. He'll brush past the staff like he always does, ignore the scrolls and letters full of notices from debt collectors. Instead, he'll retreat to his study for a drink and to relax. He'll go out riding for a few days, visit his tailor, get new clothes, and at some point, decide that he should check in on his heir. He'll invite me to dinner in the main hall—and it's always more of a demand than an invitation—and then sit as far away from me as possible at the long trestle table that spans the length of the enormous hall. At some point, he'll realize I'm not sitting opposite him.

Then, and only then, he'll realize I'm not in the hold. That I'm not waiting around for him to notice that I exist.

It would have been nice for someone to care that I'm gone, I think wistfully. After all, I'm the heir to Honori Hold. No one knows that we're broke and artifact-less except myself and Father and a few of our most trusted servants. A holder's daughter should be important.

Shouldn't someone care?

Anyone at *all*?

Squeaker makes a loud mrowr near my ear and paws at the blanket. Obediently, I lift it up, and she shoves her way under, curling up against my side. At least my cat loves me.

TWO

ASPETH

26 Days Before the Conquest Moon

THE NEXT MORNING, I read over the well-worn pamphlet yet again, just to make certain that I haven't missed anything. The Royal Artifactual Guild meets once a year, on the eve of Swansday, to say a prayer to the gods, to honor the king for his benevolence, and to update any rules of the guild itself. It's a time when artificers are officially promoted, artifacts are haggled over by holders, and those who wish to join the guild can pledge to a teacher, who will do their best to prepare their fledglings over the next year in order to take the certification test.

That's where I come in. I clutch the pamphlet to my chest and take a deep breath.

I'm ready. More than that, I *need* this. Artifacts would solve all of my family's problems. Two or three Greater Artifacts would settle us once more and give us safety. Several Lesser Artifacts would staunch the bleeding, and could hopefully be traded for a Greater, depending on how useful they are. Truly, I'm well-equipped for this job. I learned Old Prellian for amusement. I can read and speak three other languages in addition to the Prellian glyphs. I'm well educated and good with math.

They should be salivating over my skill set.

With another deep breath, I dress, casting off the last vestiges of Aspeth Honori, only child of Holder Corin Honori of the Far Reaches. Today I truly become Sparrow, applicant and fledgling to the Royal Artifactual Guild and general nobody. I pull on my underclothes, petticoats, and corset, cinching it up the front. Brown stockings go over my sensible boots. Over my head, I toss my least extravagant dress. It's made of a thick, sturdy brocade in a dull pattern, the skirts swishing at my ankles. Ties have been added to the skirts so they can be hiked up at the front for ease of walking or hiking—or tunneling, since Sparrow will be expected to venture into the dark and mysterious tunnels of the Everbelow. The bodice attached to this one is decorated with brown ribbon at the edges, all to convey a subtlety to my clothing. I lace myself up, the bodice bound at the front so I can dress myself instead of having a lady's maid do so.

Gwenna watches all of this from the bed, petting Squeaker's round head as she does. "You want help with that?"

"Sparrow dresses herself," I say, determined.

She rolls her eyes at me. "You're taking this too seriously. They're going to take one look at you and know you for a lady."

"They won't. I'm dressed like one of the common folk." I finish lacing my bodice and gaze down at myself, pleased. The sleeves are heavy and undecorated, with a button at the wrist, and I do them up, admiring the very drab pouf of fabric. Not even a bit of embroidery to liven things up. "Look at me. I'm wearing so much brown I can't possibly help but look common."

"No 'common' woman owns a gown in brocade, no matter the color." She swings her feet on the bed. "You want to swap clothing?"

I consider it, but Gwenna—Wren, I must remember, Wren!—is far shorter than I am. Her skirts would be practically indecent and she's got more in the bust than I do. "I shall be fine."

"Are you wearing your spectacles today? You haven't put them on."

"Absolutely not. Spectacles are a rich woman's accoutrement. I can't have them thinking that I don't need to join."

"Can't have that," Gwenna drawls. "Bad enough that you've got titties."

"Hush." I gaze down at said titties and they look rather prominent, thanks to the bodice I wear that's designed for exactly such an effect. That won't do. I unlace the top and do a bit of strategic tucking so I seem flatter, and then re-lace with a bit of give. "There. Better. And it's raining, so I shall take my umbrella."

She eyes me and then looks down at her own plain clothing, then shrugs. "So what do I need to know about the guild?"

"What do you mean?"

Gwenna purses her lips. "Like, am I supposed to know what they do other than tomb robbing? Who was the first tomb robber? How'd they manage a whole guild about tomb robbing?"

I sputter at her words. "'Tomb robbing'?! It's not tomb robbing! It's artifact retrieval."

"From tombs." She puts up a hand when I protest again. "I'm not judging, I'm just asking what I need to know so I can blend in and make it look like it's my lifelong dream to join the guild."

I want to protest more, because it's *not* about tomb robbing. True, some artifacts are found buried with people, but the reason behind the artifact retrievals is a noble one. Each one will be used to carefully further the power of the holders, enabling them to protect people and the lands. "What do you want to know?"

"How did it get started? The whole guild thing? It's because of the Mancer Wars, right?"

Nervous, I wonder how much I can sum up for her that she'll remember. There are three hundred years of storied and glorious Royal Artifactual Guild history, but I suppose she just needs the basics. "The Mancer Wars had shown everyone that personal magic—be it as a pyromancer, geomancer, or even necromancer—was unstable and corrupted the person using it. Because of the Mancer Wars, the king outlawed personal magic and established the holds amongst his lords. You know that part, yes?"

She nods. "And it was all three hundred years ago? Is that when Prell fell?"

I shake my head. "Old Prell was destroyed over a thousand years ago, long before the Mancer Wars. But after the Mancer Wars, without magic, people didn't know how to protect their holds. Wars broke out constantly and the lords of the holds were unhappy because they felt they didn't have enough power to hold on to their lands. A man called Spar-kanos was interested in ancient history, and he traveled to the ruins of Old Prell. Three hundred years ago it was simply a cattle pasture. He dug into the earth and pulled up an orb with a word of power on it, and brought it to the king. The nobles all wanted orbs of their own, and the ruins were overrun with thieves and vandals. Sparkanos and the king knew the flow of artifacts had to be controlled so it could be kept amongst the nobility. They walled off the caverns that led to the Ever-below and declared it owned by the Royal Artifactual Guild, and if any-one wished to hunt for artifacts to sell, they would have to join the guild. Understand?"

"I thought you were going to give me the shortened version." She winks at me. "That's a lot to remember."

It's because that is the shorter version. I'm skipping three hundred years of politics, guild maneuvering, discoveries, and holder power grabs. "All you need to know is that Old Prell went boom nearly a thousand years before the guild was created. All right?"

"Old Prell, really old." She lifts one finger and then another as she counts. "Guild came much later. Wait, when was Vastwarren built?"

"The city itself grew around the walled-off section of the Everbelow controlled by the guild. So the guild was here first, and Vastwarren came second."

"Oh, sure." Her expression tells me I'll probably have to go over it all again, but I've studied Old Prell and Vastwarren for years. I can't expect everyone else to know as much as me. She scratches at Squeaker's chin and glances up at me. "So when are we leaving?"

"You should stay here."

"What? Why? I thought we were joining together."

We are. Biting at my thumb's cuticle, I consider the situation. I would love for Gwenna to come with me, all told. I'm terrified, but if we leave our luggage and poor Squeaker unattended here at the inn, I suspect I'll never see either again. They're all I've got left, because if my father finds out I've run away, I'll be privately disowned. He won't make it public until he's got another heir lined up, and I'm hoping that I'll have my guild certification by then, and hopefully an artifact or two to bring to my family to restore our glory. If not . . .

With a lump of emotion in my throat, I grab Squeaker and haul her into my arms. Gwenna doesn't like to be hugged, so I lavish kisses on the cat, letting her lick my nose raw as I snuggle her. "I won't take long," I promise. "I need you to stay with Squeaker and guard our things. I'll find a teacher for both of us and return to collect you. Give the woman downstairs a penny and see if she doesn't have scraps of meat for the cat."

I kiss the cat a dozen times, until she's squirming against my chest and I can't put off leaving any longer. Then I set her down and try to hug Gwenna, since I've decided that I'm now a hugger. She waves me off, though. I might be a hugger now, but Gwenna is firmly *not*.

With my umbrella in hand, I head out of the inn and into the nasty streets of Vastwarren City. Today it's no longer as foul smelling, at least; the weather is washing the scent away. Unfortunately for me, it's creating quite a slog of mud, and even the raised cobbles in the center of the streets for walking upon are slick and filthy. My skirts, swishing at my heels, are still getting soaked and slapping against my stockings. I let this annoyance go on for one street, then another, and then I give up and duck into a dark alley and fasten the loops that hike my skirts up for tunneling. They now bunch up at my knees and I look a right fool, but I can walk with purpose.

With my umbrella over my head again, I stride back out into the street and squint at my surroundings. I need to find the main guild hall of the Royal Artifactual Guild, as that's where all of the artificer meetings are held.

It's just going to be damned difficult without my spectacles.

I'm nervous as I head through the crowded, filthy city on my own. It's not that anyone is threatening me—it's just that this is the first time in my life I've ever gone anywhere unaccompanied. I keep expecting to look over to a chaperone on my left, or a maid, or a guard. It's strange to walk alone. I feel exposed, vulnerable, and oddly lonely.

And damp. Very, very damp. The drizzle of rain is never-ending as I walk through Vastwarren, as if the gods themselves are spitting on my dreams.

The huddled buildings lining each street are so strange compared to Honori's tall stone walls and elegant architecture. Back home, there are not many windows in the hold, as it was originally built for defense, but

over time, my relatives have sought to beautify the place. If the room has
no natural light, gorgeous, artistic metal chandeliers hang from the ceiling. Rich tapestries and paintings adorn otherwise plain walls. Lush car-
pets ensure the stone floors are warm and inviting, and everything has a
look of elegance. Here, everything is haphazard, as if it were slapped
together overnight. The buildings sag against one another and I'm pretty
certain a few of them are made entirely of cast-off wood. There are no
tile roofs here—houses and shops are covered with battered tin or equally
battered wood. The impression is not of functionality but of "good
enough," and everything looks temporary.

Or at least, it does until you get to the heart of the city.

All roads in Vastwarren lead to the guild, because the city was built
up around the guild holdings. The guild's thick stone wall is visible from
a distance, making it easy to find—I just have to continue up to the top
of the anthill, so to speak, and head for that wall. Unlike the rest of the
city, it's impressive in its make, and taller than the tallest inn. As I approach, I can't help but think it reminds me of my family's holding, with
enormous, forbidding walls to protect the treasure inside.

By the time I find the entrance to the walled-off part of town that
belongs to the guild, I'm soaked. Once I pass through the impressive
gates, I'm lost in an entirely new maze of barracks and halls and libraries.
When I find the large, ostensibly gray building that must surely, *surely* be
the main guild hall, my clothes are heavy and dripping with water and
I've wandered over half of Vastwarren itself. I'm probably carrying all
the mud in my boots, too.

I'm in a dreadful mood by the time I see the statue of Sparkanos the
Swan, the first artificer. Triumph surges in me again, and I tilt my umbrella back, ignoring the fat drops of rain that spatter on my clothes as I
regard him. Sparkanos's statue wears a long cloak, the fabric swirling out
behind him as he clutches the Sphere of Reason under one arm, a sword
in the other. At the hem of his cloak, it looks as if the fabric is turning
into feathers, a nod to his curse. It's a powerful-looking statue, and one
I've read about and seen drawings of in books, but this is the first time
I've seen such a wonder in person. I'm utterly breathless at the sight.

To think that could be me someday, with a powerful artifact tucked under my arm, paving the way for others to bring our world out of darkness and back to the enlightenment of the ancients.

My mood lightens and I'm smiling as I race toward the long climb of stone steps that leads to the hall itself. It seems as if the entire city is here. There's a crowd on the steps despite the driving rain, and when I push my way forward with a few muttered apologies, I'm not surprised to see that the doors to the hall are wide open and even more people are crowded inside.

The hall looks exactly as I pictured it. Light streams in from outside through great windows strategically placed to highlight statues of the guild's most famous artificers. The room itself is three stories tall and longer than it is wide. High above, there are stuffed birds lining the walls, reminders that the guild chooses their namesakes. There's a long nave, much like in an old church, with a sodden brown carpet down the center of the room. People are squeezed in, and far ahead, at the front of the hall, I can see a banner and a dais.

The crowd is obnoxious, jostling to get inside the hall. A man nearby elbows me, knocking me into my neighbor . . . who promptly palms my backside. I let out a squeal of outrage, but when I snap my umbrella shut to strike my attacker, I can't tell who it is. There are several men smirking at me, dressed in fine coats and wearing hats, rain dripping off them.

An uneasy feeling starts in the pit of my gut and I wonder if I should have brought Gwenna after all. Now that I'm looking around, I don't see any other women.

In fact, I might be the only woman here.

That is . . . very interesting in a very alarming sort of way.

I draw myself up, my jaw clenched, and decide the only way to handle this is to be aggressive. I swat at men with my closed umbrella. "Step aside. I need to enter," I declare in a loud voice. "Move it! Coming through!"

There are a few grumbles, but the crowd continues to part, letting me in. I make it to the doors, and to my surprise, I'm standing behind one of the large, horned Taurians. There's another thing I never see at my father's hold—the strange bull-headed people from the plains.

Well, of course there are a few Taurians who are artificers. It makes sense, doesn't it? If a human can be an artificer, why not a Taurian? I decide to treat them like everyone else and give the man in front of me a smack on his thick arm with my umbrella handle. "Let me through!"

He growls low and angry in his throat, turning to glare at me, and the swivel of his horned head is so great that I let out a very undignified squeak and retreat, losing my balance. I stagger, arms flailing—

—only to be caught around the waist and saved by strong arms and the irritated, strange expression of another Taurian, this one with golden eyes.

THREE

HAWK

MY SKIN PRACTICALLY itches as more and more humans crowd into the main guild hall. It's recruitment day, so it shouldn't be surprising. Today's the day we try to find enough students to make a Five—a trained team for exploring the ruins. Only half of the people who are here will actually apply, but it feels like everyone in Vastwarren shows up to gawk at the normally closed-off guild buildings. It's like this every time, but this year it's particularly irksome because of the way the calendar falls.

"I hate the Conquest Moon," Raptor says at my side, his tail thrashing almost as wildly as mine. "Makes me want to come out of my skin. Or rip someone out of theirs."

I snort with amusement, because I know just what he means. Humans are blissfully unaware of such things, but Taurians are sensitive to the god Old Garesh, and the Conquest Moon is meaningful for every person with a drop of minotaur blood in their veins. Once every five years, the Blood Moon crosses over the White Moon, just as Old Garesh took to wife the queen of Old Prell. It's called the Conquest Moon amongst the Taurians, because the god conquered the queen's army and then kept her in his bed for five days. When she arose, she was pregnant with five sons.

And until the Conquest Moon passes, every Taurian is going to be agitated and on edge . . . or leaving the city entirely. Every Taurian female goes into heat, and every Taurian male is hit with the need to rut with abandon until the Conquest Moon passes.

It's not convenient.

If you have a wife, I'm sure it's fine. Fun, even.

But I don't have a wife. I don't even have a lover. My work in the tunnels takes up my days, and there's no time for a woman or a family. The only female I'm ever around is Magpie, and the thought of falling upon her in a rutting frenzy makes me shudder with horror. We're friends and business partners, but that's as far as it goes.

I scratch at the fur on my neck and try not to snarl when another hopeful scholar tries to push forward. Baring my teeth at him, I manage to keep myself in check—but just barely. The Conquest Moon is almost a month away and yet I'm already short-tempered and impatient. I'm going to be an absolute wreck by the time the moon gets here. "Timing is awful," I tell Raptor as the human moves past me with a quivering look. "I need to be here in the city."

"You'll murder someone and then rut their corpse if you stay here in the city," Raptor tells me with a smirk not even his nose ring can hide. "And then they'll lock you up and throw away the key."

He's not wrong, but he doesn't know the half of it. Magpie needs students . . . yet she can't be trusted to guide them on her own. If I count on her to pull things together, we'll find ourselves with two students (or *no* students) instead of the standard five, and then they'll quit because there's no way a team of two will pass, and then there will be no income for either of us, because Magpie will be booted from the teaching program. Magpie will spend all her time at the bars, getting laid out and moping about the past, and I'll find myself without a job.

I flex my magicked hand, the fingers aching despite the fact that they're not real. If Magpie doesn't get students, I'll never get out of my indentured contract. So I have to stay. Magpie can't be left to run things alone. "Can't leave," I say absently, flexing my hand again out of habit, just to make sure it's there. "I don't have a choice."

"I always forget," Raptor says, and there's a hint of sympathy in his hard voice. Raptor works on a Five for Lord Nostrum, with a constantly rotating roster. Lord Nostrum is cheap and also neglectful, and I'm pretty certain that Raptor only stays because he can sell some of the artifacts he pilfers on the black market. Everyone else realizes that Lord Nostrum is paying pennies and so his team constantly switches out, leaving Raptor to do all the work. Sometimes I think it's not about black-market sales, but just that Raptor would rather work alone than have to babysit the fools he's normally saddled with.

"You're leaving? Soon?" I ask, crossing my arms as another scholar pushes his way in out of the rain. It's well-known that Taurians make the humans nervous, and we know to stay at the fringes of the room or in the shadows. They can't do without us because we're far superior in the tunnels, but we also know when to make ourselves scarce. I remain in the doorway instead of pushing my way inside. It lets me see the entire vicinity while also letting me leave easily . . . or so I tell myself.

Raptor shifts on his hooves. "I shouldn't, but it's pretty bad this year. I keep waking up sweaty, and I can't sleep. It's either stay or spend my entire fee on whorehouses, and then another fee for the delousing I'll need after that."

I wince. If I don't leave Vastwarren for the Conquest Moon, *I'm* going to be the one in the whorehouses. I hate the thought. There's something cold and impersonal about having a stranger with you through your rutting. I had to utilize a sex worker last time, and it left me feeling vaguely unsettled. Took me months to feel like myself again. The whores do their job and don't discriminate between human men and Taurians, but it doesn't mean I like it.

Maybe I'm particular, but I'd rather be touched by familiar hands than a stranger's, no matter how eager the stranger.

But that's not looking like an option. Maybe I can slip away for a couple of weeks once Magpie has a team of fledglings established. Take the fastest coach I can—or find someone with a teleportation stone—and head for one of the Taurian festivals out in the plains to the south and just fuck everything moving for a week straight.

The odds of that happening fill me with a vague sense of despair, but I'm low on options. At least the Taurian festival is free. Any sex worker in Vastwarren City during the Conquest Moon is going to charge a premium. "I don't know what I'm going to do," I admit to Raptor, gazing out at the sea of people crowding into the benches in the hall. I turn back to my brother Taurian, considering. "I think—"

An umbrella comes out of nowhere and smacks Raptor on the arm. His eyes flare with anger and he turns so hard and so fast that the stranger—a woman—immediately stumbles into me, a mouselike squeak in her throat.

I automatically grab her and save her before she pitches to the floor. Perhaps it's all the years of practice with Magpie. My arm goes around a sturdy, corseted waist, and I haul the woman against me like a bride, because it's either that or dump her on the floor.

This isn't helping the latent heat pulsing through my veins. The Conquest Moon might be a month away, but I'm already feeling the effects.

The stranger's eyes go very wide and she takes in my features. I'd bet a handful of pennies that she's never seen a Taurian this close before—there's something about her demeanor that speaks of being sheltered. She gapes at me, at my bull-head and horns, at the jewelry on my ears and nose. I scowl in her direction, releasing her.

"Watch where you're going," I snap. "You could get trampled."

"It is rather crowded," she admits, straightening herself and then shaking out her umbrella, which causes water to rain all over me and a few others. "Oops. My apologies." Her gaze goes to me again, and then to my shirt. "Oh dear."

I look down. Soaked orange fur clings to my sleeve in clumps, transferred from her clothing.

"Sorry," she says quickly, plucking the clump I hold up out of my grasp. "That's from my cat. She's quite the shedder. Just ignore all that."

Raptor muffles a snort of amusement, looking at me over the woman's head as she continues to pat my arm, pulling off bits of wet fur from my linen sleeves. Maybe it's just the oncoming rut making my mind focus on all the wrong things, but I can't stop staring at her.

She's interesting, I think, in the way unexpected things are. Her cheeks are flushed pink, her clothing well-made if drab, and it's all soaked and clinging to what looks like a fine, plump, sturdy figure. She's tall, nearly coming to my chin. It's a fine height for a female, and the fact that she's built solidly makes me think about her in lascivious ways that are most definitely rut-influenced. Her face is human, so I don't know if she's what they would consider pretty or not, but her eyes are big and dark and expressive, and her fingers are blunt with short nails.

And busy. She has very busy fingers. If she pets my sleeve one more time, my cock is going to act up.

"Leave it be," I tell the drenched woman, and then because everyone in the hall is staring at her, I add helpfully, "You shouldn't be here."

It's the wrong thing to say. She stiffens, all softness leaving that face of hers. Her mouth flattens into a line of distaste and her head rears back. "Is that *so*?"

"You see any other women here?" Raptor joins in.

The woman turns to him, scowling, and for a moment, I think she's going to hit him with her umbrella again, and then I'll really have to step in. "This is the Royal Artifactual Guild's annual meeting, isn't it?"

"It is," says a nearby human man. "Are you lost?"

Her expression gets even more brittle, the color on her cheeks heightening. "Not at all. I'm here to join."

The woman's voice carries across the large chamber, and I'm not entirely surprised when all the men burst into laughter. They take one look at her—young, disheveled, female, and alone—and laugh as if they've seen nothing funnier.

"Where's your chaperone, love?" one of the men calls out.

"Go back home to Daddy," calls another.

More laughter rings out.

To her credit, the woman's expression only grows harder, more determined. "I fail to see what's so very amusing." She pulls out a soaked pamphlet from her bodice and shakes it open. "The bylaws state that anyone may join if they arrive by Swansday and present themselves as a fledgling." She looks up from her reading, scanning the room. "Is that not the case?"

The guild master approaches her, a short, elderly human with a very loudly colored vest and garishly expensive clothing. He gestures at the others, indicating they should pipe down, and moves to the woman's side. "My dear, my name is Rooster. I'm the head guild master in charge here. Please don't be alarmed. I'm sure this is all a misunderstanding."

"I'm glad we agree," she says, her chin lifting. Even though I find her annoying, I'm impressed at her bravado. "So where do I sign up?"

"I'm afraid it's not possible," Rooster continues. He holds a hand out to take the pamphlet from her, but she folds it and tucks it back into her dress. "It wouldn't be correct for a woman to join a team full of men, even for training purposes."

She looks down her nose at him, and Rooster only comes up to her chin, which I find rather amusing. Her shoulders are stiff and back, and she looks ready to go to war. "If that's your only concern, then you need not worry. My friend—who goes by the name Wren—will be joining me. We both wish to learn." She makes a benevolent gesture with her hand. "You may assign us anywhere. We are not choosy."

Raptor snorts, glancing over at me with amusement. It's not often these sorts of meetings are worth the time, and the entire crowd is now focused on the dripping woman in brown standing up to their leader.

Rooster still has that patronizing smile on his face—I've seen it many times directed at Taurians—and shakes his head. "Women do not join the Royal Artifactual Guild. Everyone knows this."

"Do they? Because I have read your pamphlet from back to front, and nothing is mentioned about gender in the slightest." She tilts her head at him, regarding him in that withering way that the holders seem to use. "Might I remind you that twenty years ago, Artificer Magpie located the greatest find of our generation? And every treatise and book I have read quite clearly shows Magpie to be a woman. So you see, *Cockerel*, you are mistaken."

If it's a slip of the tongue, it's a clever one. Rooster's florid face turns three different colors and he straightens his clothing. "My guild name is Rooster. And Artificer Magpie is different."

"In what way?" She waits, the tip of her umbrella dripping water on the floor, and holds on to the thing like a cane, her hands delicately perched upon the curved handle.

"She doesn't wear skirts," a man catcalls from the crowd, and they erupt into laughter again.

This doesn't faze the woman. "So if I take them off, you'll let me attend?"

More laughter floods the room, and Rooster looks as if he wants to choke someone. He fiddles with the ornate buttons on the front of his guild dress coat—a ridiculous concoction that no one who ever goes into a tunnel would wear—and adjusts his bejeweled sash, the material the deep gold color of the guild leader. "Madam, you are mistaken. It does not matter how you dress. Women have not proven themselves to be valuable members of our guild. Magpie was an aberration. She is *not* how we prefer to represent ourselves."

I grit my teeth, thinking of Magpie, who's no doubt curled up in a pool of her own vomit in her bed, reeking of spirits. No, I can't imagine that anyone thinks she's a good representation of the guild. Even so, they can't kick her out. As long as she's an active member, they're stuck with her. It's another reason why I can't leave for the Conquest Moon. If I abandon Magpie's side and word gets out that no one's teaching her students, she'll be removed from the guild for certain.

I'll definitely have to resort to sex workers, I realize, and the thought is as unappealing as it is impersonal. Raptor wouldn't understand how I feel, though. He's perfectly happy to share a bed with anything and anyone willing.

I can't let my guard down enough to do the same. My hand flexes again, phantom pain fizzling at my fingertips.

"But Artificer Magpie—" the woman is saying again.

Rooster clears his throat, shaking his head again. "I don't know what sorts of ideas you've gotten into your head about who we are and what we do, but I assure you that a job with the Royal Artifactual Guild is as difficult as it is dangerous. It's not a place for young women who cannot find a husband and think they can take on men's work."

"Excuse me!" Her nostrils flare with anger, her eyes narrowing, and for a moment she looks utterly magnificent in her ire. "Do you know who I *am*?"

That response—and the confident, almost arrogant way she carries herself—makes me wonder.

"I do not," Rooster declares. "Who are you? Tell us."

She pauses, and then her demeanor changes, losing its confidence. "My name is Sparrow."

The room erupts in laughter again. Even Raptor chuckles. I don't. I don't find any of this particularly funny.

"You haven't earned that name, love," another man calls out.

"Perhaps she's having a case of the vapors," yells another, and more laughter erupts from the room.

Rooster shakes his head again, both hands in the air to calm the onlookers. To most, he seems like a kindly, well-dressed leader, wearing finery that he's earned through his years of service to the guild. That he has a gut now just speaks to his leadership, that he's needed more for administration than actual ruin diving. "I understand your disappointment, my girl, but please understand. The guild's work is of an extremely dangerous nature. Many of our members do not make it ten years before retiring, or worse. Every year we lose good men. Every year, we are forced to retrieve competent men from the tunnels because it's too difficult."

Raptor coughs loudly, his hooped earrings jingling. It's a reminder—not that Rooster will realize it—that *he's* not the one rescuing men from the tunnels. That duty always falls to the Taurians. I can't count how many times I've been pulled from teaching duties or woken in the middle of the night to go on a retrieval party simply because some fool who barely passed his tests has decided that he can strike out on his own.

Taurians always clean up after the humans.

"It's nothing against you," Rooster continues. "It's your *gender.* A woman in the mix will make it unsafe for the entire team. They won't be able to focus with a woman around."

She grabs her umbrella in the middle and taps the hooked end of it on Rooster's coat like a teacher lecturing a child with her ruler. "You may write this down, *Cock.* My name is *Sparrow.* And you will hear from me again." With one last nudge of her umbrella at him, she turns, her chin in the air, and storms out of the room, heading toward the doors again.

Both Raptor and I step aside to let her pass, and the laughter follows her out of the hall.

Raptor shoots me an amused look, as if to say that he approves of her spirit. "I like her."

I don't. All that enthusiasm has nowhere to go, just like with Magpie, and I'm tired of seeing people broken by the system, myself included. My hand aches and I flex it again. It's a reminder that this very same system owns me until I've repaid my debt.

"It's Rooster," the man left on the floor yells after her with annoyance. He swipes at the wet spot left on his coat. "Rooster."

FOUR

ASPETH

I CRY ALL THE way back to the inn.

I hate crying. It feels helpless and pathetic, and it should be reserved for dire times in one's life. I cried over the death of my mother. I cried when I overheard my fiancé, Barnabus, speaking to one of his friends about me, complaining that he was being forced to marry an ugly spinster for her estate. I cried again when I found out that the estate is bankrupt and defenseless and the lives of every person at Honori Hold are in danger. That we could be conquered at any time, our people put to the sword.

I've done far too much crying lately.

But truly, what a pompous, arrogant little prick that Rooster fool is. If he'd known he was speaking with Aspeth Honori, Holder Honori's sole heir, he would have kissed my hem and cooed that he would do anything for me in the hopes of getting Holder Honori's commission . . . because he wouldn't know we are penniless. He wouldn't let me join the guild, of course, but at least he'd properly kiss my arse.

Instead, I had to swallow my pride and endure them all laughing at me because I'm a *woman*.

I knew it wasn't common for women to join, but they made it sound like it's forbidden. I know it's not. Just because they don't think a woman can do everything a man can doesn't make them right. It makes them absolute cretins and I'm even more determined to prove them wrong.

I *will* find a teacher.

I will pass that guild test. I will find artifacts and replenish my family's holdings and bring us back to greatness. And I will make sure that Rooster fool knows who I am.

My mouth screws up and I have to fight back a fresh onslaught of tears. I can handle this. I can. I knew it wouldn't be easy. I knew that joining the guild would be fraught with complications, but I hadn't anticipated that I'd be turned away the first day. I don't know what to do. I'm not going to give up, but that doesn't mean I know how to move forward.

I . . . need to hug my cat.

An hour later, I've returned to my rooms and am wearing a warm dressing gown, seated by the fire as I hold Squeaker tightly in my arms and let her lick my chin. "They were horrible, Gwenna. Just horrible." I fight back another watery sniff. "I didn't even get a chance to approach any of the guild members to speak my case. They don't know—or care!—that I can read Old Prellian. All they care is that I have . . . I have . . ."

"Tits," Gwenna declares. "I knew they'd hate tits."

"How can anyone hate tits?"

"They don't get to touch 'em," she says, shaking her head. "That makes them angry. To them we're nothing but things to grope with no brains in our heads."

I sigh heavily, feeling defeated. My sheltered life at Honori Hold hasn't prepared me for any of the challenges that Vastwarren City offers. I'm entirely out of my depth. I've always been respected and obeyed because of my holder name. Now that no one knows who I am or the family I come from, I'm finding the world very different and a great deal bleaker than I imagined. I bite at my thumb, my cuticles already nibbled to a painful level. "I don't know what to do, Gwenna."

"I do. We turn around and we leave. We go home and we figure something out. You marry some idiot for his fortune and we forget this nonsense."

She doesn't understand. Gwenna doesn't realize that Barnabus would likely get rid of me once he finds out my family has no artifactual value. That our hold has no defenses and the mystical renowned Honori faerie-fire cannons are dead, their charges expended. That our defense stones are depleted. We can't protect anyone or anything, and once that's discovered, everyone will attack us. Our neighbors, our friends, our enemies—they're going to realize we're weak and try to take over Honori Hold. If we're lucky, Father and Grandmama and I will be cast out. Unlucky? Someone will find what's left of us in the moat.

And she doesn't realize that it won't stop there. Anyone with any sort of connection to us will be either driven out or killed, simply so there will be no one contesting the new rulers.

I can't even approach the black market because Honori Hold is penniless. Our credit is gone and there's nothing to pay my father's debtors with. Father sold all of our valuable artifacts.

I haven't told Gwenna that Barnabus only wanted me for my family's holdings. That he's never been interested in kissing a spinster like me, and all the times I let him touch me, he was pretending. Even now, the thought makes me feel like vomiting. It's too shameful to bear. I know I'm not particularly pretty or charming, but finding out what Barnabus really thinks of me has made me feel ashamed. Like I'm some sort of disgusting creature that can only be tolerated because of the title I bring. I've tucked it all deep in my heart and kept it to myself. As far as Gwenna knows, we're low on artifacts and I'm here to find new ones for my family. My father's gambling problems are well-known by all the servants already, though I don't think they realize how vulnerable it's made all of us.

"I'm not leaving," I tell Gwenna softly. "I don't know what we're going to do, but we're not leaving. We're not giving up. Not after we've come this far."

"Mrrrrowr," Squeaker agrees. But she also just might want out of my clinging grasp.

Gwenna takes a deep breath and then jumps to her feet, pacing the room. "All right, then. We're not leaving. We're still going to join the guild. So if those twits won't let you in the front door to join the guild, how do we get in the side door? Who do we know that we can pull connections with?"

For a moment, I stare at her in awe. Of course we're not giving up. It's time to enact another plan. I'm humbled by her faith in me, and new tears threaten, but I blink them away. Just like Gwenna isn't a hugger (gods, I could really use a hug right now), she'd hate crying even more. And those horrible men aren't worth crying over. "I don't know," I admit. "I don't know what we do from here. Father no longer sponsors a guild Five because we haven't the funding. Even if he did, we couldn't approach them because I'm not supposed to be here."

"Right." She pauses, drumming her fingers on her crossed arms, thinking. "Well, perhaps we should find out where they drink and seduce our way into the school. A man with a tired cock can't refuse a woman anything she asks."

Seduction?

Me?

It's . . . not a bad plan. If she was suggesting this to anyone other than me, it'd be an excellent plan. As it is, I'm not sure I'm the right person for the job. "How am I supposed to seduce someone? Sit on them and recite Old Prellian poetry until they give in? I don't know the first thing about being appealing to men. The only experience I've had is with Barnabus."

And I can't trust any of it.

My cat twists in my arms, digging in her claws, and I let her go. Squeaker abandons me, leaving behind floating bits of fur in her wake, and I cough, waving a hand in the air to clear it.

"All right. Not seduction, then." Gwenna continues to pace, thinking. "But if we can find out where the guild men drink, perhaps we can bribe or trick one into getting us in."

"I'm not sure that's going to work," I tell her, uncertain. "They seemed pretty against women overall."

"Because they were in a group," she says, all confidence. "Men say very different things when they're alone with a woman."

This sounds suspiciously like seduction again. But I don't have any other plan, and I don't want to give up, so we might as well give it a try. Find a nice man at a bar. Talk to him. Get him to realize how much this

means to me and see if he can't persuade them to let me in. I don't have
the funds for bribery, but there are other things I can do. I can read and
translate. I know how to deal with holder nobility. I'm very good at etiquette. I have an excellent grasp of Old Prellian history.

And if nothing else seems to be effective, perhaps tits will work.

WE ARGUE OVER who will stay with the luggage and the cat. Gwenna
wants to go with me as I head out into Vastwarren City after dark, and I
would love for her to accompany me as well, but I also don't want to
abandon our things.

"Let's go downstairs and talk to the innkeeper," she suggests. "Maybe
she'll know something and we can go from there."

It's a good compromise, and a short time later, we're downstairs in
the raucous tavern room. There's a woman in the corner shouting a story
at a nearby man, a large mug of ale in her hand. Two other men
watch her with annoyance, and there looks to be a family tucked away at
a table in the corner, by the hearth. The room is dimly lit and smells of
smoke; the battered tables are greasy and look as if they haven't been
cleaned in years. Behind the bar, the innkeeper leans against a cask of
ale, talking to a man seated by himself at the bar. He looks . . . unsavory,
and I nudge Gwenna to make sure we keep a safe distance between us
and him.

We settle at the other end of the bar, near the door, and the woman
in the corner gets louder. "AND THEN I WALLOPED HIM," she
howls. "SHOULDA SEEN HIS FACE!"

I wince delicately and wait for someone to tell her to calm down, but
no one does. Perhaps this is a normal occurrence here. That's . . . worrying.

The innkeeper saunters over to us, and I'd swear she's wearing the
same clothing as yesterday, stains and all. She slaps at the counter with
her wet rag, and it's the same one, too, and smells awful. I swallow hard
and decide to breathe through my mouth.

"Y'hungry?" she asks us.

Oh, by the five gods, I don't think I'll eat anything in this place again. I try not to stare at the dishrag in horror. "We are seeking information—"

Gwenna puts her hand on mine, shaking her head. "What my friend here is trying to say is that we're looking for men. *Guild* men."

The barkeep eyes us as if we're fortune hunters. "Mm-hmm. I suppose it's that time of year."

What in the Lady's name does *that* mean? I open my mouth to protest, but Gwenna stomps on my foot. "Can you think of a better time to find a good man?" She beams at the woman. "Don't suppose you know where we might introduce ourselves to a few of them? See if they're lonely?"

See if they're *lonely*? Good gods.

The innkeeper shrugs. She swipes at the counter with that nasty rag again, sending a fresh wave of scent in our direction, and I press a finger under my nose as if it will make a difference. "You can ask the loud one in the corner," the woman says. "She'll know everyone at the guild. And if you get her out of my inn before she breaks something, I'll be mighty grateful."

I turn my head, craning to look at the woman in the corner with new interest. She's currently in a drinking contest with another man, both of them with their mugs tilted back and beer spilling down their faces. From what I can see of her, though, she looks to be about the same age as Gwenna and myself, though she's wearing a pair of trousers and a dark blouse that is about to be completely soaked.

"Thank you." Gwenna puts a penny on the counter and then grabs me by the arm, hauling me across the tavern room toward the carousing woman in the back. We march up to her table, and Gwenna speaks again, holding me against her. "'Scuse me, miss—"

The woman slams her near-empty mug down on the wooden tabletop, splashing us with the remnants of her beer. She looks over at us, then opens her mouth and gives the most unholy belch in all of history.

"That's very impressive," I say politely, since I'm not sure what else to say. "Good job."

"Nasty," Gwenna agrees, waving a hand in the air. "You the one who knows all the guild people?"

The woman shrugs. Her blond hair is wet around her face, and I suspect it's from beer and sweat. Tendrils hang over her eyes and I resist the urge to push them out of her way. She's younger than I originally assumed and can't be more than twenty, perhaps twenty-two. "Maybe. Who wants to know?"

"Me. I want to join the guild," I blurt out.

The man across from the blonde spews his beer out of his mouth, showering us with more booze, and then laughs as if it's the funniest thing he's ever heard.

I've had enough. I grab the drink from his hand and dump it over his head. "I don't think it's funny, you rockhead."

The room gets quiet, and then the blonde laughs even harder. "I like you," she declares. "Come and join our game." She gestures roughly at the man sitting across from her. "Get out of here, Jallus."

He gets up and leaves, and the woman pounds on the table, indicating we should sit across from her.

"Oh, I don't drink—"

Both she and Gwenna turn to me.

I know when to shut up. I smile brightly instead. "Very well. Game it is."

Gwenna and I squeeze onto the vacated bench across from the woman. I try to ignore the fact that my seat is wet, the table is, too, and I'm a little worried as the innkeeper comes over with three full mugs and drops them down in front of us.

"I'm Lark," our new friend announces. "But not like the bird, because I'm told I haven't earned it yet." She rolls her eyes. "So it's just . . . Lark. Like an adventure, I guess." She lowers her head to her beer and slurps the foam off the top, then licks her lips. "You two looking for a guild hangout?"

I nod eagerly. "Yes!"

"Because you want a guild man?" She wrinkles her nose. "They're arrogant pricks, but I guess if that's your thing—"

"I already said I want to *join* the guild."

"Oh, right." Lark holds up a finger and then lifts her beer, chugging it. She sets the mug down with a thump and I wait for her to blow our hair back with another staggering belch, but she only sniffs and eyes us. "So where are you ladies from?"

I blink, because I don't have a good answer. It didn't occur to me to lie, but telling the truth seems too obvious, like I'll be discovered for sure.

Gwenna steps on my foot under the table and takes control of the situation. "We're coming in from the north. Yourself?"

Lark brightens, and not only because a refill is brought to her. "I came in from the south. Left my troupe because it was about time I came to Vastwarren."

"Troupe?" I ask politely.

"Entertaining troupe. I was a sword juggler." She starts to get to her feet and knocks over the bench she was seated upon, then staggers.

Gwenna grabs her arm, giving me a panicked look. "We believe you! No need for a demonstration."

"Oh." She hiccups. "All right."

"So you must be good with a sword," I venture, tensing until she sits down again. "That's an excellent skill to have if you're looking to join the guild."

Lark grimaces. "Alas, the only skill I have with the sword is actually juggling it, and I don't think the ratlings would be much impressed with that."

"Ratlings? What's a ratling?" Gwenna asks. "This is the first I've heard of such a thing."

Oh, have I not told Gwenna about the dangers of our soon-to-be profession? "You know the tunnels below Vastwarren? The Everbelow?"

"The ruins, aye." Gwenna nods.

Lark leans in and mock-whispers, "They're totally crawling with these huge, oversized rats." She flings her arms out and stretches them as far as she can to indicate the size, then frowns and twists her body sideways, trying to indicate height. "That tall. Big. Nasty. Smelly. And they swarm."

The look Gwenna shoots me is one of alarm. "No one's ever mentioned ratlings to me."

"I'm sure they're not as common as they seem," I say, dismissing her fear. From what I've heard, cave-ins are far more likely. "But this is why everyone who joins the guild learns sword work."

"Mucking lovely," Gwenna mutters. "Human-sized rats."

"More like child-sized," Lark corrects. "Or slitherskin-sized." She lifts her beer and chugs it until she drains it, then pounds on her chest and lets out an unholy belch. "So you two wanna join the guild?"

"We've said that, yes." I give her a tactful smile, but it takes everything I have not to fan the air in front of my face to get rid of the burp smell.

"Three times," Gwenna adds helpfully. "Should you be drinking this much?"

Lark shrugs. "You're not drinking enough, if you ask me."

Because I want Lark to be happy with us, I lift my beer and take a sip. And then I cough. By Asteria, that is the *worst* flavor. It tastes like piss, a far cry from the expensive wines of my father's hold. But I smile between coughs and take another drink—or pretend to. Gwenna seems unbothered, taking a large swig and then swiping at her foamy lip.

"I went to the guild meeting this morning," I tell Lark. "Just like the guild pamphlets say to do. And before I could even sit down, they kicked me out. Said I didn't belong because I was a woman. That I'd be distracting to the others in the tunnels."

"Cocks," Lark swears viciously. "Cocks, all of them."

I'm a little startled by her vehemence, but Gwenna giggles and takes a larger drink of her beer. "I like her," she says, leaning over to me.

"I've met several, and they're all cocks," Lark continues, swiping my mug and taking a drink. She really is quite drunk, if her glassy eyes are any indication. "Specially the leader. He's the biggest cock of them all."

"Is his name Rooster?" I ask.

She pounds on the table and then points at me. "Yes! How did you know?"

"Because that's who I met." My heart sinks and I start to worry this is going to be all for nothing. Not that Lark isn't fun. Gwenna's having a great time, and Lark seems nice, if a little beer-happy. "He's the one who told me I couldn't join."

"That cock," Lark says again with a shake of her head. She waves at the innkeeper. "More beer for us! We've dealt with too many COCKS today." She shouts the word across the inn.

Gwenna just snort-giggles into her beer.

"I don't know what to do," I confess, my hands curling around my half-full mug of beer. "This was the plan—to show up and get accepted into the guild trainee program. I don't have the funds to bribe someone."

"Oh, that's easy," Lark says. "You can join my fledgling group. We need five and right now we've got four. The two of you join and that makes five!"

"That makes six," Gwenna corrects.

Lark squints at her.

Gwenna shakes her head and reaches over to pat Lark's hand. "Just keep drinking. So how do you know we can join your class if the guild leader said no?"

"And how is it you can join and you're a woman?" I protest. This doesn't seem fair. Lark's going to be a trainee?

Lark beams at the innkeeper when she arrives with three more mugs of beer. She pays the woman and hugs her beer to her chest, sighing happily. "I'm going to miss you," she tells it. "So, so much."

"Is it going somewhere?" I ask.

"Can't drink when you're a fledgling," she says, and then takes another hearty swig. "That's why I'm celebrating tonight."

"So you *are* a fledgling." Lark belches an affirmative, and I cover my nose with my sleeve. "How did you get in when they turned me away?"

"Oh, that's an easy one. It's my aunt's class and she promised my mother. I figure we won't be distracting all the cocks if we're a party of girls." She wiggles her eyebrows and then looks thoughtful. "Though there is a slitherskin in the class. Oh, and a man, actually. But once he finds out there's more women, I bet he leaves. He won't be able to stand the *shame* of us walking around with lady parts in his presence."

"Men do get weird around women," Gwenna agrees.

I'm about to agree, too, when I realize what Lark's just said. "Wait . . . you said it was your aunt's class? But only guild masters can teach. How is this possible? Magpie is the only woman in the current roster."

Lark swipes at her mouth and then beams at us. "Magpie's my aunt. She's gonna be my teacher. *Our* teacher."

Surely . . . surely I can't be that lucky? For the first time since arriving here in Vastwarren City, I feel a surge of excitement.

FIVE

HAWK

KNOWING MAGPIE AS I do, I shouldn't be surprised that someone pounds on the door in the middle of the night.

It's already been a particularly awful day today. Magpie didn't show up for fledgling day, being too drunk to crawl out of her bed, which left me to recruit a class of five. Given that I'm a minotaur, and humans are naturally afraid of anything that looks different or could destroy them with a single swipe, it was a spectacular failure.

I only had to recruit three, since Magpie has already given two seats away. One's for Lark, her headstrong niece, and the other is for a priestess of some kind. All Magpie would say is that she lost a bet, and I'm concerned the priestess is going to be as hard a drinker as Magpie is. But humans don't trust Taurians or even particularly like us. All I managed to recruit was a slitherskin who looks barely old enough to leave his family's hatching grounds, and a young merchant's son named Guillam who already looks as if he's going to bolt once he has a better offer.

Four isn't enough, though. Four won't qualify us to have a class of fledglings. We need five.

I should be out with the other guild Taurians, celebrating another year of business. A full class means the odds of a student passing are that much greater. Any student who completes the certification at the end of the year becomes a full-fledged guild member, and to pay back their training, they tithe a quarter of their earnings for the first five years. But I don't have enough students for this year, and last time Magpie was in charge of training, we had no one pass because she was in her cups more than she was out of them. If we don't get more students trained and working for the guild patrons, we won't have enough funds to live on. The thought runs circles in my head, making me pace.

I don't drink, though. Watching Magpie ruin herself with alcohol has killed that particular vice for me.

The pounding on the door gets louder, and I growl to myself as I throw on a pair of breeches, then storm down the hall to the entrance of the dormitory. If this is one of Magpie's drinking friends . . .

When I throw the door open, a snarl on my mouth, I'm ready to shove the idiot down the alley. It's not one of Magpie's drunken friends, though. It's her niece, Lark, who seems to be following in her aunt's footsteps. She's clearly drunk, her eyes red and slitted, a dopey expression on her face as she sees me. Her gaze roams over my bare chest and my unbelted pants, which are threatening to fall down my hips. "Damn."

"Shut up. I'm your teacher, and you should be in your room, not ogling my chest." I gesture up the stairs, angry at her carelessness. "Classes start at dawn."

"Classes don't start until we have five because five is the sacred number," she corrects, staggering in a step to get out of the rain. She belches, then waves a hand in front of her face and mine. "Whew. I'm ripe enough to scare the ratlings in the Everbelow. Glad you finally woke up. I've been knocking *forever.*"

"I should have left you out there," I growl.

"You wouldn't. You're too nice." She pats my bare arm, squeezes it just a little more than she should, and then weaves over to the bench by the door and flops down. "Nice and built. You should be glad I'm here, Hawk. I've got *solutions.*"

Not likely. "You don't tell a Taurian he's nice," I grumble. "You tell them that they're fearsome. As for you, you're an absolute tunneling *mess,* Lark. If you plan on going into the Everbelow, you need to be sober. . . ."

I trail off as two strangers step inside from out of the rain, wearing cloaks and carrying bags. One drags a muddy cart in after her, both of them dripping water and leaving a trail on the clean floors. The first stranger shakes off a hood, showing a round, displeased face as she glares at me and then her surroundings.

"What is this?" I ask—and then the second person removes their hood.

It's the woman from the recruitment meeting earlier. The tall, bossy one in brown who declared that she was going to be in the guild.

Oh, *bury me*. This cannot be happening.

"I *am* giving up the booze," Lark declares in a wobbly voice. She raises a hand in the air as if toasting, but holds no mug. "Tonight was a proper send-off. Goodbye, drink. I'll miss you dreadfully."

"You picked up a few strays," I say flatly, eyeing the two newcomers.

"I found more people for our class." Lark beams at me and then slumps over the bench, yawning.

"No, you didn't."

"Yes, I did. They're right there." Lark gestures at the women waiting nearby. "Can't you see them?"

Of course I see them. It's just that this is a spectacularly bad idea.

Eyeing the two dripping women standing in the doorway, I shake my head. "You can't just grab anyone off the street and make them fledglings, Lark. That's not how this works. It's a dangerous job."

The one from the meeting earlier—the one who called herself Sparrow—draws herself to her full height and gives me a haughty stare. "What makes you think we don't want to join? We know what we're getting into."

Lark chortles. "See?"

I cut her off with a wave of my hand, staring down the stranger. Bad enough that Magpie already has a priestess and a slitherskin and her niece. We're already not being taken seriously because Magpie's a drunk and I'm a Taurian. Two women and a slitherskin is just going to add fuel to the fire, but Magpie's made promises and I've no choice except to keep them. Might as well lump all our problems into one group and realize we're wasting our time.

Every year, something like this happens. Magpie takes in the dregs and then none of them pass the guild tests after months of hard work. I then chastise her for her carelessness and she agrees that I'm right, promises to change, and then spends her days sucking on the nearest bottle of alcohol. The moment students arrive again, she takes in more dregs. Rinse and repeat.

I'm a good teacher, but I need students who give a damn, and Magpie doesn't seem to recruit those. She picks the rebels, the wastrels, the misfits—anything that speaks to her. If she was sober for longer than an hour a day, we could probably make it work between the two of us. As it is . . . not so much.

But to add this woman who's already made herself notorious? That's just begging for problems. "We've only got room for one more in the class, not both of you."

If I put this "Sparrow" in our class, they're going to laugh Magpie right out of the guild halls.

"They're both joining," Lark says, oblivious to my train of thought. "Her and Gwenna."

"No, they're not. Five's the sacred number, remember?" I gesture at the door, indicating that the two women should turn around and head back out into the night. "You've wasted your time, both of you. Magpie won't be having a class this year."

It seems the wisest decision. Magpie's in no state to teach, and if she's not got enough for a class, I can cry off. Lark won't be offended for long. She'll find another job with a traveling troupe. The priestess that Mags owes money to will just have to deal with it. The slitherskin can find another teacher, as can Guillam.

As for me . . .

I'll just have to take on odd jobs until the annual guild fees are paid. I can run as a substitute in a group that needs five but is missing a member, or do rescue runs. We sure as shit can't send Magpie into the tunnels. We've been in worse situations as business partners, Mags and I. And I hate to say it, because Mags is the one who gave me a chance all those years ago, but maybe it's time for me to move on, too.

I immediately squash that thought. If I leave, Magpie has no one but Lark, and they certainly wouldn't be a good influence on each other. I have to stay.

And then I think of the Conquest Moon and my frustration mounts. Why is it that bad luck has to come in a chain? Why can't it be strung out between phases of pleasant monotony? As it is, all this bad luck is a cascade threatening to bury us.

"You can take both of us," the tall woman says, her expression as stony as mine. "I've done a great deal of reading on fledgling classes. Teachers have taken on additional students in the past, but only five can be sent for testing. You can teach us all, and the best five will be tested at the end of the year, correct?"

"Are you spouting guild law at *me*?" I glare at her as mightily as I can, tired and annoyed. If it were any other person and any other situation, I might be amused at the woman's bravado. As it is, I'm frustrated with Magpie and her reckless niece, and irritated that I'm being lectured by a stranger. "You want another guild law? How about the one where women can't join the guild—"

"Oh, don't start that again," the woman snaps, interrupting.

"—without a chaperone's permission?" I finish.

The woman's jaw drops, and pink blooms on her cheeks.

I think I've finally silenced her. Maybe now I can go back to sleep.

"Are we done here?" I ask, my arms crossed over my chest. I eye the two newcomers and then turn to glare at Lark. "I don't know what sort of drunken idea you've all gotten in your heads, but this isn't happening. You can just—"

"How does one get a chaperone?" the woman in brown says suddenly.

"What?" I scowl in her direction.

She gestures at me with her hand, indicating that I should continue. "You said we need a chaperone to give us permission. Are there specifics on the chaperone? Does the chaperone need to produce a letter of some kind?"

They're truly going to debate this? My glare deepens.

Lark speaks up. "Magpie's my chaperone!"

The round-faced shorter woman points at the bossy tall one in brown. "She's my chaperone."

"Very well, then," the tall one says, smoothing a hand down the front of her soaked bodice. She lifts her chin as if she's the queen herself and gives me a steady look. "I'm the only one who needs a chaperone, then. May we speak privately, you and I?"

I should say no. I should absolutely say no. Something in her manner tells me that she thinks she has the upper hand, and though I'm curious, I also sense a very bad idea in the works. I hesitate, and then think of the spectacle she made of herself earlier in the guild hall. "No."

She ignores me as if I haven't spoken. Instead, her gaze goes to the open door of my quarters. "Is this your sitting room?" she asks, striding toward it. "We can talk in private there."

And before I realize what she's doing, she's heading straight into my bedroom. Me, a minotaur.

A minotaur on the brink of the Conquest Moon. Is she . . . insane?

SIX

ASPETH

M Y DEFIANT SAUNTER into the sitting room is going perfectly well until I run into the corner of a bed.

I'm not in a sitting room at all, but in the Taurian's bedroom. Oh. Well, this is *embarrassing*. This is also what I get for not wearing my spectacles, but I didn't want him to turn us away on the off chance that he thinks my vision is going to be a liability. Plus, he'd see me as a rich lady, and I can't have that.

I'm far more talented than just a pair of blurry eyes would attest anyhow. I just need to have time for the guild to realize that.

So I act as if nothing is wrong. I pat the edge of the bed frame and confidently turn in the shadowy room. As if I always planned on confronting a half-naked Taurian right next to his bed . . . in private. Naturally. I clear my throat as he stalks toward me, a reddish-brown blur with a glint of gold at the nose. I wish I had my spectacles on, because I'm dying to see just what he looks like. If his chest is as hard and muscled as it seems, and if his nose truly looks like a bull's nose or if it's exaggerated by stories. His face is long and he's got horns, but the shadows and my poor vision hide the rest from me.

"What do you think you're doing?" he asks in a low, deadly voice, moving to stand right in front of me, a handspan away.

And then I can see everything with clarity, because our noses are practically touching. I can see the golden, strangely human eyes. The long, blunted nose that ends in a golden ring. The horns that sweep up from a proud forehead. The sheer height of him as he towers over me. He is completely and utterly alien-looking, and I want to just stare and stare like the sheltered holder's daughter I am.

I swallow hard. "I wished to speak to you in private."

He quirks an eyebrow, and it is astonishing to me to realize that he in fact does have eyebrows. They're slightly darker than the rest of his face . . . fur, but the expression is the same. He thinks I'm ridiculous.

It puts me on familiar territory. I square my shoulders and give him a challenging look. "I want us to come to some sort of agreement, you and I. You help Magpie teach her fledglings, yes? I wish to become one of those fledglings. I'm certain we can agree on terms. Just name them. Tell me your price."

He eyes me up and down, his lower lip curling slightly. It somehow looks even more insulting on a Taurian, that expression. "You don't have any coin."

"You don't know that."

"If you did, you wouldn't have walked here in the rain. You'd have taken a coach." He reaches out and flicks one of my dripping, deflated puffed sleeves.

Oh. Well, he's correct, but I don't intend on letting that stop me. "I can find the funds—"

An angry howl erupts from the hallway. The Taurian immediately turns, pushing me behind him. "What in the gods' name is that?"

I grimace. "That's my cat. I'm afraid it's past her feeding time and she's quite angry about it." Count on Squeaker to have terrible timing. "I have food for her, though. It shouldn't be a problem and she won't wake the other residents."

He turns to give me an incredulous look. "You brought a cat . . . ?"

"Well, yes. The pamphlets I read stated that students of the guild stay in their mentor's nest—that's their lodgings—for the duration of training. This is Magpie's nest, is it not? It looks like guild housing—"

"I know what a nest is," he interrupts, waving a hand at me. "You're not going to be a student here."

"Why not? Magpie is the greatest of her generation and a woman. Of course I want to learn from her."

The Taurian stares at me. Hard. "Look. You seem determined, and while you're getting on my last nerve, I am going to offer you a word of advice. You don't want this nest. We're a mess. Magpie's not the right teacher, and that means everything falls to me. Taurians aren't respected by the rest of the guild, and so if you're looking to prove yourself, I'm not the right teacher for you. In addition, the class is going to fall to pieces in the next month. You're better off looking elsewhere."

His words make me flinch, because they have the ring of truth to them. It would be better for me all around if I was accepted by the most venerable teacher the guild has, and it sounds like Magpie isn't that teacher. It's incredibly disappointing, and yet . . . now I'm curious. "Why is the class going to fall apart in the next month?"

He gives me a hard-eyed stare. "Because I'll be teaching."

I wait for clarification.

When none is forthcoming, I prompt him again. "Why are you falling apart in the next month?"

He shifts his feet, and I hear the creak of the floorboards under his hooves. His hands go to his hips and he leans in closer, and I catch the faint scent of . . . leather? Surely not. But whatever it is, it's a good, earthy smell. I'm so distracted by the pleasant scent of him and his nearness that I almost miss his words.

"Don't you know anything about Taurians?"

I blink, meeting his gaze. "Should I?"

"You're the one who touts her guild knowledge all the time. You tell me." He gestures at me with one impatient hand.

"To be honest, Taurians aren't mentioned much in the books and pamphlets I've read."

He snorts with annoyance. "Of course not."

"So why is it you're falling apart in the next month again?" I prompt. My thoughts are racing. Maybe that month will buy me time. Maybe I can convince another teacher to take me on if this one doesn't plan on instructing for the full year. Maybe—

"I can't speak of it," he says, voice gruff. "You're obviously educated, which means your family is wealthy. I don't want some merchant coming to turn me into a saddle because I told his innocent daughter filthy things."

My face grows hot and a forbidden little thrill zings through me at the thought of *learning* filthy things. The more he dances around this subject, the more I want to know what it is that happens in the next month. "I will have you know I am not a merchant's daughter nor am I innocent. I am thirty and a spinster. You can tell me everything."

Please, do tell me everything.

He runs a hand down his long muzzle and then tugs at the ring at his nostrils in a gesture that has to be pure annoyance. His hooves shift again, the floorboards creaking once more under his agitation. "I am a Taurian about to be surrounded by women on the eve of the Conquest Moon."

"And . . . ?"

I could swear his eyes grow wider. "Woman, how do you think Taurians procreate?"

My face feels scorchingly hot. Truth be told, what I know of procreation was learned from lurid novels that use words like *waves of ecstasy* and *spellbinding pleasure* and not much else. I bluster my way through it with confidence, as I do with everything in life. "I expect Taurians procreate about the same as everyone else, ahem, procreates."

"We go into heat." His voice is flat. "We *rut*."

Oh my goodness. My tongue feels glued to the roof of my mouth and I stare up at him in fascinated horror.

"Every five years, all Taurians go into season at the Conquest Moon. Our lives become about sex. About fucking. About taking a mate. About holding her down and pushing—" He lifts his hands as if grabbing some unseen female and then just as quickly stops himself, recovering. "You get the idea."

I'm still lost in the word *rut*. I stare up at him, imagining him looming over me and holding me down and then just . . . waves of ecstasy, I suppose. Heat is curling through my body in the most delicious way, though, and I feel I'm missing a key component as to why this is so very terrible. "And your wife, she won't like that you have a class full of women when you're in this moon rut?"

He paces away, and I catch a glimpse of a lashing tail before he stomps back to me, all frustration and intense eyes. "I don't *have* a wife. That's the problem. I don't have an outlet for . . . that *time*. Now do you understand why this won't work? You need a teacher and I'm going to be absolutely useless."

"And Magpie—?"

The Taurian shakes his head. "Won't be available to teach. Unless you're asking if I'd rut with her and . . . no. Just no." He shudders. "Now do you understand?"

"So . . . you need a wife," I repeat slowly. "Because of this unfortunately timed moon."

He huffs a frustrated laugh. "Sure, aye, a wife. I just need a willing woman, but a wife would be ideal."

"This is perfect," I tell him, thoughts racing with excitement. "You said I needed a chaperone, right? What better chaperone than my own husband? We can marry and solve both of our problems!"

The look on his face becomes utterly aghast, as if I've stepped into a pile of excrement. "You can't be serious."

I'm a little stung at his reaction. "I happen to be very serious. I need a husband and you need a bed partner. We can fulfill both of our needs." I pause, raising a finger. "Does there have to be a baby? I'm afraid that would curtail my career as a guild artificer."

"No baby. Just rutting." He runs a big hand down his snout again and then meets my gaze. "You're not seriously offering to have sex with me just to get into the guild school?"

Why is he so shocked? I'm a holder's daughter. I've grown up with the realization that sex and marriage would be transactional for me regardless. That I wouldn't be able to marry whom I chose, and it certainly wouldn't be for love. That's why Barnabus's betrayal was so devastating. I thought I'd truly lucked out and fallen in love.

The esteemed Barnabus Chatworth would be appalled that I'd gone and married a Taurian, which truly makes the idea all the sweeter. That I've married a common guild employee and not some titled holder or even wealthy man.

But this Taurian doesn't know that I'm a holder's daughter. He probably thinks I've been dreaming of love all this time. "If having sex with you gets me into the guild apprenticing halls, I am all for it, sir."

That strange shaggy eyebrow of his goes up again, and then he looms over me once more. Perhaps it's a Taurian thing to try to use height to intimidate, but I refuse to back down. We stare at each other, practically nose to nose, and I keep my gaze steady despite the flutter of my heart.

"What if I told you to get into my bed right now?" he asks in a low, deadly voice.

"I'd tell you to get me a marriage certificate first," I retort.

He rears back and barks a laugh, shaking his head at me. "I don't understand you. Aren't you afraid?"

"Afraid of what?"

"Marrying a stranger. Marrying a Taurian. Tying yourself to someone you just met."

"I am thirty," I point out. "I am also, as you guessed, poor. I am not a particular beauty. What options do you think I have in this world?" I don't mention the whole holder's-daughter thing because I suspect he would simply try to ransom me back to my father—or send me back to the hold immediately—and neither suits my purposes. I shake my head at him, doing my best to seem like the embittered spinster I'm trying to be. "This is my one chance to make something of myself. I'm not going to let anything stand in my way. If it means a sham marriage, then that's what it means. People have gotten married for less practical reasons." I give him a bright smile. "And if we don't find ourselves compatible, we can always divorce."

"Not until after the Conquest Moon we can't."

"Not until after that, no."

"Divorce is also a stain on a woman's reputation."

"So is being penniless, old, and ugly. I'll take my chances."

He huffs again. "You're not ugly. You *are* insane. And no, this isn't going to work."

I fight the urge to preen at the haphazard compliment. "You said yourself you don't have a wife. You said the class is going to fall apart without you. I need a chaperone and to enter the guild as an apprentice. Why can't we help each other? I'm not going to be emotional about my virtue, and you shouldn't be. You have something I need. I have something you need." I try not to blush and fail. "Let us be sensible about this."

"You're telling *me* to be sensible?"

"I am. Do you find me repugnant? Is that the problem? I realize I'm no great beauty." Am I fishing for another compliment from a half-naked Taurian in the middle of the night when I should be focusing on my plan? Absolutely.

The Taurian gives me a narrow-eyed stare. "What's your name again?"

"Sparrow. What's yours?"

"Hawk. A name I've earned. You haven't earned yours yet. What's your real name?"

Hawk. Of course it's Hawk. It's a strong, respectable, dangerous guild name. I should have guessed. I keep my chin lifted despite his dismissive tone. "Why do you need my real name?"

A hint of a smile graces his strange mouth. "If we're marrying, I need to know what to call you."

My heart flutters in my chest. Oh. I mentally race, trying to think of a good fake name and come up blank. "Aspeth," I blurt out, and then because it's not common and he might have heard of me, I add, "Like the holder's daughter. No relation, though! And everyone shortens the name. You can, too."

Oh, by the goddess, now I'm babbling to cover up my lie.

He gives me a strange look. "What am I supposed to shorten Aspeth to? Ass?"

"*Rude.* You can call me . . . Peth." Gods, even that sounds ridiculous. I tense, waiting for him to call me out. Waiting for him to point out that I also happen to be thirty and unmarried, just like the holder's daughter.

But all he says is "You're sure?" When I nod, he leans in. "If you leave me high and dry on the Conquest Moon after all of this maneuvering, I'm going to hunt you down, *Aspeth.*"

"No one is going to be dry at all on the Conquest Moon," I say merrily. "No dryness. Just conquesting! Or whatever it is you'd like to do."

Strangely enough, his nostrils flare and he gives me another long, searching look. "Gods help us both. I think I'm an idiot for saying yes."

I smile, pleased that I've gotten my way. I'm sure the moon-induced rut will be distracting, but easily handled. What's important is that I now have a teacher and a place as an apprentice. Nothing's going to stop me now.

SEVEN

ASPETH

I'M TRYING NOT to be smug as he guides me out of his bedroom. Getting him to agree to let me into the fledgling ranks was surprisingly easy. A hand in marriage? A virtue I don't plan on using? Child's play.

I'll think about the implications of it later. For now, I just feel as if I can breathe for the first time since arriving here in Vastwarren. I'm going to join the guild. I'm not going to be sent home. Everything will be fine.

"You're both determined to do this?" Hawk asks as I rejoin Gwenna in the hall. "Can't talk you out of it?"

"Not me," I say automatically, and try not to stare too hard at Gwenna. If she abandons me at this point, I won't blame her, but . . . I'll also miss her terribly. Having her at my side is the only thing that's kept me from having a nervous breakdown as one obstacle after another presented itself.

"I'm staying at Sparrow's side," my former maid says, lifting her chin. "I'm not going anywhere."

I beam at her. "We're going to have so much fun—"

"This is not about fun," the Taurian snarls at me. "If you're expecting 'fun' out of this, then you might as well turn around right now and march out that door."

Gwenna and I exchange grimaces at his sour attitude. Sheesh.

"This is a dangerous job, and that's why apprenticing is so important. If you aren't going to take this seriously—" He pauses, glancing around. "Where in the five hells did Lark go?"

"Got pukey," Gwenna explains. "She headed off to find the latrine."

Hawk sighs heavily, then rubs a hand down his long brown snout. I want to stare at him in fascination, because I've never spent so much time around a Taurian before, but it seems rude. I guess I can stare at him after we get married.

Goodness. We're going to be *married*. The thought strikes me as absurd and bizarre at the same time. If he finds out I'm a holder's heir, he's going to send me back to my father—or blackmail me for funds or artifacts I don't have. It's imperative he never know.

"Fine. Whatever," Hawk says after a long moment. "I'll show you to your quarters. Follow me before I change my mind."

And then he gives me a long, meaningful look.

"Wonderful," I chirp. "Thank you."

We pause and I gaze at my surroundings, thrilled. I've tried to picture what the nests—the dorms the fledglings live in until they get official guild housing of their own—are like. It's dark and I don't have my spectacles, but the place seems cozy enough. There are creaky wooden floors under my feet, and there's a draft coming in from somewhere. A large fireplace at the entrance has a pair of chairs near it, and on the landing of the stairs there's a painting that I can't make out. Upstairs, I imagine, is where the students stay. Overall, it's a bit ramshackle, but that just adds to the charm.

Gwenna tugs on the cart in the doorway. Before she can drag it in farther, the Taurian lets out a heavy sigh, moves toward her, and grabs the entire thing, holding it against his chest as if it weighs nothing at all. It's a display of strength more than it is of politeness, and I'm unnerved as he heads up the stairs.

Gwenna is, too. She shoots me a suspicious look as I grab Squeaker's carrier and tuck it under my arm. "Change his mind about what? What's he talking about?"

"He's going to be my chaperone," I whisper brightly. "So I can join the guild apprentice ranks."

"And how did you manage that?"

"I'll explain later."

The look she gives me is openly skeptical, but I keep smiling. I follow behind the Taurian as he stomps up the stairs, his hooves making sharp, echoing raps on the wood. He moves to the door farthest down the narrow hall and throws it open, revealing a small room with a single bed, a ragged rug on the floor, and a trunk at the foot of the bed. "Quarters" is all he says.

"Delightful," I say, and I mean it. This is the authentic experience and I'm going to savor every moment. "Looks as if we're sharing, Gwenna."

"For tonight you are," he agrees, turning to look at me over his shoulder. "Tomorrow you're with me. We'll find a priest in the morning."

"What?" Gwenna squawks.

I wave a hand at her, indicating she needs to be quiet. I'll explain everything when we're alone.

Hawk moves toward the trunk, and I can't help but notice that for his big, bulky form, he moves with a fascinating grace. Are all Taurians built like him, or is he unique in his breadth? I eye his thick flanks and the pants nearly falling down his arse behind his tail. . . .

Gwenna tugs on my wet sleeve, glaring at me furiously.

"Later," I mouth to her, giving a little shake of my head. "This is quite lovely, thank you, Hawk."

"'Instructor Hawk' to all fledglings," he corrects, and throws the trunk open, then points at the contents. "Uniforms. You'll wear these every day while you're in this house. Sash goes over the right shoulder. It's a plain white sash for a fledgling. Be up at eight for breakfast and team registration. After that, we'll go straight into training." Before I can say anything, he turns and heads straight for me, pinning me with his gaze. "You—be up earlier."

"Right. Of course, Instructor Hawk." The words sound awkward together, and I can't help but tease. "You sure you don't want me to call you 'master'?"

The look he gives me could make grass wither. "I'm not a guild master. Taurians never are." He storms out of the room, nearly knocking Gwenna over onto the pile of bags in the cart. "Get some sleep. Lark can take care of herself."

"When do we meet Magpie?" I call after him.

He ignores me and heads down the stairs. Rude. Perhaps we'll see Magpie in the morning, then. A thrill of excitement races through me at the thought of meeting my childhood hero. Dreamily, I turn on my heel and set Squeaker's carrying case down upon the floor . . . only to notice that Gwenna is glaring at me.

Hard.

"What was that all about?" Gwenna asks, her tone dangerously even.

"I persuaded Instructor Hawk that we both need to join the school to round out the numbers." I release Squeaker from her carrier and she immediately waddles out with an indignant look, her orange fur spiked with rain. She begins to sniff things, settling in. "It's all taken care of."

"What did you convince him with, pray tell?"

"My winning personality?" When she continues to scowl, I can tell she's not buying it. "He needs a wife—"

Gwenna's screech echoes in the room. *"What—?!"*

I immediately race over to her side and clap a hand over her mouth, settling on the bed beside her. "Shh! I don't want him to change his mind!"

"Are you *insane?*" she hisses. "You're going to hook up with some stranger just because he needs a wife? Does he know who you are?"

"No, and neither of us is going to tell him!"

"Aspeth, he has *hooves.*"

"Well, I'm sure his other parts are reasonably normal. Don't you think? But apparently there's some rutting situation"—I ignore Gwenna's horrified moan and continue on—"and he needs a bed companion. And I need a chaperone, so it works out quite nicely for both of us. Don't look at me like that."

"Your father—"

"Will be dead unless I get some artifacts. Me taking a Taurian to my bed is the least of my problems."

"Well, no wonder you got him to agree," she mutters. "Horny old goat."

"I don't think he's that old. And he's a Taurian. There's no goat involved there, just bull."

She points at me. "You are the worst and this is a terrible plan."

"You won't tell on me, will you?"

Gwenna sighs heavily. "No. No, I suppose I won't. But if you call me 'Chickadee' again, all bets are off."

MY STOMACH IS full of butterflies all night. I don't sleep a wink, just stare up at the ceiling in the darkness while Gwenna snores in bed next to me, Squeaker sprawled atop my breasts in her usual sleeping spot. The cat is enormously heavy and presses on my lungs, but I don't mind. It's a comforting weight, having her there, and I pet her and try to compose my thoughts.

I'm marrying a stranger in the morning.

A stranger with hooves, as Gwenna pointed out. His face isn't even remotely the same shape as mine. I suppose kissing is out . . . and then I wonder why I'm even thinking about kissing at all. I did enjoy kissing Barnabus, I think wistfully, but his kisses were a lie to get me to marry him. I'd rather take an honest man with no kisses than a liar with a sweet tongue.

Then again, I'd rather join the guild with no man, but I guess I can't have everything.

Hours pass, and when the dawn begins to creep into the skies, I ease myself from bed and feed the cat her dried rations, then dress myself in the uniform I had made for this day. I've been on my guild plans for months now, and so I've made myself a fitted version of the very basic fledgling garb. Each fledgling wears brown trousers with multiple pockets, knee-high leather boots, and a plain white shirt under a guild jacket encrusted with rows of buttons. Over the tightly buttoned jacket, an individual guild sash is worn affixed over one shoulder and showcasing the particular guild artificer's honors. Mine is plain at the moment, but I affix it anyhow. My boots are finely tooled leather with decorative sparrows dancing up the sides next to the buttons, and I have matching bracers that look very nice and keep my large, fashionably puffed sleeves out of the way. My blouse is plain white as is proper, but I've made sure that it's crafted from the finest linen, and I've paired it with a functional overskirt in brown made out of a glossy shot silk that gleams in the light.

I look rather fetching, if I do say so myself. I feel well-armored against the disparaging comments that the men of the guild are likely to make this morning when I show up for apprenticing with the rest of Magpie's crew. It's outrageous that these men think women can't hunt for artifacts as well as anyone else . . . as if gender has anything to do with it.

Putting on my spectacles, I peer at my appearance in the small mirror mounted on the wall, tuck a few stray strands of hair into a bun at my nape, and then pull my spectacles off again and hide them in one of the trunks. I can't let anyone know about my vision issues until I'm official.

Swallowing hard, I take one last look at Gwenna, still in bed, and my sweet Squeaker, who's hungrily eating the last few bites of her kibble. I kneel down to scratch Squeaker's orange chin. She'll be fine in the room by herself while we're in our schooling, and Gwenna will make sure that she's got more food and water and her toilet pads are changed out. "I have to go," I whisper to Squeaker. "I'm off to marry a Taurian. Wish me luck."

Squeaker just purrs and leans into my caress, oblivious to the chaos in my head. She's happy as long as she's got kibble and a nice comfy place to lay her head. It's Gwenna I'm worried about—what if she changes her mind and spills the truth about who I really am? We're friends, but I know she can also be stubborn when she thinks we're doing something foolish.

Marrying a stranger? That has to be the height of foolishness in practical Gwenna's eyes.

I head down the stairs, my stomach full of flutters. Someone's opened the shutters and light floods into the dormitory. It's a quaint place, with heavy wooden beams and equally heavy furniture placed in strategic sitting spots, but I suppose it makes sense given that a Taurian would break anything dainty. It's cozy, though. There's a shelf with books on it across from the fireplace, and a desk covered in papers on the route to what must be the kitchen area. There's no one around, and I have a moment to squint at the large portrait of a strong-looking woman at the landing. She's wearing a guild sash over one shoulder and pants. Her face is lit up with wonder and she holds a glittering box in her hands, extending them out toward the viewer. This must be Magpie.

A box? I wonder which of her many finds are contained in the box. I lean in closer, trying to focus my eyes. Perhaps this isn't Magpie after all? The sash she wears is the red of a guild master, though. How very confusing. I practically press my nose to the painting, trying to get the object in focus.

"What are you wearing?"

The harsh voice echoes in the quiet dormitory halls and I wince, turning around at the top of the landing.

It's the Taurian, standing at the base of the stairs. He's dressed in a guild uniform similar to mine, but his shoulder is covered with the bright blue of his guild sash and something gleaming that I can't make out. But the large russet head is most certainly his, as is the wide breadth of shoulders in the white linen shirt. He's not wearing a guild jacket, and looks so casual I don't know what to make of it. I decide to ignore his state of undress and smile instead. "Oh, good morning, Instructor Hawk. I was admiring the painting." I gesture at it behind me. "I don't suppose you know—"

"What are you wearing?"

He repeats the sentence with the same unhurried cadence, but there's nevertheless a touch of menace in his tone. It makes me bristle, and my back stiffens. He's going to need to learn how to deal with women if he plans on being married to me, because the more you order me about, the less inclined I am to listen. "Is that Magpie in the painting?"

Hawk points at the base of the stairs, as if indicating I should move there, and quickly.

Even though I'm irritated, I need him. I can't afford to anger the person I need to enroll me into the fledgling program . . . at least, not on day one. Once I'm safely ensconced in training, I don't give a god's arse what he thinks of me. Fighting back my annoyance, I head down the stairs and stand in the spot he indicates.

"What are you wearing?" he asks again.

"A uniform." I flick a strand of Squeaker's cat hair off my sleeve. "Why? Am I wrinkled?"

"That's not the uniform I gave you." This close, I can see the displeasure on his unusual face.

"That's correct. I had this one tailored before I left home."

His arms cross over his chest and he glares down at me. "Are you not taking this seriously? Is all of this a joke to you? Because we can end this right now—"

"Of course I'm taking this seriously!" I put my hands on my hips and glare up at him. "I should think that's obvious, given that I had a uniform made even before I arrived. You're insulting me by suggesting otherwise."

"Everyone wears the same uniforms when they're a fledgling," he says in that dangerous tone of his. "The same shitty uniform. You want to be taken seriously? Then you'll change."

"Having a blouse tailored doesn't mean that I'm not serious—"

He leans in, and I automatically lean back, his muzzle in my face. "Do you really want me to rip those clothes off you, Aspeth? Is that what we're going for here?"

I let out a squeak of distress, blinking up at him. He's alarmingly tall. Alarmingly tall and a little scary. "D-do you really want to start our marriage ripping my clothes off?"

"While I would love nothing more than to do that in about three weeks," he murmurs in that deadly voice, "right now I just want you to change. Understand?"

Managing a nod, I hold my breath until he steps back and gestures up the stairs again. This time I race up them, heading back to my quarters. Once inside, I pull off my tailored clothes with shaking hands and fish the much cruder set out from under Squeaker, because of course she's made a nest on them. They're wrinkled and covered in cat hair now, but if this is what Instructor Hawk wants, this is what Instructor Hawk gets.

I can't believe I'm going to marry the grump. I'm an idiot. I tuck the ill-fitting blouse into the waist of the pants and wonder if I should just lick my wounds and retreat. Return to my father's keep and . . .

And then what? Wait for a rival holder to come and behead me? Wait for someone to steal our lands and just pray they're in a benevolent mood and send me to a convent instead? No, this is my only choice.

Annoyed at Hawk—and at myself for hesitating—I return downstairs, this time clad in a blouse that is far too tight across my bust and makes me look stout and matronly because the waist isn't cinched. The pants barely fit over my backside and I suspect if I have to sit at any point, they'll split. But I'm in the uniform he wanted. "Happy now?"

"Thrilled," he says flatly. "Let's get going. You have to be at registration in two hours."

Hawk tosses a brown cloak over my shoulders and then puts one on himself. He pulls the hood up, his forward-pointing horns making the tent of fabric huge over his head, the tips just barely sticking out of the hem. Following his lead, I pull up my cloak hood as well, and head out the front door behind him.

Despite the early hour, the city is bustling. We head down the busy, crowded street, narrowly avoiding the contents of a chamber pot that someone empties above, and I trot after him. I keep close, because I don't want him to use any excuse to call this off.

I'm a little surprised when he takes me to the nearest temple of Asteria. I thought that Taurians worshiped Old Garesh, the god of war and destruction. Perhaps he's not the right god for a wedding, no matter if it's Taurian or not. Hawk marches into the temple, his hooves echoing obscenely loudly on the floor. There's a nun taking donations near the front altar, and he heads directly for her, pulling a small bag of coin from his waist. "I need a marriage, quickly. Get me a priestess."

"Please," I add politely, moving to his side and taking his arm.

"Hush now," he tells me.

"If you're going to demand things, at least have the decency to add a 'please' on the end. You'll find people much more willing to deal with you."

He lowers his hood, turning to give me an incredulous look. "Are you *chiding* me?"

I shrug. Perhaps he thinks he didn't need chiding. On this, we'll have to agree to disagree.

Hawk snorts, as if unable to believe his ears. I keep waiting for him to shrug my arm off, but he doesn't. I guess it would ruin the fantasy of our hasty marriage if he did. The priestess arrives a few moments later, a puzzled expression on her lined face. "It's the middle of the week, my dears. A marriage on the weekend, when the goddess is at rest, is a blessed marriage. Wouldn't you rather wait?"

"No waiting." Hawk sounds as gruff and cranky as ever.

"It needs to happen today," I try to explain, a gracious smile on my face.

The priestess blinks at us and then leans in, confiding to me. "My dear, if you're in a carrying sort of way, a few days won't make a difference, and your child might need the goddess's blessing more than anyone."

I stare at her in horror. She thinks I'm pregnant? I glance up at Hawk in surprise, then back at the priestess. She's ignoring Hawk as if he doesn't exist, her gaze focused entirely on me, and I don't know whether to laugh or be offended. I decide upon being offended, and pretend to lean in to confide back to her, my voice deliberately loud. "If I have to go another night without this virile buck in my bed, I shall scream. The wedding *must* happen today."

She makes a distressed sound and somewhere behind her, I can hear the muffled giggle of a novice. "I see." She composes herself and holds her hand out, and the novice puts the bag of money in her grip. "I suppose the goddess does love . . . ahem, love. Take your man's hands and I will join you."

"Wait," I blurt out, looking up at Hawk. "Don't we need witnesses?"

"The church registers all marriages," he says.

"For another coin, you can have a lovely certificate to post over your home altar," the priestess adds, putting her hand out for an additional coin.

Hawk hands it over without question, and I guess we're about to be married.

EIGHT

HAWK
25 Days Before the Conquest Moon

MY NEW BRIDE's hands twitch in my sweaty grasp, her cuticles covered in tiny scabs from zealous overchewing. Her expression is bland and composed, but the twitching gives away her nerves. She's as anxious about this marriage as I am, and when the priestess says the last of the matrimonial prayer, Aspeth breathes a sigh of relief and flashes me a quick smile that takes me aback and makes my tail flick.

I'm still thinking about earlier, replaying the moment in my head time and again when Aspeth realized the priestess was ignoring me. *If I have to go another night without this virile buck in my bed, I shall scream.* She made a fool of herself—and the priestess—simply to shut down any argument, and I know it was for my benefit.

It was . . . kind.

"There now. You are married in the eyes of the goddess," the priestess is saying. Her gaze flicks over me dismissively and then focuses on Aspeth's composed form once more. "No kiss of union is necessary."

"Oh, we'll kiss," my new wife says cheerfully. "I wouldn't want anyone to think we weren't united." And she puts a hand in the front of my clean, pressed guild shirt and pulls me down toward her. Before I can even think about how I'm going to fit my mouth to her flat-faced human one, she presses a smacking kiss on the leathery end of my nose. "There."

She gazes up at me, and then impulsively reaches forward and gives me a quick hug.

"So it is done," the priestess says, and there's a hint of distaste in her voice. "Go with the goddess."

"Our certificate, if you please." Aspeth clings to my arm and beams at the woman as if she truly is the happiest of brides.

The priestess's smile is tight. "Very well. However, I must say I'm not familiar with the ring ceremony of the Taurian people." The look she gives me is pointed. "I'm afraid you will have to go elsewhere for that."

"Ring ceremony?" Aspeth asks.

Five hells, I am not explaining that wedding custom to her. "We're skipping it. Doing things the human way," I say gruffly, and grab my new bride by the arm. "Hurry with that certificate. We're on a tight schedule."

The priestess hurries away, and Aspeth shoots me a curious look. "Should I inquire about the ring ceremony?"

In which she fits a ring around my cock and balls to show that she owns me, and I pierce her cunt with a matching (slightly smaller) one to show my side of fealty? It's a tender ceremony. It also works a lot better with female Taurians, who are as superbly wide as they are strong. I can't imagine it with Aspeth, who I feel nothing for but vague annoyance. I imagine pinching her cunt in my hand until her clit pokes free, and then piercing it with a ring to show she's mine, and my cock stirs.

All right, I feel nothing but vague annoyance *and* a hint of moon-related arousal. "Don't ask about the rings."

She nods, and we drop it.

A brief time later, we have the certificate and hurry back to Magpie's dormitory. Inside, it's all chaos, as I knew it would be. The students are in the kitchen in varying stages of readiness. Lark is hungover, her head on the table, her hair in her face. The tiny priestess who arrived last night is in uniform, but she also looks ready to cry as she argues with Lark about who is in charge. She clutches prayer beads tightly in her hands and all but falls to her knees when we return. Aspeth's companion is busy ironing her shirt, wearing nothing but a chemise as she leans over the stove in the kitchen. There are two other pots on the stove, both bubbling over and hissing. The slitherskin is the only calm one, dressed in a tiny uniform, his small hands tucked at his waist, but he's wearing his enormous house on his back despite my repeatedly telling him not to.

To top it off, there's a strange fat orange cat in the center of the table, eating the last of the salted pork.

"Where's Magpie?" I growl, trying not to lose my temper at the chaos.

"Where she always is," Lark says, grinding the heel of her palm into her eye socket. "Sleeping it off."

My temper flares just a bit more. I make up for Magpie's lack a lot of the time, but fledgling initiation is one of those times when she needs to be there. I shouldn't be surprised that she's still soused, but I am definitely growing more and more annoyed with every moment that passes. It's up to me to take care of things yet again, and make excuses for her. Even though I owe Magpie my life and would willingly work at her side for the rest of my days, it's hard to remain loyal when she doesn't even bother to do the bare minimum.

Jaw clenched, I tug on my nose ring. It's a twitchy habit, like humans biting their nails. Now, do I wake her up, knowing there will be a scene?

That she'll likely scare these students off before they ever start their training? The last time I dragged Magpie along with her students against her will, she bitched the entire time, vomited in someone's pack, and passed out on the obstacle course and had to be carried home. I heard about it from the other Taurians for weeks on end.

It's fine, I remind myself. Everything is fine. I can handle this. If Magpie wants to sleep, she can mucking sleep. I'll take over her duties like I always do. "Let's just get going."

They ignore me. Lark continues to rub her head. The priestess starts another prayer, her lips moving as she passes the beads through her folded fingers. The slitherskin continues to eat his breakfast, ignoring the chaos around him. The woman ironing her blouse by the stove holds her top up, admiring the pleats, and Aspeth moves to her side. "Oh, that's nice work. Can you do mine next?"

"No," I say quickly. "No more ironing. It's time to go." I grab the priestess by her collar—at least she's dressed—and haul her to her feet. "You. Get shoes. You by the stove, get your clothes on. Lark, get rid of the cat."

Aspeth sputters, turning to look at me. "No one is getting rid of the cat—"

I ignore her and point at the slitherskin. "You, take your house off. You need to leave it behind."

The lizard-creature takes one look at me, blinks one eyelid, and returns to eating. He does not, in fact, take off the oversized shell house he has attached to his back. He doesn't even bother to tug on one of the straps. He just ignores me, too. At least Guillam will listen—

I pause. "Where in the five hells is Guillam?"

"Left this morning," Lark offers, struggling to her feet and picking up the cat. "Said he didn't want to be with a bunch of women and a frog. No offense to you, Kipp." She adjusts the fat cat in her arms and frowns at the cat hair that floats into the air. "How often do you brush this monster?"

"Every day," Aspeth tells her. "She's just a shedder. And did you hear that, Instructor Hawk? Guillam left and now we're back to five. This is perfect."

I stare at my team of fledglings for the new season. At the half-dressed woman with perfect pleats in her blouse. At the weepy priestess and the drunk niece of my boss. At the slitherskin who ignores me.

At my new *wife*.

This is a nightmare, and Aspeth's pleasure at finding Guillam to be gone is getting on my last nerve.

I downgrade her from "sexually intriguing but vexing" back to just "vexing" again.

ASPETH

"It gives me great pride to welcome the newest class of fledglings to the Royal Artifactual Guild." Rooster beams at us from his spot behind an ornate wooden podium. He stands taller than the podium, which makes me suspect he's standing on a box of some kind. "On behalf of King Kethrin III, we look forward to working with you and training you to join our ranks."

My heart wants to burst with excitement. I tremble in my seat in the audience, thrilled to my core. This is it. This is what I've been waiting for. I don't care who I have to marry, or train with, or where I have to sleep. I'm going to be trained to be a guild member. I'm going to save my hold. I'm going to—

"You'd think he's handpicked all of us with that tone of voice," Gwenna says, leaning over to my side. "Acts like he's the king."

"Hush," I whisper to her. While Rooster is a little pompous (or rather, a lot), I don't blame him for taking pride in the welcoming cere-mony. It's an important moment in our lives to be added to the roster of fledglings, the trainees who will live in the guild nests (such a clever name!) and work with the guild masters to learn the craft.

"Once you are signed into the fledgling lists, there is no backing out." Rooster casts a stern look over the audience. "You will either pass your test or fail. Fail, and you will become one of the guild repeaters. You will work with the guild, performing menial tasks and paying off the lessons squandered until another guild master decides to let you fledge again."

Gwenna pinches my leg, leaning over. "What's a repeater?"

"He just said. Someone who fails out—"

"Yes, but what do they do? What tasks is he talking about?"

I think for a moment, trying to recall what I read in the pamphlets and books about the guild. "There are guards, and each house has an assigned nestmaid who takes care of the food and laundry—"

"Wait, so if I fail, I become a maid again, except this time I don't get paid? Aspeth! What in all the mucking hells—"

At my other side, Kipp the slitherskin hisses loudly. We both turn to him and he glares sternly at us, putting a finger to his mouth to indicate silence. Then . . . he licks his eyeball.

Right. I put a finger to my lips and give Gwenna a meaningful look. "You're not going to be a repeater," I promise her. "We're going to pass."

She growls at me. *Growls.* I'm guessing she's not going to want a hug after this. It's a shame, because I'm so excited to be here that I want to hug everyone. Even Rooster, if he came close enough. Commoners hug, don't they? Surely it wouldn't be too out of line.

I continue smiling as Rooster drones on about guild history and the Mancer Wars, and how the guild was established by the king three hundred years ago. I know all this, so I focus on my teammates instead. Lark's head bobs, her eyes closed as if she's at prayers. She looks truly focused, and I'm so delighted to see that . . . until she leans too far forward and snores. At her side, Mereden the priestess nudges her, the look on her face studiously polite. She stares ahead, her gaze focused intently on Rooster at his podium.

My gaze slides past them to the next row, where a male fledgling about my age is looking over at us. Our eyes meet, and then he makes an obscene gesture at me with his tongue. Flustered, I look away. Good gods.

"As your teachers and mentors, the guild masters expect three things from each fledgling," Rooster continues. "Curiosity. Eagerness. Honesty. Let me tell you a little bit about each one and why it matters."

Gwenna leans toward me again. "Do you think he's going to go on for much longer?"

I bite back a grimace, because I truly don't know. Already he's been up there for quite some time. The people on the benches in front of us are drooping, and I suspect more than one is nodding off, just as Lark was. "Possibly? He hasn't touched on the guild handbook yet."

She groans quietly. "How is it that he's making grave robbing sound so boring?"

I shoot her a frown. "It's not grave robbing, Gwenna!"

"Call it what you like." Gwenna shrugs, and then lifts her chin, indicating something across the aisle. "Think we'll have to deal with a lot of that here?"

A quick look finds yet another man, this one younger, making lewd licking motions with his tongue and aiming his attention at Mereden, who is steadfastly ignoring him.

"Goddess, I hope not," I mutter. Here I'd thought that once we were let in as fledglings, we'd be seen as just a few more guild recruits.

Perhaps I've been far too optimistic.

HAWK

"You *married* her?"

At the back of the main guild hall, Raptor looks at me as if I've grown another head. I understand. It's an absolutely insane move for me to make. I'm still not entirely sure why I did it. Probably thinking with my little head. I pretend to keep my focus on my fledglings, several rows ahead at the front of the hall. They're sitting with nineteen other guild teams, waiting to be initiated. "We needed a full team. And I need a partner for the Conquest Moon."

"But . . . her? The bossy one?" He stomps his hooves in agitation, idly watching the ceremony. "I thought you couldn't stand her."

"I needed students. She needs a chaperone. We'll go our separate ways after this if we need to, get the marriage annulled. I don't know why it's a big deal."

He looks over at me with that "are you insane" expression again. "You're joking, right? No one's going to grant you an annulment after it's very clear that you rutted her. And if you have to marry a human, why *that* one? No one takes her seriously. No one takes us seriously, either. Any reputation you had left is going to be shredded by that woman clinging to your arm. Did Magpie talk you into this?"

I scoff. "No."

But it's true that Magpie takes in all kinds that don't pass. There have been women who showed up on recruitment day but didn't last a week. Most didn't make it through the training, either from harassment from the male fledglings or simply because the job itself is too dangerous and unpleasant. Magpie is a sucker for a female student, but the truth is that most can't hack it like she does. Or did. The current Magpie wouldn't get ten steps underground without sucking on a bottle of liquor.

"Bad, bad idea, my friend" is all Raptor says, arms crossed.

I know it's a bad idea. I don't need him weighing in on it. I ignore his headshake of disappointment, pretending interest as Master Finch brings his five chosen fledglings to the front of the room so they can be inducted into the book of names. The five names are recorded at the beginning of the year, and when the students graduate, those names are crossed out and replaced with their chosen guild names. It's all very pompous and self-congratulatory, but that might be the Taurian side of me speaking. We hate fuss. Finch guides his students to the book of names and watches as they sign it. My students are toward the back of the hall, in one of the last rows, so I'm hoping things are cleared out before I have to go up there with them.

It should be Magpie doing that, but she hasn't yet appeared. She swore she'd dress and show up in time for the ceremony, but we've been here for hours now and there's no sign of her. Something tells me that she headed for the nearest bar instead, and I tamp down my feelings of frustration. She'll show up. She has to.

I eye the doorway, but it's empty.

Class after class heads toward the book and signs their names in, receiving their official fledgling pin from Rooster as they do. As the room clears out, the smirks and nudges become more obvious, and they're all directed toward my students. I know what they see when they look at the bench for Magpie's house. They see four women in varying degrees of softness—led by Aspeth, who has her chin in the air as if she rules the place—and a slitherskin (who is still wearing his house, much to my irritation). We're a joke to them.

I can't even be mad at the snickers they make. I look at them and I see another year that we won't have a passing class. I see another chance for commissions going up in smoke. I look at them and I wonder which one is going to peel off first, ruining the season for the others. A passing class must have five.

"The fledgling class of Master Magpie," Rooster calls out.

My students get to their feet, and despite the fact that the room is nearly empty, the whispers grow louder.

Raptor grunts. "Mmm. I'm starting to get it now." I huff, torn between amusement and sheer annoyance at Aspeth again. She's wearing her guild uniform, but it doesn't fit her the way it fits the others. Her ample backside pulls the fabric tight, outlining her rump right down to a dimple in one plump cheek. When she turns to the side, her tits strain against the guild blouse, and Raptor makes another fascinated sound. "Maybe you can gag her when she talks."

I elbow him. "That's my wife, you clod-brain."

"Rut her good, my friend." He claps me on the back so hard that I stagger past him and the other Taurians remaining at the back of the hall.

They chuckle as I move forward, crossing the long hall to stand at my students' side.

"Guild Master Magpie?" Rooster calls again, searching the room as he stands behind the massive book. "Is Guild Master Magpie here?"

I clear my throat, moving to stand in front of the podium. "Guild Master Magpie is sick. I'll sign the book in her place."

Rooster's lip curls at me, as if he's offended by the sight of a Taurian standing in front of him. "You're not a guild master. Where is Guild Master Magpie?"

"Like I said, sick." His lips thin further, and I have no doubt he's thinking of the last two classes, when I presented them, too. I continue on. "I'll present her class and she'll be here for graduation."

Even if I have to haul her bodily in front of the guild itself, she'll be here.

He takes a deep breath, as if considering, and then holds the feathered quill out to me. I sign the book with Magpie's name, the quill ridiculously small and fragile in my too-large Taurian hand. I manage not to snap it, and then turn to hand it off to the first student in line.

It's Aspeth, of course.

"I assume all these females have chaperones?" Rooster continues in that haughty voice of his. "You can provide proof of this?"   .

"They do and I can."

He eyes us and then gestures for Aspeth to sign. I've never seen a student so giddy to put their name in the book as her, only to pause over the book itself and then look at me. "What's our last name?"

NINE

ASPETH

I FUSS WITH THE sash on my shoulder over and over again, just for an excuse to touch it. Right now the sash is plain white, but I envision the day it's covered in pins representing the artifacts I've brought to the guild. Small circles for minor artifacts, and the four-pointed stars for the major artifacts. I imagine Magpie's sash must be absolutely encrusted, and the weight of it on her shoulder must bring so much pride.

I cannot wait to meet her. It's going to be glorious.

Glancing up, I eye the others in our nest. Lark looks bored and slightly hungover, slumped on a bench. Gwenna sits properly on the bench in front of her, frowning as the brown-skinned priestess at her side folds her hands and goes through yet another prayer. On the far side of Gwenna, the strange child-sized lizardman slitherskin sits, swinging his tiny feet, the massive shell of his house on his back. I haven't heard him say two words since we arrived, but maybe that's normal? I genuinely don't know.

Our teachers are nowhere to be seen. There's still no Magpie, and now we've lost Hawk, too.

I purse my lips, trying not to frown. The other nest groups have abandoned the hall, along with their teachers. I'm not sure what we do now. Do we follow them out? Wait for instructions? Gwenna looks at me, curious, and the priestess does, too. It's clear they're looking to me for answers.

All right, then. "I'll go find our teacher."

"Your *husband*," Gwenna says, pretending to study her nails. "You'll go find your husband."

"Right. Yes. That." My face gets hot. It's jarring to think that I've just married a stranger, but I don't want anything to come in the way of the classes here. "My husband," I say confidently, lifting my chin. "I'm sure he's around here somewhere."

Lark tumbles back on the wooden bench, lying flat and flinging an arm over her eyes. "Wake me up when you find him."

I frown at her, but it's not like I can scold her. She's a student, just like me. With a flick of my fingers over my coveted sash, I pretend to wipe away a speck of dust. "Be right back."

I turn and walk away, heading out of the main hall and into one of the side corridors. I've never been deeper into the actual guild hall before today, but it can't be that hard to figure out? I hope. I'm familiar with the entryway, as that was where I was humiliated yesterday, but deeper inside? Not at all.

All of the students filed out of the main doors, heading toward the Swan statue, but I head in the opposite direction. Something tells me that Hawk wouldn't leave without us. He seems to take his job quite seriously. So I head farther into the hall, turning down one curving corridor lined with doors. I pass something that looks like a blurry library (I wish I was wearing my spectacles) but appears to be empty.

Farther down the hall, I hear the sound of arguing.

"I said I'm handling things," a deep, sonorous male voice says as I quietly approach. That's Hawk, and he's in one of the nearby rooms. I peek in, and when I see his enormous, blurry brown form standing near a short, squat man who has to be that Rooster arse, I duck behind the door and hover in the hallway. Should I let them know I'm here? Say something?

"Your version of 'handling things' is very different from mine," Rooster says in a haughty voice.

I hear the stamp of hooves on the ground and a loud, bullish snort.

"Correct me if I'm wrong, but your only male candidate for your nest has fled. He signed up with Mallard's class this morning, filling their last slot. Now you've nothing but a horde of flighty females—"

"Don't forget the slitherskin," Hawk drawls.

"—and a lizardman who won't take off his house to get in uniform. Truly, it's embarrassing."

My mouth purses into an angry little pucker. How dare he?

"It's a disgrace to the guild's history," Rooster continues. "And where is Magpie?"

"Like I said, she's sick. I'm handling things."

"She was sick last year on enrollment day," Rooster counters. "And the year before she showed up late."

She was? She did?

"Like I said, I'm handling it." Hawk's tone grows more and more impatient.

"I do not doubt your competency, Hawk. That has never been in question. You are good at your job, but you're not a guild master. Only guild masters can teach a fledgling nest. You know the rules as well as I do."

Silence.

Chicken-man continues. "Twenty guild masters are allowed at one time, for twenty nests. Twenty teams of fledglings are allowed to join every year. Magpie might be a guild master due to her past exploits, but she is in danger of losing her position. If she doesn't get herself in order, do you know what's going to happen?"

More silence. I so badly want to peek around the corner but I don't dare.

"Your class will fail," he continues. "Just as they failed the year before last, and the year before that. And I will not be able to protect her any longer. She will lose her guild master position to another who can make the guild money. She will lose her house and her pension, and she will end up in the gutters. You're a good artificer and a good teacher, but you're not in charge. She'll undermine everything you do and chase your students away. Do you understand?"

His tone is so dismissive, so condescending, that I want to punch him.

What a rude, odious little man. I loathe him. I want Hawk to give him a verbal tearing-down. I want Hawk to tell him what's what. I want him to lay into that peahen of a man and tell him what to do with his—

"This class won't fail" is all Hawk says.

"How can they not fail?" Rooster continues, and I can hear the astonishment in his voice. "I saw that bunch of misfits myself. You're doomed. Magpie has doomed you."

"I'm going to push them harder than ever. And I'll handle Magpie, just as I always have." Heavy hooves clomp on the floor, and it takes me a moment to realize he's heading toward the door, where I'm spying.

Just as I jerk away from the heavy wooden door, Hawk comes around the corner.

We stare at each other for a moment, and then he grabs me by the arm and escorts me away, his grip tight and leaving me no choice but to trot alongside his much longer strides.

"You'll keep all of that to yourself," he murmurs as he hauls me back toward the others.

"Of course I will," I hiss at him. "But do you want to tell me what's going on?"

"Later." We round the corner back toward the others, much quicker than I anticipated. They all sit up as we approach, and then there's no time to ask anything else. I notice Gwenna has a tight expression on her face, and the look she shoots me indicates she wants to talk.

Well, that makes two of us.

Hawk releases my arm as we rejoin the others, and I resist the urge to rub it indignantly.

"Good, you're all here," he says in a curt voice. "Now, if you'll all follow me outside, we'll get your backpacks."

"Backpacks?" Gwenna asks.

"Aye, to fill with rocks." Hawk marches over to Lark's bench and hauls her upright by the shoulder. "We're going to see how far you can march with a full pack to determine your stamina. I need to know how fit you are . . . so then I can push you even harder."

I swallow hard.

Somehow, when I'd dreamed of adventuring through the tunnels, I hadn't thought about physical fitness. Given that I've spent most of my life seated at elegant tables or in front of a book, I suspect this is going to be a rather awful afternoon.

Hawk turns on us, his eyes flaring with irritation. "Well? Why are you all just standing there? Do you want to be fledglings or not?"

With a terrified squeak, the priestess races for the door, and we follow after her.

I'M RIGHT. TRAINING isn't fun. It's one of the worst afternoons of my life.

With backpacks loaded down full of rocks, Hawk marches behind us and forces us to walk over Vastwarren's rambling, twisting cobblestone streets. He yells at us if we fall behind. He yells at us if we want to take a break. If we ask for water, we're allowed two sips before he's demanding that we get up again. Over and over, he marches us up and down the streets, and the only thing that stops me from screaming is the fact that we pass other classes doing the exact same thing, relentlessly harassed by the teacher jogging at their sides.

Sweat pours down my face, soaking my guild blouse and making it stick to my skin. The priestess cries. Lark bitches. Gwenna doesn't complain, but she huffs and shoots daggers at me with her eyes as if this was all my idea. The only one seemingly unbothered by all of this is the slitherskin, Kipp, who trots along with the pack on his front and his house on his back.

When we turn up another twisting street—really, does all of Vastwarren have to be sloping? Can't one street be flat?—I want to burst into tears with relief when we spot Magpie's symbol hanging on a flag outside her house. We're home, just as the sun is setting and my feet are screaming in pain.

Hawk marches us up to the house and then stands in front of the door, guarding it and preventing us from going inside. He crosses his arms over his broad chest, and I'm disgusted to see he's barely broken a sweat. Meanwhile, I'm positively dripping. Lark tosses her pack to the ground, and when he doesn't chastise her, I slip mine off, too. The relief is overwhelming.

"That was pathetic," he tells us.

"Such flattery," I manage to gasp out, hands resting on my knees. By the five gods, I am exhausted.

"I mean it," Hawk growls out, glaring at me. "You think this is all fun and games? You think when you're two leagues under the city and a tunnel collapses on you that you're going to have the stamina to dig yourself out? You all need to get better. Stronger. Faster. Be ready to do this again at dawn. All of you." He points at the slitherskin. "Leave your house behind this time. I mean it."

Kipp licks his own eyeball with his long tongue, and I don't know if that's agreement or an insult.

"You're dismissed for the night," Hawk says, stepping aside from the door. "Stay in the nest. From now on, if you go anywhere, you have to clear it with me before. Tomorrow is your first full day of training and you're going to need your strength." As we file in, he glares at Lark. "And *no* drinking."

"Of course not," she says sweetly.

I walk inside and sit down on the closest seat near the cold fireplace. The windows have been shut tight and the darkness is welcoming, as I just want to crawl away and hide. My feet throb in time with my pulse, and I bend over to unlace my boots, only to have Gwenna march to my side and grab my arm.

"We have a problem," she whispers in my ear. "Let's go upstairs and talk."

I don't know that I can make it up the stairs, but at least up there I can take my sweaty clothes off. I consider this and then abandon my seat by the fireplace. The others are heading in the opposite direction, toward the kitchen. They haven't noticed Gwenna heading upstairs. With a sigh, I follow my former maid up each step with painful thumps. It eases my heart a little to see Squeaker curled on the bed. The cat looks up and howls for dinner the moment she glimpses me.

"One moment," I tell the cat with an affectionate scratch to her ears. I slip off my boots and stockings, then peel the rest of the clothes off.

They're as sweaty as a devil's arse and I don't know how I'm going to get them clean for the morning, but that's a problem for tomorrow morning. I pull off layers, finally removing my corset—damp with sweat—and scratching at the skin underneath. "Oh gods, that's better."

Gwenna puts down fresh food and water for Squeaker, then leans against the door, saying nothing. I put on a fresh chemise, and it feels like heaven. When I dramatically flop down onto the bed in the place the cat just vacated, she finally speaks. "We have a big stinking problem, Lady Aspeth."

"Just Aspeth," I remind her, fighting back a yawn. By all the gods in their realms, I'm exhausted. I continue to scratch at my waist, enjoying the cool air against my overheated skin. "We're incognito."

"That's the problem," she hisses. "While you were busy chasing after our teacher, I chatted with Mereden, the priestess, for a bit."

She seems sweet enough, if overly teary-eyed. I didn't pay much attention to her because she kept weeping and praying, as if being part of Magpie's fledgling team is the worst thing to ever happen to her. She wore her veil, too, as if protesting in some quiet way. "Dedicated to Asteria, is she?"

"Not exactly. Apparently"—Gwenna exaggerates the word, her hands on her hips as she approaches me—"Mereden is from the Convent of Divine Silence. Sound familiar?"

It's where a lot of wealthy women are sent when they are widowed. "It does."

"Also *apparently*, Mereden offered to tithe a share of her guild income if they would write her a letter of recommendation and let her come for training. The church is looking to acquire more artifacts, and so they reached an agreement with Magpie. But Mereden fears her father is going to be quite upset when he finds out she's here and not at the convent. And do you know who her father is?"

I'm too tired to think straight. Fighting back a yawn, I shrug. "Is he rich?"

"He's Lord Vatuo Morsell of Morsell Hold's youngest son. She's the lord holder's granddaughter."

I blanch. She's right, that's not good. I've met Lord Morsell at several parties. He's got a long, wiry beard and ropes of braided hair that are beaded with the finest shells. I remember that much. I also remember that his sons were quite a bit older than me and thus not considered good marriage candidates, so we didn't visit them often. But holders travel in tight circles, and we all know one another.

Still, a younger son's daughter isn't that important in the scheme of things, hence why they allowed her to join the church. It's why I didn't recognize her. "Has she recognized me?"

"I don't think so. But you're going to have to be doubly careful around her, and we need to make sure that she remains ignorant."

"Tell her that I'm named after Aspeth Honori if she inquires. Tell her I'm from the area and my father met Lord Honori once and named me after his daughter to curry favor. Tell her anything." I shrug. "It's not as if she can do much now. She needs me on the team. We've five now, and five's the sacred number."

"You're not worried?" Gwenna looks shocked.

"I'm too tired to be worried. Do you think we're going to have to carry rocks tomorrow, too?"

"We should dye your hair. Or cut it. How do you feel about being blond?" She paces, thinking hard. "The spectacles are obviously out of the question. And it's a good thing you're wearing the same uniforms we are. She'd suspect something for sure if she saw your tailored clothes. . . . Are you even listening? Aspeth?"

I force my eyes open. "I'm listening! I swear. Mereden. Younger son's daughter. Me with new hair. Rocks tomorrow."

Gwenna throws her hands up in the air. "I can't believe you're so casual about this. Why do I even bother talking to you?"

I grab the nearest pillow and tuck it under my head, too fatigued to get up. There's probably dinner somewhere downstairs but I don't want to move from this spot. "Because you have to complain to someone and no one else will listen."

"I should have stayed home," she mutters.

"But I'm so glad you didn't," I say sweetly. "Can we hug?"

"Oh, piss off." She huffs in irritation, and I chuckle. I'm so glad Gwenna's here to keep me company. This adventure wouldn't be the same without her.

A knock at the door startles us both. We exchange a look, and then

Gwenna heads to the door, shooting me a cautious glance. She leans against the door, calling out, "Who's there?"

"It's me, Lark," answers the voice on the other side.

Gwenna shrugs and looks at me. I pull a robe over my chemise, and she opens the door.

Immediately, Lark tumbles inside, followed by Mereden and Kipp. Both Lark and Mereden are in their nightgowns and Kipp is wearing his house, as usual. My spirits sink at the sight of them. All I want to do is sleep, and I'm worried something new and dreadful just occurred.

"What's going on?" I ask, scooping up my cat so she doesn't run out the door. "Is something wrong?"

"Nothing's wrong," Lark reassures us, and grabs one of the throw pillows on a nearby chair and takes a seat on the rug. Mereden joins her, primly adjusting her skirts. Kipp moves across from them, shrugging the large shell of his house off his back and then sitting atop it. Lark grins at us. "We've decided to have team-bonding time. Get to know one another."

"Oh, that sounds lovely," I say.

"Forget it," Gwenna says at the same time. Then she realizes what I've just said, sighs, and closes the door.

Lark pats the rug on the floor. "Come sit with us."

I immediately do so, settling Squeaker in my lap and stroking her ears. Squeaker loves a good pet, and settles in, ignoring the tufts of hair flying as I scratch at her thick ruff. "This makes me so happy," I confess to them. "Other than Gwenna, I've never had friends before."

"Weirdo," Lark says.

I chuckle, because it probably is a bit strange. But as someone who grew up alone, surrounded by no one but tutors or chaperones, I love the thought of becoming close friends with everyone in the room.

Lark leans on the pillow and eyes me. "So tell us about *you*, Aspeth."

"Oh. Um." I scratch at Squeaker's ears. "There's not much to tell. I'm just another person who wished to join the guild."

"Mm-hmm," says Lark, and clearly she doesn't believe me. She exchanges a look with Mereden, who raises her brows and gives us a prim expression. Kipp just licks his eye.

Gwenna nudges me, leaning forward. "She's being modest. For as long as I've known Aspeth, she's had her nose in a book about the guild. She's told everyone who would listen about Old Prell and the guild history and what kinds of adventures guild members get up to. She's studied it ever since she was old enough to read. She's here because it's *her dream.* Because she wants to make something of herself."

Her vehement response changes the way everyone looks at me. Mereden's lips quirk in a tiny smile. Lark just "Humphs" but relaxes. Kipp gives a quick nod as if full of understanding.

"Why, thank you, Gwenna," I say softly. "But yes. It has always been a dream of mine. I grew up reading stories of Guild Master Magpie and her exploits. I want to be just like her."

"Gods, no you don't," Lark says with a chuckle.

"So does your family have a lot of books?" Mereden asks politely before I can inquire what Lark means. Immediately, I know it's the wrong thing to say. Books are a rich person's possession, much like spectacles. I might as well confess that we're wealthy or powerful if I admit that I have a great many books—or that I used to before my father sold off my library. "We had a fair amount at one time," I say, hesitating. "But they were too expensive to keep. I borrowed whenever I could from the nearest monastery, or from my tutors."

"Oooh, tutors. Fancy." Lark makes a flourish with her hand. "We've got ourselves a rich woman. What about you, Gwenna? You a big reader?"

"No," Gwenna says in a flat voice. "My ma worked for Aspeth's father. That's how we know each other. I'm here because I don't want to work in a kitchen all my life."

I tense, worried they're going to ask where we're from.

Instead, Lark rolls onto her back, nodding. "I understand that very well. My family never had two pennies to rub together, and as for myself, you can only juggle blades for so long before you have to seek out other careers. My aunt said she'd train me if I ever wanted to join, and so that's why I'm here. Figure it's time to learn a new skill before I lose a finger or six."

Wincing, I keep petting Squeaker's ears and scratch her chin. "Fingers are important."

"And what about you, Mereden?" Gwenna asks. "A convent novice doesn't strike me as the type to join the guild, no offense."

Mereden's smile is tremulous. "I was sent to the convent because I didn't want to marry. After being there for a while, I realized I didn't want to devote my life to the gods. This seemed as good an option as any."

"Sounds like we're all desperate," Lark says. "Except for Aspeth. She's just a nerd."

"What about Kipp?" I ask, looking at the slitherskin. "What's your story?"

He blinks at me, then licks his eyeball with his long tongue.

Is . . . that a response? Helpless, I look over at the others.

"Slitherskins don't talk aloud," Lark says helpfully. "They gesture if it's important, but otherwise they only talk to their own."

"I see," I say, though I'm not sure I see at all.

"I worked with a slitherskin in the troupe. Nice guy. Good with coin. Better at keeping secrets." She winks at Kipp. "He'll talk to us if he feels like it, but it'll be with hands and not lips."

I'm not even certain Kipp has lips.

The slitherskin rolls his eyes at Lark and then looks at our group. He lifts his hands, and then starts to gesture. It takes a little time for me to understand what he's trying to say without words, but I think we get the gist. He and his family are wanderers. Everything he owns is in his house, which he pats affectionately. His parents have left—or died—and he's alone in the world now. He wants to join the guild because it's exciting to him. He wants to be a hero, judging from the straight-backed, arrogant pose he sets.

Strangely enough, I relate to Kipp more than anything after that. He wants to be more than he is. He has a dream of becoming someone great. He's not escaping his life, he's improving it. I love that. "Can I hug you?" I ask him, full of emotion.

Kipp recoils, an offended look on his face.

"You don't ask a slitherskin that," Lark protests. "It's rude. You don't touch them without invitation."

"I asked." My face is hot. "And I didn't mean to offend. My family doesn't hug and I've decided that now that I'm going to be my own person, I'm going to ask for hugs. I love hugs. I want hugs every day. It's just the warmest, best feeling . . . but I seem to be surrounded by non-huggers."

"I'll hug you," Mereden says in a soft voice.

"You will?" I look at her in surprise.

She nods, getting to her feet as I do. "It's a new start for all of us, isn't it? I might as well be a hugger."

Squeaker mrowrs a protest at being set on the floor, but I dust cat hair off my robe and hug Mereden. She's shorter than me, and soft, but she smells sweet and lovely, and her embrace is warm. It's a good hug.

Tight arms lock around my waist. "Come here, you," Lark grumbles. "I can be a hugger, too."

I chuckle, and then Gwenna sighs and gets to her feet, adding herself to our group hug. "Fine," she says, "but I'm doing this for you lot, not for myself."

Kipp pats my leg, the closest he'll get to the group hug.

It'll do.

TEN

HAWK

24 Days Before the Conquest Moon

MAGPIE'S NEW FLEDGLING team is arguably the worst team I've ever had, and I've had some dreadful ones in the past few years. I've worked with fledglings who didn't want to take direction from a Taurian. I've worked with fledglings who were cowards, or too spoiled to get their clothes dirty. There was one year where they all wanted to just get drunk with Magpie in taverns and none of them showed up on testing day.

They were still better than this crew.

I wash at the basin in my room, splashing water on my muzzle and wondering if everything is about to come crashing down upon Magpie's nest. This team has to pass or Magpie's going to lose her position as guild master. We'll be kicked out and homeless, and I'll never pay my hand back.

But I don't know if this is the team to get us out of the hole we've been dug into.

It's been two days of training and I haven't seen a lick of potential. They're a stunning disgrace, and I don't have much time to get them into shape so they can do test runs in the tunnels. I knew it would be bad, and yet I'm staggered anew every time I look at them. I couldn't have picked a worse team if I tried.

Lark is yawning and belligerent, but I knew she would be. She argues with all my orders and makes faces behind my back.

The slitherskin won't take off his house, and I'm not entirely convinced he's listening to a thing I say.

The young priestess cries when she has to run and says a prayer when I look at her.

Gwenna glares at me as if I'm ravishing her friend in front of her eyes. And Aspeth?

Aspeth tries, at least. Just like yesterday, she tried her hardest today. Just like yesterday, she was the worst of them. She huffs and trudges along the heavily sloped streets of Vastwarren with the best of them, gamely trying to keep up. She truly wants this, I sense, which is annoying because she's in terrible shape, athletically. It's also annoying that the more she sweats, the more her clothes cling to her figure and outline the heaving mounds of her tits. It took everything I had not to stare at the dark nipples poking through her flimsy linen top.

I stare at myself in the mirror. Is that a hint of red in my pupils or am I imagining things? I look half-crazed already, and we've still weeks to go. It's the upcoming Conquest Moon that's making me act like a rut-addled fool. Normally I wouldn't be mesmerized by a pair of sweaty breasts. I could focus on my work, on molding these students into decent guild members so they can tithe to Magpie's house and I can pay off some of my debt. I could ignore all distractions.

Instead, here I am marrying a student and daydreaming about the salty sweat trailing between her tits.

The sacred knot swells ever so slightly around the base of my cock like a band, reminding me that things are about to get worse, not better. I rub the ache of it until it lessens, and then towel off and head out of my room to find Magpie.

The kitchen is surprisingly tidy. I expected it to be a mess after training started, but there are no dishes stacked on the table, no half-eaten crusts left about. That doesn't track. Normally students are exhausted and don't clean up after themselves in the first few weeks of training. They run the poor nestmaid ragged. They sit at the table and eat (and bitch) as much as possible. But the kitchen is empty except for one notable exception. In a corner near the hearth, the slitherskin's large, swirling shell is on its side and a tiny bell hangs over the lip, indicating that the owner is inside. Tomorrow we're going to have to talk about him leaving his shell behind. He can't just take it everywhere with him. It's against guild custom for fledglings to wear anything other than their assigned uniforms.

I'm contemplating the best way to approach removing the slitherskin's house from him when Lark enters the room, muttering under her breath. She's still in her sweaty uniform, her hair in messy braids. She glances at me and then avoids eye contact, heading for the cabinets and rummaging through them. I probably yelled at her too much today. I probably yelled at all of them too much today. I see my hopes for the future drifting away with every dramatic sigh one of them makes, every time they ask to sit down and take a break.

So then I push them even harder. They're probably regretting ever joining Magpie's nest.

"There's no alcohol," I tell her, grabbing an apple from the bowl on the table and taking a bite. "You're wasting your time."

She turns and glares at me. "I did my time. I just want a quick sip before bed."

"I mean it. No drinks. You know the rules. And if I find you've snuck something in, I'll have you on belly-crawling drills for the next three weeks." I devour the apple in two bites and snag another. "I'm tired of all the drunks in this house."

"You wouldn't."

"I absolutely would. Try me."

Lark makes an irritated sound but huffs out of the kitchen, storming up to her quarters. I can't really boot her from the program—not when we need five—but I can make her life miserable if she tries anything.

I finish my apple and then eat a wedge of goat cheese and a handful of nuts before heading out of the kitchen, just in time to run into Magpie at the base of the stairs. She blinks at me, her eyes glassy. Her hair is messy and her face flushed. She's wearing a wrinkled guild master uniform, her heavy sash dripping with pins, and runs a hand over it as she gives me a distracted smile. "Did I miss recruitment?"

Irritation bubbles up inside me and I try to ignore it. "Two days ago, aye."

"Oh, *bury* me." She almost sounds upset. Then she pauses. "Am I drunk or did I hear a cat earlier?"

"I don't know, are you ever *not* drunk?"

"Ouch." She moves past me, heading to the kitchen. Her steps are even, which might be a good sign that she's actually somewhat sober for once.

Doesn't matter if she is. I follow after her, anger simmering in my chest. "We need to talk, Magpie."

"I need to eat something. We can talk after I've had a snack." She enters the kitchen and slices a bit of cheese off the wheel, then sits atop the counter and eyes me as she eats. "Rough day? You look beat."

I cross my arms over my chest. It's either that or reach out and strangle her. "You do know what you missed, don't you?" When she gives me a blank stare, I realize she doesn't. She truly has no idea. "I had to take your students to the hall for enrollment without you, and everyone noticed."

Her eyes widen, and she chews slowly. "Huh."

"That's all you can say?"

"Well, I'd like to say hearing that really makes me want to get another drink, but I think you'll lose your shit if I do." She takes another bite of cheese. "Was Rooster pissy about it?"

"To say the least. He said if your class doesn't pass this year, you'll be stripped of your guild rank and cast out." My anger builds, especially when her expression doesn't change. "What do you have to say to that?"

"He's just bluffing."

"He's not bluffing! I talked to him! I saw his face! He's just as tired of your excuses as I am! You need to get your shit together, Magpie. Having a Taurian for a teacher isn't good enough for the guild. You know that. They don't respect me and now I'm forced to work with the mess you've pulled together as students." I gesture at the door. "Have you seen that crew?"

She squints, as if trying to concentrate. "There's one of them lizard-thingies, right? With the little legs?" She waggles two of her fingers back and forth. "Cute buggers."

Indignant, I gesture at the shell in the corner that she's clearly missed.

"Right." Magpie blinks at it, then at me. "So he's a lizard. You're a bull-man. What's the problem?"

"You also gave me Lark," I hiss.

She grimaces. "Was that this year?"

"YES."

"Okay, okay. I'll talk to her. What about the others? They any good?"

"Two more women and a priestess." I tug on the ring hanging from my nose, agitated. "What am I supposed to do with this team, Magpie? If you get booted, I won't get the chance to pay my hand back—"

"I'll handle it," she tells me easily. She hops off the counter and for a moment, she looks just like the old Magpie. "I'll pull back on the drinking. I'll talk to Lark and anyone else you want me to talk to. It'll be fine." She moves in front of me and puts her hands on my arms, then pats my biceps. "You worry too much."

"You don't worry enough," I grumble. "I mean it. You need to get it together."

"I'm trying."

I don't know that I believe her, but I need to.

WE TALK FOR a little longer, me discussing the class and potential issues, and Magpie distractedly pretending to listen. I can tell when she's no longer paying attention, as her gaze wanders and her responses slow. Something tells me she's waiting for me to shut up so she can go find herself another drink, and my mood sours. I head off to bed, because tomorrow's going to be a long day and I doubt I'll see Magpie for the morning's class, despite her assurances that she'll be there.

It's when I get back to my quarters that I realize something important. I have a wife now. And she's not here.

Not that I want to fuck her tonight. Well, part of me does. But that part is easily ignored, this week at least. No, she needs to be in my quarters because she needs to get used to sleeping with me. Even if we only fuck during the Conquest Moon's rut, we still have to make people believe we're married for normal reasons. That means she needs to stay with me. We need to act like a married couple to a certain extent.

And I don't need her avoiding me and then panicking when the lust of the Conquest Moon hits me hard. I've heard horror stories of males unable to control themselves and just rutting anything and anyone close by, regardless of whether or not those people wanted to be rutted. It's why Taurians tend to leave the city during the Conquest Moon season. It's why we line things up in advance.

So there are no surprises.

My new wife needs to get comfortable with her Taurian husband before we get down to business. Rubbing a hand down my long nose, I pull another pillow from the linen closet in the hall and toss it on the bed, then go in search of my new bride.

I find her upstairs, having a lazy conversation with her friend. Aspeth is sprawled in Gwenna's bed with the big orange cat tucked at her side. She looks sleepy, her hair is disheveled, and she's wearing nothing but a thin thigh-length chemise that leaves her arms and legs bare. My knot threatens to act up again, and so I scowl at the two women. "Was today not hard enough already? You should get some sleep. Tomorrow's going to be even worse."

"Don't threaten me with a good time," Gwenna huffs. She's sitting on a chair near Aspeth's spot on the bed, and when I approach, she puts her feet up on the edge of the mattress. It's a subtle blocking move, easily missed if you don't know what to look for. "We'll handle your class. Don't you worry about me and Sparrow here."

"Aspeth," I say firmly, reminding them that they haven't earned guild names yet, "is my new bride. She needs to sleep in my quarters."

"Oh, right." Aspeth sits up with a yawn. "I forgot."

"How do you forget your husband?" Gwenna asks. "How is that even possible?"

"It's because some arse keeps making me carry rocks in a backpack and trek through the city." She slides off the bed with a half smile at me, and then picks up the cat, settling it against her breasts. "Come on, Squeaker. We need to go to bed with your new daddy."

Ugh. "Don't call me that."

She blinks at me, then moves past me into the hall, ignoring what I said and the fact that she's barely dressed. The fat cat is tucked under her arm, leaving a trail of loose orange cat hair drifting in her wake.

Gwenna clears her throat. "This better be a marriage of convenience. If you hurt her, I'll murder you."

"I've no intention of hurting her," I reply stiffly. The insinuation is incredibly insulting.

"Good." She pauses and then adds, "She's not used to dressing herself, by the way. You might need to help her in the morning if she can't reach the laces." She takes out a set of folded clothes—another uniform—and hands it over to me with an expectant look.

By the bull god, is Aspeth that spoiled? It takes everything I have not to curl my lip. If she's that pampered, she's going to be in for a rude awakening over the next several months. Guild members are the height of physical fitness and competency. They're required to be able to handle any and all situations that might arise deep in the Everbelow, because no one can rescue them when they're six leagues underground.

Well, no one but a few Taurians, sadly enough. Used to be that the guild only passed the strongest, the most capable, but now with the greed of the holders increasing, the impetus is for the guild to continually grow so more teams can be fielded. Most of them aren't prepared enough, and so Taurians go down to retrieve anyone in trouble more and more often. I've gone on far too many of those missions myself, and seen more than one useless guild member lose his life to stupidity.

Recently, Rooster and the king decided that if a Five finds a Greater Artifact while in training, they're automatically upgraded to full guild artificer status. That caused a lot of angry rumbling, but the guild ranks have been swelling, which is what Rooster wants. As long as the demand for artifacts is greater than ever, we'll keep sending people in, I suppose.

It bodes well for Magpie's team. No matter how terrible they are, if they're even reasonably competent, I should be able to get them into the fledgling tunnels at least.

Maybe there the gods will smile upon them and shove a Greater Artifact under their noses. Who knows.

Aspeth heads for my room, yawning, and I watch as the hem of her chemise plays against the backs of her thighs. They're thick thighs, which I like. Thick thighs that will feel glorious wrapped around my waist—

"So where am I sleeping?" she asks, pulling me from my spiraling thoughts.

I gesture at the bed. It's big enough for two, even if one of the two is a Taurian.

"I see." She pauses for a moment, and then sets the fat cat down on a chair near the hearth, giving the ears a scratch. Then she turns back to me, her expression placid. "Do you want me on my front or my back?"

"To sleep?"

"For sex."

"We're not having sex tonight."

Aspeth immediately brightens. "Oh, good. I'm exhausted." She brushes past me and moves toward the bed as if it has always belonged to her. "I'm taking the right side, but tell me if you want it."

She gets in and pulls the covers over herself, and then closes her eyes. I stare at her for a long moment, my thoughts churning. How is it that this particular class has only just started and yet I feel my life spinning more out of control by the hour? Eventually, I lie down in bed and stare up at the ceiling, waiting for her to say something. To start the conversation I know we should have. I'm experienced and I know what to expect with a Conquest Moon on the horizon, but I suspect I'm her first Taurian relationship.

Or her first relationship. My throat goes dry. "Tell me about yourself, Aspeth."

"Why does everyone keep asking me about myself?" She yawns.

"Because I wish to know who I married."

"Do you? Or did you just need a warm body? Because that's what I needed." She rubs her nose, a sleepy and unguarded motion. "Don't fret about whether or not we like each other, Instructor Hawk. That's not why we married."

Hearing "Instructor Hawk" while we're alone together feels . . . strange. "Muck it. Just call me Hawk."

"Hawk, then." She drops her hand and snuggles down into her pillow, clearly ready for sleep.

While I appreciate her practical nature when it comes to our marriage, we're not on the same page. I'm thinking about sex and she's thinking about whether or not we're companionable. It just makes me even more concerned that she's innocent. "We should talk."

"Mmm." She doesn't stir, but at least she's listening.

"This isn't my first Conquest Moon. I've experienced two since I hit the proper age. The god doesn't call to his sons until they're over the age of eighteen."

"That's nice." Her voice is sleepy.

I continue to stare at the ceiling, then at the crack on the wall that drips water sometimes when it rains. It's a crack that Magpie's been swearing to get someone to fix, except she owes the carpenter money. "It's so if we breed a child, we can support it. Take care of it. I've had no children despite two god-callings. This will be my third."

She's silent, and I wonder if she's worried about children.

"I'm not looking to have children this time, so we are in agreement," I say before she can stress over it. "I need to handle my debts first." I raise my magicked hand into the air, twisting my wrist and admiring the strength of the runes carved into the metal. Every day, I'm grateful for my hand. It's a reminder that I've been in worse situations, and flexing it calms me. I can handle this. I can handle what this season brings. "Besides, if you're pregnant, you can't excavate."

"Mmm."

"So we'll need to talk about birth control of some kind. The Conquest Moon makes our seed exceptionally potent. . . ." Especially because I'll be buried deep inside her, knotted tight, and the thought sends heat curling up my spine and makes my tail twitch. I clear my throat, steadying myself. "What have you used in the past?"

"Haven't," she mumbles sleepily.

I turn my head, and then pull back a little because her pillow is even with mine and one of my horns nearly took her eye out just now. We'll have to figure that out. Later. "What do you mean, you haven't?"

"Haven't had sex." Her eyes are closed, and she looks half-asleep. "Was waiting for marriage."

I sit up on my elbows, aghast. "How old did you say you were again?"

"Thirty." She pulls her pillow over her head. "Do we have to talk about this right now?"

"And you haven't had *sex*?"

"My father would have murdered my suitors." Her voice is muffled. "And I'm going to murder you if you keep talking while I try to sleep. Can we discuss this later?"

I relax back into bed. Right. Later. Tomorrow.

Fine. It's fine.

I stare at the ceiling for a while.

"Your father must have been exceedingly protective," I can't help but comment. I've got a picture in my mind of some fat, wealthy merchant—maybe even an illegal artifact broker—who caters to all the prosperous holders. Of course he'd be protective of his daughter, letting her choose who she wishes to marry and when. And if that daughter is as bookish and spoiled as Aspeth, she probably gets her way in everything.

Even so, something isn't adding up. Why wait so long to marry and then fling herself into a hasty wedding with a Taurian who needs a rut partner? Am I going to have to deal with an angry father showing up on my doorstep? Demanding my head for deflowering his little girl?

I eye Aspeth again. The pillow is over her head still but I have a mental picture of her in my mind's eye. She's not that young or innocent. My gaze steals down to her tits, which slope indecently toward the mattress, her nipples outlined by the thin cloth of her chemise. It's like they're taunting me.

"This is damned inconvenient," I point out to her. "You being a virgin."

"Why?" She rolls over and presents her back to me, as if done with the conversation. "All I have to do is lie there, right? It'll be fine."

I sputter, glaring at her back.

Lie there?

Lie there?

"You are aware I'll be *rutting* you?"

"Mmm."

"Do you not know what that means?" I shake my head, bitterly laughing at my own folly. "Of course you don't. You're a virgin. Your father probably kept you locked away from anything that hinted at sex. I've seen the type." My head pounds and I rub my hand over the aching spot between my horns. "Allow me to educate you a little. Are you listening?"

"Mmm."

I take that as an indication to continue. It saps at my damned dignity to explain this to her like she's a small child, but I don't want any surprises.

"I take it you have heard the story of Old Garesh and the Prellian queen? The Taurian people have a different version of things than most. Our story goes that the bull god conquered Prell and stole the queen away from her husband. He was so taken with her beauty and courage that he claimed her for himself, and rutted her for five days straight. And when she arose from his bed, she gave birth to five strong Taurian sons. From there, the Taurian race was born. It is why we are part bull and part man."

It's not something humans like to hear, so I hurry onward with my explanations.

"Because we are the direct descendants of the bull god, it is he who guides our matings. Taurians are extremely fertile during a Conquest Moon. Every five years, when the moon returns, we seek our mate and do our best to impregnate her. If there is no mate, a Taurian seeks to spread his seed everywhere he can and in as many willing females as he can."

She has no response to this, and I suspect I've shocked her.

"You need not fear. Since we are married in the eyes of the gods, I will seek only to mate with you. And . . . I will be gentle. Or I will try to be. That is why we must talk." Just thinking about the upcoming rutting is making parts of me twitch. "Taurian males are not like . . . other males. When the Conquest Moon rises, so does our sacred knot. It only appears every five years, and it carries our seed. There are some minotaurs who carry the hand of the god permanently upon them, but I would not wish such a thing upon my partner." I can't imagine how those males function, constantly needing to breed, to rut, the knot always pressing, pressing, pressing. . . .

Aspeth is silent.

"I will try to be gentle," I remind her. "But it's not always easy for us. As the Conquest Moon rises, I will grow more and more unable to control myself. Your very scent will distract me. I'll want to touch you."

Lick you.

Drag my muzzle over that pretty cunt of yours and just drink in your taste . . .

My words grow strangled even as my cock stirs. "I'll grow jealous of other males in your vicinity, so if I seem like I'm in a bad mood, it's not you. It's the moon. And I'll want to mark you as mine. Not in a bad way, and not physically, of course. Just to show the world that you're mine. Some of the more flagrant Taurians take their mates out for public displays of lust, to remind the world looking at her that she's claimed. I've yet to do that, but . . . I understand it."

By the five gods, do I understand it. The thought of placing Aspeth on a platform in the market district and spreading her thighs wide so I can claim her in front of all? It appeals to the dark, base side of me. The side I've never really given free rein.

I swallow hard, because I can feel the knot rising, even now, weeks away from the Conquest Moon. I desperately stare at the crack on the wall, wishing Aspeth would say something. Her silence compels me to continue explaining, even though every word heats my veins. "When the hand of the god is finally upon me, you'll know it. My eyes will turn red and my thoughts will be of rutting you, and only rutting you. Any birth control will have to be done by you, because if it's left to me, I will try to stop it. Instinct will demand that I impregnate you."

Hot, wild instinct.

The need to fill my mate between her thighs with my seed. To fill her cunt so full of my cum that there's no chance she can rise from our bed without a child inside her. And because the moon is coming, the thought is an enticing one. It's all wrong, but my baser instincts love it.

"I've heard from my mother's brother about a Taurian who had a mate. She used a sponge to stop his seed inside her, and the hand of the god was so heavy upon him that he fished it out and then shoved it into her mouth to stop her protests while he plowed her. Heard she had twins, too, because the god was teaching them a lesson. But don't be too alarmed by that. The god will understand when it's not a good time, and I'll make a plentiful offering to Old Garesh to appease him. But during the Conquest Moon? I'll be lost, Aspeth."

Even though she's a stranger to me, and an irritating one, I can't deny that her body is enticing. I can't deny that a willing partner for the Conquest Moon is an exhilarating thought. I can't deny that I'm looking forward to things. Just thinking about it has made my cock hard, seed dribbling down my shaft as I lie next to my woman and tell her all the filthy things I'm going to do to her.

"I'll take you hard and fast," I tell her, and my voice is a growl of pure unadulterated lust. "I'll want nothing more than to shove my knot deep inside you and fill you with my seed. I'll fuck you hard and bury myself inside, and then we'll wait for my knot to go down. During that time I'll be tied inside your body, locked to you. And then once it goes down, I'll probably want to fuck all over again. Some Taurians don't come up for air until the moon passes entirely. We'll have to keep food and drink nearby. I'm going to be in an absolute frenzy. When we're done, you won't be able to walk straight for a week. That's not bragging—that's a fact."

I reach for my aching cock and then pause, glancing over at the form of her in the bed. "I know it'll be your first time, but I won't be gentle. Can't be gentle. I won't brutalize you, but we need to get comfortable with each other before the moon fully rises. I'm not saying that to get my rocks off, no matter how it seems. I'm saying that for *you*. You should be comfortable with my body, and I should know how to please yours. That will make things easier for both of us. You should know Taurians aren't built like regular humans. Just like we're built bigger overall, we're bigger everywhere. If you want an anatomy lesson, I'm happy to give you one."

The idea pleases me. Not just the thought of shoving my hard cock into her hand and letting her explore it, but the practicality of it.

"Actually, we should add that to your lessons. We can meet after class. What do you think?"

Aspeth lets out a gentle snore.

Shock courses through me as I stare at her back. How can a female sleep at a time like this? When I've just explained to her in great detail how I'm going to *rut* her? *Take* her? In public if the need upon me is too great? That I'm going to fuck her so hard—

She shifts in the bed and as she does, I notice a smear of dirt on her arm. She was so tired from the rock carrying earlier that she must have opted not to bathe but just crawl straight into bed.

And here I am trying to have a conversation with her.

I snort at my own arrogance and adjust my aching cock under the blanket. Tomorrow, perhaps I won't push them so hard. Or I'll at least make certain Aspeth is awake before I launch into a conversation about my anatomy.

ELEVEN

ASPETH

23 Days Before the Conquest Moon

"Y̲OU FELL ASLEEP last night," Hawk hisses at me as I trudge up one of Vastwarren's sloping streets. Truly, are there no level places in this blasted city? Not a single gently meandering road? Does everything have to be an uphill climb?

At my side, the Taurian practically stomps his hooves as we struggle up the street. He's sulking, I suspect, because I fell asleep while he was nattering on about gods and how Taurians are sacred. "You mean I fell asleep after a hard day of training when you decided you needed to lecture me? Like I'm some idiot girl who's never seen a cock before?"

I mean, I haven't, but he doesn't need to know that.

His nostrils flare and the ring in his septum jumps. He glances up the street, where Kipp the slitherskin is bounding away happily, carrying both house and backpack as if he was born without fatigue. Behind him, Gwenna is doing a good job of carrying her pack, and both Lark and Mereden are lagging behind both of them. I'm at the rear, limping along in my boots and wondering what ever possessed me to try to become a guild artificer.

Oh, right. Because the enemies of Honori Hold will execute us to steal our lands. Can't forget that.

And now I've got to deal with a pouty bull-man who tried to lecture me when I wanted nothing more than to sleep.

"Have you seen a Taurian cock? With the sacred knot engorged?"

Oh my, the word *engorged* just makes me all kinds of flustered. "I . . . well, no."

"Then save some energy for tonight, because you're going to see one." Hawk leans in. "You need a lesson because I don't plan on being the villain in this. It was your idea to marry."

"So it was." I can handle a cock showing. Truth be told, I find the entire idea a little fascinating. "But if you want me to stay awake, you'll have to stop lecturing me and actually let me catch my breath today." Already the backpack straps are burning two strips of pain on my shoulders.

"This is for your own good," he reiterates, and casts a stern look in my direction. "Don't think you can get away with anything simply because we're married."

I gasp in outrage. "I wouldn't! And I'm offended you think I would use our connection like that."

"Wouldn't you?"

"No!" I sputter. "You're the one who brought up your cock, not me."

He arches a brow at me. "Don't pretend like it's never crossed your mind to milk your advantage here by milking my cock."

I sputter again. "Rude!"

He snorts.

"Let it be said that I wish to learn everything there is to be taught here," I tell him indignantly. "I didn't come here to be coddled. I came here to be part of the guild. Anything extracurricular is going to have to wait until I'm rested so I can be a beneficial part of the team, and that means bed sport."

My teacher grunts. Is Hawk relenting? Have I convinced him that carrying rocks isn't the way to teach us? "We still need to train with Magpie, too."

I have to admit, I am more than eager to meet her. I want to hear all her stories. I want to learn what she knows. I want to absorb everything there is she can teach.

"Soon." Hawk's voice is terse. He jogs ahead, agile on those enormous hooves, and moves to Kipp's side. "I thought we talked about the house?"

The slitherskin ignores him.

UP AND DOWN we go, marching all over Vastwarren's streets until I'm heartily sick of backpacks and guilds and, most of all, Taurians. Sweat drips down my face, and I'm relieved when Hawk calls for lunch and a rest break. We eat and drink water while sitting on the curb of a busy lane, watching donkeys pull carts up to the apex of the city, where the ruins are walled off.

"When do we get to go up there?" I call out. "To the tunnels?"

"You're not ready yet."

Humph. Of course he thinks that. "Yes, but *when* will we be ready?"

Hawk crosses his arms over his chest. "How long do you plan on keeping your arse on the curb and resting, fledgling?"

Grumbling, I get to my feet.

We march for a little longer, until we've circled the upper quadrant of the city again and returned to Magpie's home. At Hawk's instruction, we deposit our packs by the door for tomorrow's drills, and then head inside after him. To my surprise, we enter an empty, narrow chamber. If I put my arms out on each side, I'll be able to touch both walls at the same time. At the far end of the room is a weapons rack.

"If you're not wanting to build your endurance, we'll have to work on your combat skills," Hawk tells us. "Each excavation team sent into the tunnels consists of five people, and each person on the team has a particular job assigned to them. Someone will be the navigator, ensuring you don't turn in endless circles. Someone will be the healer, in charge of keeping the party healthy. Each team will have a gearmaster in charge of supplies. A good gearmaster won't let you run out of food three days in. And then we have our combat members, our sword and shield. The shield—or bulwark—will protect the other members of the party while the sword takes point on combat. Even if you're not the assigned sword for your group, you'll be expected to handle yourself with your weapon of choice. Sometimes the sword gets killed early on and someone else has to take over the role. Understand?"

Mereden raises her hand, trembling.

"Speak," Hawk says.

"Do we have to fight ratlings? Or will they leave us alone?"

"Not just ratlings are in the Everbelow," Hawk says, voice ominous.

"What else?" Lark asks.

"Spiders, for one," Hawk says. "Big, nasty beasts with too many legs that come out of nowhere and crawl over your shoulder. Monstrous things."

"How monstrous are we talking?" asks Gwenna, a frown etching her face.

"Monstrous enough." Hawk shakes his head and moves over to the weapons rack. "And ratlings, of course. They moved in when Old Prell collapsed, and they're not keen on anyone digging around in the ruins. If they hear you in the tunnels, they'll come after you. You will need to be on guard. And then there's other teams."

"Wait, did you just say 'other teams'?" I blurt out. "They'd attack us?"

"It's not unheard-of. We all know of teams that die down to a man and yet someone else makes it out with a fantastic artifact but they can't exactly describe where they found it. No one would accuse them directly, but . . . it's best to be careful." He gestures at the weapons rack. "Does anyone have experience with any of these?"

I stare at his broad back, agog. I knew that there would be ratlings in the tunnels. I knew that there would be other problems, like collapsing paths and rockslides and things nature presented to us as we crawled leagues under the earth for ancient treasures. It never occurred to me that other teams might attack and rob us simply to get what we've uncovered. Gooseflesh pimples my arms and I rub them tightly. I wonder just how common "accidents" are in the guild.

"Anyone?" Hawk turns to look at us, and I'm pretty sure he's frowning.

Kipp moves forward and grabs a sword from the rack. It's the smallest one. Actually, it's probably more like a dagger. He twirls it around his wrist expertly and then sheaths it, gazing up at Hawk.

The Taurian glares down at him. "You want to be the sword?"

Kipp shrugs.

"You're half the size of anyone else, and you're still wearing your house, despite me reminding you repeatedly that you can't do so. If you won't listen now, what makes you think I'll trust you to listen when your team is in the tunnels?"

Kipp shrugs again, and this time the twirled shell of his house slips off his back in a fluid motion, clanging to the floor like a dropped bowl. He flourishes the blade again and then races up the side of one of the narrow walls, then onto the ceiling, his sucker-like toes clinging to the wood. When he's upside down, he twirls the sword again and assumes a warrior stance.

Hawk sighs heavily and tugs on his nose ring again. "Fine. Great. You're agile. I meant it. You're not a team of one, you're a Five. Understand?"

The slitherskin licks his eyeball, his long, sticky tongue darting out. He sheaths the tiny blade at his waist and crawls over to a corner, watching.

Our teacher turns back to us. "Anyone else?"

Gwenna raises a hand. "I'm good at cooking. And mending. Used to be a maid, right up until I came here. I could manage the gear."

Nearby, Mereden claps her hands. "Oh! I could be the healer!"

"What, I'm supposed to navigate?" Lark asks, belligerent. "I can't even find my way out of a pub. I should be the sword."

Kipp growls, the sound adorably cute instead of alarming. He clearly doesn't like that idea.

"You could be the shield," Gwenna tells her in a reasonable voice. "Aspeth can't."

"Why not?" Lark demands.

"Yes, why not?" I ask.

Gwenna glares at me. "Reasons. There are lots of reasons for her to be safe in the back and not at the front."

And I'm sure most of them deal with the fact that I'm nobility, but of course we can't say that. I just shake my head at her. "I want to do whatever I'm best at. And if it means to be the bulwark, then I shall happily contribute."

Hawk raises his hands in the air. "This is a lovely conversation and I'm glad you're all working together, but I didn't *ask* what position you wanted. I asked what you had experience in. It's clear to me that some of you are useless."

"Hey," Lark protests.

"Not you," he says. "Aspeth. She's the weak link in your chain right now."

"Rude!" I'm mortified at his words. I'm a holder's daughter. I'm educated. I cannot be the weak link. "You haven't even assessed me yet!"

"I can tell just because of how soft you are."

"Hear that, team? He thinks she's soft." Lark chortles.

He points at her, furious. "You made it sexual, when all I meant was that she has no muscles or stamina. She's . . . she's . . . pillowy."

"Please, stop," I say dryly. "My ego can't take much more." Pillowy. How humiliating.

Hawk glares at both me and Lark, as if I had anything to do with his assessment of my fluffiness. "It's crucial that your skills are tested because if the wrong person is put in the lead, you could all die." He crosses his arms over his chest and I can't help but notice that his guild coat is missing again today. It's almost as if he prefers to wear as little as possible when training us. . . .

And then my face goes crimson at the thought.

"I'm going to be placing you based on your performance with weapons," he continues. "You'll all need *some* competency level, and whoever is the best at attacking—or defending—will take the front two positions. Understand?"

The slitherskin growls again.

I can already tell I'm going to be at the back, since he considers me "pillowy."

"Enough. All of you get a weapon from the rack. Let's practice for now and see what natural skills you've got." Hawk moves aside, gesturing at the array of weapons.

Oh dear. I'm reasonably confident that I have zero weapons skills. The closest I've ever gotten to a weapon is choosing which knife and fork to use at society dinners. Delicately, I move forward and consider the selection. There are more knives, of course, and what looks like a rather short and skinny sword with a pointed tip. The shields at the end of the rack are excessively curved, as if cupping the body, and seem rather small for, well, shielding.

"You wear both at the same time," Hawk says, answering my unspoken question. "There's a bracer for each shield, and a good bulwark can utilize both at the same time and expand and combine them to provide the most shielding possible for his team."

"Ah, I see." I don't, but I'm pretty sure he doesn't want me going toward shields just yet. I move past Mereden, who picks up a spiky-looking club, and take the sword gingerly in hand. It looks, well . . . stubby. At my side, Gwenna jostles me, picking up a pair of daggers. "How come everything is so short?"

"The same reason you're in a narrow room," Hawk replies. "You need to learn to fight in close quarters. You're not going to have room to swing a massive sword in a narrow tunnel, so you have to learn to fight with smaller ones. It's why you won't see a full-on quarterstaff or training with a bow and arrow. These are tunnel tactics."

Oh. It makes sense, I suppose. "What about a crossbow? Or a blow dart?"

He tilts his head, and his horns look surprisingly rakish when he does. Not that I'm noticing such things about my new husband. "Are you good with either?"

"Well, no—"

"Then it doesn't mucking matter, does it?"

Grr. I bite my lip to keep from retorting something impolite.

He takes my hand and curls it around the hilt of the sword I'm holding. "You practice with this. Learn the basics. When you master them, then we can talk about other weaponry."

I hold the delicate sword in front of me and wave it in the air, trying to emulate Kipp's effortless swings from earlier.

"That," Hawk says, putting a hand over mine to lower it and stop my movements, "is a stabbing blade, not a swinging one. And you're going to put someone's eye out. Let's work on your grip first, all of you. Get a sword and stand in line, and we'll work on the basics."

TWELVE

ASPETH

THE BASICS ARE surprisingly difficult. I'm supposed to hold a sword tightly, but not too tightly. I'm supposed to keep my wrist loose, but not too loose. I'm to stab with expertise, but not slash, and pull back quickly. I'm to avoid bones so my weapon doesn't get caught in them. I'm not to twist, or jerk, because I can just as easily snap my own wrist as I can stab a ratling.

By the time we're done, my arms are throbbing and I want to stab Kipp with my blade, because the slitherskin is a bit of a show-off. It's clear he knows how to do everything already, and I've caught him looking at my grip as I do exercises, an expression of dismay and disgust on his face.

So I'm not good with a stabby little sword. I'm positive I have other skills that can be of use. It's fine.

Gwenna's good with weapons, though. "Just like stabbing a roast that keeps sliding across the pan," she declared confidently as she jabbed a stuffed leather dummy. "Or a man who won't shut up."

Lark hooted at that. I didn't find it quite so funny, mostly because I'm bollocks at stabbing. I don't like being terrible at things. I prefer to do things I excel at, like reading books and studying ancient languages. The sheer physicality of being a fledgling is starting to intimidate me.

I wonder if I've gotten in over my head. If I've made a mistake. But what other options do I have?

None. So I need to stop whining and simply get better at everything.

Hawk forces us to lunge and jab, stabbing at the leather dummies until my shoulders and arms ache. My calves ache, too, from all the lunging and the hiking from earlier. By the time we put our weapons away, I'm ready to pass out again.

"Break for the evening," Hawk finally says. "We'll pick up with our hiking at dawn. Be ready."

"It's supposed to rain in the morning," Mereden pipes up, her voice timid. "It doesn't rain in the caves."

"Oooh, she's got you there," Lark crows. "I think I'm hearing a day off."

"I think I'm hearing a bunch of lazy students," Hawk retorts.

"Not lazy," Gwenna says. "Opportunistic."

Hawk shrugs his big shoulders. "Fine. If you want to avoid the rain, we'll stay in and do weapons practice. You need to learn to fight in low light or none at all, so we'll be using blindfolds."

I groan aloud.

Hawk turns to me, quirking that impossibly heavy eyebrow. "Not enjoying practice?"

"It's fine," I say, determined not to be the problem here. "That was a positive groan."

"No such thing."

"Very much so. I love sword work," I enthuse, lying through my teeth. "It was a groan of . . . of pleasure."

Hawk stares at me. Just . . . stares.

Lark grabs Gwenna and Mereden each by the arms. "Let's get out of here before the newly married teacher shows his wife his 'sword work.'"

"Ew," says Mereden, casting an appalled look in my direction.

And I blush, my face hot and my stance awkward. Apparently talking about groans of pleasure and sword work wasn't the way to handle things. I watch as the others file out of the room, Kipp snagging his house and slinging the massive shell over his back before trotting after them. It's just me and Hawk in the room now.

Teacher and student.

Husband and wife.

Definitely not a complication I expected to have.

Hawk just continues to stare at me, his gaze hot. He hasn't moved a muscle, but I still feel intensely aware of his scrutiny. It's like he's looking right through my clothing and it makes me quiver deep inside. I wipe a drop of sweat from my brow. "I . . . should go bathe."

"You should," he agrees, voice low and smooth.

Nodding, I race out of the practice room and run for the stairs . . . only to pause. When is it going to get through my head that I'm staying with him and not Gwenna? That I'm married now? Slowly, I turn around and head back toward Hawk's quarters, trying to compose myself. I can do this. It's fine. I enter the room and I'm relieved to find that it's empty.

A short time later, I'm less relieved. How exactly does one bathe oneself? Surely there's an easier way than simply dropping pitcher after pitcher of warmed-up water into the copper tub in front of the hearth? That's entirely too much work and I'm far too fatigued to even consider such a thing. I stand in front of the tub (with less than a finger of water at the bottom) because two pitchers in, I realize this could take some time and I don't have the energy for it.

Perhaps I can just be grimy and sweaty for the rest of my life.

There's a knock at the door.

"Come in."

Hawk enters slowly, his great horned head poking in first. He frowns at me and then closes the door behind him, leaning on it. "Something wrong? I left you time to wash up before I came in."

I put a trembling-with-fatigue hand to my brow. "I'm too tired to fill the tub. I had people do this for me at home."

"Of course you did."

I can't tell if he's jeering at me or not, but given how ruthless he is to me in training, I'm going to go with jeering.

"I'll just stay dirty another day. You did say it would rain tomorrow, yes? That will wash away the grime." Right now that sounds far better than anything else.

He nods, eyeing me. "Wait right here."

As if I have the strength to go anywhere else? I sink into the nearest chair, leaning against the tall back. "Sounds lovely."

The door closes. I'm nearly asleep when it opens again, and this time Hawk has returned with a massive bucket many times larger than I could possibly manage on my own. He fills the tub for me and then gestures. "All yours."

"Bless you for your kindness." I strip off the sweaty layers of my fledgling uniform and toss them onto the floor, then remove my corset and chemise, and cast them aside as well. I step into the tub and sit, my knees against my chest, before I realize I just stripped in front of my new husband. I've spent far too many years with servants bathing me and I didn't even stop to think.

I glance up at Hawk to see if he noticed my actions.

Oh, he noticed all right. There's a peculiar look on his bovine face, even though he doesn't say anything. After a moment, he clears his throat and gestures over at me. "You want me to wash your back?"

Should I? Part of me does, because there's nothing nicer than being scrubbed by someone else when you're tired, but I don't know what the boundaries are between us, him and I. "I don't know," I answer honestly. "Is it just washing?"

He rolls his eyes at me. "It is unless you want more."

"Right now what I want is a nap and to never see another bag of rocks again."

"Well, you won't get either." He chuckles with a touch of amusement and settles down next to the tub, picking up the washcloth I haven't touched yet. "Sorry the water's not hot."

After the long sweaty day I've had? Cool water is lovely against my skin. "It's fine." I hug my knees. "Thank you for the help."

"You're my wife . . . at least for now. It's the least I can do . . ."

What a thoughtful thing to say.

". . . considering I have to sleep next to you and smell you."

I take it back. All of it, I take back.

He wets the cloth near my feet, and I'm suddenly very aware of how close he is and how naked I am. We're married, of course. It's to be expected. But in a few weeks, I'm going to have sex with this man. That was my part of the agreement and I truly haven't given it much thought . . . until now. Now I'm noticing the size of his forearms and the vein that traces along the bulge of one. I'm noticing the warm reddish-brown of his skin and how he's lightly furred all over, with a thicker pelt going down the front of his chest. I'm noticing that even when he kneels next to the tub I'm folded into, he's absolutely massive. . . .

Hawk rubs the cloth across my shoulders, and my fatigue wins over my curiosity about his body. I close my eyes, hugging my legs, and bite back a groan.

"I've forgotten how long it's been since I joined the ranks," he murmurs in a low voice. "The first few weeks under Magpie's tutelage were pure hell."

"You weren't in shape?" I cannot imagine such a thing.

"Oh, I was. But Magpie said that humans were spoiled arses and expected Taurians to be the best of the best, so she pushed me harder than everyone else. She wasn't wrong, either. I can't count the number of times I've had to go in and save a human who wasn't able to hack it. That's why I'm going to push your group hard, Aspeth. It's not out of cruelty. It's out of necessity. You understand, don't you?"

I do. "I want to learn. And I want to be the best. So just ignore my griping. Everyone else does." I manage a weak smile. "When do I get to meet Magpie?"

He sighs, the sound heavy and defeated. "Soon." He ditches the cloth, tossing it onto my knee, and then rubs one shoulder gently. "You've got a bruise here."

It takes everything I have not to whimper with pleasure when his fingers dig in. "Keep doing that. I'll wash."

Hawk grunts, and then continues to massage my shoulders, working out all the stress of the last few days. It feels so damned good that I'm barely aware of my surroundings. I want to just close my eyes and lean into his touch and stay there forever. I half-heartedly swipe at my arms and legs, but when he strokes big hands over my back, I give up and just rest against my knees, enjoying the relief. Hawk digs into my muscles, kneading them with expertise. "This isn't going to lead to anything, in case you're worried. You just look like you needed a bit of loosening up."

"What would it lead to?" I ask with a yawn, my brain in a pleasurable fog.

He pauses. "Sex. Your father really did keep you sheltered, didn't he?"

"Pfft, no," I lie. I don't consider myself sheltered. I had a fiancé once. I let him pet my breasts and caress my thigh. I let him kiss me dozens of times. It's not as if I've never been touched before. But a massage leading to sex? That's ridiculous. No one's ever touched me to massage me except maybe a brisk hand massage from a maid when my fingers were cold. "Do a lot of people in the guild massage each other and then have sex?"

"How would I know? You're the only one I've ever massaged."

Oh. Huh. I wonder if he likes hugs.

His thumbs dig into a knot near my shoulder and my lips part. I arch in pain-pleasure as he works the tense muscle, and this time I can't help the gaspy noise that escapes me.

"Fuck," Hawk growls. He flings himself away from the tub, storming across the room. I glance over at him and his tail is flicking back and forth wildly, smacking against the legs of his pants in agitation. I should feel a little guilty, but all I really feel is sad that he stopped. He composes himself while I finish washing with quick, brisk movements, his gaze locked on the wall. When I'm done and I wrap a towel around myself, he turns back toward me. "Remember what I said earlier?"

My brows furrow. "You've nagged me all day. You're going to have to be more specific than that."

I can see him grit his teeth, setting his shoulders. "Don't be dense, Aspeth. You know what I mean. When I said we were going to have an anatomy lesson."

"I do remember that." My pussy clenches at the reminder, and I desperately hope he doesn't notice me twitching. "You said you didn't want me to have any surprises. That we were going to go over everything prior to the, ahem, rutting time."

"Good. You actually listened." His dry humor makes me prickle. "Fine, then. If you've no objections, I'm going to show you what an engorged Taurian cock looks like so you're prepared."

And he unbuckles his belt.

THIRTEEN

HAWK

T O HER CREDIT, Aspeth doesn't run away the moment I make my announcement about showing her my cock.

I feel a little strange about it, because it's not in my nature to whip out my genitals to women I've barely met, but we're not going to have much time to prepare for the Conquest Moon and we both need to be comfortable. I ignore the lecherous feeling in the back of my mind and cast aside my belt, letting my pants fall to my knees. My cock—already hard and aching—falls out and stands proudly at attention, an arrow pointing directly at my new wife.

She blinks at the sight.

Blinks again.

Squints.

"Sorry," she says after a moment, gesturing nearby at the candles. "The lighting in here is terrible. Can I get a closer look?"

I gesture at my length, indicating it's hers to examine as she likes.

Aspeth moves closer, still squinting. She leans over and continues to peer, moving so close to my throbbing cock that I could swear I feel her breath. What in the five hells is she doing exactly? She examines me with less than a handspan between her face and my cock, moving back and forth and eyeing me with such focus, as if she's examining a fascinating artifact she's never seen before. It makes me twitch, my tail slapping against the back of my leg. It shouldn't be arousing to watch her stare at me so intently, but I can't help it. Her lips part, and I imagine pushing the bulbous head of my cock between those parted lips and feeling her tongue brush against my skin.

"There's no knot yet," I murmur. "Give me another three weeks."

Her gaze flicks to me and then back to my cock.

"Well?" I prompt after a long wait, barely holding my breath.

Aspeth squints again, and then glances up at me. "I don't mean to alarm you, *sir*, but you're dripping."

Is that all she has to say? I huff with amusement, shifting on my hooves, and resist the urge to stroke my length and watch her reaction to that. Glancing down, I notice the head of my cock is indeed slick with pre-cum. "It's because I'm aroused, *wife*. Don't you get wet when you're aroused?"

She looks up at me, her face flushing red. Aspeth straightens, touching her nose, and then her hand flutters away. It's a strange motion, as if looking for something and not finding it. "That is a very personal question and I won't answer it."

I bite back a laugh at her prudish response. "I'm showing you my cock, Aspeth. We're going to have sex in a few weeks. I think we have to get comfortable with personal questions."

She chews on her lip, staring up at me thoughtfully. "Are you aroused?" Her voice is soft, husky. "Right now?"

My cock twitches in response. "Yes."

"Because you just bathed me?"

"Because you're staring at my cock and I'm thinking about fucking you," I admit. "Because I'm thinking about touching your body." I'm thinking about her thick, solid thighs and the softness of her belly. I'm thinking about the heavy weight of her breasts and how they'd feel in my hand. How they'd move in time to each thrust I make inside her. "I can't help but think about touching you."

Her hand goes to her throat, her eyes soft, her cheeks pink. She wets her lips, gazing up at me. "Do you need to see me? All of me?" She gestures at the cradle of her thighs.

I don't need to. But by the five hells, I'd love to—

Before I can answer, something crashes in the hall outside and thumps down the stairs.

Aspeth jerks in surprise, clutching the towel to her body, and I hastily shove my cock back into my pants. "What was that?" she asks. "An intruder?"

A dish crashes to the floor, followed by a curse, and I wince, shaking my head. "No, I suspect that's Magpie."

My new wife brightens. Her fingers go to her mouth and she bites on her thumb's cuticle. "Oh, I've been waiting to meet her. How do I look?"

Like I'm about to fuck you, I want to tell her, but I know the moment is gone. I bite back a sigh of irritation and hold a cloak out to her. "You're wearing a towel."

"Right." She tosses the cloak around her shoulders and gives a girlish giggle, moving to my side and grabbing my arm. "Will you introduce us?"

Oh gods. I could tell her that she doesn't truly want to meet Magpie. That she shouldn't meet her hero. That it's only going to break her heart. But I can't avoid this forever. With an agitated tug on my nose ring, I nod. "Fine. Come on."

It's only a few steps down the hall to the kitchen of the house, but each step is incredibly uncomfortable. My cock is throbbing and stiff and shows no signs of receding. I'm glad that Aspeth's too distracted to grab a candle because the last thing I want is for Magpie to see just how aroused I am. I haven't yet told her that I married one of our students, and I'm not looking forward to that conversation.

There's another crash of pans in the kitchen, and when we enter, I see Magpie bent over, digging through one of the larders, knocking dried onions and a wheel of cheese to the ground. A lone candle flickers on the table nearby, providing just enough light for me to see my boss's disheveled appearance. She's wearing a guild uniform, but it's so wrinkled and filthy that I know it's the same one she'd been wearing the last time we talked. A quick glance over at my side shows Aspeth's excitement giving way to confusion.

Hells. I clear my throat.

Magpie turns to face us, her hair a tangled mess around her head. Her gaze flicks to me, the woman on my arm, and then back to me. "Where's the brew?"

"I had it removed from the house. You should go to bed, Magpie."

She scowls at me and turns back to the larder. "I had a stash here."

"Yes, and I removed that, too," I say calmly. "You said you'd stop drinking."

"Tomorrow," she promises, and shoves aside a row of jars, nearly knocking them to the floor.

I glance at Aspeth. Her grip on my arm is tight, her face bright as she regards Magpie. "Madam," she calls out, and then her smile grows broad. "It is such an honor. I've dreamed of meeting you for years. You're the reason I've come to Vastwarren. You're the inspiration that's made me determined to join the guild. You . . . you're a legend." Aspeth's voice grows hushed with awe. "And it is a joy to be one of your students."

I roll my eyes.

"One of *my* students?" Magpie turns, squinting. She seems to notice Aspeth for the first time and then saunters over, weaving in a way that leaves no doubt she's been hitting the bottle hard. No matter how many times I hide the liquor, she somehow finds more. She looks Aspeth up and down, frowning. "I don't know you."

"My name is Sparrow—"

Magpie barks a laugh in her face, the sound rude and affronting, and my entire spine tightens with the urge to grab Magpie by the arm and march her to bed like a naughty child. "That's not your name, fool," Magpie laughs, spit flying as she announces this. "You ain't got that name yet. And you ain't my student."

"Yes, she is," I say quietly. "She's one of your fledglings this year, along with Lark."

Her expression contorts, and for a moment, I think she's going to apologize.

Instead, Magpie leans forward and vomits at Aspeth's feet.

Aspeth looks at me with horror and betrayal in her eyes. I feel like an arse, because I know she's looked up to Magpie all this time. I should have coordinated a meeting between them. Should have figured out a way to gently point out that Magpie prefers to spend her time soused instead of searching for adventure like she did when she was younger. That she's not the same Magpie. Hasn't been for years now.

"I really should get to bed," Magpie says after a moment, straightening and wiping her mouth. "Got fledglings to train in the morning. Right after I get another drink."

She wanders away, knocking one of the canned jars to the floor with a crash. Glass and sticky peaches spill all over the floor, and Magpie doesn't seem to notice.

I bite back a sigh and pat Aspeth on the shoulder. "Go to bed. I'll clean this and make sure she ends up in her bed and not in a gutter some-where."

"She . . . You . . ." Aspeth's gaze blinks from me back to the door Magpie pitched herself through a moment ago. "That was . . ."

"I know." I give her shoulder a squeeze. "We'll talk about it in the morning. Go sleep."

"She's . . ."

"A drunk. I know. And that's why we're in danger of losing every-thing. Now you know why you have to pass this year. If our class fails out, Magpie loses everything."

And I do, too.

FOURTEEN

ASPETH

22 Days Before the Conquest Moon

MY HANDS ON my hips, I stare up at Guild Master Crow, trying to pay attention. It's difficult to be in the moment this morning, be-cause in my head I'm still stuck on last night, watching my hero vomit at my feet.

Over and over again.

"The goal of this drill is to maneuver," Crow is saying. He clasps his hands together, walking along a wooden beam high above the obstacle course. A thin rain drizzles down on us, turning the dirt course into mud.

I hate this. I hate Master Crow. I hate mud.

I hate that Hawk canceled on us this morning and instead of him training us, we're with strangers as he goes on a retrieval mission.

Behind me, a man flicks the hanging edge of my fledgling sash, earn-ing chortles from his teammates. I ignore him, but at my side, Lark growls in her throat. If Guild Master Crow notices anything, he doesn't acknowledge it. Instead, he points at each section of the obstacle course designed to test our dexterity. "Tunnel. Then climb over the boulders. Tunnel again. Sprint past the falling rocks." Point, point, point. "Belly-crawl under the fallen wall. Tunnel again. Grab a pack and then make it across the finish line before the hourglass runs out of grains of sand. If you don't, you'll have to do it all over again."

"Not much of a challenge, boss," calls one of the fledglings. "Maybe we should all be tied together again like yesterday?" He grins over at us, showing off a gap-toothed and evil grin.

"Monster," Gwenna mutters. "I hope your dinner gives you the shits."

"Excellent idea, Rosto," Master Crow says, producing two long lengths of rope. "Master Magpie's team, tie yourselves together. My team, you do the same. We'll have you both on the course at the same time just to keep things interesting."

"Oh, they're interesting all right," Lark mutters. She catches the rope when Crow throws it in our direction and moves toward me. I take it and loop the end through my belt, handing it wordlessly to Gwenna. She watches me with a curious look but says nothing. We all tie together—Mereden at the end and Kipp at the front, ahead of me.

Then we march to the starting line, and I squint at the muddy obstacle course as it rains down even harder upon us. The group of men at our side are nudging one another and smothering laughs, no doubt at our expense, but I ignore them.

I have to, or else I'm going to start screaming.

She's a drunk.

"Go!" Master Crow shouts, flipping over the hourglass and setting it down on the beam next to him.

Kipp races ahead, his pull so strong that I stumble. The team of men alongside us today—Crow's fledglings—push past us, sweeping Kipp off his feet and giving me a violent shove. I stumble and Gwenna catches my arm.

"What's wrong with you, Aspeth?" she whispers. "You're not your-self today."

If our class fails out, Magpie loses everything.

Everything. Everything's wrong.

I jerk forward as Kipp rights himself and races toward the first tunnel. I stagger after him, getting on hands and knees to crawl through the damp tunnel made of rotting wood and more mud. It narrows down until I have to turn my head to the side and crawl forward using my elbows, but I manage to wriggle through and stand up, only to drip with mud, my boots and pant legs holding an obscene amount of the filth.

"*Keep moving*," Crow screams at us. "No one told you to stop, Magpie fledglings!"

Gwenna sticks a hand out of the tunnel and I grab it, hauling her forward. She collapses on me and pants, waiting for Lark to push through. As we wait, she looks over at me. "What's wrong?"

I shake my head. If I start to vent about how wrong things are, I won't stop. Kipp is pulling at the rope, desperate to get to the nearby boulders and continue on the obstacle course. Lark pulls herself through, and then we wait for Mereden.

"Something's wrong," Gwenna hisses at me.

Mereden stumbles toward us, hauled up by Lark's hand, and then we turn toward the boulders. Kipp makes an excited sound and races toward them, tugging us along. He skitters up the side of one boulder, taller than a staircase, and then holds his small hand out to me. I take it—

—and immediately pull him down. "Whoops, sorry about that." I set him on his feet. "Apologies for the touching."

He pats my hand as if to say *Apology accepted* and then turns back to the boulders. He climbs halfway up the first one and then watches us, pointing at a ripple in the otherwise sheer surface that might act as a handhold. I put a hand there and try to haul myself up.

And fail.

And try again.

Lark gives my backside a shove. "Everyone, help out."

My face burns with humiliation as the others pitch in and more or less push me up the rock's surface, until I'm at the top of the boulder next to Kipp and gasping for air. It takes far too long and I'm sure I'm going to have bruises in unmentionable places, but I'm up there.

"Put a hand down for me," Gwenna says, reaching up and pressing herself against the boulder's surface. "We can do this together."

I reach down for her, and Gwenna latches on. Holding on to her threatens to pull me back down and I yelp in distress as her sweaty hand slips out of mine.

"Time!" Master Crow roars.

"Time? Already?" Lark puts her hands on her hips, glaring off at the distant fledgling team that is already at the far end of the obstacle course. "What the mucking fuck? We barely got started!"

Master Crow claps his hands. "Let's do it again, Magpie fledglings. Try to do better this time."

"Again?" Mereden echoes, her lower lip quivering. "He's joking, right?"

I haul myself up to a seated position atop the boulder and look up at Crow. From the sour expression on his face and the smug ones of his fledglings, no, I don't think he's joking at all.

As I watch, one of Crow's fledglings rubs his hands under his eyes, pretending to cry.

Another grabs his chest and pretends like he's jiggling his breasts, and makes kissy faces as he does.

I exhale heavily. Cretins, all of them. "Come on. Let's get back to the start and put Lark next to Kipp. Maybe that will make a difference."

NO MATTER HOW we rearrange our team, we're terrible. By the time the day is over, we're all covered in mud, scratched up, scuffed, bruised, and thoroughly defeated. Even Kipp isn't his normal perky self. The moment we return to Magpie's lodgings he dumps his shell in the corner and crawls inside, not wanting to socialize with us.

I don't blame him. I'm disappointed in us, too.

"That wasn't training," Gwenna protests as we sit down in the kitchen. "That was abuse."

"At least they helped us wash off before we came home," Mereden says in a timid voice. She sits delicately at one of the seats at the table, manners elegant despite her fatigue. "It could be worse."

Gwenna makes a face at her. "They weren't helping us. They were throwing buckets of water on us because we lost. That was their reward for 'winning' each round of the obstacle course."

"Yeah, but at least our clothes are cleaner." Lark shakes out her rumpled sash and then thumps down upon a chair at the table. She grabs a couple of slices of bread and a wedge of cheese, shoves the wedge between the bread, and takes an enormous bite. "Why were we training with Master Crow anyhow? He's an asshole."

Everyone looks at me.

I say nothing at first, because I'm too tired. I'm relieved to see that the nestmaid assigned to Magpie's house stopped by earlier today and left fresh bread and snacks out for us, because I don't think I have the energy to get out of this chair and make myself something to eat. I pick one of the nuts out of a bowl decorated with guild designs and nibble on it thoughtfully. "Hawk left this morning to go on a retrieval mission." He woke me up before dawn to let me know, dressing quickly in his leathers as another Taurian waited near the front doors to the dorm. "He was the one who arranged our training with Master Crow."

I believe his exact words were *He owes me a favor and no one else will have you*, but I keep that part to myself.

"A retrieval mission?" Mereden echoes, her dark eyes wide. "What's that?"

"Taurian," Lark answers between bites. When she doesn't elaborate, Mereden indicates for her to continue. Lark clears her throat. "Taurians are really good in the tunnels. They're strong and sure-footed and have excellent direction sense. They've got an excellent sense of smell, too, and they can keep going when humans get tired. Whenever someone gets lost in the tunnels, they send in a few Taurians to fish 'em out. Happens all the time."

"It does?" Gwenna wrinkles her nose, glancing over at me. "So why don't they just send in teams of Taurians instead of humans?"

"Control," Lark announces. "Arrogance and control. Humans want to be in charge of everything. Humans want the artifacts. And there's not enough Taurians in the city anyhow. I think they get tired of our shit and retire after a few years to go live in the countryside and raise little baby Taurians with the lady bulls." She shrugs. "It's the guild's dirty little secret. No one has to be as good at surviving in the tunnels as they used to be because the Taurians will bail them out. Aunt Magpie would joke that passing the test is the hardest part of the job." She opens her sandwich and stuffs another slab of cheese between the bread.

I eat a few more nuts before posing a delicate question to her. "You knew she was a drunk?"

Lark makes a face. "Everyone knows. Everyone keeps hoping she'll turn it around, but she never does."

"Why is she like this?" I ask, puzzled. "She has everything she could want. She's legendary in the guild. She's found some of the most fabled artifacts—the Sword of Starflame, the Claw of Guidance. Legends are going to be sung about her. How can she be miserable enough to try to drown herself in a bottle constantly?"

Lark takes another large bite of her cheese sandwich and glances over at Mereden. "Holders."

My hackles prickle with alarm.

Gwenna kicks me under the table.

"You . . . you don't say?" I manage delicately.

Mereden makes a sympathetic noise, then reaches for the cheese to make her own sandwich. "She had trouble with a holder? Contract troubles? I know my family can be difficult with negotiations. I've heard the stories."

I wait for her to look over at me. To say something about my family, the esteemed and ancient Honori holders that have been in the northern mountains for centuries. But Mereden only nibbles on her sandwich and watches Lark.

Lark shakes her head, turning her sandwich and ripping a piece of the crust off with her teeth. "Love troubles. She fell in love with a holder's heir. He was using her for her connections and the artifacts she'd find. Magpie always had an amazing sense for locating things even in the biggest piles of rubble, you know? Incredible things. Some people say she was like Sparkanos the Swan reborn, but with a vagina."

Gwenna clears her throat.

"What? I didn't say it. I said *some* people say it." Lark shrugs. "Anyhow. Aunt Magpie had everything except the man she wanted. She waited for him to marry her, and waited. Five years or more, I think.

Then she found out he was marrying some other holder's daughter. Magpie confronted him and asked him to marry her instead, and he laughed. Said she didn't have the right bloodline. I think it broke something in her. She hasn't found anything good since." Her expression becomes melancholy. "Growing up, my aunt was just the most exciting person I'd ever met. But for the last ten years she's been a mess. I'm surprised Hawk hasn't abandoned her. I think he's the only reason she hasn't been booted from the guild. He picks up the slack. He's a good guy."

I nod thoughtfully, eating a few more nuts. He might be a good guy, but he sure is grumpy to me. If there's one thing I can say about Hawk so far, it's that he's protective of Magpie all right, and determined to help her out. And that means we have to try harder as a team. "Tomorrow is a new day," I tell my fellow fledglings. "Let's eat and get some rest, and if Hawk isn't back in the morning, we'll have to do that horrid obstacle course again. But at least we'll have a better idea of what to expect."

Gwenna groans. Lark does, too. Mereden purses her lips and looks ready to cry again.

"I don't like it, either," I tell them, grabbing some of the cheese and slapping it onto some bread. "But if this is what it takes to pass, then we just have to conquer it. We'll figure it out, one way or another."

We talk for a while longer, eating all the food set out for us and putting away the dishes. Kipp joins for a bit, not talking, just listening and nibbling delicately on bits of cheese and bread. Before long, we head to bed, and it makes me feel a little strange to return to Hawk's quarters without him. Squeaker is there, curled up on the bed, and lets out a happy *mrrp* at the sight of me. I wash up and undress, climbing into bed and hugging the cat.

Here I'd thought joining the guild would solve all my problems. That I'd coast to graduation and shower my family in artifacts and save the day. Everything is far more complicated than I expected, and twice as difficult.

I'm not going to give up, though. Even if Master Crow humiliates us daily. It's just going to make my eventual success all the sweeter.

FIFTEEN

ASPETH

21 Days Before the Conquest Moon

THE NEXT MORNING, Hawk still hasn't returned. I fight back my disappointment and dress in a fresh uniform, braiding my hair and pinning it up. I desperately want to pull out my spectacles for today but Master Crow will probably blab all about that to Hawk and so I don't dare.

I'm heading to meet the others when a thunderstorm crackles overhead, the sound loud and terrifying. Gwenna and Mereden are in the hall, cloaks in hand. Mereden peers out a window, watching the rain slash down onto the cobbled streets. "We're not going out in this, are we?"

"There's still no sign of Hawk," I tell them. "I don't know how long he'll be gone, and we need to make every day count."

There's a knock at the door, and Gwenna opens it. A soaked slither-skin stands there, his house dripping and his skin bright orange compared to Kipp's leaf green. He holds out a folded note and races away the moment she takes it.

Gwenna unfolds it and reads it aloud. "All classes are to meet at the main guild hall today. No exceptions." She glances up at me. "Guess that answers that."

Once we're all gathered, we head out into the rain in the guild-assigned waterproof cloaks. They're ugly things but I have to admit, they do keep you dry. The fledgling nests—the dorms for each guild master—are only a few streets over from the main guild hall, and when we arrive, the place is filled with damp students standing in the entryway and talking amongst themselves. There's a ripple of laughter when we arrive, and one of the men grabs his crotch, only for Lark to grab hers back at him.

"Behave," Gwenna tells her, swatting her arm.

"I will if he does," Lark protests.

Before I can step in, a chime sounds and everyone looks up to the landing at the top of the hall. Several men with heavily encrusted guild sashes stand up there above us, and I grit my teeth to see that one of them is none other than Rooster.

"Today we have an esteemed guest visiting us," Rooster says in a somber voice. "Archivist Kestrel from the guild archives is spending time with us to discuss our next year's plans. We thought what better way to test our new fledglings than to have a little competition amongst our students?" He beams down at us as if he's the most clever man who ever lived. "Please proceed to the Artifact Training Hall when your teacher's name is called." He glances down at a scroll in his hands. "Masters Thrush and Vulture, please bring your teams in."

"What's this?" I whisper to Lark.

"No clue. Showing off?" She shrugs.

"What's in the Artifact Training Hall?"

Lark blinks at me. ". . . Artifacts?"

Clearly I'm not going to get anywhere by asking her questions.

The teams settle in, waiting in the hall. Mud is all over the gorgeous marble floors and there are puddles of rainwater by the entrance. I manage to squeeze a seat on a bench when one of the men vacates, and I share my spot with Gwenna. Kipp takes off his shell house and sits atop it, looking bored as only a slitherskin can. Mereden bites her nails and casts anxious looks at the door, and I try not to do the same. Are we going to get in trouble because Hawk isn't here and neither is Magpie? I try to think of a lie to cover for them both. Hawk doesn't need one, but Magpie . . . Magpie . . . perhaps Magpie has food poisoning. Bad clams, I decide. She got a batch of bad clams and has been vomiting violently for two days now. No, there's no need for a guild healer. . . .

Or is two days of vomiting too much? I lean over toward Gwenna. "Exactly how much would you expect to vomit if you ate bad clams?"

She narrows her eyes at me. "Is this some sort of weird innuendo?"

I bat at her arm. "No. I'm thinking of a cover story for Magpie—"

"Masters Magpie and Crow, please bring your teams to the Artifact Training Hall."

Oh, of course we'd get stuck with Master Crow's team again. I bite back a growl of frustration and get to my feet, smoothing my nonexistent skirts. We head through the doors that the other students disappeared into, following behind Master Crow's team of boorish thugs. One of them tries to kick Kipp, but the slitherskin just hops onto the wall and scrambles along it, as if he's completely unbothered by their bullying.

I'm busy rehearsing my excuse for Magpie, intent on getting the story straight, and then we're led through a set of double doors and into a room that takes my breath away.

It's like a library, except instead of books upon the shelves, there are trinkets and objects of every kind. As we step inside, I see jewelry boxes and ewers, spoons and blades and flutes. I see a bowl on its side with what look like bright red glyphs written on the belly. I see a few books, a quill, and a variety of other things I can't make out without my spectacles on. I want to squint and examine all of them but there are people at the far end of the hall, staring at us with smirks on their faces.

"I am Master Tiercel," the man announces, and his sash glitters just enough that even with my poor sight I can tell he's important. He's a slender man with a balding head and a blurry face. "Are both teams here? Master Crow?"

"My men are all here," he states, stepping forward. "Ready for the challenge."

Before anyone can ask about Magpie, I step forward. "All of Magpie's team is here. Hawk is currently on a rescue mission in the tunnels and Magpie couldn't make it this morning," I blurt out. "Clams. Lots of bad clams. Vomit everywhere. *Really* terrible. Never seen *anything* that color before. And the smell was just horrific—"

Master Tiercel recoils, raising a hand to stop my babbling. "We don't need the details, thank you." He looks down the line at us, pausing. Then he straightens and continues. "Very well. Teams, this is an exercise to show off your knowledge of artifacts to Archivist Kestrel. He is not a member of the guild but is very important as the official archivist for the guild itself."

An archivist? Who isn't in the guild himself but gets to catalog and pick through all of the guild's artifacts? I'm hit with a strong surge of envy. It sounds like the ideal job, and for a moment, I wish I were him. No tunnels, no obstacle courses, no backpacks with rocks. Just sitting inside and enjoying time studying artifacts to learn what we can from Old Prell and its ruins.

"Our friend has brought several legitimate and no longer functional artifacts here with him today. We've hidden them amongst the training duplicates on the walls here." He gestures at the laden shelves. "There will be three rounds. Each person on each team will select an object and bring it to their team's table. The archivist will give you a point for each correctly identified artifact. By the end of the game, the team with the most points wins."

"Oooh, what do we win?" Lark calls out.

"Honor for your house," Master Tiercel announces in a stiff voice.

Lark groans.

"I can see it's not much of an incentive for Magpie's students," Master Crow says in an infuriating voice. "So I'll sweeten the deal for you. The losers have to do the obstacle course in the rain and the winners will eat dinner inside."

"I'm sold," Gwenna mutters.

"Take a moment to discuss strategy and then select the order your team will go in," Tiercel continues.

We huddle, our heads together, with Kipp in the center of our small group.

"We're fucked," Lark whispers. "Two of Crow's men are repeaters."

"That means they suck, right?" Gwenna asks.

Lark makes a sound of distress. "You'd think that, but they have an advantage. They'll be familiar with the training artifacts already. They've probably done this several times before."

Mereden looks crushed. "I don't think I can do the obstacle course again today."

Gwenna shoots me a warning look, and I know what she's thinking. She wants me to stay quiet, to hide the fact that I know how to read Old Prellian glyphs. But I'm with Mereden—if I have to hear Master Crow scream for me to "tunnel" one more time, I might lose my mind. "I should go first," I tell them. "Each round, let me go first."

"No—" Gwenna begins.

"Yes." My expression is firm. "I can see if there's a legitimate artifact and try to get it before they do."

"How do you know if it's legit? What, are you some kind of artifact expert?" Lark scoffs.

"No, but I can read Old Prellian," I say, and before I can add onto that, Master Tiercel rings a bell. I straighten and move to the front of the line of our group, ignoring the curious looks that Lark is shooting in my direction.

When he nods, I step forward for our team, and so does someone for Master Crow's team.

"Each of you select one artifact and set it on the table in front of your team, and then someone else in your team will take their turn and select."

I stride forward to the shelves with crisp, authoritative steps, and then move my face a mere handspan away, squinting and examining each thing as best I can. There's a music box. A spoon. A plate. A tool of some kind. A wand. A goblet. A lamp. An ewer. The scatter of objects ranges from the mundane to the fantastical, and all of them are highly ornate in the style of Old Prell. My vision is terrible without my spectacles, so I pick up one object and hold it practically to my nose, trying to read the writing painted on the underside of a vase.

"Is there a problem, fledgling?" Master Tiercel calls out.

"No, I'm just making sure I don't miss anything," I tell him, and set the vase back down on the shelf. It looked authentic and appropriately old enough, the porcelain surface cracked and crazed, but the tidy writing on the underside was absolute gibberish, mimicking Old Prellian glyphs without knowledge of what they mean. It's obviously a fake.

I squint my way down the rest of the shelf, looking for obvious issues. Several of the "artifacts" have a bold yellow paint on them that makes me pause. Prellians crafted their dyes from minerals and foodstuffs and most of their yellows were murky at best. Blues and reds and earth tones are the colors prominent in Old Prellian artifacts, and I pick up a yellow cup and eye the glyphs crawling along the edge.

Cup of Neverturnal Milks from a Great Pigeon

Yeah, it's a fake. I suspect all of the yellows are fakes, and that helps me rule things out. My opponent picks up an artifact with confidence and returns to his table, and then all eyes are on me, waiting.

"Do we need to set a timer, fledgling?"

"No, I'll pick something." I just don't know what. I eye the next shelf, worried, and then spot what looks like an ugly, stone-encrusted egg behind a comb and mirror set. I pick the egg up and look for glyphs, as Prellians labeled everything that had a function.

Weight of Crushing. Charges Left: Zero.

Prellian artifacts with a specific set of charges always have a countdown glyph engraved on them, magically updated as each charge is used. Pursing my lips, I turn the egg over in my hands and then set it back down on the shelf as if it's a fake. I walk toward a series of glassware and pick up an ewer, then say, "Does the artifact need to have charges?"

"What?" Master Tiercel demands, clearly annoyed at the time I'm taking.

I turn, facing him with the useless ewer in my grasp. "Does the artifact have to have usable charges or does it just need to be a legitimate artifact?"

He tilts his head and gives me an annoyed look. "Do you think we would put working artifacts in here?"

I want to say *I don't know, would you?* Because some artifacts are absolutely useless other than being amusing at parties. Like the only artifact we have at home that still works—an ewer of delicate water. It makes any water it pours have a light floral taste to it, a nod to some spoiled noble's taste preference. But I'm probably not supposed to know that and everyone's staring at me with resentment. I put the pitcher back, intending to head back for the egg when I see the perfect solution.

It's a small bowl with a glyph on the metal lip, and a pretty red enamel on the edges and the two fluted handles. I recognize that bowl, because my mother gave one to my grandmother long ago. It's a bowl of infinite olives, another kitchenware nod to some Old Prellian nobility who couldn't be bothered to make their own snacks. I snatch it up, glance at the bottom to confirm that it is, indeed, a bowl of infinite olives, and then return to my table proudly.

"Finally," Master Tiercel says. "Next up, choose your artifact."

Lark heads out for our team, and as she does, I cough and cover my mouth, bending over. As I do, I whisper, "Don't pick anything with yellow on it. They're fakes."

"How do you know?" Mereden whispers back.

Gwenna grabs her hand and squeezes it, then gives Kipp a meaningful look. "Just listen to her, all right? She knows what she's doing." Her gaze moves to Lark, who has a bright yellow flute she's bringing back to the table and purses her lips.

I try not to wince, because everyone knows that wind instruments weren't popular in Old Prell. It was in the Mancer Wars several centuries ago that flutes became popular in music. But no one's perfect.

I manage to keep a straight face as Gwenna picks up a knitting hook of some kind that has the *domen* sign on it, the one of the bird with its wings spread that is a favorite of forgers everywhere. She wouldn't know, so I'm not going to judge her. Kipp picks a delicate knife and Mereden chooses something that looks like a clasp, and then all the artifacts have been chosen for our team.

Master Tiercel and Archivist Kestrel stroll past our table, picking up each item and then setting it aside. "Fake," Tiercel declares loudly as he picks up Lark's object.

"Fake," he says to Kipp's blade.

"Real," to Mereden's clasp, and she lets out a gasp of pure delight.

"Fake," to Gwenna's knitting hook.

He pauses and eyes my bowl, then looks over at his companion. Archivist Kestrel nods sagely.

"Real," Master Tiercel says in a sour voice. "Two points for Master Magpie's team."

I grab Lark's hand with excitement, and I'm pretty sure Kipp's tail curls around my boot with delight. Two points is good considering our team has never gone over the finer points of forgery. Or even the less fine points of forgery. Or any points at all, really.

The points are tallied for Master Crow's team and they only have one artifact declared real. "One point for Master Crow's fledglings. Let us begin round two. Fledglings, please come and choose."

Master Crow looks like he could spit nails, glaring at me as I get to my feet. I smooth sweaty hands down the front of my pants and wonder if I need to get a fake this time to seem as if I'm like everyone else, or if

I want to score points for my team. I debate this mentally as I continue down the long row of packed shelves. To my surprise, the man opposite me hurries over to the ewer I'd held last round—the one when I'd asked if items needed charges—and snatches it up.

Too late for hiding under the radar, I suspect.

Everything I touch now will come under scrutiny, I realize. They're all watching my every pause to read glyphs, my every hesitation in front of an object. I need to go back to the egg from before, but as I turn around, I see a thick palm-sized disk on a chain, the metal tarnished and scuffed. It has glyphs at four equal points on the surface, one of them the ornate eye used to denote the home of the gods, which the Old Prellians believed was in the great north, past the mountain range of my home. I pick it up and turn slowly until the medallion shivers in my hand, indicating that I'm facing north.

Well, I can't very well put it back now and pretend like I don't know what I'm doing. I return to my table with the medallion and set it down as discreetly as possible. Mereden, Kipp, and the rest of the team pick items, and I do my best not to wince when each forgery arrives on the table. At least they're avoiding the yellow like I'd asked. But it's clear from what they're choosing that they have no knowledge of Old Prellian art or enchantment, or even the basics of glyphwork. I make a mental note to bring this up to Hawk. My team needs classes on how to spot forgeries.

Well, and how to spot artifacts.

Really, we just need classes on everything.

"One point for Master Magpie's team," Master Tiercel declares at the end of round two.

One point is then declared for Master Crow's team, this person a different one from before. If I had to guess, I would say there's not an expert on Crow's team. They're just guessing out of luck. But now I need to go back and get that egg. I have a feeling that if I don't, we'll end up with a tie, and I'm willing to bet that a tiebreaker would not go in our team's favor.

This time, I head straight for the Weight of Crushing egg with no charges left. I pick it up and bring it to our table, and sweat as I watch the others pick their choices. When everything is chosen, this time Master

Tiercel goes to Master Crow's team first and picks through their objects with the archivist at his side.

"One point for Master Crow's team again," Master Tiercel declares. "Total points—three." He strolls over to our side as I busily do mental math. Okay, we're at three points at the moment. My egg should get us to four, which is a win, unless they don't count it because of the lack of charges. If someone else on the team has picked a winner—

"No points this round for Magpie's team."

"What?" I blurt out, looking up. "So deactivated artifacts don't count after all?"

Archivist Kestrel seems puzzled by my reaction. "They do count. You do not have any real artifacts at your table. We have a tie."

I glare up at both of them. "That's not right. Mine is a real artifact. It just doesn't have charges."

"The guild frowns on poor losers," Master Tiercel begins.

Archivist Kestrel turns the object over in his hands, peering down at it.

"I'm not a poor loser," I declare, stabbing a finger at the stupid thing. "It's a legitimate artifact. Read the glyphs on the bottom. It's a Weight of Crushing but it's out of charges. They're a common sort of thing. Look at it again." Master Tiercel gives me a pitying look that only pisses me off more. "Just look, all right?"

"This is not very becoming of your team," Master Tiercel continues. "And if your teacher were here, she would hear about it. This is the reason why teams need to be supervised. You can't be left alone. The rules are rules for a reason—"

"She's right," Archivist Kestrel says suddenly.

All eyes are on him. And me, but I keep staring at the archivist, waiting for him to elaborate.

"She's right," he repeats, and shows the underside of the egg-shaped weight to Tiercel. "Look at the markings. Look at the usage of lapis. There's one like this in the archive and it's got the same angle of cuts in the stone."

They bend their heads together, scrutinizing the artifact. Lark nudges me but I ignore her. My every fiber is vibrating with anxiousness as I watch the two of them. For some reason, it's very important to me that I be correct about this. I've always prided myself on my Prellian scholarship. If I'm not right, then I've got nothing to my credit. Not looks, not wealth, not holder name . . .

Master Tiercel grunts after a long, interminable pause. "I suppose."

"It's truly a shame it no longer has charges," Archivist Kestrel says in a bright voice, clutching the egg to his chest as if it is precious. "I would love to see how much weight the Prellians considered to be crushing. It would be a fascinating bit of scholarship, don't you think?"

"Absolutely," I force myself to reply. I want to talk about other weights that were mentioned in prior tomes and the units of measurement that Prellians used depending upon the situation, but now isn't the time. I eye Master Tiercel. "So this means we have four points?"

The master's jaw clenches and his nostrils flare. It's clear he doesn't want to announce us as the winners. He looks over at Master Crow, who seems equally irate, and then turns back to me. "The game is canceled. No winners, no losers."

"That's not fair!" Lark protests. "We fucking won!"

"You," Master Tiercel snarls and points at my face. "You stay behind. The rest of you are dismissed. The rest of the games are canceled. Spread the word with the remaining teams."

The room empties out with the sound of scraping chairs and grumbling voices. There's more disappointment as others file into the hall and announce the cancellation, and my face burns as I remain in place. The others on my team stay at my side, and Gwenna moves to link her fingers with mine.

Master Tiercel gives Lark, Gwenna, Kipp, and Mereden a dismissive look even as Archivist Kestrel continues to study the egg in his hands. "The rest of you can go," he says. "You're not in trouble."

"But I am?" I ask.

"The guild frowns upon cheating—"

Gwenna's hand tightens on mine and she steps in front of me. "She did *not* cheat. How could she possibly?"

"This is horseshit," Lark declares. "You just don't like us because of Magpie!"

Mereden and Kipp make angry noises of assent.

I'm flattered they're all so quick to defend me, but I can tell from the guild master's expression that it's useless. He doesn't know how I managed to identify the objects and I can't exactly tell him that I've been studying rare tomes ever since I was a tot. No one would have access to those kinds of books save for a guild member or a holder who'd paid a great deal to buy or borrow them. I can't point that out, or that I had a tutor—a retired artificer who was too old to go tunnel crawling—who taught me how to read glyphs.

I can't say any of that. I'm supposed to be just another person here, learning with the rest of them. So I give Gwenna's hand a squeeze and then detangle myself. "It's all right. I'll stay behind and answer their questions. I've done nothing wrong. You should go on back to the nest."

Mereden and Lark reluctantly head out, with Kipp at their heels. Only Gwenna remains behind, scowling at everyone. I have to give her another reassuring hand squeeze and a gentle shove toward the door. She stumbles forward and then glares at Master Tiercel and Archivist Kestrel. "If she's not back by dusk, I will have every Taurian in the city at your doorstep."

Then she turns and leaves and I'm left alone with the two men.

"Sit down, fledgling," Master Tiercel says in a furious voice. "I want to know all your tricks."

"My tricks?"

"How you did this. How you managed to cheat the system." He gestures at the artifacts. "How you guessed right all three times." He indicates the egg cradled in the archivist's hands. "How you knew this was legitimate when even we did not."

"Luck?" I answer weakly.

He leans forward over the table, the look on his face hard and unyielding. "Sit. Down. You're not leaving until we get some answers."

The archivist looks up as if seeing me for the first time. "Are . . . are you the one who married the Taurian? Your guild master's assistant?"

I didn't think it was possible but Master Tiercel's expression gets even harder.

I sit.

I imagine I'm going to be here for quite a while.

SIXTEEN

HAWK

FUNNY HOW THINGS change the older you get. When I was a young bull, I wanted nothing more than to be in the tunnels at all times, exploring the ancient grottoes and ruins of Old Prell. It angered me when we had to return early due to an injury in the party, or when Magpie started her descent into the bottle, because it meant we couldn't go out hunting. Not without five, and not without our leader. Now, though? As we finish another retrieval mission?

I'm glad to be home. Glad to be done with the soft idiots who pass for guild members these days. After two straight days in the tunnels, I'm sweaty and dirty from the hiking and digging. I'm tired, and more than that, I'm irritated and disgusted because the team we rescued made poor choice after poor choice and ended up with empty hands to show for it. If they'd run into a nest of ratlings in an unexpected location, I could have some sympathy for them.

Instead, they'd eaten mushrooms they'd found in the tunnels and ended up injuring themselves. They'd used a rescue signal stone for no reason and wasted our time.

I know I'm not the only Taurian who feels that way. Raptor, myself, and a big older bull named Osprey went down to retrieve the team, because a sacred five isn't needed for a rescue party, it seems. We were all three in a foul mood when we left, and are in an even worse one now as we head through the cobbled streets on the way home, our guild pay for the retrieval mission jingling in our pockets.

The three of us pause at an intersection, the general guild housing the next street over. Across from us is a popular pub frequented by the guild members, and it's packed to the gills with human men laughing and drinking and having a great time.

"Idiots," Raptor mutters, shifting on his feet, his hand on the strap of his pack. "Ten crowns says that our 'team' is going to head straight for the bar once the healers are done with them. They won't learn a thing."

"Do they ever?" Osprey harrumphs. "Whoever's in charge of the guild criteria for testing is clearly on the take. In my day, these fools wouldn't ever leave the training grounds, much less head into danger. Mushrooms, of all things." He shakes his shaggy head. "Insanity."

"At least we get paid," I say, like I always do. Normally it appeases me, knowing that the extra funding is going to a good cause, another step toward repaying my debt to the guild. Today, though, it just makes me bitter, because I know in another few weeks, I'm going to be back in the same tunnels, retrieving the same idiots . . . and the guild thinks a few coins tossed our way makes everything better and excuses poor behavior.

But no one ever asks Taurians what they think of things.

Before I let that path of thinking sour me, I adjust my pack against my shoulder. "I should get home. New wife and all that."

Strangely, just thinking about Aspeth waiting for me is pleasing to think about. She'll be in bed, no doubt snoring that little feminine snore of hers, her mouth slightly open. She'll fuss at me over training, because she likes to fuss and protest. I'll bathe . . . and maybe she'll give my cock that intense stare again, squinting at it as if she's never seen anything like it before and flattering my ego.

"So you decided to stay after all?" Raptor asks me, pausing. When I nod, he claps me on the shoulder. "Can't decide if you're an idiot or brilliant for taking a wife to handle the Conquest Moon, but I'm leaning toward idiot."

"Definite idiot," Osprey agrees.

"Thanks."

Raptor glances up at the sky. "Moon's gonna be ripe in another three weeks. Gonna be some kind of hell on the lead-up. Maybe a wife is smart after all."

"I'm heading back to my village," Osprey says. "Lots of eager widows looking for a few nights of fun and not much else. If you change your mind, you can come with," he tells me. "I leave in three days."

I nod, though I know I won't take him up on the offer. "Appreciate it."

"I leave tomorrow," Raptor says. "Take some time off. My Five fell apart, so it's a good break for me before returning to work once Lord Dipshit finds more for the team. I'll be back in time for the fledgling tests later this year, since we all know what a fuck-storm that will be."

I'm trying not to think about it, but he's not wrong. To pass the guild test, every person must take part in both a team exercise and an individual one. For the team exercise, every Five has to make a quick trip to the tunnels to retrieve an artifact placed there by guild masters, or to find a brand-new one. Those who pass both their tests return and celebrate their inclusion in the guild. Those who fail are fished out quickly (if they're alive) or slowly (if they're not), and it falls to the guild's Taurians to clean things up. Individual tests are usually tailored to the student's particular weaknesses, which is why I have to push Aspeth so hard. She can't stay soft and naive, not if she expects to become a guild artificer.

We're months away from anything like that, however.

"I'll see you when you return," I tell my friends.

We part and I make the brief trek back to Magpie's dorm, my thoughts full of Aspeth. Is it weird that I just want to sniff her? To breathe in her scent and let it wash over me? I'm sure it's the Conquest Moon making me obsess over a woman's scent, but I imagine what she smells like when she's aroused, and the thought of it makes my cock stiffen.

Definitely the Conquest Moon. I surreptitiously adjust my cock so walking home isn't quite so difficult.

The moment I step inside the dorm, though, all is chaos. There's shouting in the kitchen, and equipment is strewn all over the entryway to the house. I step over it, heading toward the source of the noise. The kitchen is even messier than outside. Magpie is by the stove, trying to pull a too-tight guild blouse over her chemise. Lark is stabbing a wheel of cheese into small chunks with her sword, Mereden is crying and packing the cheese chunks into small pouches, and the slitherskin is trying to pull a too-large jar off a shelf, three other broken ones near his feet. Gwenna is shouting at Magpie, who looks as if her head is about to split open.

I'm also pretty sure every weapon from the practice room is on the table. "What happened? Where's Aspeth?"

Mereden bursts into fresh tears.

Gwenna storms across the room toward me, her expression one of pure fire. "You! High time you showed up. You think you can just gallivant off and leave us behind?"

I arch a brow at her. "I was on a rescue mission. I left a message with Aspeth."

"Yes, well, we need you more than anyone else does." She puts her hands on her hips and glares at me. "Now that you're here, you need to go and save Aspeth before they torture her for information!"

"No one's torturing anyone," Magpie declares. "I've said that twice now. Can someone help me with my sleeve?"

Gwenna scowls at her and doesn't move to help. No one does. Instead, Gwenna turns back to me. "This is all your fault," she hisses. "If you hadn't left, Aspeth wouldn't be in this mess."

Her anger—as well as my own fatigue—make me unpleasant. I lean in, looming over her. "You want to tell me exactly what mess it is I'm supposed to be responsible for?"

She leans back, but only a little, her expression remaining fierce. "We were playing some sort of artifact game against the other teams of fledglings and they decided that Aspeth was cheating. They're holding her hostage at the guild hall and won't let us in to see her. That's why Magpie's getting dressed." She casts a dismissive look over at the guild master. "For all the good that will do."

"I'm helping!" Magpie protests.

"You're a soggy mess is what you are," Gwenna declares. "If you weren't such a waste of skin, we wouldn't be in this mess, now would we?"

"Hey," Lark protests. "That's my aunt."

"Your aunt is a drunken waste of skin," Gwenna repeats. "Tell me I'm wrong."

Lark glances at me and then drops her gaze, sullen. "I mean . . . she's trying."

"She's not trying very *hard*." Gwenna glares over at the two of them again. "And now Aspeth is suffering because there was no one to speak up for her. So someone in charge needs to fix this. Now."

I look over at Magpie. Her head is stuck in her clothes, one hand flailing above her head.

Sigh.

I set my pack down. "Someone help Magpie with her sleeve. I'll go get my wife."

BY THE TIME I make it to the main guild hall, I'm a tired, angry, cranky mess. My hooves are still crusted with mud from the caverns and I smell like old sweat. I want nothing more than to change out of my old clothes and take a bath, but it seems I'm having to retrieve my wife instead, and my mood grows more dire with every moment that passes.

When I storm inside, wild-eyed and tail swishing, an apprentice spots me and immediately runs down a hall. No doubt he's been told to notify someone of my arrival. Sure enough, Master Tiercel appears in the hall from one of the doors, his mouth tight and his expression troubled.

That makes me pause. Master Rooster is a fool, as are many of the other masters, but I've always respected Tiercel. He's hard but fair, and as a teacher, his students never end up needing a rescue.

"I'm here to retrieve my wife," I say, but some of the fire has left my voice. "What's the problem?"

"Hawk." His greeting is accompanied by a friendly handshake, and my mood smooths out a bit. "I'm glad you're here. I wish it were under different circumstances. We need to talk about your wife. When did you marry?"

"Recently" is all I say. "Where is she?"

"She's being questioned," Tiercel says. "This is the first I've heard of your marriage. And to a student? You have to know this is rather unorthodox."

"But not against the rules. Just like having a female student," I remind him. "As for my wife, she likes to argue, but I'm not entirely certain that's a crime," I point out, and mentally I'm imagining how Aspeth has managed to piss off Master Tiercel. "What's going on with the artifacts?"

"First, I would like to know how you came to know her." He tilts his head, regarding me. "Did she approach you or did you approach her?"

I narrow my eyes at him. What is he getting at? "I'm not sure why that matters. She wanted to be a student at the guild. Remember that she approached Master Rooster and wanted to enroll?"

He blinks. "Was that her?"

"It was. Called herself 'Sparrow'?" Recognition dawns on his face, along with an amused smile that for some reason makes me want to punch him. "You remember now."

"I do." He chuckles, and the sound grates on my nerves. "She certainly doesn't lack for boldness. What made you decide to marry her?"

I decide to lay it all out. "There's a rut coming up."

His expression remains blank.

Just as well. He wouldn't get it. He's not Taurian. "Mating ritual. Once every five years. Unavoidable."

"Ah. To appease the family, then?" His brows go up.

"Something like that."

"And you trust her?" At my puzzled frown, he goes on. "We have reason to believe your new wife is either a very skilled antiquities thief or possibly a holder spy."

When I sputter, he tells me of the game that afternoon. How Aspeth took a great deal of time to choose certain items, and how she'd chosen perfectly each time and corrected them on the third one. "She knew it was discharged. Either she was already in the know of that particular item or she reads glyphs."

That makes me pause. "Only archivists and a few of the masters read glyphs."

"Exactly."

I know Magpie recognizes some of the more common glyphs, and I've learned to pick a few out, but the Old Prellian written language is complex and requires a great deal of study, which is why it's only truly mastered by archivists, who aren't active members of the guild for one reason or another.

"My question is, did she position herself with you in order to get an in with the guild?" He gives me a worried look. "Everyone knows that Magpie's students tend to be a bit unorthodox. Perhaps she deliberately sought you out?"

I give my nose ring a tug before shaking my head. "I was the one who suggested we marry," I lie, trying to calm the situation. But I think about that night, and how Aspeth and Gwenna showed up with an obviously drunken Lark and asked—no, demanded—to be students. Surely not. Surely they're just two women who have decided to take on a particular challenge, and not spies. "If you want my opinion . . ."

"Please."

"She's not a spy. She's a spoiled rich woman. She's hinted before that her family comes from wealth, and she arrived with tailored guild clothes in expensive fabrics. She's incredibly sheltered and her physicality is terrible. If she truly was a spy, they would have sent someone who would easily pass the physical tests. As it is, I'm going to have to work her hard to ensure that she doesn't fail the basics." At Tiercel's slow nod, I continue. "It's far more likely that her father spoiled her and purchased artifacts on the sly. You and I both know that some merchants love to acquire contraband. That could be why she recognized them."

Tiercel nods again. "Most of the items she recognized seemed to be trinkets. You could be right. Who is her father, if you don't mind me asking?"

"I don't know."

His expression darkens again.

I raise a hand in the air before he can go down the "spy" route again. "I will keep an eye on her, and the moment I find out anything, I'll pass it along. But if you're asking me if she's dangerous, my answer is no. Not hardly. She'll be lucky if she passes the guild tests at all. She might have scholarly knowledge, but you and I both know that it only gets you so far in a dark tunnel."

He grunts, stepping aside. "You're right. Perhaps I'm just panicking. You'll alert the guild if you find out anything in particular?"

"You know I will."

We shake hands again and then he leads me into a waiting room. Aspeth sits next to an enchanted reading lantern, her hands clasped in her lap, her lips pressed into a firm, unhappy line. I can feel Tiercel's gaze on us so I move to Aspeth's side and rub my muzzle against her forehead, pretending affection. "Come along, wife. You've caused enough trouble today."

"Trouble?" she echoes, indignant. "I've caused no trouble!"

I take her by the arm and give Tiercel another knowing look, one that indicates I'm a man put-upon by a needy wife. Aspeth catches the look and makes another angry noise, jerking at my grip. She has every right to be annoyed at my expression, but I have to sell it to Tiercel so he doesn't suspect anything.

Leading her out of the building, I don't speak until we're in the streets and I know for certain that there's no artifact hidden in an alcove and capturing our conversation for the guild to spy upon. I sling my arm over her shoulder, and the lecher in me can't help but notice that she fits under my arm perfectly, as if she were made to be a Taurian's woman. "You want to tell me what's going on?"

She scoffs. "I don't know. Do I? Or are you suspicious of me, too, simply because I can look past a shoddy paint job? Whoever made those artifact duplicates should be ashamed. Even a child could pick them out."

"And yet no one else did except you," I muse. "Every single time, if Master Tiercel is to be believed. Are you just amazingly lucky or is there something else I need to be aware of?"

She pauses, glancing up at me, and for a moment, I worry that everything Tiercel said was right. That she truly is a spy of some kind looking to steal information about artifacts to take back to holders or to underground merchant rings. Her expression is guilty. "I haven't been totally forthcoming about my past."

"You don't say."

Aspeth stares straight ahead, but she doesn't fight off my arm. If anything, she leans into me. It's like she's seeking support. It's both gratifying and slightly terrifying. "When I was a child," she begins slowly, "I read a lot. My father was busy and my mother was dead, so my father's manservant had a standing order to find me any books I should like to read and he would buy them. Early on, I was fascinated with Old Prell and decided I would teach myself glyphs."

"That's impossible," I point out. "It takes years to master glyphs, even with a teacher."

"It takes twice as long when you don't have one," she says, voice wry.

"And you're telling me you taught yourself?"

"Some. Then I had my father hire a tutor who was a retired artificer, and he taught me the finer points. But I learned much on my own. I had nothing else going on and no friends." She shrugs. "No siblings. What else was I going to do with my time?"

Instead of suspicious, I feel a surge of sympathy for her instead. I imagine a small Aspeth, young and bossy and desperate for knowledge to make up for the lack of companions. I picture her with her annoying, shedding cat in her lap, a book in hand as she sits by the fire.

It would explain why she's so terrible at the physical aspects of guild life. It would explain a lot of things, actually. It would explain why she married a Taurian. She has no people knowledge, just books. I grunt. Things are falling into place. I squeeze Aspeth's shoulder. "Let's just get home, all right?"

"Am I in trouble? Is the team in danger?"

"No and no."

We walk through the curving streets in companionable silence, and I keep my hand on her shoulder. It feels good to have her at my side. Feels strangely good to realize that Aspeth might need a friend and that I can be that person for her. Not that I lack friends, but there's something different about Aspeth. She's infuriating and a know-it-all . . . and incredibly vulnerable, too. Returning to the dorm, everyone hugs Aspeth, Mereden cries, and Gwenna fusses over her like a mother hen. Magpie is still with the others, but silent. At least she has her clothes on properly now. I'm a little surprised she's still awake, but am too tired to deal with it. "Aspeth and I are going to bed," I tell them. "You should all do the same. We have drills in the morning."

They all groan. Kipp disappears into his shell house and the others scatter.

SEVENTEEN

HAWK

THE CAT IS waiting in our quarters, and Aspeth pets it and feeds it as
it howls and makes a ruckus while I fill the copper tub near the fire.
I've never heard such a loud creature, but she pets it (and fur flies everywhere) and talks to it as if it were human. "I know," she tells the orange
beast. "You've been sorely neglected today but I promise I'll make it up
to you. What do you think of that?"

I pour the last of the water into the tub and then shuck my clothing,
glancing over to see if Aspeth has noticed me. She's still petting the cat,
utterly focused. I yawn, extending my arms out. By the bull god, I am
fatigued.

"Oh, big stretch," Aspeth coos, startling me. I turn and she blushes,
her face bright red. "The cat!"

"Right." I adjust my cock, stepping into the tub, and notice that her
gaze follows me as I move. I sink into the tub and groan as the hot water
soaks into tired muscles. Gods, it's been a long week. I relax in the water,
and then grab the cake of soap and rub it into the washcloth I've hung on
the side of the tub.

Aspeth clears her throat. "Should I wash you? Since we're married
and I should be learning about your anatomy?"

I glance over at her. Her cheeks are pink and flushed, her eyes bright.
I don't know at what point she became attractive to me, but I can't look
away from her. There's something so very earnest about Aspeth. It's as if
she puts everything she has into whatever task she's focused upon, be it
guild business or something else. I suspect that she'd put all that enthusiasm into bed, too, and the thought makes my cock harden. "While I
appreciate the offer, you should know that if you touch me, it's not going
to stay just a wash."

"Oh." She sounds dazed.

She also doesn't get up from her spot on the edge of the bed, which tells me everything. We're not there yet. We're not at the carnal stage of our marriage, and I fight down the lick of impatience that curls up my spine. She's gone through a lot in the last week. Hells, I've gone through a lot, too. It's perfectly fine to wait. It's only the moon—and the knot I'll be forming—that's making me addled with lust.

"How was your trip?" Aspeth asks in a bright voice as I scrub at my skin. "Was it a rescue mission?"

"Oh, it was." My tone sounds bitter, even to myself. I try not to let guild politics get to me, but this season I can't seem to get away from them. "It took us two days of hard tunneling to find a brand-new team laid out with three broken ankles. They weren't even in a newer tunnel, or a deeper one. Just idiots doing idiotic things, I guess."

"Did they find anything?"

I turn toward her, immediately suspicious. "Cave mushrooms, hence the broken ankles. They started hallucinating and ran off a ledge. Luckily it was a short drop. Unluckily for us, we had to carry them back."

She makes a sympathetic sound. "So no artifacts? That's a shame."

"Why is it a shame?" I'm still prickly, thinking about Tiercel's comments from earlier. About Aspeth being a spy . . .

Aspeth sighs heavily. "I'm vicariously dreaming through them, I suppose. I've always wanted to find an artifact. Not just any artifact, but something important. Something world-changing." She chuckles, her expression wistful. "I suppose I should settle for 'any artifact' before I start going on about world-changing ones, right? It's just . . . it must be so exciting. I can't imagine wasting your time in the tunnels with getting high."

I relax, because I understand what she means. There's a rush you get when you first discover something of importance. It's a heady feeling that's only compounded when you turn it in to the guild and find out what it truly is . . . or you're devastated to find out that it's a dupe. Or broken. "This is a heartbreaking business," I tell her. "It gives you the highest of highs and the lowest of lows."

"More highs than lows, I hope."

I think of Magpie, and how often she returns to the bottle despite swearing that she'll quit. "That's the hope, aye."

"Mmm." She's quiet for a long moment. "May I ask you something, Hawk?"

"Of course." I dunk the washcloth again, trying to focus on getting clean.

"Do Taurians kiss?"

And there goes my focus. My cock stiffens, surfacing through the water like some sort of hungry leviathan. Aspeth isn't thinking about artifacts entirely. "Kissing is a human invention. It's not as comfortable for Taurians. Our mouths don't work quite like yours. We prefer tail play to show public affection."

"I see."

She's quiet for another long moment, and it takes everything I have not to look over at her. If I do, I worry she'll see the smolder in my gaze and get skittish. It's too soon for my eyes to turn red with the Conquest Moon but five hells, I'm feeling its nearing presence in every throb of my cock.

Aspeth is oblivious to my internal turmoil, however. Her voice grows bemused. "I suppose I shouldn't find it strange. My parents were a marriage of convenience and I don't recall ever seeing them kiss. Lots of marriages are for convenience's sake and I know I'm not the first human to marry a Taurian. I suppose I'm not missing out."

Missing out?

Missing *out*? Because of marriage to a Taurian?

I stand fully upright, letting the water sluice off my form. My cock is fully hard and dripping water just like the rest of me, and I look over at her, making sure she sees every last bit of what is on display. "I'll make sure you don't feel things are lacking. Trust me."

She's comfortable on the bed, snuggled up with her cat. At the sight of me, her gaze goes to my cock and stays there, her eyes wide as if she's just now realizing our size difference. She blinks. Squints. Blinks again. Bites her lip.

Doesn't look away, though. Not even when I reach over to pick up a towel and dry my arms off, making sure my cock continues to swing free, stabbing at the air with hungry need.

Aspeth sits up slowly, setting the cat on the floor and hanging her legs over the side of the bed. Her expression has changed to thoughtfulness even as she continues to stare at my cock. It prickles with the heat of her gaze, and I can feel pre-cum sliding down the domed head.

"I—" she begins, her voice a croak.

I bite back a chuckle.

She clears her throat and tries again. "I cannot help but think about how you showed me your cock. Would you like to see my body, too?"

"You *know* I would." If bulls could purr, I'd be purring right now.

She gets to her feet and tugs at the front of her boxy blouse, at the brown buttons that line the front. It's the most unflattering of garments on her, but I know what she looks like underneath. I know what she looks like wet. The guild uniform is just a tease. "If I was a bolder sort, I'd make a joke that I welcome critiques." Aspeth gives me a nervous little half smile, glancing up. "But I confess that I'm an absolute ninny when it comes to my body. If you find something repugnant, please don't tell me about it. I'm nervous as it is."

As if I'd ever tell her that she was anything but splendid.

She fiddles with one of the buttons and then glances back at the bed. "Should I be sitting or standing?"

"You should be however you're comfortable."

"So in the library with a book upon my lap, then?" she jokes, tossing her blouse to the floor. Next go her boots and stockings, then the trousers she wears. She strips it all off methodically, and when she's down to nothing but a corset and her thin chemise, she pulls her hair down from its pinned bun and shakes it loose. With trembling hands, she pulls the laces free of her corset and tosses it aside. Her chemise follows after it a moment later.

Then she slides back onto the bed and lies atop it like a corpse at a viewing, her legs tightly together, hands folded at her waist, eyes closed.

It's not the sexiest of positions, but I'd have to be an idiot not to realize how unsettled she is. I move toward the foot of the bed, giving her space, and eye her pale, plump legs. I like them. I like the rounded curve of her calves, her delicate ankles, and her large feet. She's tall and solid and made as such, and I'm dying to skim my hand up one strong, thick thigh so I can watch her legs part.

But I can tell she's nervous. It's the whole corpse thing, her eyes squeezed shut as if she expects me to take her measurements with a tailor's tape and tsk over what I find. I curl my fingers around her ankle, lifting it up, and rub her foot.

Her gaze flies open. "Oh—"

"It's fine," I tell her. "You're fine. We're just a naked married couple in our room together. There's nothing to be nervous about."

"Says you. You're beautiful." She watches my hands move over her foot, her gaze heavy-lidded. "You're covered in muscle. I don't think I have a single one."

I bite back the laughter that threatens to huff out of me. "I'm pretty sure I spotted one. At least one." I let my gaze move over her again, lingering at the gentle swell of her belly. She's soft here, too, an indication of her pampered life, but I rather like it. I like the thought of cuddling up to pillowy softness in a wife. Her breasts are just as large as I expected them to be. Flat on her back, they pull toward her arms, her nipples dark and prominent and tight. All of her looks soft and touchable, and I can't stop staring.

"There we go," I tease. "There's a muscle."

She laughs, trying to crane her head to gaze at the foot I'm holding near my chest. "Where?"

I lean in, nuzzling her ankle. "Right here."

Aspeth whimpers, the sound soft and utterly enticing.

"Is this all right?" I ask, even as I run my muzzle against her soft skin. "Or should I stop?"

"I'm fine," she promises, breathless. Her fingers twist in the blankets at her sides and she watches me with parted lips. "You . . . my . . . this is fine. All fine."

I drag my mouth against her skin. She's so damned soft. So pettable. "I wanted you to touch me the other day. All you did was look."

"Oh," Aspeth breathes, and her flush goes right down to her pretty tits. They jiggle as she shivers, her nipples tightening, and I nip at her calf. "I wasn't bold enough. Not yet."

"I'm bold," I tell her bluntly. "Can I touch you more? Or are you not ready for that yet?"

The look in her eyes grows soft. Sensual. Her hands clench the blankets again. "You can touch me."

Good. Because I'm aching, my cock as hard as stone. This is about easing her into pleasure, though, and I'm dying to touch her. I want to run my hands all over her skin, to feel her quiver when I caress her. I want to show her what it's like to be in bed with a Taurian. That she's not going to *miss out* on a single thing. That I can make her feel better than any human can, if she'll just give me a chance.

And now's my chance. I push her thighs apart, spreading her legs, and lower my head between her thighs before she has time to think about what I'm doing.

Aspeth squeaks in surprise the moment my tongue brushes over her skin. The thing with Taurians? We have long, mobile, thick tongues. I can lick my own eyebrows, if I'm so inclined, and human men can't compete with a Taurian who knows how to use what he's got. Kissing be damned. I've got better things to do with my mouth. Leaning in, I drag my tongue over her entire pussy in one smooth stroke.

Her breath hitches and then a moan escapes her. "You . . . oh . . ."

"You said you'd been touched before, Aspeth. How much?" With the tip of my tongue, I tease her cleft open, rubbing against the bud of her clit and making her squirm. "Did your human lover do that to you?"

"He—he touched my thigh," she babbles, her fingers gripping the blanket next to her hips. "No tongue. I—I thought you were going to touch me with your hands."

"Tsk. You're going to have to be more specific, wife." I flick my tongue over her cunt again, and she shivers in response. "Tell me if you want me to stop, then. If this is too much for you."

"Not too much," she breathes, and then parts her thighs wider, bending her legs at the knees. "Do you . . . should I . . ."

"You stay right there and let me taste you." I run a hand along the inside of her thigh, watching her reaction, and then lap at her cunt again. The taste of her hits my senses—musky and somehow sweet. She moans again, her hands fluttering toward me before settling back down to the bed.

With amusement, I grab one of her hands and place it firmly on my shoulder. "You can grab the horns, if you like."

Her fingers curl against my skin and her eyes flutter closed. I tap my tongue against her clit again, and she arches. "You . . . no, that's really good. Really, really good. You can do that all you want." Aspeth's voice takes on a dreamy quality. "Feels so nice."

I'm both amused and offended by her commentary. "Nice" isn't what a bull wants to hear when he tongues his wife. He wants to have her screaming. But Aspeth is a little more virginal than I'd expected, so I need to go slow. Make sure she doesn't get overwhelmed.

Which is fine, because it allows me to savor every moment of this. I love the squirming she does with every tap of my tongue. I love the taste of her, as soft and delicate as her skin. My cock throbs in time with my pulse, dripping pre-cum all over the floor and the edge of the bed, but I can't be bothered with such trivialities. I've got my muzzle between my wife's thighs and everything else in the world—including my own pleasure—can wait for a bit. I push her legs into the air and wrap my hand around the base of my cock, squeezing to stop myself from coming before she does.

Because I need to taste her release. Badly.

I tease the tip of my tongue over her clit again, rubbing against the underside of it. I've had females in my bed with prominent clits in the past, and they're easy to tease to climax. Aspeth has sweetly thick folds hiding her bud from my sight, and when my tongue teases over it, it's barely more than the tiniest of bumps. Perfectly fine. It's delicate and hesitant, just like her. No matter a woman's shape or form, I can figure out how to get her off. It just takes a little attention to detail.

Squeezing my cock again, I tongue her and push into her core, using my thick tongue length like I would my cock. She sucks in a breath of surprise, squirming against my mouth. Something tells me that she's never had that happen before and she doesn't know what to make of it. Her cunt clenches around my tongue and I thrust into her, but she's no longer making those little pants of delight—time to change plans. I go back to licking her pussy, using firmer and firmer strokes of my tongue, until she's wet and juicy and making those sweet sounds again.

This time I focus on her clit, that intoxicating, half-hidden little bit that I know she'll like attention on. Using my free hand, I push the folds of her cunt apart, exposing her, and it forces the tiny, flushed bud into prominence. I lick her again, and Aspeth's hands fly to my horns. The gurgling sound that erupts from her throat would make me laugh if I wasn't so mucking hard. As it is, I stroke my hand down my cock, my fingers messy with pre-cum. I should stop rubbing myself, should play with her pretty, jiggling tits and give them the attention they deserve, but I can't stop myself. Just like I can't stop myself from wrapping my lips around her now-prominent clit and sucking lightly.

The cry Aspeth makes is sharp, her hips rearing against my face. I try to pull away, only for her to arch her hips, following my mouth, and so I give her what she wants. Fuck drawing this out. She wants to come? I'll make her fucking come. I run my tongue over her clit, teasing along the underside before sucking on it again. She cries out once more, then she's riding my face while I frantically stroke my cock, desperate to get her off before I erupt. The moment I feel the burst of her release against my tongue, I spray against the coverlets, bucking my hips against the mattress as I nut, my face buried between her thighs.

Goddess Asteria's fabled paradise could not bring me more pleasure than this moment.

Aspeth is panting, her hand to her brow as she struggles for breath. Her face—and her glorious, heavy tits—are flushed and the insides of her thighs are damp with her release. Mine is all over the side of the bed, but I can deal with that. Soon.

For now, I'm happy to pay attention to her pussy, giving it slow, contented licks, and loving the way she trembles with each stroke of my tongue.

I bet I could make her come again without too much effort. The thought feeds some primal urge in me, and I give her a wicked grin before pushing her pussy open wide again and lowering my head.

This time, Aspeth reaches for my horns.

EIGHTEEN

ASPETH

20 Days Before the Conquest Moon

I BLUSH ALL THROUGH breakfast the next morning.

For his part, Hawk is quiet, but when I glance over at him across the table, he's got a smug look on his face, as if he's quite pleased with himself. He seems more relaxed today than he has been in the past, which just makes me blush harder.

Luckily no one else has noticed my silence. Gwenna is arguing with Lark and Mereden about the best type of toasted cheese sandwich, and Kipp is watching them with an amused expression as Mereden goes into great detail about the perfect amount of butter that should be spread upon the bread before applying cheese. And while I have definite opinions about toasted cheese sandwiches, I can't focus on anything.

There are parts of my brain that still haven't recovered from last night.

I can't stop thinking about where he touched me. His tongue. The hungry noises he made as he pleasured me. The way I curled my legs around his shoulders and rocked shamelessly against him while he licked me to climax. I've read a few naughty books and touched myself a few times, but never in my wildest dreams did I imagine anything quite like that. I poke at my porridge, wondering how I'm possibly going to be able to hold a conversation with him today, because I distinctly remember the ring through his nose resting upon my mound as he licked me. . . .

"Good," declares a loud, brusque voice that makes me jump. "You're all here. Saves me the effort of locating your asses." I glance up in surprise as Magpie bustles into the kitchen. She's wearing her guild uniform, and while it's wrinkled and faded, it's the first time I've seen her look something like a guild master. Her normally disheveled, gray-streaked hair is pulled back into a tail and she wears her sash over her shoulder, so encrusted with pins that it pulls the side of her blouse down.

A spark of excitement races through me as she sets her pack on the table in the midst of breakfast, making the dishes rattle. What's going on?

Hawk leans back in his chair, his arms crossing over his broad chest. It makes the muscles in his biceps bulge, and I can't stop staring. Gwenna catches my eye, a curious expression on her face, and I immediately turn bright red, shoving another mouthful of porridge into my face and trying to look anywhere but at her.

Or Hawk.

"Well, now," Hawk drawls, tilting his head and eyeing Magpie. "Look who's decided to be upright before noon. Going somewhere?"

"Shut up, you," Magpie tells him, but there's a grin on her face. "You all kept bitching about teaching, well, now you get your teacher. I'm taking charge."

"You are?" Lark grins at her aunt.

"Are you, now." His tone is even. Unruffled.

"I am." She puts her hands on her hips. "You going to fight me over it?"

"Not at all." Hawk seems guarded, but he nods after a moment's thought. "Glad you're feeling like joining the team. It's been a while."

"Yeah, well, yesterday's scare with this one"—she gestures at me—"made me realize that if I didn't get off my ass and teach these idiots, they'd go back to their villages, and then where would I be?"

"Did you just call us the village idiots?" Gwenna stiffens in her seat, scowling at Magpie.

"I did. But you can prove me wrong." She points at the pack she's placed in the center of the table, almost atop poor Kipp. "I assume you all know how to pack your bag for tunneling?"

Everyone pauses. I exchange a worried look with Gwenna and then glance over at Hawk, but he's not looking at me, thank Asteria.

"We haven't gotten that far yet. We've been working on drills," Hawk says. "Physical fitness."

"Spoken like a true Taurian," Magpie continues, and gives her head a little shake. "Look, I won't say that you don't need to be in good shape to hold your own in the tunnels, but as long as you're smart and know what you're doing, it's not that important."

There's a smack against wood, and I realize when Hawk stands up that the smack was his agitated tail hitting the nearest chair. He leans forward, his hands braced on the table. "Not important? Do you know how many idiots Taurians have to retrieve out of the tunnels every year because humans deem it 'not important' to be competent at their muck-ing jobs?"

"I'm the teacher here," Magpie says in a hard voice. "You want me to teach or not?"

Hawk's nostrils flare so widely that the ring in his nose jumps. He looks furious, his tail lashing back and forth hard. It smacks Mereden in the arm, but her eyes are just as big and worried as mine.

"Fine," he says after a moment. His voice is flat with distaste. "You teach. Prove me wrong."

"Good," Magpie declares. She stands a little straighter, looking more authoritative by the moment. "You're all going to get a lesson on what to pack, and then we're going camping."

"Camping?" Gwenna sputters. "What the muck does that have to do with tunneling?"

The guild master's eyes gleam. "That's what I'm about to show you."

A FEW HOURS later, we've all got bags packed, Squeaker has enough dried food for several days (plus I've left instructions for the nestmaid to look after her), and we head off. Hawk wants us to march from Magpie's dorm all the way to a camp somewhere in the distant trees far outside the city, but Magpie insists that we catch a ride instead.

"Won't do us any good if they're all too tired to learn," she tells Hawk. "And like you said, they're not in great shape."

She wins this battle, too, and I worry that Hawk's going to be in a terrible mood by the time the day is over.

We ride out on the back of an empty vegetable wagon leaving the market now that its goods have been dropped off. It's not the fastest ride, but it's the right price, apparently. We all climb on and sway along as the mules pull down the cobbled, twisting streets. The pack on my back feels cumbersome, but not as heavy as the ones Hawk has been making us carry. I sit next to Gwenna on one side, Mereden and Lark on the other side of the wagon. Kipp races back and forth, his house a large shield on his back, and doesn't seem to want to conserve his energy at all. Maybe he doesn't need to. He seems to have enough enthusiasm for all of us. Master Magpie rides with the driver, talking his ear off, and Hawk sits on the back of the wagon, his heavy legs hanging over the edge, almost as if he doesn't want to be with us. It makes me a little worried. I glance over at him on the far end of the wagon but he's not been very talkative today. Is it Magpie? Or is he regretting what we did last night?

As we leave the city behind, the rutted road curves past the "Dig for Artifacts" field, which makes Magpie point and laugh as people shovel away at holes in the midst of the loose dirt. "Look at those fools."

"Are they fools for wanting to find something?" Mereden's voice is wistful. We all watch the people in the field digging and sweating, using shovels and buckets to move mountains of dirt aside. "Most people can only dream of finding an artifact. I understand why they'd spend a few pennies for the chance."

"No one ever finds anything," Lark admits, shrugging. "It's just people fleecing the tourists."

I'm not as jaded as Magpie and Lark. Part of me still wants to go out there and try my own luck. I'd be one of the people out there with a spade and pail, happily digging away. I squint-watch the blobs of people with wistful admiration. They have a dream, and they're going after it in the best way they can. Nothing wrong with that.

Gwenna nudges me. She's seated next to me after making both Mereden and Kipp switch places with her. "Everything okay?"

"Why wouldn't it be okay?" My face immediately colors bright red, making a mockery of my casual tone.

If she notices my blush, she doesn't say anything. "You're normally not quiet about all this," she whispers, gesturing at the wagon. "You're usually nattering on about how they did things in Old Prell or how traditional guild members do things."

I fuss with the hem of my sleeve, agitated. Keeping my voice low, I say, "Do you think Hawk is upset over Magpie being here today?"

"Why would he be? Isn't she the one in charge?" She nudges me. "Or are you afraid your lover is going to be upset?"

I clap a hand over her mouth. "Shhh!"

Her eyes widen. She licks my palm, forcing me to release her, and I wipe my hand on my clothes, glaring. "What the fuck," she whisper-mouths. "Are you—are you blushing?" Her gaze moves to Hawk and then back to me and she leans in closer. "Are you two fucking already? I thought you were waiting for this moon shit?"

My face feels as if it's on fire. "We are. It's just . . . he . . . I . . ." I shake my head, unable to continue.

"He . . ." she prompts, giving me an encouraging look. "Rearranged your organs? Gave you the dicking of your life? What?"

I twist my blouse in my hands. I don't have anyone to share such things with. Never have. Even when I had my heartbreak over Barnabus, I couldn't confess to anyone how hurt I was, how foolish I'd felt. Gwenna had been my servant and it would have been inappropriate of me. But now we're both just guild fledglings. And I desperately want to talk to *someone* about it.

I lick my lips, and then lean in to whisper. "He licked me. Inappropriately."

She blinks, and then a sly smile curves her mouth. "You do know it's not inappropriate if you're married, right?"

"Hush. I just . . . I was taken by surprise."

"I am, too. He seems kinda like a stern type, but that's a good sign. A man who isn't afraid to make his lady come first is a good man in my book. He did make you come, right?"

That does it. My face is going to be permanently red. When they paint my portrait, I'll look like a ball of fire from neck to hairline. I do hold up two fingers, though.

Gwenna nods slowly. "My esteem of him grows by the day."

Mine does, too, so help me.

WE ARRIVE AT our campsite near dusk. It's a pretty area, with a lot of trees growing near a winding stream. On one side of the water are fields and pastures with cattle grazing. On the other side, things are a little more wild and unkempt. The trees cluster together tightly, not a single path to be seen, and the underbrush is so thick that I can't imagine crossing it. Scrubby bushes mingle with weeds and lead to taller trees in the distance.

It's in this rather unimpressive place that Magpie smiles and waves a hand in the air. "Here we are!"

"Where is 'here' exactly?" I ask, glancing around. I don't see any sort of buildings nearby, or a tunnel into a cave. If we're camping, surely there's going to be a cave involved, right? Since we're training to be familiar with caverns and ruins and such things?

"This is the perfect spot of land for terrain practice," Magpie declares, rubbing her hands together.

"You always did love terrain practice," Hawk says from nearby. I want to turn to look at him, but my face feels rather hot again, and instead I tug on my collar, trying to get air in my blouse. Sure is warm here.

"Terrain practice?" Mereden asks, glancing over at Lark, who shrugs.

"Terrain practice," Magpie repeats.

Gwenna slings her pack off her back, ever the hard worker. "Great. Shall we set up tents and get started, then?"

"No tents just yet. It's too bright out." Magpie squints at the sky.

"It's sunset," I point out. At my side, Kipp snorts, and I don't know if he's amused or irritated.

Magpie just grins at me. She's got deep hollows under her eyes and her skin has a greenish cast to it, but if she feels poorly, she's hiding it well. "Sunset, aye. We want it to be fully dark."

"Why?" Gwenna blurts.

"Because it ain't well lit in a tunnel," Magpie says, enunciating each word slowly. "Just like it ain't all even and level, either. Or dry. Some tunnels are wet. Some are nothing but rocks. There's nothing about it that's easy. So we're going to keep those packs on your backs." She points at Gwenna's pack, indicating she should put it back on. "And then we're going to go marching up the stream. The water here is only ankle-deep. It makes the rocks slippery and treacherous, which means it's perfect terrain practice. I haven't been in a tunnel yet that's as smooth and easy to navigate as the streets of Vastwarren."

Considering that the streets of Vastwarren are cobbled (terribly cobbled, I might add) and slant heavily, this is a rather alarming piece of news.

"And we do this in the dark?" Mereden asks, her voice timid.

"It's all good, Mer," Lark says in a confident voice. "We'll be tied together, just like in the caves, right?"

"Exactly," Master Magpie says. "You're getting it now."

"But it's going to be too dark to see anything," I point out. I can barely see as it is. In the dark? I'll just be stumbling.

Magpie turns to me. "Then light a fucking torch and quit complaining. You think it's bright in the caves?"

"I think I preferred it when Hawk was teaching us," Gwenna mutters.

I do, too.

NINETEEN

ASPETH

DESPITE OUR GENERAL helplessness, the evening isn't as bad as I expect it to be. Gwenna makes a fire and we light a torch, only to find that the torch doesn't burn for very long at all. Magpie then produces an oil lantern and lectures us. "When I say come prepared, I mean it."

After the oil lantern is lit, we're tied together. Kipp takes up the front, followed by Lark with the lantern. Gwenna follows behind her, then Mereden, then me in the back. We march up the slippery stream, and Magpie's right—it's only ankle-deep. It's still incredibly treacherous, though, and we end up slogging with each step, our boots heavier with water every moment. I decide that I'm going to get myself a staff before anything else. A short one, so no one can gripe about my having it in close quarters. Maybe just to bosom height instead of past my shoulder. I like that idea—a staff to assist with walking, and to put a lantern atop because not being able to see is maddening. Right now, I can't see anything except Mereden's backside and the coiling puff of her dark hair.

We march up the stream.

Down the stream.

Up the stream again, this time in a different order with me at the front. This goes badly for all involved and Magpie barks things at me like "Are you blind?"

(I don't point out that in fact I am quite night-blind without my spectacles.)

We march up and down the stream until all three moons in the sky have disappeared again and the night grows bitterly cold. Our teeth chatter and Kipp gets too cold to function, so we take turns carrying him.

"Enough," Hawk finally declares. "You've shown them you know what you're doing, Mags. Let them rest."

"Oh, fine," she says. "Though I know Hawk's just griping because he wants time with his wife. I suppose you all get a break." She claps her hands together. "Now we make camp and another fire."

"What happened to the last bloody fire I made?" Gwenna demands.

"Were you tending it?"

"No! I've been marching upstream all night and scaring all the fish!"

"Then it's out, isn't it?" Magpie's smile is evil in the shadows. "So make another fucking fire. You're not going to have anyone to depend on in the tunnels to keep things lit for you. Don't expect different out here. My job is to prepare you."

Gwenna shoots me an agitated look, as if she's blaming me for everything. I can't fault her for that—it *is* my fault that we're here, as fledglings. I suppose I deserve any and all blame. "I'll make the fire."

"I can make it," Gwenna says. "I know how."

"You *all* need to learn how to make fire," Magpie corrects. She points at me. "You make the fire. The others can set up their sleeping packs. Tomorrow we practice sword work."

We all groan, with Kipp's hiss carrying above the rest. I'm not sure if he's delighted or irked about the sword work. Probably a mixture of both, knowing Kipp. Sometimes I'm not sure if he likes us or is just tolerating us to get to his endgame, being in the guild. Come to think of it, there are no slitherskins in the guild at the moment but no one objected to his fledgling-ship. Meanwhile, anyone with a pair of breasts was deemed a problem.

I want to prove them wrong and make them regret their silly prejudices. I want them to have their eyes opened when we pass. I want them to be dumbstruck when they realize just how capable we are. It's yet another reason why we need to try so very hard to pass this first time around. Magpie won't get a second chance, and I suspect neither would we.

It takes a long while (and Magpie barking some terse instructions) before I manage to figure out how to make a fire, but when it's finally going well, camp is set up. There are mini-tents, and we can sleep two to a tent, with Kipp preferring his round, cozy shell. Mereden and Gwenna will sleep in a tent together, and Lark will bunk with her aunt for tonight. When we're in the tunnels of the Everbelow, I won't be able to sleep with Hawk, of course. I blush just thinking about it.

But it's not time to sleep just yet. Gwenna tosses a bunch of ingredients into a stewpot to start a meal and we all relax by the fire, waiting while it bubbles.

"So," Magpie says.

Everyone's quiet, regarding her. She seems awkward now that we're relaxing and there are no orders to bark at us. I discreetly look around for Hawk, but he's on the edge of camp, leaning up against a tree and just watching us from afar.

"I'm glad you're with us," Mereden says in her sweet voice. She clasps her hands over her knees, looking young and innocent, her dark eyes gleaming in the firelight. "You have such a reputation with the guild. I was so excited to meet the legend of so many stories."

Instead of being flattered, Magpie looks embarrassed. She pats her pockets, grimaces, and, when Lark passes her a skin of water, takes a swig from it instead. "Stories are just that. Stories. Sometimes exaggerated, and sometimes they don't matter at all. What matters is now." She grimaces at the water and hands it back. "Speaking of the here and now, have you all thought about names that you'll take? When you pass?"

I inwardly preen at her assumption that we'll pass. "Sparrow," I say proudly. "You can call me Sparrow."

Lark groans, rolling her eyes. "We know. We *know*."

Mereden giggles, her sleeve masking her smile.

"There's nothing wrong with anticipating success," I point out, my back stiff. "Your name is Lark, after all, and you don't see me harassing you about that."

"That's because my mother named me that at birth," Lark points out. "It was her idea. When I pass maybe I'll change it up. Be 'Mudlark' or something."

Mereden just giggles louder. "'Mudlark' is a terrible name."

"Oh, shut up," Lark says, but there's a hint of a smile on her face. "Like you've picked out something better?"

"I haven't," Mereden admits. "I haven't thought that far ahead. Maybe you can think of one for me."

"'Tit.'"

She scowls at Lark. "You know what? Forget I asked."

"'Bushtit,'" Gwenna says suddenly. Lark howls with delight.

Mereden frowns in her direction. "You're not helping."

"I don't know. I thought 'Bushtit' was pretty good," Gwenna says with a smile. "It beats 'Chickadee,' which is what Aspeth thought I should be at first. I think we settled on 'Wren.'"

"'Chickadee' is a great name," I protest. "They're very industrious birds. Happy and busy. They make me think of you." Perhaps I'm not very good at picking out names. "But if you don't want to be 'Chickadee,' you don't have to be. Mereden can be 'Chickadee.'"

"Or not," Mereden says.

Magpie caps the waterskin and slings the strap over her shoulder. "'Wren' is a nice, unassuming name. 'Chickadee' might be too feminine for all the cock-swinging you'll have to endure with the guild itself. Luckily enough, these names aren't taken. If I had a coin for every swaggering man who wanted to call himself 'Raven' I'd be rich."

"Or 'Hawk,'" I blurt out immediately, thinking of him.

"What about Hawk?" Magpie asks, and all eyes turn to me.

"Yes, what about Hawk?" he says, chiming in, his gaze on me.

My face flushes hot. "I mean, it's just a common name, you know? Very masculine. I'm sure a lot of men want that sort of name. Something with a lot of swagger and testosterone. Not that it doesn't suit you. It does. You're very masculine. Very suited for something that aggressively male." I pause, realizing that my words might make it seem as if Hawk is the type to beat me in private if I keep using words like *aggressive*. "Not aggressively male in a bad way. I just mean—"

"Go on," he continues, his mouth drawing up in an amused smile. "Please continue to extoll my masculinity."

If my face got any hotter, it'd be aflame. "I mean, it's just very lucky that you managed to get the name that's perfect for you. You would think it wouldn't be available."

"So you think it's perfect for him?" Mereden's voice is *so* sweet. "That's adorable."

"I didn't say that!"

"You did." Hawk is giving me the most hard-to-read look. I can't tell if he's choking on laughter or just wants the conversation to end. "As for the name, it was timing. I knew the old Hawk. When he passed, I put in for the name first. I could have just as easily been 'Goose.'"

"'Goose'?" I sputter, forgetting we have an audience. "Oh, you're far too masculine for something like 'Goose.'"

"She sure keeps saying 'masculine' a lot," Lark mock-whispers to Mereden.

Goddess, I'm just making things worse. "Kipp," I blurt instead, trying to distract. "What about you? What name do you want?"

The slitherskin shrugs, touching the tip of his tongue to his eyeball, and then moves to Magpie's side and pats a hand on her. The message is clear. She can pick it.

"Something clever and quick," Magpie says. "'Swift,' maybe."

He nods, and I suspect he's pleased.

Lark snaps her fingers. "I just thought of the perfect name for Mereden!"

The once-priestess perks up. "Oh?"

"'Swallow'!"

Mereden throws a stick at Lark while we all try desperately not to laugh.

TIME AROUND THE fire is nice. It's pleasant to laugh together and relax, to talk about our hopes and tease one another about names. We linger for an hour or two, until Magpie pushes us off to bed. "Enough gossiping. Tomorrow's going to be a tiring day. You'll need your strength. Get some sleep."

We head off, and for the first time in hours, Hawk approaches me. He puts a hand to the small of my back, guiding me to the tent we'll be sharing. My face scorches again, as I suspect everyone is staring at us. I bite my lip as I duck into our lodgings. "Your tent is bigger than the others."

"Taurians are bigger than humans."

So they are. I've noticed Hawk has distinctly . . . nonhuman proportions on certain parts of his anatomy. His thighs are absolutely enormous and nothing but rock-hard muscle. His biceps are as thick around as *my* thigh, and I'm not a small woman. Of course he'd need a larger tent.

I lie down on the pallet—a guild-issue pad to make sleeping on rock a little more bearable and a matching scratchy wool blanket—and Hawk settles his big body next to mine, dominating the narrow space. I'm intensely aware of how big he is now that we're pressed close together, and the sheer size of his head and horns. His shoulders are huge, too, and he turns on his side, getting comfortable.

He leans in, his muzzle near my ear, and his breath steams my skin. "How's this?"

"H–how's what?"

"Are you comfortable?"

I clasp my hands over my blouse, because I'm not sure where else to put them as I lie on my back. "I mean, I don't have a pillow," I whisper. "But I'm certain I'll get used to it."

"Sit up," he says, and when I do, he adjusts his large form and then indicates I should lie back down again. I do, and I'm cradled at the curve of his shoulder, resting against him.

Oh. That was . . . kind.

"Better?" he asks.

My skin prickles with awareness, my nipples tightening against my clothing as I think about last night. About *licking.* Somehow when I'd imagined our marriage of convenience, I hadn't factored in pleasure. I thought we'd have sex, of course, but I hadn't thought beyond that. Now I can't stop thinking about Hawk touching me again. Hawk and his delightfully strange—and thick—tongue.

A tongue that went all over me. Everywhere.

Mercy, it's warm in this tent. I tug at my blouse, trying to air my cleavage.

"Is something wrong?" he asks, voice low and secretive.

"No." I undo the top button on my blouse and pretend that was all I was up to. "Just getting comfortable." I pull my hair down from its bun as well, tugging free tightly bound strands and fussing with it until my hair spills loose over his arm. "There. See? All comfy now."

He grunts.

His grunt reminds me that he's been rather stony all night. Ever since Magpie took charge, Hawk's demeanor has been downright sour. Does he feel as if he's been passed over as a teacher? That we don't need him anymore? I turn and glance up at him, and his mouth is pulled down in what can only be a Taurian frown. "You've been acting strange tonight."

That gets his attention. "Strange?"

"Yes. Dare I say it, disapproving. Like you don't appreciate that Magpie has returned. That she's taken charge. Why is that?"

He rears back slightly, studying me. "I'm not disapproving. It's just . . . well, I've seen her like this before."

"Like what?"

"Like her old self. Smart. Capable. Attentive." Hawk shakes his head. "I've seen it happen before, when she comes out of the bottle. She's great for a few days, and then something pisses her off or is difficult, and she reaches for the drink again. Then she's worse than before. I just don't want to get my hopes up."

I gaze up at him, sympathetic. He sounds so glum, and I want to fix this for him, somehow. I wish I could. Sadly, I know he's right. There was a stable hand back at Honori Hold who drank too much. He'd get fired, only to come crawling back, swearing he'd changed his ways. The "new" changes would last only a few days before he'd turn into a drunk again, and he'd get fired once more. The only reason he got another chance was because his wife was one of the cooks. I remember her crying constantly, her face buried in fistfuls of her apron. How she swore he was a good man when he wasn't drinking.

It's just that he was *always* drinking. I think of Magpie, and it makes me ache with sadness to see my childhood hero like this. That today is likely just a fluke and she'll go back to being the puking, miserable drunk she was before. "Why do you stay with her if she's this bad, Hawk? It's clear everyone in the guild respects you. You could work for the guild masters directly. Work with the archivists. You could substitute in until you found a permanent Five. Anyone would take you. Why are you wasting your time with Magpie? If she's a lost cause?"

He's quiet for a long moment, thinking over my question. Then, when he speaks, his voice is soft. "I owe her my life."

"Go on." Hawk's so private that I wonder if he'll actually tell me.

To my surprise, he doesn't hesitate. "I grew up in a very poor family. Many Taurians who live outside of the city are impoverished. They farm and grow crops, and that doesn't exactly bring the wealth the holders have."

I say nothing. I know all too well that holders have a great deal of coin. Well, usually. The venom in Hawk's voice makes me pause, though. Such vitriol has a history behind it, and I'm afraid to ask.

"It's not uncommon for a young Taurian man to leave home the moment he's old enough to earn coin on his own. I was twelve when I left home."

"Twelve!" I'm shocked. It's so very young.

"Aye. I had three brothers and four sisters and there was never enough food to go around. So when I hit the ripe old age of twelve, I set out for Vastwarren to make my fortune. I was young and arrogant and full of myself. It went about as well as you'd expect."

There's a hint of amusement in his voice but I can't even laugh. I just ache, thinking of a twelve-year-old forced to leave his family behind because he wanted to have a full belly. Then there was me, still living at home at thirty and fretting because I didn't have enough coins for finery. For parties. Meanwhile Hawk was just trying to survive to the next week. I'm a little ashamed of how disparate the fortunes of holders are in comparison to the poor. I know all too well that holders have a ridiculous amount of wealth, and tax their landowners heavily so they can continue to acquire more artifacts to protect what they already have. It's a vicious cycle, and the moment you fall behind, everything collapses.

Just as my father has had everything collapse around our family.

A knot rises in my throat as Hawk continues. "I showed up at the guild hall and declared myself to be as capable as any students they had here already, and that even though it wasn't Swansday, I should be allowed to apprentice. They laughed in my face, and when I didn't give up, they told me if I could beat Osprey at the obstacle course, I would be allowed to join. He beat me handily and all I got for my pride was a public shaming and the realization that I didn't know what I was going to do for a living. I slept two nights in the gutters before Magpie offered to buy me a drink. Said she felt sorry for me. I followed her home and showed up on her doorstep the next day, asking for work. Any work, no matter how difficult. At first she declined, but I kept showing up, and she started to give me errands. Running things to the guild hall. Grabbing supplies from merchants. Making sure the practice swords stayed sharp. I made a nuisance of myself but I also made sure she saw that I could do the tasks she set for me. She gave me a place to stay, but I wasn't considered part of the guild. When I was eighteen, I was allowed to join as a fledgling. *Her* fledgling. I passed my very first testing. Excavated for two years, and then I lost my hand."

"Lost your hand?" I squint into the darkness, not sure I've heard him correctly.

"Yes. I was in the tunnels with my Five. They were idiots, looking back, but I was just happy to have work. Our navigator took us down a wrong turn and a tunnel collapsed over us. My arm was pinned and our healer buried under the rock. The others left us for dead."

I gasp. "They left you?"

"It was self-preservation," he says, voice bland. "If they'd have stayed, they'd likely have run out of air or encountered ratlings. They swarm after a tunnel collapse, looking for carrion. But aye, they left us behind. I was there when the healer died, crying out for help until the end. I thought I was a goner, too, that it was just a matter of time. Don't know how long I was down there, pinned. Two days? Maybe? But then Magpie showed up. She'd heard they'd left me and brought her students down to come and save my arse. Rescued me and carried me out of the tunnels. My hand was crushed, so there was no choice but to amputate it. And just when I thought I couldn't owe her more, Magpie used her connections to acquire me a hand." He lifts an arm and flexes it. "A magical limb from Old Prell, grafted to my stump with words of magic."

I'm shocked. "I didn't realize you had a false hand."

"Most don't. It changes its appearance to match my skin and moves just like a real hand." He rotates his hand in the air, flexing his fingers, and I can barely make out their outlines in the shadows. "There's naught but a small line on my lower arm to show where it's connected, but if you run your fingers over my wrist, you can feel the glyphs carved there."

It's a siren call if there ever was one. "May I?"

"Of course." He extends his arm toward me, his palm open.

Hesitant, I brush my fingers over his hand, wondering what it'll feel like. I'm not entirely surprised to find that it's warm, his skin like normal Taurian skin under my touch. Magic, like he said. I trace each finger and then run my hand over his palm. I move lower, encircling his wrist, and sure enough, I can feel the etchings of glyphs as if they've been carved into his skin. "That's incredible."

"It is. It feels like a real arm, a real hand." He makes a fist, as if proving to himself that it's possible. "But because it's an artifact, it's expensive. The guild agreed to sell it to me rather than to one of the holders. I suspect it would have been a different story if one of the holders was in need of a right hand, but since I was the only one, it came to me." He flexes his fingers again. "Now I must pay the guild back for its largess, and to do so, I need students that tithe to Magpie's nest."

Of course. Because that's how guild brokering works. Teachers don't go into the tunnels, so they're paid via tithe from graduating students. If no students graduate, there's no money coming in. No wonder Hawk is so very stressed. Magpie is at risk of losing her job and becoming homeless, and Hawk . . . well, Hawk could lose his entire hand. "So it's more important than ever that we get things right. Not just for Magpie, but for you, too."

"Indeed."

I reach up and play with his fingers, thinking. There has to be something I can do. Some sort of string I can pull. As a holder's heir, I'm used to being the one with all the power. People listen to Lady Aspeth Honori. People fear getting on her bad side. But here, I'm just Aspeth who wants to be Sparrow. I'm just another student, and if I interfere, it'll cause more problems.

Money would solve things. Money would solve things for both of us, but it's the one thing I don't have, even with all the power of my family name. I think of my father . . . and then I think how he would react if he knew I married a Taurian just so I could apprentice. He'd be horrified at both the Taurian and the apprenticing. My father is a holder who believes firmly that grunt work should be left to, well, grunts. Lessers.

I don't think of Hawk as my lesser, though. If I'm being honest, he's better than me—and most humans—at absolutely everything he puts his mind to. I don't think of Magpie, Lark, and the others as lesser, either. Or Gwenna, despite the fact that she was my servant for years prior to coming here. We've bonded over the last several days of exercises, helping one another with the ropes that tie us together, or laughing when someone makes a mistake. We share our successes and pick one another up when we fail.

They're my companions.

My . . . friends.

I don't think I've had friends before now, and the thought is a sobering one. I know of every family in society, of course. I know which holder's son is married to which daughter and who lives where and their crests and who tithes to them. I know about them all, and yet I don't *know* them. The thought of telling any of them of my guild adventures is utterly terrifying. They wouldn't understand.

I grew up with the nobility, and yet I'm a stranger to all. Sad.

I continue to toy with Hawk's large fingers, marveling at the magic that makes it feel as real as flesh and blood. It's strange. His hand is so warm and so big and yet I wouldn't know it was magical if he hadn't told me. It's fascinating to think of how much he's overcome. There are sides to him I'm unaware of, pieces I haven't yet learned. That's rather exciting. He's an interesting person, my strange new husband. I tug on one fingertip, wondering how it must have felt to lose a hand and then regain it. "Tell me more about this. What does it feel like? Does it feel different or does it feel like your hand? How does the magic work? Can you do fine movements with the artifact? Is there loss of motion?"

His chest rumbles, and I realize after a moment that he's laughing quietly, the chuckles vibrating his big body.

"What's so funny?" I turn and frown up at his form in the darkness. "It's a legitimate question, and we're in this business because of artifacts, yes? Why wouldn't I want to learn more about one that's attached to you?"

Hawk strokes his magic hand over my belly, his fingers teasing at my blouse. "Do you truly want to know how it feels?"

"Isn't that what I asked?" I sound breathless and uncertain as he toys with the waistband of my clothing. Is he . . . ?

My breath completely escapes me as his hand slides under my clothes and cups my pussy. One thick finger strokes in the cleft of my sex and I'm shocked to realize I'm already incredibly wet. He circles my clit, teasing it, and whispers in my ear. "Tell me if you think I have good control over my hand, hmm?"

Lips parted, I make a choked sound as he continues to toy with the sensitive flesh. His finger feels scorching hot against my skin, and he moves slowly and maddeningly, each languid circle driving me more and more insane. I look up at him, at his big, strange face, his eyes gleaming in the dark. My hands curl against his chest and I have no words to speak. I can only feel, and feel, and feel.

He adds another finger, and then he's rubbing back and forth, caressing my clit from both sides. I make a whimpery noise and he leans in closer. "Shhh. You're supposed to be sleeping, naughty thing."

I grab double handfuls of his shirt, twisting the fabric as his fingers slip over my slick heat. Gods, I'm so wet. His strokes are just gliding over my skin, and every so often I can hear the wet sound of my pussy, just loud enough for it to fill the tent. I should be horrified, but instead I'm so aroused that it only turns me on more. Panting, I cling to him, trying to keep quiet. The climax builds, and I lean forward, grabbing a mouthful of his shirt and biting down on it to stifle the scream in my throat as my legs jerk and I come, soaking his hand with my release. He keeps rubbing me, whispering my name, until he wrings a second orgasm out of me in quick succession.

"Does that answer your question?" he murmurs in my ear.

I can't even *remember* the question.

TWENTY

ASPETH
19 Days Before the Conquest Moon

DAY TWO IN the woods is miserable. It rains upon us all night long, and we're shivering and cold. The fire won't stay lit, and no one's in a good mood. We're beset by swarms of bugs that bite and sting every exposed inch of skin, and I slap at my arms and legs repeatedly, because the dratted things even bite me through my clothes.

Hawk seems to be in a foul mood after that night's training, and after being bitten by bugs and listening to Magpie screech at us about how terrible we are, the last thing I want is to be stuck in a closed tent with an equally grumpy Taurian. He's been so snarly all night and it irritates me. I'm reminded of my etiquette teacher's words—that you can win far more suitors with sweets than with vinegar—and so I paste a smile to my face despite my fatigue.

I'm going to charm my husband, damn it all.

So I take off my sweaty guild coat and unlace my corset so I can breathe, relaxing. I pull off my boots and lie back atop the blankets because the day is warm and the sun is beating down upon our tent outside. At least it's somewhat dark in here. Since we're training in the night, we're having to sleep during the day. Hawk stomps in, his mood as foul as it was earlier, and I don't comment upon it. I just stretch, enjoying the feeling of being able to relax and not carrying a heavy pack upon my back.

He tosses his coat down on the bottom of the tent, his jaw clenched, and then all but rips his shirt off.

That gets my attention.

I watch as his broad muscles flex, the russet color of his body and coat fascinating and shiny. It makes each muscle seem highlighted, as if drawing attention to just how corded and taut his arms are, or how his pectorals are nothing but thick planes built by even more muscle. He scratches at his waist, and my fingers twitch with the need to touch him, to run my hands over all that physical power.

Goddess, I never thought I was one of those women to get the vapors at the sight of a strong chest, but I see now that I was wrong. Because looking at a half-naked Hawk is making me feel fluttery and distracted. If I reached for him, would he slap me away with a flick of his tail? Or would he welcome my exploring hands?

I wish I knew.

"Hawk . . . ?"

He grunts, acknowledging that he's heard me.

My nerve deserts me. I curl my fingers into fists and decide to go for conversation instead. Propping my head on my folded arm, I turn on my side and watch him as he pulls off his belt in preparation for sleep. "Tell me about you."

"Tell you about me?"

"Yes, please."

"I have a new wife who needs to go to sleep," he says in a terse voice.

A mosquito lands on my arm and I slap it with annoyance.

Hawk goes still. "What was that?"

"Mosquito."

"Ah." He shakes his head. "Pests are out today. The Dark God must be in a good mood to send so many of his servants to annoy us."

"Or they're just plentiful because we're in the woods," I reply, and then return to my initial subject. "So you won't talk to me about you?"

"You should go to sleep."

"No, I should get to know my husband. Since we're going to be sharing a marriage bed and all." I keep a smile on my face, though it's not hard to do now that he's nude except for his pants and is easing his big body down onto the ground next to me. I think about being in the tent with him the other night and how he'd pushed his fingers into my pants and touched me until I came, and my thighs clench together because I want to do that again and I don't know how to ask.

Hawk rolls his eyes and adjusts the blankets under his body. I notice he's not getting under the covers, either. "Fine. What do you want to know?"

"You don't have to sound so put-upon. It was a simple request."

He tugs on the ring on his nose. "I just . . . none of this gives me a good feeling."

"You and me?" I'm hurt, because this feels as if it is coming out of nowhere. I know we're still getting to know each other, but surely he doesn't feel the marriage was a mistake, does he?

But Hawk glances over at me in surprise. He rolls onto his side, facing me. "No. Sorry, I should have been clearer. I meant I don't have a good feeling about your Five. About Magpie being involved." He reaches out and runs a fingertip down my nose, tracing the length of it as if fascinated by its size. "You're actually the only one I do have a good feeling about."

Warmth threads itself through my body, and I'm desperate for more touching. I didn't realize how much I craved it until I married Hawk. I always wished the staff—or my father—would hug me when I was back at the hold, but I knew those embraces wouldn't happen. Now that I'm married and Hawk touches me? It's an addiction I want to feed. I need him to touch me constantly. I need him to reach for me. I need him to pull me close and tuck me against him.

Or put his hands in my pants again. Truly, I'm fine with either.

But his words of flattery—as lovely as they are—are just as surprising. "If you think I'm competent, why are you so mean to me?"

Hawk chuckles, the sound low and sensual, and my nipples harden in response. "I didn't say you were competent, little bird. But I trust you to have good sense when it comes to being in the tunnels. It's clear you've studied the guild and the ruins, which is more than I can say for the others. If anyone in your group will pass, I think it's you." He traces my nose again, and then moves down to the divot between my nose and my lip. "But that's why I have to be so hard on you. The guild will be suspicious because we are married. You have to show that you're an excellent student no matter what is thrown at you."

His teasing finger is making my blood heat. I want to suck on his fingertip. I want to touch his cock. I want—

Something crawls over his bare arm. A tiny spider. Automatically, I reach out and flick it off his shoulder.

"What was that?" he growls, his tail thudding hard against the ground.

"Spider. It's gone now. Nasty little creatures." I fight back a yawn. To my surprise, Hawk jerks to his feet and abandons the tent. "I . . . Where are you going?"

"Need to talk to Magpie" is all he calls back, voice strangely tight.

Rude. Rude to just up and leave after teasing me like that. With a huff of annoyance, I close my eyes and try to go to sleep.

HAWK

Being in the tent with Aspeth each day is the sweetest torture. At night, when they're marching through the woods, it's easy to push down any feelings of affection. It's easy to focus on the task ahead of us—of training the fledglings. Magpie seems to be in a good mood—almost too good. She swears she's not drinking, but she also won't let me sniff her breath, so I don't know that I believe her.

It's hard to trust again after so long.

But Aspeth's presence makes this better than most fledgling trainings. After I checked everything thoroughly for spiders, I returned to the tent to find Aspeth still awake. We talked when we should have been resting. Just lay on our sides and discussed everything and nothing. It was . . . nice. Real nice. Nice to have someone I can talk to and who sees the situation for what it is. Nice to have an equal who isn't a staggering drunk.

I might be Aspeth's teacher, but it's clear after a few hours of conversation that she could teach me a lot about Old Prell, and I enjoy her intelligence.

I actually look forward to our next rest period in the tent.

Once the training is done for the night and Magpie is sweaty and pale with fatigue, I tap Aspeth on the shoulder. "Time for bed."

"Oooooooh," Lark coos, because she's ridiculous. At her side, Mereden giggles behind her hand.

"You all need to get some rest," I tell them sternly. My cock is reacting to the Conquest Moon—and to Aspeth's nearness—and by the time we get into the tent, I'm rock-hard and aching. Not that I'd rut my soft little wife here in the woods. But bury me, I sure do think about it.

We undress in silence, and then Aspeth lets out a sigh of pleasure, scratching at the chemise she wears under her corset. "Gods, that feels good."

I grunt, adjusting my cock surreptitiously. "Get some sleep."

But my wife never listens to anything I say. I can't decide if I find it amusing or irritating, but I'm leaning toward amusing. She lies atop the blankets again, her nipples poking against the fabric of her chemise, and stifles a yawn as she gazes up at me. "No sleep. This is our get-to-know-each-other time and I plan on taking full advantage of it. What's the most beautiful thing you've ever found in the Everbelow?"

Her question makes me chuckle, because of course Aspeth wants to know all about the job. "You mean the most expensive thing? The most powerful?"

She turns on her side and tucks her arm under her head again, gazing at me as I lie down. "No, I mean the most beautiful. Old Prell was full of all kinds of beautiful works, and not just magical ones. I've seen drawings of Prellian frescoes that would put modern artists to shame. I've read about glorious architecture. I can't wait to see it all. I was just curious what you'd seen. It doesn't have to be an artifact." Her eyes gleam with a dreamy expression. "I wish I could have seen Prell in its height of power. I bet it was splendid."

"It also fell into the ground at its height of power. You wouldn't want to be around for that."

Aspeth bats at my arm, chuckling. "Don't ruin my dreams."

I consider her words, lying on my back and gazing up at the ceiling of the tent, a blanket strategically placed over my cock. Her hand remains on my arm, touch lingering, and it's making my erection remain as hard and aching as ever. "I used to go in the tunnels all the time when I first joined the guild. I do it less now—or rather, I do it for artifacts less now. I end up on more retrieval missions than anything. But I remember that I found a mirror once, and it made me stop in my tracks."

"A mirror," she breathes. "How incredible. Was it broken?"

I shake my head. "It was wrapped in fabric in a tunnel, just wedged in some rocks near an old cave-in. Perhaps a thief tried to steal it and decided not to bother and left it behind, but when I found it, there was nothing else around. No ruins, no other artifacts, just that solitary wrapped mirror." Holding my hands in the air, I try to shape it with my fingers. "It was about the size of a platter, and as clear as day. All around the edges the metal was worked so delicately that it looked like vines covered in flowers, and every flower was a different size and shade. Every leaf, every petal, all of it was made from colored gemstones. A few of them had chipped and cracked but it was still gorgeous."

"How beautiful. Was it magical?"

"That's the ironic part." I chuckle at the memory. "The only thing the mirror did was make your hair seem a dark, rich black in the reflection. Got rid of the grays. And if your hair wasn't black, it adjusted your reflection. Useless."

"Someone was sensitive about his hair, then," Aspeth replies with a soft smile. "How funny that they were a people who imbued magic into everything they owned and we're a people with no magic at all."

"That's because all the mancers went crazy three hundred years ago. Better to not have magic. At least with a magic mirror, you can put the mirror away."

"I suppose." Her smile grows broader as she gazes up at me. "Have you ever found something you wished you could keep?"

You.

The foolish thought bubbles up and I push it away, because it's likely moon-induced. Ours is a marriage of convenience, nothing more.

TWENTY-ONE

ASPETH

17 Days Before the Conquest Moon

WHEN NIGHT FOUR in the woods arrives and we're still doing drills, I decide they're doing this to torture us.

We go up the stream.

Down the stream.

Up the stream again, but this time tied in a different formation.

We go up and down the stream with weapons drawn.

Without a lantern. All of us carrying lanterns. All of us carrying lanterns with our pack weight doubled to simulate if we found a stash of treasures.

Not even a few stolen touches in the tent can make this any better. Not that there's been many of those lately, either. After that first explosive interlude when Hawk made me come, I've been aching for him to touch me again. Aching.

Instead, we just *talk*.

And while I find talking to him joyous and incredibly satisfying—he's as fixed on Old Prell as me in some ways—I wish he would touch me again. I think it's my fault. I told him I wanted to get to know him during rest times in the tent, and I think he interpreted that to mean I didn't want to be touched until we knew each other better.

Is it greedy to want both? I certainly don't think so.

Magpie grows steadily more ornery as the nights pass as well. She doesn't look so good. Her hands shake with tremors constantly and she sweats even when it's cold. Her face is pale, her eyes are hollows, but she's determined to keep us moving. She's grumpy, too. She yells at us constantly to pick up our feet, or to move faster, or to swing a sword harder. To make a fire faster.

In short, she's horrible.

Hawk isn't much better. He doesn't speak much outside of our rest times inside our tent, alone, and when he does, it's to point out something our Five is doing wrong. That we're going to fail if we keep going as we are. That we need to shape up, do better. We're giving everything we've got and yet it's still not good enough for him, or for Magpie.

"YOU'RE USING YOUR eyes too much," Hawk tells me, batting aside my attempts to stab with my training sword. "I can predict where you're going with your weapon. Quit projecting."

"I'm not projecting."

At my next stab, he makes another growl of frustration and bats me aside again, as easily as batting away a fly. "Eyes."

"What else am I supposed to do?" I sputter, even as I stab and feint again. My vision is blurry and I'm focused more on shapes and colors than actual objects, but I can't let him know that. "They're eyes! They're meant for looking!"

"And in the tunnels, your lighting is going to be almost nothing. The shadows are going to trick your vision. You need to rely on your other senses when you fight, Aspeth, or we're going to have to break out the mucking blindfolds again."

I make a frustrated sound and stab again, just as he's taught me.

Hawk parries me easily, and when I stab at him wildly a second time, he smacks my hand with his blocking staff.

Yelping, I drop my blade and bring the back of my hand to my mouth. My skin stings at the contact, but more than anything, I'm humiliated. I can't tell him that I can't see enough to follow his lessons other than the broad gestures. I can't tell him that I'm doing good just to not run into walls. I have to pretend like I can see as well as anyone else. This is something I can't master, and I can't tell him that. "I need a moment."

I walk away, sucking on the back of my hand, determined not to cry. Tears of frustration don't solve anything. They won't make me better at sword work. They won't fix my vision. They won't get me into the guild, so I need to channel that helpless anger into something else.

"Aspeth," Hawk calls after me.

"I said I need a moment," I call back, walking into the thick copse of trees. "Let me be and then I'll come back to training." I keep walking, and my frustration mounts when I can hear him crashing through the underbrush behind me. I hike a little faster, only for him to keep following me as if what I want doesn't matter. It only adds to my bad mood, and by the time I hit a good spot to sit and relax, I turn and glare at the big bull-man who has followed me all this time. "What part of 'I said I need a moment' did you fail to understand?"

He ignores my bad mood and marches right up to me and takes my hand, turning it over and examining it. "Did I hurt you?"

Oh. "It stung, but you did the same to the others."

"I'm not married to the others." He lifts the back of my hand to his muzzle and rubs his nose against my skin. "I'm sorry. I was trying to be gentle with you and instinct kicked in."

"I don't want you to be gentle with me," I tell him, distracted as he continues to rub his muzzle against my skin in a way that makes me feel shivery inside. "I want you to treat me the same as the others."

"But you're not the same," he murmurs, and his golden gaze meets mine. "You're my wife, and I'm supposed to be teaching you about pleasure. I don't like seeing you hurt."

His response leaves me flustered. "It's not like it's been about pleasure over the last few days. You haven't touched me since the first day we got here."

"Missing it?"

Oh gods. My face heats. "I mean . . . no . . ."

"Liar." He grins, his expression practically feral as he releases my hand and takes another step forward. I automatically take a step back, and stumble over roots, only to find myself with my back against the nearest tree. His hand goes to my waist, and then he flicks open my belt and slides his hand into my pants.

Sucking in a breath at the feel of his warm fingers against my skin, I flick my gaze up to him. "What are you doing?"

"Making you feel better." The heat in his eyes is playful, even as he cups the back of my neck with his other hand and draws a teasing circle around my clit. The pose makes me gaze up at him, and when I brace a hand on his chest, I can see a smile curving his mouth. "You sounded sad that I haven't touched you lately. I'm making it up to you."

"You—you don't—I wasn't—"

"Shhh. I know, little bird." He strokes against my clit, and my knees almost buckle. "I have you."

My lips part, and anything I want to say, to protest, disappears from my mind as he keeps touching me. His fingers dance through my folds, slicking them with my juices, and when he dips a finger into the heat of my channel, my body makes a wet squelch. I jerk, startled and embarrassed.

Hawk only hums with pleasure. "Feel how wet you are, Aspeth? When the moon is upon me, the more I touch you, the more slick your body will create so you can take me. You're going to be twice as wet as this, so wet that it runs down your thighs and soaks the bed. It's all so I can stretch you to take my knot, and it'll make you feel so good." He eases his finger into me again, his thumb moving to rub my clit as he does, and then starts a slow, regular motion, pumping into me with his hand. His gaze is locked on mine as I curl my hands in his shirt, clinging to him as he pushes me toward a climax.

When I come, it's with a muffled cry, my face pressed against his chest as he keeps fingering me. Pleasure bursts through my mind and sweeps down my legs, and then it rolls through me, leaving me sated and weak-kneed. "Oh. That was . . . nice."

"It was, aye." He rubs his muzzle against my ear, as if drinking in my scent.

"I wasn't begging for you to touch me," I tell him primly. "I just thought that we were supposed to be spending our time here in the woods getting to know each other. Our time alone, that is."

"Oh, we are." He chuckles, amused at my prissiness. "I'm getting to know which touches make you squeal, and that you talk about Old Prell in your sleep."

I wriggle until I free his possessive hand from my body and slip away from him, flushed with embarrassment. "I do not."

He licks his fingers clean of my taste with lascivious strokes of his tongue that make me think all kinds of naughty things. "You do, and it's charming. Last night you were discovering bowls in your sleep."

"Last night" was actually "last day," since we've been sleeping in the daytime, but I don't correct him. I'm a little too mortified that he's right. I do have vague dreams of unearthing glowing bowls from a big pile of rocks. "What kinds of bowls?"

Hawk chuckles, his expression amused and full of affection as he gazes at me. "I don't know. You kept saying it was a secret."

Normally I'd be fixated on the soft expression my new husband is giving me, but all I can think about is that I'm talking about secrets in my sleep. Is real life bleeding over into my dreams? Have I mentioned anything about my father and his hold? His need for artifacts? I need to distract Hawk from this line of thought so he doesn't pay too much attention if I do so again. "You know, Prellian bowls were a very important part of mealtimes. They had different-sized bowls and different colors of bowls depending on what was being served and at what time. It was considered poor manners to serve anything in a large bowl at the first meal of the day, for example. It implied you were greedy. If a wife wanted to get on her husband's bad side, she'd keep increasing the size of a bowl, a subtle insult."

The Taurian chuckles, shaking his head at me. "That's one of the things I like about you, Aspeth—when you get cornered, you start teaching history lessons about Old Prell. By the time you get to be a guild master, I'll be as much of an expert as you are, because you'll have told me so much."

His words make me pause. "You truly think I'll get there?"

"If anyone will, it's you." He smiles.

I want to preen at his approval.

THE AFTERNOON WHEN we start our fifth day in the woods begins with a drizzling rain, and my boots squish with every step I take. It's the breaking point. The cloak I wear is wet. The socks on my feet are soaked. Everything is covered in mud and damp and cold and I've had enough.

"This is ridiculous," I exclaim, parking my feet at the edge of the stream before we can tie ourselves together for yet another water hike. I turn around to glare at Magpie and Hawk. "Why are we doing this to ourselves?"

Gwenna, Lark, and Mereden look just as miserable as I am. Even Kipp looks a little weary. The big shell of his house hangs lower on his shoulders than it should, a sign that even someone with his expertise can grow tired of this nonsense.

"You know why," Hawk says, voice harsh. For a moment, I regret I didn't ask him to go easy on me because I'm his wife. He's just as hard on me—if not harder than anyone else.

Next to him, Magpie winces and holds her head. She's looking just as sorry as the rest of us, her clothes wet and muddy, her eyes hollowed out. She acts as if she has a headache, too.

"We're going to be in tunnels," I feel the need to point out. "Not—this!" I extend my hands, gesturing at the rain pattering down on us, and then indicate the mud at my feet. "There's no rain in the Everbelow! There's no bugs! There—"

"Spiders," Hawk says immediately. "There are spiders."

I pause. "They're just spiders."

"Not *just* spiders. They're great big ones. Terrifying creatures." His lip curls and he looks absolutely revolted. "I wish there weren't, but you need to be prepared for such things."

"You say they're big? How big?" Lark asks. "Like . . . the size of a plate?"

"Big as my thumbnail," he declares in a grave voice, his expression somber. "Trust me when I say they're horrible."

My lips twitch, but I promise myself I won't laugh. "While I hate a spider as much as anyone, I don't see how this camping excursion continues to help us. We're more in danger of mosquitos and getting a cold from being rained upon than running into cave spiders. If you really want to teach us what it's like in the tunnels, we'd be better off indoors, don't you think?"

He shakes his head. "This is about—"

"I know what it's about," I protest, exasperated. "All I'm saying is that there has to be a better way to teach us than to trudge us through a forest full of mud!"

Hawk storms over and plants his hands on his hips, looming over me. Mereden makes an alarmed squeak but I only glare back at the Taurian. If this is an intimidation tactic, it's not going to work on me. "Do you have something you want to say to me?" he asks in a deadly voice. "Wife?"

"Yes." I lift my chin. "This is madness. If you want to teach us how to move about in the tunnels, find us a nice dry basement instead and—" I cut off as he puts a finger in my face. "Put that thing away."

"Aspeth," he says, his tone full of warning. "*I* am your teacher. *Magpie* is your teacher. If we tell you to trudge through the mud for a week straight, that's what you're going to do."

"I really don't think—"

"Tut!" The finger is under my nose again, raising higher with the sharp syllable. "You're not here to think, you're here to learn."

Now I'm the one making an angry sound. "I'm not some idiot—"

"No, just a terrible listener. *And* you don't seem to like being told what to do." He eyes me balefully, looking nothing like the heavy-eyed bull who fingers me to climax when we're alone. "I'm thinking you've picked the wrong line of work."

"You're not here to *think*, you're here to teach," I snap back, using his words against him.

Gwenna hisses between her teeth.

Kipp takes a delicate step away from us.

Hawk gets in my face, his muzzle practically to my nose. "If you were a man, I'd turn you over my knee and spank you like a child, since you're acting like one."

I'm not sure why, but the angry flick of his tail hitting his thighs and the loom of him over me doesn't make me any madder. If anything, it makes heat uncurl deep in my belly. "My gender shouldn't matter."

His eyes narrow. "So you *do* want me to spank you."

Now we're both breathing hard.

"Hey, uh," Lark says. "I think I speak for all of us when I say 'What the fuck?'"

"Mind your business," Hawk says, not looking away from me. I don't look away from him, either. If I continue to meet him glare for glare, is he going to make good on his word? Is he going to turn me over on his knee and spank me, his hand on my bare buttocks, me helpless and splayed over his lap . . . ?

Mercy, that should not be as arousing as it is. I blink up at Hawk, and I could swear I see a hint of red in the gleam of his eyes. Is it the moon making him act like this . . . or does he really want me? It's most likely the Conquest Moon, as he's drummed into my ears over and over again, and the realization dampens my arousal.

I'm just convenient, nothing more.

Before I can come up with a response, there's a distant sound in the woods like that of branches snapping. We all turn, and then a voice calls out, "Ho! Is someone there?"

"Ho," Magpie calls back in greeting, cupping a hand to her face. "Over here! By the stream!"

To my surprise, the pack I have on my shoulder slips. One of the straps falls away and I turn to grab it, only for the entire thing to tumble to the ground with a wet slap. The blankets, foodstuffs, dry boots, and everything else spill out into the mud, and I want to scream in frustration. Just what I needed.

Gwenna kneels down next to me, picking up one of my boots. "You clumsy, silly thing," she loudly exclaims as the riders make their way toward us.

I pick up one end of the strap, noticing it's been unbuckled. What the—

"Pull your hood up," Gwenna whispers to me. "Do it now. Quickly."

There's an urgency in her voice I've never heard before. I pull my sodden hood over my hair, looking up at her in surprise. I reach for the boot but she holds on to it, and her gaze meets mine. There's a warning in her eyes.

"Greetings, greetings," a man says in a cultured voice, his accent that of the north. Like mine. "Is there a better place to cross this water? My lord Barnabus's horse has lost a shoe and is too expensive to risk laming on the rocks."

I freeze, ice going up my spine. Lord Barnabus Chatworth? He's here?

Gwenna gives me the boot, her expression firm, as if to say *See?*

Oh, I see now. I take my time shoving things back into my pack, determined to make it last as long as possible. I wonder if I can get sick on command? Right now my stomach is roiling enough that I wouldn't have to try too hard. Barnabus is here. Why? He's made it clear to me in the past that busy, dangerous Vastwarren holds no interest for him. Surely he hasn't come to retrieve me.

"The stream crossing narrows farther down the hillside," Magpie explains. "You're heading in the wrong direction if you want things to get easier. Only gets wider from up here, but it ain't deep. If your horse can't cross this you've got bigger problems."

Hawk chuckles. Mereden and Lark do, too. I don't hear anyone else laughing, though, and my pulse pounds in my ears. Barnabus is here. I've been found out. Woodenly, I pick up a soggy piece of clothing and pause, panic rising in my throat. I'm going to lose everything. I'm going to be destroyed. Not only will my father and grandmother be in danger, but our hold will go down in flames. And Hawk—

"Clumsy twit," Gwenna says in an exasperated voice. "Let me help." And she kneels next to me and pulls everything back out of my pack. "You're not going to be able to fit everything in again. Watch how I do it."

"Thank you," I mouth to her, squeezing my trembling hands into fists.

The horses grow louder, the sounds of their hooves in the mud and the jingle of harnesses like death knells to me. I glance over, peeking out the side of my hood, and there are at least a half dozen horses around the edge of the stream, the men wearing a familiar livery. I recognize the house colors of their jerkins, the Chatworth Hold deep blue with the bold yellow trim that stands out even to my bad eyes. One of the men is walking, leading a horse by the reins. And then to my horror, Barnabus himself rides up, eyes the stream, and turns to look at our group.

I quickly hide my face again.

"What is going on here?" he asks, voice just as cultured and haughty as I remember. I used to love how precisely he said each syllable, as if he were biting them. Now I know it's just a tactic to put himself above others. To show them that he's superior because he has holder blood.

That, or I'm still bitter about him calling me ugly.

His words make me freeze in terror, though. I clutch my canteen tightly, a knot in my throat.

"What do you mean, what is going on here?" Magpie's voice is an amused drawl. I imagine her with her hands on her hips, confronting him with that world-weary stare of hers. "What does it look like is going on here?"

"It looks like a religious ceremony of some kind," Barnabus answers, his voice stiff. "Are you some sort of nature cult?"

Gwenna snorts, a sound so low that only I can hear it. I want to be amused, too. Normally I'd laugh at the idiotic suggestion that we're a nature cult . . . but I'm too afraid that I've been caught. That I'm going to be dragged back to Honori Hold in disgrace, without a single artifact. That everything has been ruined.

"Why in the five hells would we be a cult?" Hawk sounds annoyed.

I can almost see the dismissive look that Barnabus would send in his direction. "You're all wearing the same clothes. It looks like a religious training program."

"Your men are all wearing the same clothes," I hear Lark mutter loud enough to be overheard.

Mereden giggles.

Magpie shushes both of them. "It's a uniform. This is a training program for fledglings of the Royal Artifactual Guild."

I tense, waiting for him to remember my fascination with it. How I was always reading books about the greats of the guild. How I'd been obsessed with learning Old Prellian glyphs.

"Ah."

I wait.

"That explains the colors. Carry on, then," Barnabus says, as if we needed his permission.

I slowly help Gwenna restuff my pack as the horses splash across the stream. When I dare to look up, they're on the far side of the stream, nothing but horse withers and Chatworth cloaks meeting my stare.

They're gone. I'm still incredibly rattled, though.

I'm shaking, and Gwenna puts a hand over mine, as if to comfort me. "I don't think he noticed you," she whispers. "He barely glanced in our direction."

Taking a deep breath, I nod. Then my stomach churns, and I realize I'm going to throw up the cold breakfast I ate a few hours ago. I barely manage to crawl away a foot or two before I'm puking in the mud, bent over.

When I recover, Hawk is looming over me, a heavy frown on his face. He hauls me up to my feet, brushing me off, and then cups my face in one hand, studying it. "What's wrong with you?"

I manage a faint smile, downplaying the situation. I don't want him to realize why I'm so stressed. "It's nothing. Just feeling a little ill."

He pulls his canteen out and pops the cork free, offering it to me. "Drink." Turning, he says to the others, "We'll go back to town. Let you rest. We're pushing you too hard." And then his gaze lingers on me. He reaches out and tucks a lock of scraggly hair behind my ear. "I'm sorry."

I just sip the water, feeling like the worst woman alive. I should tell him that we haven't been worked too hard. That I'm not sick because I'm overtired, I'm sick because the knot of anxiety in my gut seems to be growing larger by the moment. But I can't say anything.

It never occurred to me that my two lives might collide. That someone from my past might show up in my present . . . and now I have no idea what to do if it happens again.

TWENTY-TWO

ASPETH

14 Days Before the Conquest Moon

HAWK HIRED A nearby woodcutter to cart us back to Vastwarren that night, and we spent the whole next day catching up on sleep. The next morning, we head to the guild library. There, Magpie goes over the history of Old Prell and common types of artifacts that are found in the tunnels. Normally I'd love this sort of thing. I love talking about the Prellian

Empire with others, and nothing excites me more than artifact discussion. But I can't concentrate. Barnabus's return hangs over my head like an executioner's axe.

I've been woefully blind to the dangers here. Anyone who recognizes me could blackmail me. They could demand funds from my father—funds that aren't there. We could be exposed in an instant.

Destroyed in a heartbeat, and no one would do more than shrug. Their fortune was gone, someone would point out. Their artifacts gambled away. What did they expect?

I stare at the book in front of me, not seeing a single page. It's a book on the pottery of Old Prell, and there aren't enough copies for all the students, so I'm sharing with Kipp, who turns the pages with the sticky end of his tongue. The Prellian Empire was famous for its ceramics and the sorts of things they enchanted the jars and vases with. I know everything in the book already, but I've never seen this particular reference and part of me knows I'm going to regret being unable to concentrate. Yet every time I try to focus, I see Barnabus on his horse. I think of what will happen if he finds out I'm here in Vastwarren and not high in the mountains, safely ensconced in Honori Hold and weeping bitter tears over our broken engagement.

He'll make a move if he knows I'm here. At home we're surrounded by retainers and guardsmen who have no idea that our artifacts are gone. They blindly trust in my father's might. Their lives are at stake, too.

Should I turn around and leave, then? Go back home and marry someone like Barnabus and reinforce our family's holdings through a connection? Or is it already too late because Barnabus knows I'm here? If he lets that out, I'll be ruined.

There's also a small matter of my Taurian husband, but I'm tackling one problem at a time. Even if I can't make our marriage work long-term, I at least owe it to him to be here for the Conquest Moon. He needs a partner, though he acts as if any woman wouldn't be falling all over herself to get together with him and that mouth of his—

"Aspeth?"

I look up, startled. "I—yes?" I grab the page to turn it, pretending like I was paying attention. My fingers encounter Kipp's slithery, sticky tongue instead and I squeal in horror. The slitherskin makes a choked sound, pulling back and putting a hand to his mouth with a wounded expression that reads *How dare you.* "I'm sorry," I manage, embarrassed. "Could you repeat the question?"

"I asked if we were boring you," Magpie says. Her graying hair is pulled back from her round face in a tight braid today, emphasizing a hint of cheekbones. She looks better than she has in the last while, though her hands still shake with tremors at times. Lark says this is a good sign, though. Hawk doesn't agree. He's still waiting for her to falter again.

"Oh, I'm not bored," I exclaim, putting on my simpering noble-woman act and beaming at her. "I love Prellian pottery."

"Excellent. Remind me of the piece we were just talking about and the common things to look for?" Her dark, heavy brows go up.

Um. I eye the page in the book in front of me. There's a drawing of a fluted, thin bud vase with a rounded flare at the base. Looking at it makes me think of Hawk and the knot he's supposed to get at the time of the Conquest Moon. I stare at it, trying to think of non-phallic characteristics. "Ah . . ."

"Leave her alone," Hawk says, voice gruff at the back of the room. "You know Aspeth's knowledge isn't a problem when it comes to arti-facts."

I hadn't realized Hawk was even in the library with us. He must have joined after we'd sat down. I glance over my shoulder at him and see his big form stretched on a bench near the wall, his hooves sprawled out in front of him, arms crossed over his chest. He slouches like a man of lei-sure, ironic given that his guild coat is taut over his thick arms. . . .

"If she's so knowledgeable, she needs to share with her companions." Magpie's expression is unyielding. "We don't have time to waste. Not now."

He straightens in his seat, hooves squarely upon the floor. Hawk leans forward, one hand on his knee as he studies Magpie. "What do you mean, exactly?"

"Remember when Lord Jent decided to go to war with that big coastal hold? And he called in a special request to the guild? We sent out teams of students fresh from the schoolroom and only half of them made it out alive, but that wasn't a problem for Lord Jent because he got the artifacts he needed and quickly. We've a similar situation now. Lord Chatworth has asked for additional teams to be sent to the tunnels to look for artifacts. He's going to war and he's willing to pay top price to do so."

I can feel the blood drain from my face. My entire body, actually. I'm just a numb lump of flesh, unable to move, to speak, to breathe.

Chatworth Hold is going to war.

I can guess who he's going to attack. I want to shoot a panicked look to Gwenna but I don't dare turn around to meet her gaze.

This is the nightmare situation I was dreaming of. Worse, even.

"What does that mean for us?" Mereden asks.

"Lord Chatworth's younger son is paying for additional teams to head into the tunnels. This happens occasionally with the guild—sometimes a lord will need an emergency supply of artifacts. Whenever this happens, the teachers take any team of fledglings in that is deemed competent enough. It'll give you an edge when it comes time for your final exam."

"And we're competent enough to go into the tunnels? As a team?" Lark sounds openly skeptical. I can't blame her. I wouldn't think of us when I think of competence, but maybe . . . maybe . . . maybe we can find something good, something big, and I can claim it for Honori instead of turning it over to Barnabus. Maybe I can find something big enough to change our circumstances. After all, it was the Sphere of Reason that established Sparkanos and the guild after the Mancer Wars. If there's one artifact like that, there are bound to be others.

Maybe this is where I need to be after all. If we find something big, I can do my best to make sure it doesn't fall into Barnabus's hands. He must need additional firepower of some kind if he's paying for more artifacts. He needs an edge over my father in some way and is counting on us to deliver it.

Okay. Okay. I can fix this. I can save the day still. I take a deep, shuddering breath.

"We're not ready," Gwenna states in a firm, reasonable voice. She sits behind me so I can't see her expression, but I know she's thinking the same thing I am—we can't help Barnabus. We just can't.

"It's not like you'll be going in alone," Magpie retorts.

I glance up. "Hawk's coming with us?"

She pauses. "A good idea, but no. He's going to be needed for more retrieval missions, most likely. Just today, another team got stuck in the ruins of an old temple despite that area being off-limits. Idiots."

Wait, he is? He mentioned the other Taurians had left the city due to the oncoming Conquest Moon. Why is he here with us if he's heading out on an emergency mission? I shoot a look over to him but his face is impassive. "Isn't that dangerous for him, too? The other Taurians are gone."

"It's not a dangerous area. They're safe where they are. They just can't get out." Magpie shrugs.

"I'm training a retrieval team, too," Hawk adds. "Since the guild is realizing it would help to have additional trained teams. Once they have their gear together, we're meeting at the drop station and heading in. Hopefully it won't take too long." His expression is carefully blank, but I feel like he's annoyed at being on call. I can't say I blame him.

"Don't you worry about Hawk," Magpie says. "Just give his balls a good jiggle when he comes back."

Hawk clears his throat.

My face heats. "Must you be so crude?"

"Only if I'm awake." She smirks in my direction. "And we all know you're giving his balls a jiggle, so it's not like this is a secret."

Kipp makes a hissing noise and I realize he's laughing. I scowl over at him.

"So fucking pay attention in class," Magpie says, leaning forward. "Because we're going into the tunnels in a little over a week and you need all the information I can shove in your head."

Over a week. It's enough time to send a letter home. I need to warn Father somehow, to let him know that Barnabus is going to make a move against Honori Hold. But mucking hells, I don't even know where Father is. Is he at court? At his mistress's home by the sea? At our hold? Do I send out anonymous letters to all those places and hope I catch him? It feels foolish, but what choice do I have? Not warning him seems even more foolish. I have to tell him something. Perhaps I can hint that Father has a friend here in Vastwarren who is looking out for his interests. I don't have to point out that it's me. He wouldn't recognize my handwriting anyhow.

I contemplate what I'm going to write through the rest of the lessons, lost in thought. It's not like I need to know the shape of an urn that carries a particular spell, or what it means when a jar is found magically sealed (nothing good). I already know these things. I'm able to tune out Magpie and not feel too guilty. I've got bigger problems on my mind.

By the end of the day, I'm feeling relatively good about the message I'm going to send. I have the perfect, concise statement ready, and I'm mentally going through the rooms in the barracks that might have stationery I can purloin. Then it's just a matter of getting it delivered. But when we arrive back at the dormitory, any thought I had of being in control goes out the window.

There's a message waiting for me, the vellum envelope sealed with plain, unadorned wax. The others look at me curiously when I tuck it into my blouse and head to my room to read it in private. With trembling fingers, I open it and read the brief spatter of text.

> *Tomorrow night.*
> *King's Onion tavern.*
> *Midnight.*

It's from Barnabus. Has to be. Somehow he's figured out where I am. And I have to go. I don't have a choice.

IT'S NOT UNTIL later that night that Hawk heads out with the retrieval team trainees, all of them wearing the black sashes of the repeaters. I wave goodbye from the doorway of the nest like a dutiful wife, but I'm glad he's gone. With Hawk out, it's going to be surprisingly easy to sneak away. I go to bed early the next night, pretending to be tired from a full day of sword work. Once I'm alone in the quarters I share with Hawk, I change out of my guild uniform into my darkest, most somber dress and cloak, slipping on my delicate boots. I don't know why I'm bothering to try to pretend like I'm not in the guild. Plausible deniability, I suppose. Either way, it feels safer to show up as "Aspeth" instead of "Sparrow." After giving Squeaker's ears a good scratch, I open the door as quietly as possible . . .

. . . only to see a glaring Gwenna waiting on the other side.

"What are you doing here?" I ask, dumbfounded.

"Stopping you." The look on her face could peel paint. "What do you think you're doing?"

"Nothing."

"Aspeth, you are a terrible liar! You're going out to meet Barnabus, aren't you?"

I scoff. "No."

She reaches out and plucks a tuft of orange fur from my cloak. "Pulling out our old clothes, sneaking away at midnight . . . sure sounds to me like you're meeting him."

"How do you know he's even asked to meet me?"

"I snuck in and read your note."

"Gwenna!"

"What? It's obvious you weren't going to tell me." She marches into my room and sits on the edge of the bed, her arms crossed as she glares at me. "So again, I'll ask, what do you think you're doing? Because going to meet him is incredibly stupid."

"What other choice do I have?" She continues to give me a look of disbelief, so I explain. "He knows where I am and what I'm doing. If you think he's not going to use that information for his own purposes, you're being naive. I have to see what he wants and what it'll take to keep him quiet."

Gwenna purses her lips, hesitating. "You know he doesn't want anything good."

"I know he doesn't. But again, what am I supposed to do?"

She sighs. "I just don't like it, Aspeth."

"Me, either."

Gwenna stands up, and I think she's going to push me back into my room. Instead, she envelops me in a hug. Surprised and touched, I hug her back, feeling awkward and yet somehow happy. I don't know what I would have done if I'd come here alone. Probably have given up a half dozen times already.

She pats my back. "Let me come with you, hmm?"

"You can't. We both know you can't." I give her a squeeze of affection and then pull away. "If I don't return, you have to tell the others what happened. If you come with me, we both could get in trouble. At least this way you're safe."

"Yes, but you're going to go into the city alone after dark? That's dangerous, Aspeth."

She's not wrong, but again, I don't have a choice. It's not as if I can ask Barnabus to meet somewhere more convenient. "I'll wear my cloak and keep out of sight as much as possible. And don't forget, I've been practicing with a short sword."

Gwenna stares at me and then we both burst into laughter.

We giggle until tears stream down our faces, because I'm absolutely rotten with a sword. Comically bad. I'm in far more danger of wounding those around me with my sword, to the point that Magpie has instructed me to use a club and only a club. No sharp objects, especially not in confined spaces.

Gwenna doesn't give up, though. Wiping tears from her face, she shakes her head again. "Ask Kipp to go with you. He's good with a sword and no one will pay much attention to a slitherskin."

"What if he says something to someone?" I ask, worried.

"Kipp? Please. He's the soul of discretion." She tugs me by the arm, pulling me into the hall as if it's already decided. "Come on."

Maybe she's right. We head down to the kitchen (Kipp's favorite spot to tuck into his shell house and relax) and talk to him. A short time later, I'm out in the streets of Vastwarren, heading for the tavern with Kipp keeping a careful distance ahead of me. He seems to know where he's going, which is good, because it's dark and I can't see anything without my spectacles. I weighed the idea of wearing them, but it would ruin my disguise with Lark and the others, so I have to stagger around blindly in the darkness. It's all a blur of shadows, but I can keep my eye on Kipp's pale shell that he shoulders as if it weighs nothing, and it makes it easy to track him.

The night in the city seems dangerous. Even though I know I can take care of myself—probably—I'm still a little alarmed at the crowded streets. Vastwarren's winding, crooked streets are packed with men of all ages after dark, most of them drunk and rowdy. Things are peaceful behind the guild's high wall at the center of the city, but here in the common streets it's a mess.

Once you get away from the center of the city where the guild holds sway, the inns and shops all cluster together like people crowding and jockeying for space. If there's a fingerbreadth of ground to be found, someone has built a booth on it and is selling wares. We pass an alley that's crowded with blankets and stolen goods laid out for buyers. Kipp hurries past but part of me wants to pause and look to see if there are artifacts being sold.

Not that I have the funds, of course. But you never know. I've heard all kinds of stories about what can be found here in Vastwarren if one knows the right people to talk to, and I'm here to acquire artifacts to protect my home above all else. I need to remember that.

It's a sobering thought. I speed up, clutching my cloak tighter to my body, and follow behind Kipp as he winds through the crowds. Luckily the cloak—and the nasty, damp weather—keep anyone from bothering me. I get a few sideways looks from people who lose interest when I don't pause and just continue on my way. Then I see it.

A wooden sign hangs out over the street from the balcony above, designed to move back and forth in the wind. It's hand-painted with a busty woman holding out a bright yellow goblet that pours round white shapes that must be onions—of all things—like they're liquid. THE KING'S ONION is written in bold lettering at the top of the sign, large enough that even I can read it.

Kipp pauses directly underneath it and looks over at me, then at the tavern. A raucous crowd is inside despite the fact that it's the middle of the night, and someone screams with laughter, only to be drowned out by more shouting. His expression is displeased as he eyes me.

"It's not my idea of a good place, either, but I don't have a choice," I tell him as I come to his side. "Thank you for the guidance. I wouldn't have made it here without you."

He gestures at the wall and mimes leaning against it and waiting, then looks at me.

"No, you don't need to wait for me."

Kipp taps his heart and then gestures at his sword. Then he gives me a firm, emphatic nod. I'm pretty sure this is a *We're a team* sort of gesture and it makes me feel warm inside. Even a quiet slitherskin has my back.

"I know," I say softly. "And I appreciate you, Kipp. But I promise I'll be fine."

He nods again and adjusts the straps on his shell house, then trots down the street, heading home. I'm left alone in front of the raucous inn, and my gut churns with unease. I don't want to do this. I don't want to see Barnabus. I want to go home and sleep and not think about anything.

I can't, though. My past is coming to fuck things up for me. I bite back a sigh of frustration. Nothing to do but move forward. Get Barnabus out of my hair and then move on with my life.

Taking a deep, steeling breath, I exhale and step inside the tavern, lowering my hood as I do. The stink of sweat and humid air from so many people crowding into the place hits me like a wall, and I flinch. It's warm inside here, the fire merrily blazing in the large hearth at the far side of the inn, and every wooden table is crowded full of people. It smells like spilled ale as I move toward the crowded bar, looking for Barnabus. The wooden floors creak and groan as I wind my way through the busy cluster of people, and when I spot an empty section at the far end of the bar, I move toward it quickly.

As I approach, a barmaid comes toward me. She could be my age, her smile bright despite the tired circles under her eyes and the many stains on the front of her apron that speak of a long day. "Can I get you something, hon?"

I didn't bring any coin with me and want to kick myself. "I'm waiting for someone."

She fills a couple of mugs and slides them down the bar, eyeing me as she does. "Alone? In a place like this? Everything all right?" She leans in to wipe an imaginary spill and her voice lowers. "You need me to get the constable?"

I shake my head. "Much as I would love that, I'm afraid I need to hear what he has to say."

"That's always the worst, isn't it? When you don't want to hear their shit and you have to anyhow. Old flame?"

"Something like that."

"Been there." The barmaid shakes her head. "Here. Have a drink on me." She rinses out a stoneware mug and then fills it from one of the barrels behind her.

"Oh, I really couldn't—"

"You're pale, hon. Take the drink. Think of it as free advertising."
She finishes pouring and then shoves a wedge of white onion on the
edge, like a garnish.

"Oh, um, an onion. A great big one, too. Thank you." I turn the
mug, trying to figure out how to drink without touching the onion
itself.

"Comes from the name of this place." She gestures behind her, where
a basket perches atop another aging barrel. It's full to the brim of peeled
white onions, and as I watch, one falls from above, joining its brethren in
the basket. I look up and see a golden goblet—the selfsame goblet that
was on the sign—turned upon its side. There's a foggy circle in the middle, and as I watch, it coalesces into another peeled onion, then rolls out
of the cup and drops into the basket below.

An artifact. "Fancy. From the king, I suppose?"

The barmaid nods proudly. "Owner here did a favor for the king
once and was rewarded. Everyone comes here for the free onions with
their beer. We have fried onions, too, if you're more into that. Pickled
ones, too. Baked, breaded . . ."

"I'm good, thanks."

She offers me a wry smile and leans in again. "Just between you and
me, I'd avoid the privy, though. It's pretty rank and oniony."

Ew. I wrinkle my nose and nod.

Just then, I see a feathered purple hat bobbing as it moves through the
crowd, and I know immediately who that is. Barnabus has always had a
taste for the most ridiculous, showy hats. I take a large gulp of my beer
to brace myself, then grab the onion and take a huge chomp out of it,
because fuck Barnabus. If he wants to talk to me (or worse), I hope I reek
of onions.

"Atta girl," the barmaid says.

I nod at her, eating the onion like an apple, and get to my feet to approach my former betrothed. Is he going to be glad to see me? Beg me to
run away with him and leave this place? Or is he going to threaten me
somehow?

Knowing what I know now—that Father has no money and we've no
artifacts left—it's tempting to consider leaving with Barnabus. To marry

him and let Honori Hold become his problem. Let him figure out how to pay for the knights and their annual fees. Let him figure out how to get more artifacts.

But I'm already married, so I can't do that.

And even if I did, he'd probably murder me in our marriage bed once his claim on Honori Hold was secure. He wouldn't need me any longer, and a widower can marry again, of course. So no, marrying to solve my problems isn't the answer, much as I might entertain the idea for a brief, shining moment.

I chew on the last of the onion, hoping that my breath is fragrant and terrible, and raise a hand in the air to signal him. He can come to me, I decide, and not the other way around. So I sip my beer and watch as another magical onion rolls into the basket. The barmaid grabs it off the top, slices it into quarters with a deft knife, and then wedges them onto the rims of four more mugs and sends them flying down the counter. She knows her stuff, and I'm impressed.

Then Barnabus is standing in front of me, a look of regal horror on his face as he eyes my rumpled, damp clothing and my frizzy hair that's probably fallen completely out of its knot at my nape. I smile tightly at him, wondering if we're going to bother with a polite hug and cheek kiss of greeting as all holders do.

He moves toward me and oh, I guess we are. "Barnabus," I exhale as I say his name, brushing my cheek against his and making sure to get a lot of oniony air into my words.

Barnabus recoils, gazing up and down at me. "My gods, Aspeth, look at you. How has it come to this? What are you doing in this cesspool of a city?"

"Come to what?" I flutter my lashes and decide to play it stupid. "And I'm just visiting friends. What are *you* doing here?"

"Visiting friends? In that? Hardly." He flicks a hand at my clothing. It's creased from sitting in my trunk and covered in cat hair, and the colors are unflattering, but I didn't think it was that bad. "Are you actually working with the guild? In the *dirt*?"

It's more a matter of "excavating" than digging in the dirt. And I haven't even gotten the chance to go excavating yet. Not that he needs to know that. "You set up this meeting. What is it you want?"

The look of incredulousness on his face turns to one of sheer calculation. "I want to know why you're here. We were supposed to be married."

Is he still going on about that? I broke off the engagement months ago. "You're not in love with me, Barnabus. We both know this. So tell me what you want by dragging me here, because it's obvious you want something."

"I want Honori Hold." His voice is soft. "It was in my grasp and you took it from me."

"It's not yours—"

"I'm a second son," he continues. A mug with an onion decorating it is shoved in front of him by the barmaid and he draws back with a look of disgust. He nudges it away from him and turns back to me. "My brother is ridiculously healthy and his wife is pregnant. There's no chance I'll inherit my family's hold. So I want yours."

"You can't have mine." Not that I want it much at the moment, but I'll be damned by all the gods if I just hand it over to this arse. "How did you even know I was here?"

"I didn't." He leans back and studies me. "It's coincidence, really. But I saw your maid by the stream the other day. You two were as thick as thieves back at Honori, so I had my men ask around. Everyone in the guild is quite eager to tell me all about the women who have fledged to Guild Master Magpie and her Taurian brute."

I purse my lips, irritated.

"You didn't even go by a false name, Aspeth darling. It's as if you were begging to be caught."

"I had one. They wouldn't let me use it," I mutter.

He reaches for my hand on the bar. "We can ignore all of this. Come home with me."

Just as he touches me, I snatch my hand away. "I'm not going anywhere with you, and we're not marrying. You're not getting Honori Hold."

Barnabus ignores me. "I won't even tell anyone that I found you here. We'll simply say you were overcome with passion for me and we eloped. No one has to know the truth. Your family will be ruined if anyone finds out that you're here, pretending to be a guild stooge."

I bristle at that. He makes it seem as if I'm an idiot. That I have no idea what I've gotten myself into. I know—and have always known—that traveling without a chaperone isn't done for a holder's daughter. I know that coming to a rough city like Vastwarren makes it ten times worse, because the reputation of this place is less than savory. The guild is considered a necessary evil by most holders—required, but disliked.

I know all this.

I just don't *care*.

Being a pristine, virginal holder's daughter with an impeccable reputation got me nowhere for the past thirty years. I haven't married. My father's hold is broke. Our artifacts are gone. We're in danger of losing our lives if the truth comes out, and frankly I'm tired of all of it. I'm here in this rough, despicable city, preparing to do the dreaded *manual labor* of a guild member, because I'm out of better choices.

I'm finally doing what I want. What I need to do.

And Barnabus is here, sticking his nose in and trying to ruin things. My anger rises, and I grab the onion from his mug and crunch down on it, not caring that I spray bits of white onion flesh everywhere. I hope he finds me disgusting. "I'm not going to marry you."

"Wrong." He leans back, his expression downright smug, as if he has me trapped. "You marry me, and I'll keep your little secret about all of this. Otherwise, your reputation is destroyed."

"I'm not going to marry you," I say again calmly. He doesn't need to know that I can't. That I'm already married to someone else. Seeing him here has just cemented the fact that I would rather walk across broken glass than marry this jerk. To think that I once enjoyed his kisses. I try to imagine this selfish, self-absorbed boor tonguing me the way Hawk did and the onions in my stomach churn. "Don't make me say it again."

"Well, then, enjoy hunting artifacts for me," Barnabus says, voice light. "I've paid a lot of money to the guild to get everyone possible down there scouting for artifacts, and they'll all come to my hands. They know I'm planning to go to war. To take down another hold. And do you think they care? No. All they care about is getting a commission, so I made sure it's an enormous one." He smiles, all teeth, and leans back confidently. "You're of course welcome to commission teams on your father's behalf. It can be a race between us."

My nostrils flare as I seethe in silence. He knows I can't stop what he's put in motion. The guild is neutral when it comes to the squabbles and power plays of holders. They have to be. It doesn't matter who is fighting whom, just that the guild gets paid for the artifacts they retrieve.

"So you should marry me," Barnabus continues. "Marry me and I won't tell everyone that I saw Lord Honori's spinster heir Aspeth pretending to be a guild lackey. That she was slumming with commoners and thieves. Trust me, you *want* my silence."

My mind is racing. I can't even tell my father about this. Can't warn him. If I get connected to the guild itself, Father will show up and drag me home and marry me off to Barnabus anyhow, just to stop the oncoming bloodbath. A marriage to me stops everything.

Which is why I threaten Barnabus instead of cowering. "You're not going to tell anyone that I'm here."

"Won't I?"

"No, you won't." I straighten. "If you do, I'll marry someone else—the first holder I see—and make him the heir to Honori Hold."

His face flushes with angry color. "You wouldn't."

"Oh, I would. There are other holders with sons who aren't married. What about Vurlith from Morsell Hold?" Mereden has mentioned her brother is courting another man, but I don't care. "He seems nice enough, and he's not married. We don't have to be compatible, understand? We just have to be married for me to make him the heir."

Barnabus leans in toward me. "You little bitch, listen here—"

I slide out of my seat, moving away from him before he can grab at me. I'm playing a deadly game—there's nothing that would stop him from dragging me out of here with him tonight and hauling me in front of a priestess to marry me forcibly. I need to extricate myself, and quickly. "I have to go."

And just then, I see a huge, hulking, angry Taurian shape in the doorway, horns swinging back and forth as Hawk scans the room looking for me.

Uh-oh.

"I'll be in touch," I tell Barnabus, and then race toward Hawk before he can see me with my ex.

TWENTY-THREE

HAWK

13 Days Before the Conquest Moon

NOT EVERY RETRIEVAL mission goes smoothly, no matter how many skilled Taurians are sent.

This one? This one was a fucking nightmare.

Everything that could go wrong did. The flags were in the wrong tunnel and we had to backtrack once we realized it. The trainees were useless. The tunnel we actually needed was collapsed. Then when we dug them free, it turned out they had found a nest of ratlings. I'm covered in bites and bruises, and one of the idiots I was trying to save slashed me with his blade because he was waving it about so crazily.

My shoulder throbs under the hasty bandage. My artificial hand aches as if to remind me that it worked doubly as hard as any real hand down in those tunnels. I'm tired, sore, and most of all, fed up with humanity for a day.

I want to go home and sleep and not think about anything until dawn. Maybe two dawns.

I want to go home and roll over the innocent, nubile human woman in my bed—my wife—and lick her cunt until she squeals against my tongue. I want to jerk my cock to the scent of her bathing my muzzle. I want to drink in her soft cries and her panting, let it soothe my irritations like a balm.

That's what I want.

I want to forget all guild business for at least a night, and focus on plump thighs wrapped around my ears. Nothing would be finer.

When I open the door to Magpie's, though, I'm surprised to see Gwenna in the hall. She sits in one of the chairs facing the fireplace, a blanket wrapped around her shoulders and a candle on the table next to her. She jumps to her feet at the sight of me, a worried look on her face.

"What are you doing here?" I ask. It's late and all students need to be in bed, because drills start early.

She hesitates and then sighs, shoulders slumping. "Don't get mad."

My hackles rise. "And why would I be mad?"

She smiles brightly, her expression brisk. "Aspeth will be back very soon. Any moment now."

Aspeth is . . . out? At this time of night? I narrow my eyes at Gwenna, taking in the worried expression she's trying hard to hide. "Why is Aspeth out and where did she go?"

"It's nothing—"

I dump my mud-encrusted, heavy pack on the ground and cross my arms over my equally dirty shirt. "If it's nothing, then why is it happening at midnight? And why are you waiting on her?" When she hesitates again, I continue. "If I wake up Magpie, is she going to be aware of this excursion?"

The look on Gwenna's face becomes panicked. She clutches her blanket tighter around her shoulders. "She had no choice."

"What do you *mean*?" I'm trying to keep the infamous Taurian temper in check, but it's growing more difficult by the moment. Aspeth is somewhere out there in the city. Alone. Against her will.

When she should be in my bed.

It's the moon's influence on me that makes the last part growl through my mind. But nothing good can come of a lone woman being coerced out alone into the streets. "Who is she meeting, exactly?"

Gwenna hesitates. "An old friend."

"Who's blackmailing her into going out alone at night?"

She hesitates again, and then falls silent. Whatever she knows, she doesn't want to speak of. "You have to understand," Gwenna says after a long, long pause. "No one has ever looked out for Aspeth. She's the one who thinks she has to protect everyone else. Tonight is no different."

"Who's she protecting?" I demand.

Gwenna doesn't answer. "Aspeth has never had anyone who cared for her. Not enough to look out for her. Not enough to say 'No, Aspeth, that's a terrible idea. You can't meet a man at midnight—'"

"So it's a man?" Hot, possessive fury coils in my guts. Has she lied to me about everything? "An old lover?"

Gwenna shakes her head again. "I can't say more. I'm sorry. I can't betray Aspeth."

Her loyalty to her friend should please me, but it only heightens my frustration. I want to shake the answers out of her. Just shake her and shake her until the truth drops from her like leaves falling from a tree. But she's clearly doing what she thinks is best for Aspeth, and I can't hate that, as much as I'd like to. Loyalty amongst a Five should be praised. The last few days wouldn't have been such a shit show if the Five we were rescuing had given a damn about one another.

"She always had everything growing up, except people. Her father thought that wealth was more important than affection, and her mother died young. She doesn't have anyone except me."

"And me."

"And you," she adds, but her expression is clearly doubtful. "As long as you don't murder her tonight."

I give her a tight smile. "I need my wife alive."

She tugs on the blanket at her shoulders again. "I know you don't understand and I know I'm only giving you half-arsed answers, but just trust me when I say she's doing this because she thinks it's the right thing to do. I know Aspeth pretends like she has it all under control, but in her heart, she's a people pleaser. Just because she hasn't had anyone love her back doesn't mean she doesn't want to be loved. Do you see?"

I'm starting to. I've suspected all along that Aspeth was some rich merchant's headstrong daughter. A fuller picture is forming in my mind—of a neglected daughter who had everything but affection, and the only one who cared for her is a maid who felt sorry for her. Whatever is going on tonight is tied to her past, something she feels she has to do in order to please or protect those she loves.

I'm still fucking furious, but it's making sense.

With a frustrated tug on my nose ring, I shake my head. "Just tell me where she went and I'll retrieve her."

꩜

A SHORT TIME later, I'm stomping wearily through the streets of Vast-warren. At this time of night there's nothing but troublemakers and drunks out. Luckily they know not to mess with a Taurian on a mission. The scowl on my face probably could stop a parade in its tracks. I find the inn after wandering through a sketchy district and glaring up at each sign as I pass. The area isn't great—but what part of Vastwarren is?—and I grow more and more annoyed by the moment that Aspeth thinks it's fine for her to wander around alone after dark with beggars and thieves.

Foolish, foolish human female. Does she think she's invulnerable? Gwenna is loyal to her but that only means she's helping Aspeth with her ridiculous schemes. I'm going to put a stop to this. I'm going to put As-peth over my knee and paddle her bouncy, delightful bottom to teach her a lesson.

But then I start thinking about smacking her arse and how it would jiggle and the noises she would make, and I bite back a groan. I can feel my knot rising, a ring of tightness at the base of my cock that feels like a vise. It's affecting my thoughts, because now I want to find Aspeth—not to punish her but to pleasure her.

Well, maybe a little fun punishment, too.

Adjusting my cock, I glare at all the drunks loitering around the en-trance of the bar. There are a few men off to one side wearing militia uniforms of some unimportant holder, but I ignore them. Every soldier needs to get his throat wet. I'm looking for Aspeth . . . and whoever had the poor judgment to blackmail her.

My magical fist clenches, and I wonder idly which one hurts more when I throat-punch someone, the real fist or the fake one.

I step inside and scan the place, noting that there's only one other Taurian in the room, and he's by the fire with a human male in his lap. There aren't a lot of females of any race, either. I see a wench behind the bar, slicing onions, and other than that, nothing but human men as far as the eye can see. It's crowded in here, elbow to elbow, and I'm tempted to wade in and just start shoving people aside until I find Aspeth.

If someone's harmed her . . .

"Oh, look," calls out a bright, familiar voice. "You're just in time."

Then Aspeth is in front of me, her expression cheery as she pushes through the crowd. She's wearing her cloak over a dress, her hair is mussed, and her cheeks are flushed from the heat of the bar. Am I imagining things, or are her eyes shining with relief? She tucks her arm into the crook of mine and steers me toward the door. "It's late and you're here to see me home, right?"

I know what she's up to. She's leading me away from whoever it was that she met in this bar. I'm not an idiot. I ignore her tugs on my arm as she tries to drag me outside, pausing to look around at the crowded room again. Everyone is staring at us, but I don't know if it's because a human woman is leaving with a Taurian or if there's something else at play. I wait for one man in particular to sack up, to separate himself from the crowd and announce that I can't leave with his woman, but after a moment, they all turn back to their drinks.

No one's going to admit that they were here with Aspeth. I glance down at my wife's overbright smile and realize she's not going to tell me anything, either.

The urge to spank her grows stronger by the moment. Scowling, I go with her when she tugs on my arm this time.

We're in the street and heading away from the tavern before Aspeth looks up at me. "You're growling."

Am I? It's probably because I hate this. I hate this place full of men who probably wouldn't think twice about groping my wife. I hate that she's put herself in this situation. I hate that no one's telling me anything.

So aye, I'm probably gonna growl for a while. Anyone would in my situation. "You want to tell me what was going on in there?"

She blinks up at me. "Not really?"

It just makes my temper flare. I jerk to a stop in the street and resist the second urge to shake a woman this night. I grab Aspeth by the shoulders tightly. "You foolish woman. Why are you out here alone in the middle of the night? Don't you know it's not safe?"

Her expression grows uneasy. "I know."

"Then why? Why?" When she doesn't answer, my tail slaps against my thigh, as furious as I am. "Why were you meeting a man out here?"

Her brows furrow together. "I didn't say I was meeting a man—"

"Why would you meet a woman at a pub in Vastwarren? At mid-night?" I gesture back at the bar, furious, because I remember Gwenna's words about how Aspeth had no choice in the matter. "Is someone blackmailing you?" Another thought blisters through my mind and fills me with an incoherent rage. *"Did someone touch you?"*

I might have to go back and murder everyone in the bar.

There must be something unhinged in my gaze as she reaches up and pats my chest. "I'm fine, Hawk. Truly, I do appreciate your concern, but I promise you that no one has molested me. Everyone was very polite and focused upon their drinks."

I eye her, trying to determine if she's lying. If she's covering up for the situation because she knows I'm already furious at her. I cup her chin, tilting her face up, and look for bruises or marks. There's nothing, and her clothing looks rumpled but every button is in place, even the tightest one at the throat. I release her, resisting the urge to run my thumb over her pretty, plump mouth. "Humph."

"I ate a lot of onions to be as repellent as possible," she tells me in a hopeful voice. "If that helps anything."

It doesn't, because now I know that *she knows she was in danger* and went anyhow. "I'm going to ask you one more time, and you need to answer me honestly," I say, voice low and careful. "Do I need to go in there and kill someone? I won't ask any more than that. Just tell me who and I'll make it happen. I can hide the body where it will never be found." Already I'm thinking of tunnels that would be easy to collapse, who I'd need to bribe to look the other way when I descend into the ruins.

She blinks up at me, then a smile spreads across her face. "You'd do that for me? I'm flattered."

"It's not meant to be a compliment." I'm back to wanting to throttle her. I grab her by the arm and note that she does smell quite oniony. "Just . . . come on."

Aspeth is silent as I drag her through the streets. Good. I hope she realizes what a mistake this was. I hope she's realizing that her loyalty is to the guild first. To *me* first.

It occurs to me that I'm jealous.

I don't like that. I don't like that at all. But as she won't tell me anything about who she was meeting, my mind continually circles back to the worst possible scenarios. Who else would you meet at midnight except an old flame? Is she looking for a way to back out of our marriage, then? Trying to get away from the beast she finds herself hitched to? Is that why she won't tell me what's going on?

The thought makes my temper flare and the painful tightness swell at the base of my cock. It's possessiveness that makes me furious. Aspeth is my wife, has sworn that she'll take part in the Conquest Moon with me. Has sworn to help me out as I help her. This isn't about feelings, I remind myself even as I furiously stomp my hooves on the cobblestones and glare at anyone who dares to walk down the same darkened streets as we do.

Does it matter if she has a lover? I ask myself. *A flame she left behind? She married you. She's in your bed. It shouldn't matter.*

But . . . it does. The Conquest Moon and Taurian instinct are fucking with my head, demanding that I claim my woman, demanding that I fight anyone who tries to take her from me.

A drunken group of men spill out of a nearby tavern and she instinctively moves closer to me. They look rough and rowdy, and my protective instincts prick. There's an entire lineup of taverns in this part of town, all of them seedier than the last. Rather than drag Aspeth past and ask for trouble, I steer her toward the darkened alley to the side. "Come on."

"Is this the right way?" she protests, trotting after me.

"Shortcut."

"It doesn't look shorter to me."

I want to growl at her to trust me, to quit asking so many questions, but instead I simply tighten my grip on her arm and hurry her along. I know I'm rushing her, but I can let her yell at me when we get back to the dormitory. I know of far too many guild students who have been accosted by thieves on these streets after dark simply because someone thought they might have an artifact of value upon them. Stupid, but most thieves are stupid. Or drunk. Or both.

We turn down a second alley, only to see a crowd of people outside another tavern, and then I realize my mistake. It's not a tavern. It's a brothel.

Aspeth sucks in a sharp breath. "Are those . . . What . . . what are they doing?"

The musky scent of sex carries on the breeze, making my knot tighten at the base of my shaft. It's an orgy in the street. I recognize it immediately. As the hand of the god falls more and more heavily upon his sons, the Taurians, we become far more hedonistic. It's not uncommon for Taurians to use sex workers to slake their thirsts as the moon rises, and public sex just adds another titillating edge to things. It's not surprising to me to see the multiple Taurians out in the alley with the brothel's women. It likely started with just one Taurian looking to get relief from one of the women who ply their wares against the alley wall due to the crowd in the brothel. From there, it escalated with multiple other sex workers and males joining in until the alley seems full of writhing, rutting bodies and the wet slap of hips meeting hips.

At my side, Aspeth makes a strangled sound and immediately turns her back to them. "They're in the street," she hisses. "Fornicating!"

For some reason, her prissy words just piss me off. In less than two weeks, I'm going to be doing the exact same thing to her, just not in an alley. There's no time left to be missish about things. "You should watch."

The look she gives me is incredulous, her head jerking up. Her breathing is rapid and in the low light, I can see there's a stain of a blush on her cheeks. "It's not polite—"

"*Damn* politeness." When one of the Taurians raises his head and looks in our direction, I step to the side and pull her into the shadows so we won't get invited to join. She lets me tug her along, and I try to turn her around. She immediately tries to turn her back to the orgy once more, and I grab her and forcefully turn her around. I tighten one arm around her waist, pinning her against me, and with my other hand, I clamp her jaw in my grasp and force her head in their direction. "Look at them, Aspeth. This is as good an education as any as to what you've agreed to do."

She whimpers, going still in my arms. Her breath remains quick, panting.

Holding her like this sets my senses on fire. I can smell all of her like this, erotic despite the oniony perfume. Her form is hot against mine, supple and firm. It makes my cock rise, and the sound of bodies slapping and the grunts of the bulls in the alley in front of us isn't helping.

"I want you to watch," I murmur in her ear. She trembles, and I hesitate. "Am I hurting you? Are you scared?"

Aspeth shakes her head as much as she can in my grip. She pants, and I follow her gaze to the nearest couple. It's a Taurian who has a woman bent over, her hands on the wall in front of her. Her tits spill out of a low-cut corset, bobbing violently with the force of the thrusting Taurian behind her. Her skirts are piled up to her waist and the male has her by the hips, dragging them back as he works her over his cock.

"Watch them," I croon into her ear, still holding her jaw. I nuzzle against her neck, and when she makes a strangled sound of pleasure, I realize that Aspeth is enjoying the sight of them. It's her prudish upbringing that made her turn away.

That ends tonight. I want her to see everything. I want her to get a good fucking look. I want her to sate her curiosity because I want her to want this—want me—just as much as I want her.

I glance over at the male as he thrusts vigorously into the squealing woman. There are other couples twined together farther down the alley, but these two interest me. He's giving her quick, shallow thrusts, and I realize why. The female he's rutting reaches back and slaps at his hip, indicating that she needs a break, and he releases her, his wet, hard cock slipping free.

Aspeth trembles at the sight of it.

"He's bigger than you expected, isn't he?" I rub my muzzle against her ear, my hips grinding against her backside as I do. My cock is just as hard as the stranger's, need making me ache. I can't stop myself from pressing up against Aspeth, letting her know just how aroused I am. "That's how big my cock is, little bird. I'm going to hollow you out when I take you, but I'll make it so fucking good you won't even care."

She whimpers against my hand, and I stroke her cheek with my thumb.

The Taurian gestures and another female comes running forward, her bare tits bouncing. Her dress is falling off of her, and she's clearly enjoying the attentions of multiple Taurians tonight. She immediately assumes the position that the other female vacated, shoving her arse into the air as she plants her hands on the wall. There's an eager expression on her face.

"He's got a knot," the exhausted woman tells her, leaning against the wall nearby. "Mind your cunt."

Aspeth twitches in my grasp.

"It's a bit early for that, ain't it?" the first woman says.

"I like 'em" is all the new woman says, and gives her ass a cheeky jiggle. "Do as you like. I can take it."

As the Taurian mounts her, I lean in close to whisper into Aspeth's ear. "Some Taurians have the god's hand upon them at all times. Those males are cursed—some say blessed—to have a knot at all times. He must be one of them. Can you see it?"

"I can't see anything," she whispers back to me. "It's too bloody dark."

I love that she sounds disappointed. I'd love to know what she's thinking. If the thought of the male knotting the woman in front of him arouses her like it does me. Then again, a gentle brush of fabric arouses me right about now. I rock against her hips again and groan when she presses back against me.

"Describe it to me," Aspeth whispers. "Please."

"His cock is thick, engorged with blood." I rub mine against her backside. "At the base, there's a swelling that makes it thicker than usual, like a fist wrapped around the shaft. When I sink into you"—her breath catches and she trembles, and at the same time, the sex worker cries out with pleasure as the Taurian plunges into her—"I'm going to fill your tight cunt so full. Some women don't like it, but it's because they've not been prepared. I'll make sure you're soaking wet and hungry for it, Aspeth. You'll want my knot, won't you?"

"Please," she whispers, her gaze locked on the rutting couple.

One of the Taurians gets impatient when his partner leaves. He grabs the nearest woman—who's being taken from behind—and shoves his cock into her mouth. She clasps his hips hungrily and he shuttles between her lips.

Aspeth makes a gaspy sound. "Is he . . . Are they . . . ?"

"In her mouth, aye. Not his knot. Just sucking on his cock."

"Ohhh . . ." She draws the word out in a long, gusty sigh. "Gods have mercy. I can't believe we're watching her."

"You like the sight of it?"

She whimpers, and I think she does. "It looks . . . so big."

"Aye, but you can take it." I stroke my thumb against her soft jaw. "Your mouth won't fit everything, but you can just lick a cock like a treat. Like she's doing." A new sex worker arrives to the group and immediately drops to her knees, licking at the exposed sac of the Taurian fucking the woman's mouth.

Aspeth moans, the sound soft and yearning. "But . . . are you sure it will fit inside me?"

Ah, the age-old question of virgins everywhere. "Aye, I'll fit in your cunt, Aspeth. With my scent in your nose, you'll get slick. Slicker than you've ever been. It'll ensure you can take me. I'll ease into you gently at first, getting you stretched around my cock."

She moans, the sound soft and yearning, and her hips rock against mine. I thrust against her backside again, and then because it feels so good, I keep doing it. I'm using her to rub myself off, but I don't fucking care and I don't think Aspeth does, either. I keep grinding against her plump backside, the rustle of fabric as I thrust betraying our actions.

"When I come, my knot swells. I'll be trapped inside your pussy, locked there until I've flooded you with my seed." I let my hand fall from her face and cup her between her thighs. She gasps again and then rocks against my hand. "You'll come so hard, over and over." As the woman in the alley cries out and the Taurian's hooves clack against the pavement, I suspect he's doing just that. I'm not looking at them any longer, though. I'm too focused on Aspeth's heavy-lidded eyes, the part of her lips, the hunger on her face. I drag my fingers over her clothed pussy, rubbing, and love when she bites down on her lip, her eyes fluttering closed.

"And I'll make you feel so fucking good," I promise her. "I vow it, Aspeth. Because I like to watch you come. I like to watch it too damn much."

"Please," she whispers again, her eyes closing. "Make me come right now."

I groan, and any shred of control I had disappears. I turn Aspeth until she's pressed to the stone wall of the alley, against an armorer's stall. Her cheek presses against the stone as I tilt her hips out and mimic the position of the couple we were watching. Her little whimper excites me, as does the spreading of her thighs. She's still fully clothed—as am I—but it doesn't matter. I push her thighs farther apart and then thrust against the juncture there.

Aspeth moans, the sound encouraging me.

I push up the front of her skirts and rub harder against the bloomers she wears underneath. I'm not sure if this'll feel as good for her as it does for me, but if she needs more, I'll give her more. I shove my hand into the front of her bloomers and seek out her clit. Her cunt is soaked, slippery with arousal, and I drag my fingers through it before circling her clit. She jerks against the wall, gasping, and I rest a finger against her clit, then drive into her from behind, letting the momentum of our bodies do the work for me.

"Gods," Aspeth whimpers, shuddering against me. "Oh gods."

"They're watching us, just like we were watching," I tell her with ragged breaths. "Give them a show, little bird."

When she comes, quaking against my fingers, I lose it. I burrow against her, driving between her thighs as if sheer force can somehow tear the layers of clothing between us and let me sink home into her cunt. I buck, holding her in place and using her as she trembles, my breath so hot and heavy that it steams the air around us. I'm so lost in the moment that when I come, it's surprising to feel the heat soak my pants instead of shooting into her. My thighs shiver with the force of my release, and my tail lashes so hard that it smacks the wall next to her.

I collapse over Aspeth, pinning her against the stone as she gulps in deep breaths. A quick glance over at the orgy shows that the couple we were watching is still there, the male with a sated expression as he rubs the sex worker's shoulders. He looms over her, their hips joined, and as I watch, he reaches up and squeezes her tit, enjoying the moment.

Unlucky bull. What must it be like to have a knot every day? To be constantly grasped in the insistent fist of lust? To know that every time you take your female, you're trapping her under you? Old Garesh must truly test those that he places his hand upon.

Then again, I can't complain about how he's treating me. I ease off Aspeth, catching my breath, and adjust the now-wet crotch of my pants against my throbbing cock. I want to pull Aspeth against me and cradle her tight. I want to lick the taste of her off my fingers and savor making her come again. I want to drag her to the nearest bed and lap between her thighs for hours.

But then I'm reminded that we don't have hours, because she needs to sleep. We've been running her ragged with drills and training, and instead of resting . . . Aspeth has spent her time sneaking off to meet someone.

Someone she won't tell me about.

It's like cold water poured over my ardor. I shove her skirts down and step away, but the small, vindictive part of me can't help but lean in as she adjusts her clothing. "Let that be a lesson for you."

Her huff of outrage tells me that my comment stings her pride.

TWENTY-FOUR

ASPETH

5 Days Before the Conquest Moon

YAWN AS WE stand in line at the guild hall, ignoring Gwenna when she elbows me. I know what she'll say. It's my fault I was up so late. And it was. The past few days of training have left me so exhausted that I should be sleeping like a babe. But I couldn't fall asleep last night. Too many things were racing through my mind.

I fret over my husband. I fret over my friends. I fret over Father and the hold. Father loves to feast and carouse and attend parties. What he doesn't love is the actual day-to-day minutiae that comes with tending to a hold. He doesn't think he should have to worry over debts or bills or purchasing artifacts.

He'll be completely clueless about the attack until it's too late.

Can I send a message somehow? Do I worry him knowing that there's no money to pay additional knights anyhow? That there are no artifacts to defend the hold should Barnabus continue with this takeover?

I worry that saying nothing is the wrong choice. The selfish choice.

Because if I say something, it will almost certainly be traced back to me. Is it better to try to influence things here? To possibly offer up the promise of funds—or some other sort of compensation—if anything is found? The fact that Barnabus is throwing money at the guild means that his father is low on useful artifacts . . . or isn't supporting Barnabus in this particular venture. If no one finds anything useful, will he give up?

I wonder if Hawk is going to miss me while I'm gone.

Things haven't been cozy between us since that night in the alley. I still throb with arousal every time I think about it and how he'd held me. How he'd pounded between my thighs . . . and then pushed me away. It's been days and we've been cordial during training, but bed has been lonely. He either doesn't come to bed or doesn't speak to me.

I feel like I've lost something precious, and it hurts. The bed feels cold without him, and entirely not right. It's strange to be in his quarters without him, and even though Squeaker loves to sprawl on Hawk's side of the bed and rub her orange fur all over his pillows, I still find the bed strange when it's just me.

After our interlude in the streets, he didn't come to bed that night. Said he had work to do. Since then, it's been a round of excuses in private. He's made it clear that no one else needs to know we're having problems, but each time he leaves me alone to go "on patrol" or to check gear, my heart aches.

And like every other night in which he isn't in bed, I barely sleep.

I'm regretting it now. I should be full of enthusiasm and excitement this morning, and instead I'm dragging behind the others in my Five as we crowd into the guild hall behind Magpie. There's something about her that seems a little off this morning. It's hard to describe—like the hard edges have been softened. There's something almost lackadaisical about her demeanor, and it's puzzling.

She yawns as we wait in line. "Not too much longer and then we'll get going."

"Somehow when I thought of wild adventure and tunnel crawling, this wasn't what I had in mind," Gwenna tells me as we shuffle forward in line.

I have to admit that she's right. The reality is far more . . . bureaucratic.

We're standing in line in the guild hall along with a dozen other fledgling teams, waiting to be recorded in the logbooks. We have to request which tunnel we'll be heading into and we'll be assigned a series of colored, numbered flags to denote where we're excavating.

"It's to ensure teams don't tunnel on top of one another," Magpie had explained as we got in line. "And to avoid tunnel collapses if too many people are working the same area. Also, if we tell the guild where we're digging, it makes it easier for them to rescue us if something goes wrong."

"What could go wrong?" Mereden had asked.

Magpie had just laughed in her face.

So . . . *that* didn't give us a ton of confidence. I glance over at Mereden. She's near the front of the line, standing behind Magpie, her pack on her back. Her tight black curls are covered in a festive head wrap, and as I watch, one of the men from the next line over reaches out and tugs on the jaunty bow over her ear.

She turns, glaring.

"I don't think this cap is guild standard, fledgling," the man sneers.

"Who are you, the guild uniform monitor?" Lark immediately comes to Mereden's defense. "Leave her alone."

"Bold of you to wear that at a guild event when you're trying to be taken seriously," the man says, flicking at her bow again.

Mereden blinks rapidly, her lips pressed together, and she looks as if she might cry.

"They're not trying to be taken seriously," jeers another. "Everyone knows they're trying to fuck their way into guild membership." He turns toward me and gestures. "Just like that one did."

Ouch. But . . . he's not wrong. Isn't that what I'm doing? I married my teacher just to have a chaperone.

As Lark argues with the team in line next to us, I scan the room for my husband. Hawk didn't come to bed last night, and he wasn't at breakfast this morning, nor did he show when we packed our things. It's almost as if he's avoiding me, though Magpie didn't seem concerned.

Then again, she's not concerned with much of anything right now. Lark looks as if she's ready to brawl with the men in line next to us, and Magpie couldn't care less. Her gaze is wandering the room, eyeing the other teams that are clustered in line waiting for their assignments.

"All right, all right," Gwenna says, moving forward and separating the men from Mereden and Lark. "A man can suck a dick as easily as a woman can, so someone sleeping their way into guild membership isn't a female-exclusive sort of thing." She gives the men a tight smile. "And I'm sure your teacher wouldn't want to hear about what you've been up to late at night, fledgling."

The man flushes and steps away, only to have the other men in line jeer at him.

"You know him?" I hiss to Gwenna when she turns back to us.

"I know his type. Every servant does." She shrugs. "Where's your husband this morning?"

"I have no idea." My face heats. "He's avoiding me."

Her brows go up. "He is?"

I nod. "He might be mad at me. I didn't tell him who I was meeting the other night."

"Nor should you," she whispers. "No good can come of any of that."

Gwenna knows things with Barnabus didn't go well. That he threatened me and that I threatened to marry someone else. That things ended up going nowhere and I've been uneasy ever since. "No more messages have come in, have they?"

She shakes her head. Gwenna's been getting friendly with the repeater who brings the mail just so she can snatch it up first and hide any messages I might get. There's been no other contact from Barnabus, and that makes me just as nervous as that first message.

"I don't know what he's up to," I fret. "If he's making moves or if he's lying low and waiting to see what is found in the tunnels."

"He might be waiting to see what you do," Gwenna suggests.

Ugh. She might be right. I wish bad people came with a glowing beacon over their heads that said **AVOID**. We need an artifact like that. "Mucking prick is trying to ruin everything I've been working for."

"Ooh, strong language for a lady." She nudges me playfully.

"I just wish he hadn't figured out I was in the city. He said he recognized you that day in the woods."

A guilty expression comes over Gwenna's face. "I was hoping he hadn't remembered me."

"He said he recognized you because we were always together."

She nods. "He tried to get me to go to his rooms once and I turned him down. I didn't think he'd recognize me because, well, it happens to all servant women far too often. Perhaps he's more sensitive to rejection than most."

I stare at her, agog. He propositioned my maid? "When was this?"

"Right after your engagement party, I think?" She winces. "Don't hate me?"

After my *engagement party*? When he'd declared love to me? When we'd kissed in the gardens and I'd allowed him to fondle my breasts and thigh? That *arse*. "I'm not mad at you. I'm furious at him."

"Yes, well, most nobles can't be trusted to keep it in their pants." Gwenna shakes her head. "I think they're too used to getting everything they want. Hawk's different, though."

I blink at her. "I married him for the chaperoning, nothing more."

"It might have started like that, but I've seen the way you two look at each other. Tell me there's nothing there except for convenience. No fascination at all?"

My face grows hotter by the moment. I can't think of anything to say. How are we looking at each other? Like he's tongued me between my thighs? Like he's shoved his hand down my bloomers in an alley and made me come? Like he made me watch other people having sex so I could see what a knot is like? Like—

"Thought so."

"Shut up."

"NEXT IN LINE," the guild clerk calls out, and then we're up.

Our names and positions are carefully recorded. I'm listed as bulwark and Kipp is listed as our sword. Gwenna's the gearmaster in charge of supplies, Mereden's the healer, and that leaves Lark as our navigator. We all look a little alarmed at that.

Magpie just waves a hand. "We're just trying it on. I won't let you get lost. Have a little more faith."

The way she says it is so loose and lazy it doesn't exactly fill me with confidence, however.

The guild clerk licks his fingers and thumbs through the pages of a logbook, expression one of complete boredom. "I show that Magpie is the guild leader and Hawk is the guild leader's assistant. Which will be going into the tunnels with the fledgling team?"

"Me," Magpie says. "Hawk's away on a rescue mission."

"Another?" I blurt out before I can help it. "Seriously?"

She turns to look at me and then shrugs. "Someone needed rescuing and the pay was right. We're shorthanded on Taurians right now due to the Conquest Moon . . . but I'm sure you know about that."

The smug way she says it makes me want to scream . . . or fall into a puddle of shame. "He's tired."

"We're all fucking tired," Magpie says in a weary voice. "Work still has to be done."

I am really starting to dislike her.

I'm also strangely hurt that Hawk left on another mission without saying anything to me. I know it's just a marriage of convenience, but surely he could say something to me as I head off to the tunnels for the first time? Wish me luck? Tell me he's going to miss me?

Gods. My head is scrambled over him.

The clerk scribbles something else down and we're assigned a set of slate-blue flags for our Five. "Lucky" is all he says, not looking up from the book he's furiously scribbling in. "Bringing any artifacts with you?"

"Just a dowsing rod," Magpie says.

He looks up and smirks. "Really? That party trick?"

"What's a dowsing rod?" Mereden asks.

"It's a stick," Magpie tells us. "But they say if you have Old Prellian ancestry, you have magic in your blood. The dowsing rod will point you toward whatever you're looking for."

"So it's a stick," the clerk says flatly, expression deadpan. "You're bringing a stick."

"A dowsing rod," Magpie states again. "Don't discourage my students."

"I'm going to write down 'stick,'" the clerk replies. "Any other items to declare?"

Kipp walks up to Magpie and taps on her leg. *Tap, tap, tap.*

She glances down at him and then nods. "Right. We've also got a slitherskin house."

"Gods help me," the clerk says, but writes it down anyhow. He slaps the flags down onto the table along with a pass. "Please declare any tunnel with your guild flags. Please do not intrude upon another's flagged tunnel. Should you run into trouble, activate your beacon and a rescue team will be sent down as quickly as possible." He grabs a small glass ball with a swirling fog inside it and sets it on the table. "Your beacon. Any questions?"

Magpie scoops up the objects. "None. Thank you. We're heading for Drop Thirteen."

His eyes widen as he writes, and I realize it's not a great choice. "Mmm. Luck to you. You'll need it . . . but then again, maybe you won't. You do have a stick after all." He smirks.

Magpie ignores him, turning to gesture at us. "Follow me, fledglings."

The guild clerk waves a hand as we shuffle behind Magpie, carrying our packs. "Next team, move up!"

I'm shoved from behind, my backpack jostling. Someone sticks a foot out and Lark nearly falls on her face. The room fills with male laughter and her face turns apple red with fury. She whirls around, but Mereden grabs her by the arm and drags her away before she can pick a fight. "Let's just go," she whispers. "We have better things to do."

With the pass in hand, Magpie leads us out of the hall and down another corridor. My heart thumps as I realize we're heading in a direction we've never gone before. There are guards down the hall, all of them wearing guild uniforms, and I see tapestries and bird symbols of the great guild masters who came before—Blackwing and Stonebeak, the legendary Stork, and of course, Sparkanos the Swan, the guild founder. Magpie's symbol is there, too, but it's small, and for a moment I feel such pride and joy that I'm on her team.

This is my dream.

I'm about to do what I've always dreamed of. My heart is in my throat, tears pricking my eyes. My heart feels so full. No matter what else happens, I will cherish this day forever.

There's another guild member at the end of the hall, and we present our pass to him. "Drop Thirteen, eh? Good luck."

I glance over at Gwenna, brows furrowed. "Is there something wrong with Drop Thirteen, do you think?"

She shrugs, adjusting her pack as she walks. Her gaze goes to Magpie.

But then the double doors at the end of the hall are opening and I hold my breath, ready to get my first glimpse of the secretive entrance to the ruins of Old Prell. It's something none of the books I've read have ever gone into detail on, and I've wondered about it. Is it a giant tunnel mouth? Another door with multiple doorways? Layers like a cake? I'm so very curious that I'm practically bouncing in place, waiting for my turn to pass through and see.

Magpie leads us out . . .

. . . and into a muddy courtyard full of holes.

For a moment, I'm reminded of the field outside of town—the one where you can dig up your own artifacts. Disappointment crashes over me. There's a large wall encircling the courtyard, closing off what must be leagues and leagues of the crowded city's apex, and it looks strangely deserted compared to the clustered buildings outside. I can still hear people talking in the streets nearby, which is jarring. There's mud everywhere, true, but there are also a lot of rocks, and the pathway we take is cordoned off with rope.

Magpie walks briskly through the strange courtyard as if she knows exactly where she's going. We follow behind her, single file, and pass another team clustered up near their leader. As we move farther in, I see crumbling walls of old brick amidst the muddy paths and my heart clenches with excitement once more. These truly are the ruins of Old Prell.

There are holes all over the place, too. Not small holes dug by spades—these holes are big enough to drive a wagon through, and I think of the small spade in my bag and the staff I carry with the pointed end. Neither of these tools seem big enough to do the level of digging I'm looking at. As I watch, someone pushes a mine cart forward, and a guild member runs a wand through the air. A shimmering portal opens, and the cart is pushed through. Another one comes through the portal, this one empty.

I gasp and tap Gwenna on the shoulder. "Did you see that?"

"Seems like a shitty use for an artifact," she says, and sounds spectacularly unimpressed.

"Where do you think it goes?"

"Does it matter? Nowhere important if they're just using it to dump dirt instead of selling it to some holder for top coin."

Hmm, she has a point. I'm still entranced, though, and I watch as the portal wavers and then flickers out again. The exasperated guild man waves the wand in the air again, reopening it, and another man pops through with an empty mine cart.

I eye the men crawling all over the anthill of the ruins. Everyone's wearing guild uniforms, but only the one with the wand has the patch of someone who's passed the guild tests. Everyone else is wearing apprentice colors. I move forward and tap Lark on the shoulder. "Ask Magpie why there are so many apprentices here."

"Magpie has ears," our guild master calls back. "And those aren't apprentices. At least, not right now. Those are repeaters."

Oh. Repeaters—the fledglings who didn't pass guild testing and were dropped by their masters. They're doing manual labor to assist the guild in the hopes another master will be impressed by their work ethic and give them another chance. I stare at the men hard at work, at the resentful looks they shoot in our direction as we walk through. This doesn't seem good at all. It's a setup that's positively asking for abuse. I need to say something to Hawk about it, but then I spot a broken cornice at the edge of a crumbling brick wall at knee height. The blurry form is obvious to me, and all the thoughts fall from my head at the sight.

It's an Old Prellian carving, late period.

I rush forward and collapse next to the cornice, touching it with hesitant reverence. By all the gods. Even though it's been worn down by time and weather, I can still see the stylized eagle that was so very popular with Late Prellian architecture. It's an amazing example and looks to be made out of the marble they favored in the late period. My fingers trace along the outstretched wings, and I'm in awe. To think that I can see this up close. To think that people just walk past this, every day, as if it's nothing.

Someone clears her throat nearby.

I turn and see Magpie, her hands on her hips. "If you're done fondling the rocks, can we get going?"

"Oh, but—the cornice—the eagle—" I stammer, covering it with my arms as if to protect it. "Late Prellian architecture. It's just sitting here in the courtyard. Someone could hit it with a shovel—"

She gives me an exasperated look. "Where are we going, Aspeth?"

Is . . . is this a trick question? "Drop Thirteen?"

"We are going into the ruins of Old Prell. It's full of rocks just like that one. So get up and let's go look at those other rocks, yes?"

Reluctantly, I get to my feet. I don't want to leave it behind—it's so damned beautiful, I don't understand how they aren't scooping it up to put into a museum or a treasury—but I want to see Old Prell, too. And I want to dig in the ruins.

And I *need* artifacts.

It hurts me physically to leave the carved cornice behind. I feel it in my heart, but I can't stay behind in the mud and with all these glaring men with shovels. I get to my feet, dusting off my trousers and adjusting my ill-fitting clothes. Satisfied that I'm following again, Magpie turns and marches once more. Gwenna gives me a sympathetic look. More than anyone, she understands my obsession with Old Prell.

We follow behind Magpie as she makes her way through the enormous field littered with rocks and gigantic holes surrounded by scaffolding. As we walk past, a flag with the number eight—in bold yellow—is hung on a pole. Behind the pole, a cluster of guild men are being lowered into a hole in what looks like an enormous basket.

I have to admit, I didn't picture this. When I imagined guild life, I thought of adventures in the tunnels, but not of how anyone got to the actual tunnels. It's not very . . . glamorous. Again, I'm reminded of an anthill with all the holes dug out.

Magpie turns, holding our blue flag out to a pit monitor. "Drop Thirteen," she announces. "Magpie and her fledglings."

He laughs. "Drop Thirteen, eh? Good luck with that."

"Why does everyone keep saying that?" Lark asks.

The man waves us forward, taking us to the last of the four holes open in his quarry area. We walk past the other three and I lean over one, but it's too dark to see anything inside except the rope and pulley leading down. "Thirteen is just a bold choice is all," he says. "Unlucky number thirteen."

"Why is it unlucky?" she prompts.

"Because no one finds fuck all at Drop Thirteen," the man says helpfully.

We all turn to stare at Magpie. "Why did we pick it if it's notoriously bereft of artifacts?" I ask.

"Because you're fledglings and it's most important that you get practice? Calm down." She lifts her chin at the attendant. "Show us to our basket. We're late already."

He pulls it from its anchored tether at the side of the hole that must be Drop Thirteen. There's a bit of rock skittering in as he drags the basket forward. Magpie steps forward and helps him steer it over the large, gaping hole the size of a well. I watch them work, a little fascinated and a lot alarmed.

Gwenna leans toward me. "She might have a good feeling about things, but I don't. You think she picked this one because she doesn't expect us to find anything? That it's just an excuse to look busy?"

I glance over at our leader. She's climbing into the basket and adjusting the ropes with a skill that speaks of years of practice. "Why would she go to all that trouble?"

"Just to get away from Hawk judging her for a few days? You know he's not happy with her."

"I think Hawk isn't happy with anyone." I can't help but think of that night in the alley. How he'd grabbed my jaw and made me watch. How he'd flung me away from him afterward like I was garbage and then immediately abandoned me when we got home. It made me feel small and dirty and unwanted.

"Mmm, I don't know about that. I've seen the way he watches you. If he's not into you, he's fooling us all."

Her words make me flush. "Let's focus on Magpie." Because talking about her doesn't make my belly flutter. "You think she's setting us up? That she doesn't want us to find anything?"

Gwenna shrugs, her gaze locked on Mereden and Kipp as they climb into the basket. The slitherskin is agile as he trots in, his shell bouncing merrily, but Mereden looks terrified as she peeks over the edge. "All I'm saying is that the simple answer to weird behavior is the likely answer."

"And what's the simple answer?"

"That she's drinking again."

"She swore she'd stop," I protest. "She wouldn't."

"Promises are easy," Gwenna says with a shrug. "Come on. I think it's our turn to get into the basket."

I want to continue arguing, but then Lark steps into the basket and the entire thing sways, banging against the lip of the hole and sending a scatter of pebbles down into the darkness. Mereden squeals in distress, clinging to Kipp's house . . . and knocking poor Kipp flat onto his belly. Lark topples on top of him, and Magpie nearly falls over as well.

"Hold on to the basket," Magpie barks, and the next few moments are chaos as everyone rights themselves. The basket sways above the hole dangerously, the basket handler clinging to the rope on the other side of the pulley and frowning mightily at us. "You two, quit whispering and get on. The sooner we descend, the sooner we can make some coin."

Her words cheer me up. Maybe she wants this to go well after all. Gwenna's just imagining things. I move forward, climbing into the basket and clutching at the side when it sways crazily. "Oh gods!"

"You get used to the movement," Magpie says. "You just need practice."

Gwenna is the last to get on board and clings to me as she squeezes in. The basket is full, and Mereden's pack is pressing into my side even as Gwenna holds on to me. We're packed like salted fish in a barrel, and it's a good thing that teams are Fives, or else they'd need bigger baskets. I imagine a basket with Hawk's hulking form in it, and imagine pressing up against him, and my stomach flutters again.

"Ready to go?" the basket handler calls.

"Send us down," Magpie calls back, slapping the side of the basket. "We'll let you know when we're ready to come up."

The basket jerks and we all give a little scream. Well, except Magpie, who just laughs at us. Then it begins to lower slowly, and again, I feel like I'm being sent down a well. I crane my head (even as I cling to the side of the basket) and eye our leader. "So how does this work? How do we get back up?"

"Someone always monitors the basket lines," she says. "Rain or shine, morning or night. We run one of our flags up the rope and they'll send a basket back down for us."

It sounds like an imprecise system and I have a million questions. Like, what happens if we can't send the flag up? What happens if a rope breaks? What happens if we're down here too long? Magpie's short with her answers and dismissive, as if she's bored already. I'll have to ask Hawk when I see him again.

If he doesn't hate me, that is. If he feels like talking to me after our alley incident.

Then again, I'm his wife. He'll have to at least talk to me to say "I want a divorce" even if he doesn't want to knot me anymore. My thighs tighten at the thought. Surely he'll want at least that, right? Surely . . .

My mind blanks out as the basket lurches lower, and then faint lighting glimmers through the cave. As we go down, I see a pocket watch hanging on a nail, the face of it glowing bright and lighting the cave. Farther down, there's a teacup hanging by the handle, also glowing. More scattered objects light the way down, artifacts that have been determined to be useless except for their ability to light the well of the cavern, and I want to grab each one and examine it to see the glyphs. What symbols did they use for the magic? Are they Late Prellian or Early? Why would you want a teacup to glow with the brightness of the sun?

The basket creaks lower and lower, and I crane my head to glimpse each artifact as we sink lower. I'm pretty sure I see Magpie raise a flask to her lips, but I say nothing. I don't want to lose a moment of this.

Because the narrow "neck" of the cave that we've been descending—Drop Thirteen—opens up, and then I can see the enormous cavern that is the ruins of Old Prell. Tears spring to my eyes as the sight spreads before us.

It's the most beautiful, wondrous thing I've ever seen.

I've heard all the stories a thousand times. That Prell was a mighty kingdom full of wizardry and magic, and that a thousand years ago, the gods (or a nasty earthquake) struck and it sank below the earth. It turns out that the city itself was built upon a network of caverns, and so the ruins themselves are scattered in a warren of tunnels, some big and some small, and it's this that the guild guards so fiercely.

There's a large open chamber in the cavern, and the ruins of ancient buildings spill from every rocky ledge. Toppled columns are covered with moss, and water drips onto broken pieces of statues. Everywhere I look, there are pieces of Old Prell scattered like a puzzle, and I'm left with the impression that if only I had the time and strength, I could pull it all together again and remake the city once more. I can't wait to get out and explore.

But then our basket continues to descend, and I have to bite back a whimper of protest as we pass through the massive, fascinating cavern and keep going lower. The walls grow tighter, our basket smacking against the side and jostling us.

"Not much farther," Magpie says as it gets dark again. There are no artifacts this deep to light the way.

"Can't we go back up?" I ask. "I'd love to get another look at the big cavern."

"It's all picked over. Trust me, there's nothing there."

A faint light gleams from below the basket, bleeding through the slats we stand upon. It grows brighter as the basket lurches farther down, and the well opens up wider. A crystal egg gives off faint light, illuminating the newest tunnel and showing more ropes off to the side and what looks like a side tunnel.

"Everyone hold on," Magpie says. "This next part requires some skill."

She pulls a giant staff from the side of the basket. There's a hook on the end of it, and she maneuvers it out to the ropes dangling nearby. When she hooks it, she pulls hard, and we surge forward to the lip of the side tunnel. Everyone clings to the edges of the basket, but I'm relieved to note that we stop descending, and Magpie slowly pulls us toward the side.

Once we're close enough, I see additional rope loops hanging from the walls, and at her indication, we reach for them. With a few more tugs, we manage to pull the basket onto the edge of the platform of the side tunnel.

"Everyone out! Don't forget your gear." Magpie sounds cheerful, as if she has great affection for the tunnels. I can't blame her. I'm excited to explore down below. Who knows what wonders we're going to see? Anticipation makes me twitchy, and I almost leap out of the basket after Lark, eager to get started.

One by one, we get into the tunnel and have a look around. It's one of the smaller tunnels that we've passed and yet it's still large enough that Mereden could stand on my shoulders and not touch the ceiling. There are layers of rock here, the walls striped horizontally with different layers of sediment, but it's all been cleared enough that we can walk comfortably.

"Formations please," Magpie calls out, and then makes a strange noise.

"Did you just belch?" Lark asks her, suspicious.

"No."

Gwenna nudges me, an "I told you so" look in her eyes.

Great. She's drinking, and that means we're probably on our own with barely enough training. I wish Hawk were here. He can yell at me all he wants—I just feel safe when he's around.

But he's not here, and we've got to make the best of things until we get back to the surface. I'm torn between wanting to find something so we can emerge in triumph . . . and not wanting to find anything at all, because fuck Barnabus.

"Formation," I echo. "All right, should we tie ourselves together now? The sword goes at the front of the line, right?"

"No need to tie yet. See that rope?" Magpie moves to the wall and tugs on something I'd missed—there's indeed a rope bolted to the wall here, spaced-out metal hooks holding it in place. "Once we run out of handrails, then we'll be in proper digging territory. Then you can rope yourselves together."

"So this isn't where we're digging?" Gwenna asks.

Magpie laughs. "Oh, gods no. This is the entrance. We've got to go much deeper in if we expect to find anything at all. It'll take a few hours to get to where we're headed."

Instead of being dismayed, I'm rather excited. Several hours means a lot of ruins to view. I'll take it. Kipp trots ahead of me and I take my place behind him in formation, as the bulwark. The shield I've been as-signed is still strapped to my back, holding my pack in place, but I guess we get that one out when we tie together? It feels strange to have to trust Magpie . . . and I come to the realization that I don't really trust her at all.

That's depressing. My childhood hero is utterly tarnished.

Nothing to do about it now. I grab the rope on the wall—and squeal in disgust because it's damp and feels gross to the touch. Mereden also makes an unhappy noise about the rope. "It's wet!"

"Don't be such a baby," Magpie chides. "You'll be wishing for that rope in a few hours."

TWENTY-FIVE

ASPETH

IT FEELS AS if we're walking forever into the shadows. The artifacts lighting the way get fewer and farther between, and the rope handhold leads us deep into the tunnels. It slopes ever downward, and at one point the descent is so steep and slick that Gwenna almost falls, and it's only the rope—and Lark's hand grabbing her pack—that keeps her from sliding ahead of us.

The caverns are wet and drippy. I'd always wondered why there were so few textiles and books from Old Prell and now I know—nothing would survive in this constant damp. Our clothes are warm at least, and I'm grateful for the layers I have on—the trousers and the skirt over them, as well as my corset, my blouse, and my thick cloak. I've taken to wearing skirts over my trousers on the rainy days, because my arse clings to my pants when the fabric's wet and Magpie said it was indecent. So far she hasn't said anything about my modification to the uniform, which is good. Neither has Hawk—I wonder if he thinks my arse is too obvious when it's wet outside, too.

There's not as much to see as I'd hoped, either. Oh, there's the occasional bit of a broken building jutting from a wall, but around it the rock has all been hollowed out, like a cored apple, and there's nothing left to investigate. True to Magpie's word, though, there are plenty of cornices and broken statues and bricks littering the rubble. After a while, even those aren't exciting, especially when you can't stop to investigate them.

The tunnel opens up into a large bowl, and then the cavern splits two ways. Off to the left side, there's a bright green flag hanging in front, the tunnel cordoned off. There's a 32 on the flag.

"We go right," Magpie tells us.

"Why are they Thirty-Two and we're Thirteen?" I ask.

"The tunnels were dug out at different times."

Oh. "Is Thirty-Two unlucky also?"

She snorts. "I wish."

Strange. So one tunnel in the same area is a good one, and ours is a dud. Great. I eye the differences in the tunnels. Thirty-Two seems to be larger, the walls of the tunnel itself a little more smoothly hewn. Thirteen is rough, the entrance low. I hope that's a good sign, but something tells me it's not.

Kipp pulls the rope from his pack and holds one end out to me. Right. I loop it through my guild belt the way I've been shown, and pass the end on to Lark, who's going to be our navigator. She belts herself in and as she does, I shrug my pack off and pull out the shield that's part of my assignment. I've got my short staff for a weapon, but I can't use it while holding a shield. As the bulwark, my job is to protect, not strike, so I strap it back to my pack again.

When we're all roped together, Kipp pulls out his tiny sword. He grins up at me, and then licks his eyeball. I think that's a sign that he's ready to go. We all look ready, with our packs on our shoulders and Gwenna at the rear. I glance back at Magpie to see where she's going to be as we head in . . .

Only to see that she's dropped her pack. As I watch, she sets down her lantern and unrolls her bedding. She reclines on it with a yawn, her pack working as her pillow.

"What are you doing?" I ask. "I thought this wasn't the place!"

Everyone turns to stare at her.

Magpie flicks a hand down toward our tunnel. "You're going to want to head that way for about another hour or two and see what you can find. I'll wait here."

I stare at her in shock. The others do, too. I'm pretty sure that's not what our leader is supposed to be doing.

"You're not coming with us?" Mereden asks, voice timid.

"Nope. I'll stay here and guard camp. Keep a light burning for you and all that." She gestures at the cavern. "When you're ready to retire for the evening, come back in this direction. You can drop your packs here, too. Lighten your bags."

I'm not sure I like that suggestion, but when Lark shrugs and tosses her pack down, I do the same. I pull out my sleeping pallet and a change of clothes and set them down. My bag feels deflated and half-empty like this, and I'm pretty sure Hawk would have disapproved.

But Hawk isn't here.

Once our bags are settled and I've got nothing in my hands but my shield, Magpie holds out the flag. "Tie this across your tunnel. It means that if another team comes by, they can't dig where you are. You've claimed it already."

Gwenna takes the flag and gives me an uneasy look. "What's the point of doing this if we don't expect to find anything?" she asks, her voice carefully neutral. "Wouldn't it be wiser to continue our lessons up top?"

"Oh, we get paid simply for the attempt," Magpie says, folding her hands over her belly and getting comfortable in her makeshift bunk. "That's the beauty of it. In a situation like this, these lords are paying for the number of teams sent out, not what we retrieve. We can waste our time and his money as much as we like, and you guys get to practice. It's a great system." She reaches into her belt without opening her eyes and holds out her stick. "Don't forget your dowsing rod."

Lark takes it from her. "Do we say anything to activate it?"

"Hell if I know."

I frown. "Let's just go, see what we can do. If nothing else, we'll gain experience."

Kipp tugs on the rope as if in agreement, gesturing at the tunnel awaiting us. I nod and head after him, and the others follow.

WE'VE PRACTICED WALKING while roped together so we're not as bad at it as we could be. No one stumbles into one another, and we keep enough slack between us that we can walk comfortably. Our new tunnel—in Drop Thirteen—doesn't have a guide rope to hold on to and the floor is wet and slick and slopes downward. We move carefully, and I'm glad that Kipp is in the lead—even with the wet floor, his steps are sure-footed.

We lose all light and then we have to pause as Lark readies a lantern for us. She holds it aloft on a stick, but the ceiling is so low that it bangs against the rock, sending a rain of pebbles down onto our heads and making Gwenna yelp in surprise.

"Sorry," Lark says, but she sounds on edge. We all are. This is our first experience in the tunnels and I can't shake the feeling that we're not quite ready.

Well, maybe Kipp is ready. He trots into the encroaching darkness with confidence, little sword at his side. If he's as rattled as the rest of us, he doesn't show it.

"I didn't realize it'd be so dark," Mereden whispers as we move deeper into the tunnels. "I mean, I know we're underground. I guess I just wasn't prepared . . . for this."

I understand what she means. The circle of light given off by our lantern feels small, the darkness at the edges oppressive, like it's pushing in on us. Like it's an ocean being held back by the flimsiest of barriers, just waiting to sweep over us once more. She's right that our training in the darkness, at the river, didn't quite prepare us. At the river there was moonlight and the stars overhead. Here, there's only the ceiling overhead, so low I can touch it with an outstretched hand, and leagues and leagues of rock just waiting to collapse our tunnel. . . .

I shove those thoughts out of my head. If large, hulking Hawk can do this—if dozens of other Taurians can do this—I can do it, too. I ignore the resentment that bubbles inside me. Magpie should be here. Hawk should be here. Someone should be at our side, guiding us. Instead, Hawk's busy trying to save the guild from itself, and Magpie's taking a nap. We're on our own.

We're silent as we creep along in the tunnel, until it opens up. Then, suddenly, it goes from a cramped passageway into a warren of side tunnels. There's a discarded pickaxe off to one side and a broken rope, proof that others have been here in the past.

Kipp stops, and Lark swings the lantern around to the entrance of the other tunnels. Five—no, six—spread out like a fan before us. "Which way?" she asks, looking at me.

How am I supposed to know? "You're the navigator."

"Shit. Right." She makes a face. "I don't feel much like a navigator, gotta admit." She gestures at the nearest tunnel. "That one, maybe?"

We head down it for a time, only for the tunnel to twist and turn and branch off repeatedly. Some of the branchings go for nothing more than a few feet, but some descend into the darkness for quite a ways.

Lark gets skittish as we pass yet another deep, branching tunnel. "I don't know that we should go down."

"You don't have a good feeling about it?" Mereden asks.

"I don't have a good feeling about any of this," Lark confesses. "I don't want to be the one who gets us lost."

"You won't," I reassure her. "If we get lost, Hawk will come and find us anyhow. They sent us down with a retrieval beacon, and Hawk knows these tunnels better than anyone. He's always down here."

My belly flutters at the thought of my husband. Not for the first time, I wish he was here with us instead of Magpie. He wouldn't have abandoned us to take a nap in the larger cave. He'd be right here with us, offering advice. I try to imagine what Hawk would say if he was with us. "Let's just consider today a scouting expedition," I tell them. "We'll get a feel for things, explore a little, and then return to camp to rest and check in on Magpie. Once we're comfortable, then we'll start looking for something to bring back."

"How will we know where to start digging?" Gwenna asks. "You've read a bunch of books about this place. What did they say?"

I'm starting to realize just how much information my books have left out. Because everyone in those books always seemed to automatically know where to dig and how deep. They'd just stick their pickaxes into a wall and magical artifacts would fall out. Looking around me, I know that's not the case. One rocky wall looks the same as the next, and the farther we go in, the less of Old Prell there is. There are no broken bricks here, no bits of pottery or statues, and I'm reminded that Drop Thirteen is considered unlucky. Bare, even. "We'll know when we see it."

We continue exploring for the next while, just to try to get comfortable with the caves. I can't help but notice that every time I look back, Gwenna, Lark, and Mereden are all clustered together, holding on to one another. I don't blame them. I want to do the same, but only Kipp's brave exploration keeps me from joining their huddle. Somehow when I'd pictured myself as a fearless excavator, it had been more glamorous—and more well lit—than this. I'd pictured artifacts just falling into my hands with a bare modicum of digging.

This? This is going to be a *lot* of work.

"Let's try one more tunnel before we head back," I suggest after a time, when we make it back to the fanned array of passages. "We can tell Magpie that we were looking for the best place to spend our efforts. Lark, pick us a tunnel."

She points at one, and Kipp heads off in that direction. I follow after him, holding my shield up even though it feels as if it's made of lead at this point. Maybe Lark and I should switch, I muse as we head into the dark tunnel. The ceiling is a little lower here, but nothing we haven't seen before. I'd rather be navigator, I think, than carry around a heavy shield all day long—

Something brushes against my hair.

I look up, and Lark's bobbing light illuminates a maze of spiderwebs on the ceiling. Long black legs move, and then my hair twitches again. I raise a hand to the top of my head—and encounter something that shouldn't be there.

With a shriek, I fling the spider off my head and onto the floor of the cave. It's the size of my hand, the legs long and disgusting and with hairs so thick even my bad eyes can make them out. Another spider drops onto my shoulder, and then Mereden gives a horrified squeal, knocking one from Lark's cloak.

"Back!" I scream. "Back the way we came!"

We race from the tunnel, crying out in horror and shaking out our clothes. The lantern bobs, making me dizzy as the light wobbles back and forth. But then we're back at the fan of tunnels, and I drop my shield, shaking out all of my clothing over and over again in disgust. Hawk did mention he hated spiders. I should have listened. I glance over to see if Kipp has followed, since the rope between us is taut. He emerges a few moments later, a long dark leg disappearing into his mouth.

Eww.

"I think that's enough for me tonight," Gwenna says, raking her fingers through her now-loose hair. She shudders. "Can we please just go back to Magpie and decide on our next steps?"

I'm totally fine with that. I nod, and Mereden is in agreement, too. Kipp shrugs, and then puts a rock in the center of the tunnel entrance, marking it. Good idea, though he might be marking it for snacks while the rest of us want to mark it as NO, NEVER AGAIN.

Picking up my shield, I gesture that Gwenna should lead the way now, since she's at the front of the line, and we head back the way we came. We're all a little quieter now that the truth of what the tunnels are like is setting in. My thoughts are swirling, comparing the reality of the tunnels with what I had imagined. I'm not disappointed, not precisely . . . but I can't help wishing that Hawk was here. Something tells me he'd understand more than anyone else.

Or maybe I'm just making excuses because I really want to talk to him.

When the caverns open back up and we see the faint, distant light of Magpie's encampment, I realize I'm exhausted. Some of the dampness of my clothing is sweat, as we've been hiking through tunnels all day long. Gwenna looks as tired as I am, and Lark and Mereden, too.

"How long do you think we've been gone?" Mereden asks. "How do we tell time down here?"

"Well, my stomach won't stop growling," Lark says, patting her gut. "And I normally don't get hungry until well past dinnertime, so I'd say it's late. I'm ready to eat some shitty rations and go to sleep and . . ."

She stops, silenced, and I peer around her.

The camp is a disaster. Our bags have been tossed about, our food supplies flung onto the ground. The extra canteens we left behind are sitting in puddles of their contents. Our bedding is gone or slashed to ribbons, our changes of clothing equally destroyed.

Magpie is sprawled, face down, amongst the mess.

"Auntie!" Lark cries, surging forward. Immediately we're all knocked off our feet—Lark included—as she forgets we're all still tied together. She crawls forward as we struggle to stand upright again. "Auntie Magpie! Is she dead?"

Gwenna helps Mereden to her feet just as a loud, garish snore echoes in the cavern. "She's not dead," Gwenna retorts. "She's fucking drunk."

Lark goes to her aunt's side, flipping her onto her back and shaking her awake. The rest of us focus on untying the ropes, not saying anything.

"Auntie Magpie?" Lark says, tapping her cheek. "Wake up."

Magpie comes awake with a snort, then rubs her eyes. She rolls out of her blankets, and the sound of empty bottles clank overloud in the cavern. I exchange a look with Gwenna.

"Wh-whuh," Magpie says, wiping her mouth. She peers at Lark. "Whuh is it? Whuh happened?"

"You tell us! What happened to the camp?"

Magpie sits up, blinking. It takes her a moment to realize our supplies have been destroyed. She picks up one chunk of hardtack and nibbles on it despite the dirt on the cavern floor. "Ratlings, mebbe."

"Oh, come on," Gwenna protests. "It's not ratlings."

Magpie flops back onto her pallet. "You don't know that."

"Would ratlings have left you alone while you sprawled, passed-out drunk? Or would they have attacked you?" Gwenna shakes her head and picks up a torn piece of blanket. "This was clearly someone trying to sabotage us."

Oh gods. Is it Barnabus? Is he somehow sending his minions after us?

"Who would want to do that?" Mereden asks, handing me the unknotted rope so I can free myself.

"Literally anyone with a penis!" Gwenna exclaims, gesturing at our group. "Look at how they've been treating us since we've arrived! They don't like the thought of more women in their precious guild—or a slitherskin—and they're doing their best to let us know that we're not wanted."

Oh. Or that. It could be that. I pull the rope free from my belt and collapse on the floor, overwhelmed. I want my spectacles because I don't want to run into more spiders. I want to lie down and rest my head but my blanket is shredded—or gone entirely. I want to eat and go to sleep with my arms around my cat and not have to worry about Barnabus, or about other men in the guild sabotaging us. I want to not have to worry about Magpie spending her time drinking instead of teaching us. I want to not worry if my Taurian husband hates me or if Barnabus is going to expose me to the guild or simply just try to take over my father's hold.

I'm so fucking *tired* of it all.

"Seriously, Auntie Magpie, how could you?" Lark gives her aunt a disappointed look. "How are we ever going to succeed if you're sabotaging us, too?"

"Oh, grow up," Magpie snaps at Lark. "You think they're ever going to let any of you in? They hate women in the guild. Trust me, I know. They're going to let you play at being guild artificers and never pass you. I figured if I brought you down here, you could at least get a taste of things. Don't fucking blame me."

Her words just make the ache in my chest even worse. She's right. The men of the guild have made it clear that they don't respect us. Even if we did find something, what would be the point? It'd just help Barnabus.

I'm damned if I do, damned if I don't.

Gwenna cleans up around camp while Mereden and Lark work on helping Magpie sober up. Kipp takes the waterskins and heads off to the nearest drip in the rocks to refill them, and I sit on my ass and feel sorry for myself, swiping tears as they fall down my cheeks. When things are tidied, Gwenna comes and sits at my side. "Are you done?"

"I feel pretty done at the moment, yes." I sniff harder. "I don't know why I ever thought I could do this."

"No, no. I meant are you done feeling sorry for yourself?" She nudges me with her shoulder. "I recognize that look on your face. The 'woe is me, I'm just a holder's daughter, life is so hard' expression."

Shame moves over me. "I'm not—"

"Look. Is this a shit show? Absolutely." She watches Mereden and Lark help Magpie do laps around the room, trying to walk off the alcohol and sober our teacher up. Then she turns back to me. "Is every-thing stacked against us? Undoubtedly. But when have you let that stop you before?"

I rub my brow. "There's no way I come out ahead in any of this, Gwenna. I'm so tired of fighting against the tide."

"You don't give up. That's not who you are, Aspeth. You make the best of whatever you're given, always."

"And the best-case scenario here is what, finding an artifact?" I spread my hands wearily. "And then it's given to Barnabus, who's going to use it against my father and steal his hold. I don't want to help Barnabus."

"Then we don't," Gwenna says, as if it's that simple.

"What if we find something? A treasure of some kind? A magical ar-tifact? We have to turn it over. That's guild law."

"We're not in the guild yet, are we?" She gives me a pert look. "If we find something—and that's a pretty big 'if' from where I'm sitting—we talk to Mereden and Lark and Kipp. We explain the situation and offer to compensate them in some way. Maybe we give up our shares for a few finds in order to pay them back."

My eyes get misty. "You'd do that for me?"

"Of course I would. I think they would, too. You're part of our Five. You're our friend."

I manage a smile.

"Or maybe we sell whatever we find and keep the funds and you can send those home to your father." Gwenna brightens. "Or maybe it will all be made easy for us. Maybe we'll find an Urn of Ever-Giving Nether-Pox and we hand it over to Barnabus after all. Who can say what the future holds?"

I giggle. I can't help it.

"My point is, my friend, that you've come this far. Why would you let a man like him defeat you now?"

I gesture at our surroundings. At the dank cavern, where somewhere spiders are still lurking, waiting to drop onto our hair. Where another team is out there with our stuff, laughing and patting themselves on the back for screwing us over. "This just isn't what I expected it to be, you know?"

"What in life is?" She nudges me with her shoulder again, the gesture friendly. "We'll get some sleep and things will be better in the morning. We'll rough it tonight like the professionals, and then we'll wake up in the morning and we'll go looking for artifacts like we're supposed to. Like we want this job. Because I would much rather dig for buried treasure in a cavern than change out the chamber pots of spoiled nobles . . . no offense."

"None taken."

There's a nudge at my other side, and then Kipp is there, holding out a chunk of hardtack. He offers it to me with a little smile, and I take it from him gratefully. He holds another chunk out to Gwenna. "This is marvelous of you," she says. "Where did you have this stashed?"

He pats the edge of his house, as if that answers everything, and then trots away to share with the others.

"I love that little guy," Gwenna says. "He's good people. Or slitherskins. Whatever." She takes a bite of her hardtack and watches the others. "You know, it's not just your life that's difficult. Mereden doesn't want to go back to the convent."

"Oh?"

"Her father made her join the church. She didn't want to, but he's very religious and felt that one of their children should be an offering to Asteria to bring fortune on their house. She told me once that no one at the temple would talk to her, though. That it was a sect of silence and they believed they were closest to the goddess when they were quiet. That's why she pushed to come here and join the guild. She was desperate to get out of there."

"It sounds awful."

"I imagine it was. And has Lark ever told you about her parents?"

It feels a little like I'm being lectured, but it's all information I should probably hear. "She hasn't."

"Their family was poor. Magpie joined the guild but her sister didn't have the skills. She ended up working in a brothel. She named her daughter Lark because she was jealous of everything Magpie had. Wanted her to have a bird name so she could be as special as Magpie, too. Of course, we know that's not how it works, but what can you do?" She shrugs. "The father wasn't known. Lark almost ended up whoring, too, but she ran away when she was a teenager and joined a troupe of traveling fortune tellers. She's pretty good with cards, by the way. Absolute shit with juggling. No idea how she managed to make a living at it."

I had no idea about any of this. I've been wrapped up in my own situation . . . and, well, in my relationship with Hawk. "I didn't know."

"You've had your new husband monopolizing your time, so no one blames you." She pats my knee and takes another bite of hardtack. As she chews, she continues. "Kipp . . . well, I'm not entirely sure what's going on with him because he doesn't talk. But I imagine it's not perfect. My point is that everyone's life has shitty aspects to it. You're just getting all of yours piling on at once, but you'll get through this."

She sounds so confident, so certain. "What if this all goes horribly and I have no choice but to marry Barnabus after all?"

"Then we give you the Urn of Ever-Giving Nether-Pox and you make his life a living hell."

I laugh again, but it's sounding a little hysterical. "I'm already married, though. And Hawk doesn't want me, either."

Gwenna gives me an impatient look. "Why are you making problems for yourself, Aspeth? It's a marriage of convenience, remember? It's still convenient for both of you. Figure out what's going on between the two of you once it's no longer convenient. Until then, stop worrying about it."

She's right. Gwenna's practical advice sinks in, and I can feel the truth of it. Why am I making problems for myself? Does it matter if Hawk likes me as much as I like him? He needs a partner for his Conquest Moon and I need someone I can point to and say is my chaperone.

Nothing else is needed.

I reach over and give her hand a squeeze. "You're a good friend."

"I'm a mediocre friend," she corrects. "I'm an amazing maid, but I'd rather be a mediocre friend." Her smile grows wider. "Or an even more mediocre guild fledgling."

"New goal," I agree, laughing. "We both shall strive to become the height of guild mediocrity."

"Hear! Hear!" she says, and holds up her hardtack in a toast.

TWENTY-SIX

ASPETH

4 Days Before the Conquest Moon

WHEN I WAKE up from sleep, I'm sore but resolute. My neck aches from using my scrap-filled backpack as a pillow and I'm a little chilled from sleeping on bare rock. My clothes are damp and my stomach is empty, but I'm determined.

I'm not going to let Barnabus beat me. I'm going to join the guild. I'm going to figure out how to protect my father and his hold and everything will be fine.

Everything will be fine, I repeat to myself over and over as I rub my aching back.

Everything will be fine, I chant silently as Magpie groans and pukes on the floor nearby, clearly hungover.

Everything will be fine, I tell myself as I pick up my shield for the day and it feels as if it weighs a thousand pounds. If men like Rooster can do this, I can certainly do this. Strangely enough, thinking of Rooster helps. I picture that squat, odious little man besting me at anything guild-related and it lights a fire under my arse. I straighten and beam at the others, who look as if they've had a rough night. "Let's get ready to head out, everyone. Time's wasting."

"What do we do about Magpie?" Lark asks, glancing over at her aunt.

"Same as we did yesterday," I tell them briskly. "She can guard what's left of our things. It won't do us any good to drag her along."

Kipp hands out more bits of hardtack—smaller bites than yesterday's portion, but I'm still grateful to have them—and we rope ourselves together while Magpie pulls a shredded blanket over her head.

"Which way should we go?" Mereden asks, looking to Lark.

Lark shrugs. "As long as there's no spiders, I don't care. Anyone else have a preference?"

Gwenna looks to me. So does Kipp. It makes sense—I'm the expert, after all. I think for a moment. "One of the tunnels sloped downward for a bit. I think we'll head there and see if there are any changes in the rock. The other sections of the cavern were littered with rubble from the city. If we can see a crosscut of the rock itself, maybe we'll know how far down—or up—we have to go to hit the ruins." I don't know if what I'm saying is accurate, but it sounds pretty good to me.

Kipp gives his shell a firm, hard rap, as if agreeing. He hops to his feet and looks over at us, his hand on his sword belt.

I nod and follow after him.

It's hard to track time in the tunnels. Lark's using an oil lantern with a slow-burning wick, so it's impossible for me to tell if hours pass as we travel deeper, or if it simply feels like it. We take our time today, looking over the rock walls carefully. If we go too deep, we could miss the levels of the ruins entirely, so we need to find the layer of rock and debris where the ruins are. It's just that we keep finding nothing at all, no matter how many twists of tunnel we head down or how much we stare at the rocky walls of the cavern.

We take a break, and when Kipp pulls more hardtack out of his shell, I realize it must be lunchtime. I try not to think about the spider legs disappearing into his mouth and focus on being grateful for the food he kept stored away for us. So far the morning has been a bust.

"What about the dowsing rod?" Mereden asks, looking up at me as she licks her fingertip and uses it to pick up the crumbs on her cleavage, then eats them. "You think that would work?"

I shrug—I have no idea. "Don't dowsing rods find water?"

"Aunt Magpie thinks that anyone with Prellian blood will be able to find artifacts," Lark offers. "Magic calling to magic and all that."

"I can safely say I do not have Old Prellian blood," I point out. The ancestry of my father's hold goes back three hundred years at the very same spot, and even before that, our ancestors were mountain folk. Old Prell was not anywhere near the mountains. Shame. I would love to have magical blood.

"We can take turns," Lark says, pulling the stick out. "It can't hurt, right?"

I want to point out that it sounds like a silly waste of time, but what if I'm wrong? They've been relying on my so-called expertise all morning and I've led them nowhere. "Can't hurt," I agree, and gesture at her. "You want to give it the first shot?"

She hands the staff with the lantern over to Mereden, and takes the dowsing rod in her hands. It's a simple stick with a fork on one end—an uneven fork, I can't help but notice—and she closes her eyes and concentrates. "Lead us to the riches of Old Prell."

Lark holds it out and turns around slowly, making a full circle. After she does this twice, she squeezes one eye open and looks at us. "I'm supposed to feel something, right?"

I have no idea. I shrug. "I've never used a dowsing rod."

No one else has, either. Kipp takes it next and closes his eyes, turning in a circle before shrugging and handing it back. Mereden looks equally uncertain when she takes her turn and says she doesn't trust herself to tell if it's tugging or if it's her imagination.

"Oh, come on," Gwenna protests as I take the rod. "Someone has to feel something, don't they?"

"You would think." I try closing my eyes and turning, but it just feels like I'm holding a stick and spinning in a circle in an underground cavern. Which . . . I am. I open my eyes and shrug. "Are we sure we're supposed to feel it or do we just have to go on instinct?"

"Here, let me give it a try and then we'll give up on this stupid thing," Gwenna says, holding her hand out. I hand it over to her. She gives it a little flick as if shaking it into submission. "Now, show us something so we can move on with our lives—"

The stick jumps in her hands.

At least, it looks as if it does. We all gasp—even Kipp—and take a step back. Gwenna flings it away from herself, and the stick skids across the floor. At the edge of the light, I can see it slowly come to a stop, pointing down one particular tunnel.

I look over at my former maid. "What did you do?"

"I didn't do anything," she protests. She wrings her hands, frowning. "All I did was pick it up."

Lark nudges her from behind. "Pick it up again."

Gwenna looks reluctant. She eyes me, seeking advice. I shrug, because I have no idea. This wasn't in any book I ever read. She takes the rod between two fingers, as if it's filthy, and grimaces. "I don't have magic in my blood."

"Maybe you do," Mereden breathes, her eyes wide. "Maybe you're descended from a secret line of Prellian kings."

"It's more likely that I was descended from Prellian maids," she retorts, but slowly, calmly grips the stick again and points it at the nearest cavern wall. "All right. If you can show us to the artifacts, please do."

The stick twitches in her grip and we all jump.

As I watch, she turns slowly, and it's as if the stick is pulling her forward. She surges ahead, the rope pulling taut as she takes the lead.

"Wait," I cry. "Let's turn around. Lark, get closer to her so you can light the way."

We reshuffle ourselves while the stick twitches and jumps in Gwenna's grasp, as if impatient. When Kipp and I are at the back, Gwenna takes the lead again, letting the stick point the way. We follow behind it as it takes us down one of the tunnels we've already walked a half dozen times, surging forward. The tunnel ends in a rock fall full of massive boulders, and it's far too much for our measly pickaxes to handle, so we had turned around.

"I promise I'm not doing this," Gwenna calls back to us as it leads us on deeper into the collapsed tunnel. "It's like it's alive when I touch it."

"Just find us something to take back," Lark tells her. "We won't tell anyone that you're a mancer."

Gwenna jerks to a halt. "I'm not a mancer!"

"But someone in your family lineage might have been," Mereden says helpfully.

Gwenna's jaw clenches and she gives me a worried look. "I'm not a mancer," she says again, and continues down the tunnel.

"No one's accusing you of being a mancer," I say soothingly. It's a valid fear—personal magic has been outlawed since the Mancer Wars, and all mancers were put to death by the king. Poor Gwenna is going to be terrified if Mereden keeps bringing it up, and I make a mental note to talk to her about it later.

We follow along for a time as the tunnel narrows. Gwenna frowns to herself as she lets it drag her along, and then the stick seems to turn, leading us back the way we came and away from the rock fall. The stick stops her halfway down, pointing at the wall of the tunnel. "I wasn't sure, but . . . right here. It keeps finding something right here."

"It's a wall," Lark points out unhelpfully.

"Well, there's something on the other side."

"You're sure?"

Gwenna sputters at Lark, furious. "Of course I'm not sure! We're following a fucking stick!"

I put a hand up and step between the two. "All right. Let's calm down. It's the best lead we have, even if it's a stick, so we might as well give things a try." I glance over at the cavern wall. It, well, looks like solid rock. "We can try to break through and see what we find. Does everyone have their pickaxes?"

Mereden raises her hand. "What if we collapse the tunnel because we hammer too hard on the wall?"

I stare at her. By the gods, does she have to bring up something like that? "Then Hawk will come and rescue us," I say promptly. "But if you've got a better idea of a place to dig, I'd like to hear it." When no one speaks up, I gesture at the wall that the dowsing rod had singled out. "All right, then, let's give it a try. And if you feel like the tunnel is about to collapse . . . say something."

Kipp huffs at that, but he's the first one to strike the wall.

I pick up my pickaxe and strike at the wall, too, though I don't know how much good I'm doing. I can't swing full strength because we're all still roped together and standing close to one another. I'm also tired and hungry, and a little wary of hammering away at what looks like solid rock.

But we set to work anyhow, because a stick told us to.

It doesn't take long before the solid-looking rock cracks under one of Mereden's strikes. Then, like a fragile eggshell, it shatters in a dozen places as we poke at it. Soon we have a hole in the wall, and when Lark shoves the lantern toward it, we can see a chamber on the other side. "It's hollow?"

I exchange a look with Gwenna. The dowsing rod wasn't wrong. There really was something on the other side. "Should we go through?"

"Unless you just wanted to knock a hole through the wall and leave?" Lark retorts. "Come on. Get the rod again and let's see what's on the other side."

"So brave now, are we?" Gwenna murmurs.

Kipp is the first one through, the slitherskin seemingly fearless despite this newest reveal. I step through after him, clutching my shield at the shadows around us. The tunnel behind us was smooth, but even with Lark's bobbing light still on the other side, I can see there are a lot more shapes here. I squint at the shadows as something decidedly human looms in the darkness.

I step over someone's pack, my heart pounding. Have we broken through the wall to the other team? Are we going to get into trouble now?

But then Lark's light bobs its way onto our side, and with relief, I can see that the form isn't human at all. It's a statue of a man, the stern expression on his face and the headdress denoting it as Prellian. It stands nearly upright, a beautiful work of art amidst the rubble.

"Oh my gods," Mereden cries.

"What?" Gwenna asks from the other side of the rock. "What is it?"

"It's a body," Lark replies, and her voice is hushed with horror.

I chuckle. "I thought the same thing, too, but it's a statue. A lovely one." I want to move forward to touch it, but the rope is taut between us, and no one seems to be stepping deeper into the new cavern except me. I can't take my eyes off the thing, though. The face is expressive, the lines around the mouth conveying a stern disapproval even as the figure cradles a child with a circlet to his breast. A king and his heir, possibly? I've seen that in other Prellian art—

"Aspeth." Lark moves to my side and grabs me by the arms. She points at the carving I'm so enamored with. "*That* is a statue." She forcibly turns me and points at the ground. "*That* is a fucking body."

I stare.

I thought I'd stepped over a backpack. That in our efforts to get through the new hole into the chamber, someone had discarded their pack and I'd simply moved over it, far more fascinated with the ruins in front of us.

But it *is* a body. Gwenna kneels next to it, peeling back an old, faded cloak that falls apart in her grasp. There's nothing left of the body but a skeleton and some rusty bits of armor. At his side is a lump that might have once been a pack but is now just another rotted blob. Fuzzy green-ish lichen grows over everything, and a worm crawls out of one of the empty eye sockets of the skull.

I scream.

Mereden screams.

Lark screams and bolts for the other side of the wall. We stumble after her, the rope tugging on us and adding to the sense of urgency. I'm dimly aware of Kipp racing at my side, of Mereden's hand on my back as we run through the tunnel, following after Lark's bobbing light.

"Where are you going?" Gwenna cries, her voice behind us.

"I don't fucking know," Lark cries back. "Away!"

Away sounds good.

I race with them, and the tunnels slope upward. No one points out that we're heading toward Magpie and camp. No one needs to. Camp feels the safest right now. The tunnel walls seem to close in around us, the darkness and stale air oppressive, until I'm sobbing with fear, and I'm not the only one. I can hear Mereden's thin whimpers filling the tunnels, along with Lark's heaving breaths.

We don't stop until a figure appears at the end of the tunnel. It's Mag-pie, holding up a lantern. Lark collapses at her feet, gasping. "Oh, thank gods. You heard us."

"Heard what?" Magpie asks. There's a tight, unhappy look on her face.

I clutch at the stays of my corset, gasping for breath. I want to tell her what we found, that the dowsing rod worked . . . but then the shadows behind her move.

And I realize she's not alone.

A very large—and very grim-faced—Taurian is right behind her.

Hawk.

Shit.

TWENTY-SEVEN

ASPETH

3 Days Before the Conquest Moon

APPARENTLY WHEN ONE finds a dead body in the tunnels—a not-uncommon occurrence—one must call in the guild authorities. Our tunnel is roped off, sealed with guild flags, and Magpie wastes no time shouting at us as Drop Thirteen is closed off to our Five.

"You were supposed to be looking for artifacts, not for bodies," she tells us. "Idiots!"

"Why is anyone even dowsing at all? That's nothing but mucking fairy tales," Hawk growls.

We're silent, chastised. Well, except for Gwenna. She glares at Magpie as if she's responsible for our troubles.

"Maybe he had an artifact on him," Mereden says in a small voice.

"He didn't." Hawk's voice is harsh, and he hasn't stopped scowling since we ran into him.

It's been nearly a full day of guild rigmarole and politics since we returned. The guild wants to claim the new chamber because guild law states that a dead body must be investigated. Magpie wants to have the drop because she claims that it's ours until we release it back to the guild. That we've staked our claim and anything found there will belong to her house.

In the meantime, a team has returned with preliminary information while we rested, cleaned up, and ate and guild healers looked us over. It seems that our collapsed tunnel was not always collapsed, and that the spot we'd dowsed at was the thinnest spot in the walls to get through to the other chamber. The new chamber is the remains of an old bathhouse, which excites me. Some of the most interesting things have been found in Old Prell's drains, and now that I'm over being scared of a corpse, I want to return and see what we can find.

"Absolutely not," Hawk says, and he's in agreement with the guild. His expression is ice-cold as he regards us, as if we've done something wrong.

"It's our claim," Magpie argues with him. "And that body was ancient. He wasn't guild. He wasn't even a guild ancestor. He might have dated back to Prell himself."

"How was there so much of him left?" Gwenna asks.

"There was hardly anything," Lark protests. "He was nothing but bugs and bones."

"Natron," I say absently. The others in my group turn to me, and I continue explaining. "It's well-documented that the lichen that grows in the tunnels produces natron. It slows down the decay of everything. It's one reason why the bodies in the tombs last for so long down in the Everbelow."

"I find it creepy that you know that," Mereden says. Kipp looks rather disgusted, too.

Hawk doesn't budge. "I don't care if that corpse was from yesterday or from Old Prell. Let the guild determine if it's safe before you send a pack of *fledglings* back down there."

"Then you come with us," I say brightly. "You can watch over us and we can excavate and look for artifacts." Truly, I'm thinking of all the things my father's pipes master has found in the hold's sewer lines. Rings. Necklaces. Carved toys. He'd once found a hand. And while I don't relish the thought of finding that, I'd be happy with nearly everything else, especially if the cavern has been collapsed for so long that it hasn't been ransacked by the guild yet.

The look he shoots me is positively hair-curling, and for a moment, I wonder what I've done wrong to incite such anger from him. "You and I need to talk."

"We're talking right now—"

He moves to my side and grabs me by the arm, escorting me out of the dorm's kitchen, which has become our unofficial meeting area. I trot at his side, a knot in my throat and a flutter in my stomach because the last time he was high-handed with me, we'd practically fornicated in an alley.

And I'm utterly shameless because the thought of doing so again excites me.

"You're not going down there again," he tells me the moment he has me in the hall. "Absolutely not."

"If you go with us, we'll be safe," I say, my expression encouraging. "I trust you."

"Do you?" He arches a brow and then looms over me, his arm braced over my head. I get the impression that I'm supposed to be afraid, that he's using his power and build to try to intimidate me into seeing things his way, but it just turns me on.

"Of course I trust you. You're my husband."

"Then tell me who you met at the tavern the other night, and I'll go with you," he says, voice silky smooth. "I'll tell Magpie to send you down again and I'll supervise. I just need a name, Aspeth."

My entire body locks up and I go cold. "It's no one important, I swear."

"Then tell me a name."

"I can't."

He gazes down at me, his expression full of frustration. "I wonder about you sometimes."

"I promise I'm not very exciting," I tell him, my expression falsely bright. "I'm just a woman who loves Old Prell and wants nothing more than to study it." I reach up and caress his face, so strange from my own yet so comfortably familiar already. "That's all there is to me."

"Is that so?" He leans in ever so slightly. "I think you're lying, Lady Aspeth Honori."

The breath catches in my throat. My name. He knows my name and who I am.

I'm fucked.

TWENTY-EIGHT

HAWK
Earlier
5 Days Before the Conquest Moon

There's nothing quite like having a new wife to make you question your sanity.

I should be upset over the stranger she met at the inn. I should be furious. I should march down there and question every person who's ever gone in and out those doors and not let up until I get an answer. But the Conquest Moon is coming closer and closer, that annoying circle in the sky shining brighter with every day, and it's making me irrational.

I'm upset over Aspeth meeting a stranger, true, but when I try to think about that night, all I can think of are the soft cries she made as I ground my cock against her skirts. The way her slick cunt felt under my fingers. The way she watched the others with such avid interest. It's the rut that won't let me focus on anything but her, and I don't trust myself to climb into bed next to her that night, or any of the next several. Last night, I stayed in the kitchen, drinking an herbal tea that's supposed to deaden the hunger that the Conquest Moon brings on.

Magpie's up early, and when she sees me, she pounces. "Good. You're here."

"Where else would I be?"

"There's a quick job the guild needs done today," she says. "A retrieval. Some idiot left his sword in Drop Seven's tunnels and it's got sentimental value to him. He can't get it because he broke his foot. I told Rooster you'd do it."

I get to my feet, my thoughts flooding with Aspeth in bed, Aspeth pinned to the alley wall, Aspeth squinting at my cock . . . the last thing I want to do is leave her side, which is exactly why I should. "Fine."

It's a job. It's a distraction, and I can put everything off for a few more hours.

But . . . "You're taking them into the tunnels for a practice run today, aren't you? I should be there."

"That got delayed," Magpie reassures me. "I had to file for an additional permit so we could have an extra teacher. It's going to take another day before we're able to head down. You have time to do this."

I don't think anything of it. The guild is constantly asking for more permits, as people like Rooster—who loves bureaucracy—take charge. I head off and retrieve the sword, and it's exactly where it was supposed to be. Foolish to waste manpower picking up someone else's discards, but if they want to pay for this, I'll take the coins.

But when I return, the nest is empty. All is quiet, the lights out. Aspeth isn't in bed, and the only person at home is her fat cat, his face planted in his overflowing food dish. I reach down and give him a pet, only to huff with annoyance when a fistful of loose cat hair comes up. Has any creature ever shed as much as this one? "Where's your mistress?"

"Mrowr?" is all Squeaker says.

Fucking Magpie. I know what's happened here. I bet if I went to the guild, there'd be no permit for a second teacher on the excursion. She just wanted me out of her hair so she could be in charge of the team. But I've taken the last few down without her putting up a single word of protest. I don't understand why she'd maneuver around me now.

Unless . . .

I cross the house, looking for the place I stashed her liquor. I'd pried up a floorboard when she'd told me to hide it all from her, and when I get to the place in the cellar where it's hidden, the bottles are still there. That doesn't tell me much—she can just buy more if she's determined. But I'm suspicious of her actions.

She doesn't want me around for a reason. Until I figure out what that reason is, I'm not going to rest easy.

I pet the cat for a moment more, thinking about his mistress. Even though Magpie can't be trusted, Aspeth should be safe enough with her . . . I think. I'm reminded of how cagey Aspeth looked when I dragged her from the bar and think about Gwenna's words. She knew who Aspeth was meeting, I'd wager. Went on and on about how people in Aspeth's life didn't give her the love she needed. People in Aspeth's past.

So it's someone from her past that she met at the bar.

The next morning, I decide to find out what I can about my bride. I have connections with other Taurians in the city—we all look out for one another. Most are employed by the guild in some manner, but there are some who choose to work alongside humans in a variety of jobs. I know one old Taurian who used to work security for a network of merchants along the coast. Now that he's older, he organizes security for those same merchants, and he knows everyone. It's a good place to start.

I bring him a gift—a box of vegetable buns from a popular Taurian baker in Vastwarren—and drop by his house in the merchants' quarter. We catch up for a while, eating sticky buns covered in carrot shreds and dried fruit, and talk about the upcoming Conquest Moon. Hadder has a wife—an older human woman—and so he's not troubled by it, even though I'm surprised he's still in the city.

He chuckles. "The god's hand is a problem only for males younger than me. I'm too old for his grip to hold me strongly. All it does is give my wife a few exciting nights in bed and then we go back to our normal lives." His eyes twinkle and he tosses his white-streaked mane. "But it's good to know the equipment remains functional."

"Do you still work with merchants?" I ask, even though I already know the answer. "I'm looking for one—or his daughter, specifically. We have a merchant's daughter in the guild apprentices this year. Her name's Aspeth. Older daughter. Very bookish."

"Pretty?"

I can feel my face heat and resist the urge to tug on my nose ring. "Yes. Dark hair. About thirty, I think? Nice figure. Won't tell anyone where she's from but I get the impression that it was money. Lots of money. Know of any merchants who fit that profile?"

He rubs the tuft of goatee under his chin, considering. "A merchant with a pretty daughter that's unmarried? Very unlikely. Most marry them off as soon as they get tits, looking to make another connection. Is it possible he's not very wealthy? A niche market of some kind?"

I think of Aspeth and her knowledge of Old Prell. It would be someone who could get his hands on obscure tomes, someone with a lot of clout. Someone who wouldn't need the money marrying off his only daughter would bring in. "No, I think wealthy. Exceedingly so. And someone in the household has more than a passing interest with Old Prell."

"Who doesn't? It's a land of riches." He chuckles and shakes his head. "No one comes to mind on my end, but I know another Taurian who works with holders."

I turn my head and spit. "Bah. No holders. Spoiled lordlings."

He raises a hand in the air. "I know. A necessary evil. Trust me, I'm not thrilled to work with them, either. But I know Sterian and he works with a lot of holders. If you have a rich merchant, he'll work with holders, too."

I grunt, because he has a point. "Give me this Sterian's address and I'll pay him a visit tonight."

"Is your mission this urgent?"

"It might be." I think of Aspeth and wonder what secrets she's holding.

A SHORT TIME later, I'm in another part of the merchants' quarter in Vastwarren, in the section that passes as a mercantile district here. Vastwarren's only export is artifacts. As those are typically handled by the guild, the mercantile district is more of a black market than anything else.

I don't judge, though. I just want answers.

The big Taurian—big even by my people's standards—is as genial as he is loud. He shakes my hand, his laughter booming and overly boisterous. "Rooster sent you? An honor indeed! What can I help the guild with this fair day?"

"I'm not here on guild business. I'm here on personal business. I'm looking for information on a merchant."

The moment I say I'm not on guild business, he relaxes. He knocks on the table and a woman steps out of the cabinet, exhaling with relief. She flashes me a smile and hurries on to the back of the shop.

"What kind of merchant are you looking for?" The look he gives me is sharp. "Are we talking legal goods?"

"I'm not wanting to buy something. I'm looking for the name of a merchant who might have a daughter, about age thirty. Bookish. Loves anything Old Prell. Goes by the name of Aspeth."

"You mean Lady Aspeth Honori? She's a holder's daughter, not a merchant's."

I shake my head. "No, this is a merchant's daughter."

"Mmm." He doesn't look convinced. I tell him the criteria and his expression doesn't change. "I've sold a great deal of books on Old Prell to Lord Corin Honori up in the mountains. His heir is his daughter, Aspeth. Pretty girl? Tall with nice tits? Spectacles?"

Spectacles? I shake my head. "That's not her."

"Probably not. That one's fond of cats, too. Has this great orange beast she carries everywhere with her." He chuckles. "You haven't seen a creature shed until you've seen that one. I swear it has a new coat every week."

I grin, but inside, I'm ice. Nothing but ice. We converse for a bit longer and I leave my contact information, telling him to send a runner if he gets the information I'm seeking. I know he won't, of course. Because I know now that my wife, my Aspeth, was lying to me.

She's not a merchant's daughter looking for adventure.

She's a holder's daughter. And that means trouble.

AND SO I storm the tunnels to retrieve my lying wife. The fledglings have found a body, which makes it easy to pull them out of the Everbelow. It takes everything I have to keep calm when all I really want to do is grab Aspeth and hold her close until the truth falls out. Or just hold her close.

It's impossible to think straight with the rut almost upon me.

Aspeth does her best to seem composed as we return to Magpie's nest, but she won't speak to me for most of the day. I can tell she's nervous. It's in the little twitches she makes, the constant adjusting of her sleeves and fussing with her cloak. The way she bites her cuticles.

She's right to be nervous. I'm furious with her for her lies, and for putting everyone in this dorm at risk. Holder business is bad business. Holders trample over everyone to get their way, and people let them.

Holders live in a different reality than the rest of us—we're all underlings to them. We're nothing to them.

Maybe that's what pisses me off the most—that Aspeth as my wife felt attainable. Real. And now I'm realizing it was all a lie. That she never intended to be my partner. That she's using me for her own ends, because holders always use and don't give a second thought to the discarded pieces.

Aspeth doesn't respond to my accusations immediately. Instead, she charges into our quarters, and when I follow her, she's on the floor with her cat, stroking the fat beast. Tufts of fur float in the air as she affectionately snuggles the animal, oblivious to the shedding. "I missed you, Squeaker," she tells it, pressing a kiss on the orange head. "Maybe we can get you a leash and you can come with us in the future."

"The Everbelow is barely safe for humans. You don't want a cat down there," I tell her, voice gruff.

"No?" She looks wistful, rubbing the cat's ears. "I just hate to leave her side. She misses me when I'm gone."

"Then perhaps this isn't the job for you."

She winces at my harsh tone, burying her face against the cat's fur once more.

Her reaction makes me feel like an unreasonable bully. Like I'm the one at fault here. I need to remember that she's lied to me constantly every step of the way, putting my livelihood—and Magpie's—in danger. Aspeth's actions are selfish, which is to be expected from a holder's daughter. So I move to one of the dressers and open it, pulling out the spectacles I found after retrieving her from the inn. I thought they belonged to a former lover, but now I know the truth. "You might as well put these on. No sense in pretending any longer."

Aspeth hesitates, and then takes them from me. She laces the ear hooks in place with practiced motions, and then blinks up at me with eyes made owlish by the lenses. "I didn't want anyone to realize who I was because I had expensive spectacles."

"No, far better to just fumble around half-blind," I say caustically. I think of all times she's squinted at me and I mistook it for concentration. How have I been unable to see this for so long? It's downright insulting. "Is this all a joke to you?"

Aspeth straightens, frowning up at me as she continues to pet her cat. "Why would it be a joke?"

I gesture at her, at a loss for words. When she tilts her head at me, I realize she truly has no idea of the magnitude of this. "You're a holder's daughter. A holder's heir. And you're pretending to be a guild fledgling?" My magical hand clenches into a fist. "You're sabotaging the chances of the others with your lies. You fucking *married* me, Aspeth."

"So what if I did?" Her chin goes into the air. "You said I needed a chaperone, and you said you needed a wife. Our marriage suits both of our needs."

"You're a holder's daughter! A virgin! I'm pretty sure they'll hang me just for dirtying your sheets—"

Aspeth rolls her eyes. "They will not. I meant it when I said I have no personal attachment to my virginity."

"You might not, but your father, the lord holder, might have other ideas. Tell me, do you think he'd approve of you marrying a Taurian?"

Some of her bravado disappears. "He wouldn't approve of any of this," she admits, adjusting the heavy cat in her arms. "Not the guild, not me leaving, none of it. But he's why I left in the first place, so . . ." Aspeth shrugs. "He can just deal with it."

Just deal with it. Words that a holder has never, ever lived by. I'm imagining an army descending upon Vastwarren, looking to liberate Aspeth from her drudgery. I'm imagining myself drawn and quartered in the guild square for daring to touch her. Gods. And she truly thinks this isn't a problem. I tug on my nose ring. "Who here knows that you're Lord Honori's daughter?"

"Just Gwenna. When I told her I was leaving, she offered to come with me. Said I shouldn't be alone." Aspeth meets my gaze and her chin lifts again. "We tried to go by guild names, you know. Had them all picked out and everything. I was going to be Sparrow and she was going to be Wren. Nice, anonymous names. But you wouldn't let us."

"That's because you haven't earned them, which you would know if you knew anything about the guild."

"Oh, I knew. I was just hoping if we showed up with our own names, we'd get to keep them, provided they weren't already in use. I thought it would show initiative."

"You mean you thought you could have the rules bent to accommodate you," I correct. "Typical holder thinking." I shake my head, disgusted. "Pack your things. I'm sending you both home. You're dangerous to everyone here."

It'll mean dissolving the Five for this season. It'll mean no funds coming into Magpie's coffers once more. She'll lose her teaching job and I will, too, but at least we'll be alive. We'll regroup. Figure out how to recover.

Aspeth jerks to her feet, spilling her cat onto the floor. More cat hair tufts float in the air, surrounding her like a cloud even as she shakes out her skirts. "You can't send me back. You'll get me killed. You'll get my entire family killed."

That makes me pause, as does the very real fear on her face. "What do you mean?"

She gestures at me. "You think I came here on some sort of . . . frivolous fancy. That I have no idea what I'm getting myself into." Aspeth points at the floor, emphasizing her words. "But I came *here* because this was my only chance. My father might be a holder, true. But if you send me back, he'll be a dead man, and I'll be killed right alongside him."

TWENTY-NINE

HAWK
3 Days Before the Conquest Moon

WHAT DO YOU mean, you'll be killed if you're sent home? You're the holder's daughter, the holder's heir."

Aspeth grimaces, giving her head a little shake. "What do you know about my father? About Honori Hold?" When I gesture that she should continue, she does, clasping her hands in front of her in a refined pose that looks both natural and utterly rehearsed at the same time. "Honori Hold is one of the oldest holds in the land, one of the original five allotted by the king and the only one still intact. Over the centuries, kings have changed and more holds have come about, but Honori Hold is old and venerable, and we can trace our lineage back to the founding." She pauses. "And because it is such a very ancient hold, we are broke."

"Broke?" Of all the things I expected to hear, this isn't it.

Aspeth nods. "Honori holders are known for their lineage but not their monetary savvy. We've prided ourselves on our bloodlines and so Honori heirs have married other holders, but the problem with marrying holders is that their wealth is tied up in artifacts. Consequently, when my father took the lord holder's seat, he had a great deal of prestige, a great deal of artifacts, and no funds to repair the hold that was falling down around his ears." She wets her lips with her tongue. "So he decided that the way out was gambling. And since he had no actual money, he sold off artifacts. I'm sure you can see where this is going."

"Your father sold his family's birthright?"

Her expression grows tight. "He gambled away the small artifacts at first. Lamps that glowed a certain shade. Mirrors that adjusted your reflection to become more flattering. A bowl that would have endless sugar cubes. Silly things that merchants would love to pay for so they could say they owned an artifact, but nothing that would harm the family's standing. But gambling is like drinking—no one ever stops drinking with just one glass, yes?"

I think of Magpie, and how many times she's sworn to stop drinking only to grab the closest bottle and break her promises. With a heavy sigh, I nod. "Aye. It's a pit that grows deeper with every drop."

"So it is with gambling." She moves to sit on the edge of the bed, her posture prim and proper as she speaks of her father and her life at the hold. "Father swore he would give it up. Or he'd promise that his luck would turn around. It was always something, and I'd watch as a favorite lamp would disappear from the drawing room, or an enchanted portrait would vanish."

"Enchanted portrait?" I ask.

Aspeth makes a soft sound of agreement. "Painted upon wood. Late Prellian portrait of a young man in repose. There was a word of power inscribed upon the back, and using that would allow you to spy upon anyone in the room. It was a truly lovely portrait, too." Her expression grows wistful. "It was one of the last things my father sold. All the treasures I loved disappeared, and I thought, well, it's lucky that I'm going to marry the man I adore. Once he's established as the holder's heir, because you know a man is valued over a woman"—her words are light but her mouth twists—"I thought maybe my father would listen to him."

"The man that betrayed you?"

Her expression grows stiff as she tries to hide her hurt. "He told me he loved me. That I was special. Beautiful. That he loved my mind. I was so very dazzled that I wanted to be with him all the time, but propriety wouldn't allow it. I remember one day he was visiting with a friend, and I had to leave the room. I watched him through the enchanted portrait, just to see what he would say about me. Then I heard the truth. He told his friend that he found me old and ugly and was marrying me only for my title and my estate." A bitter laugh escapes her. "My title. My estate. It's ridiculous."

Even though I'm furious at her, I ache at the pain she must have felt. For all that Aspeth is a holder's daughter and more powerful than I could ever imagine, there's a strange vulnerability to her. She trusts too easily, makes her heart too readily available.

She always had everything growing up, except people. Gwenna's words ring in my thoughts.

"I broke off the engagement once I heard that," Aspeth says, calm and recovered. "I couldn't marry Barnabus. It wouldn't have been so bad if I'd thought the marriage was transactional the entire time, but he'd made me think it was more. He lied about his reasons for marrying me, and I realized that once we were wedded and he'd cemented his position at my father's side, I'd be useless to him. He'd find some way to get rid of me so he could marry an heiress with money. If I'm dead, my father has no other heir and no choice but to take my widowed husband, right? So I'm not needed, not after the marriage ceremony. I don't even need to bother with giving him an heir. There's no rival to his claim."

I grunt.

"After that, I decided to assess just what we had left in the hold. A holder is only as strong as his arsenal, of course, and I kept finding more and more evidence that my father was no longer paying his debts, even with the artifacts he wasn't supposed to be selling." Her smile grows thin. "I found nothing but our old, depleted defense artifacts, because he can't sell those. There were also two broken cups that once held liquids, a few useless toys, and a sword that previously had five charges of a word of power that caused quakes. It has no charges left and it's just a regular sword." She shrugs. "There was nothing left to defend the keep, and no way to purchase more artifacts. My father's debts are enormous and even his regular lenders will no longer do business with him. He hasn't been able to afford sponsoring a guild team for years now, so there's no hope on that front. So I thought, well, I love everything Old Prell. I can read the language. Perhaps I can join." She spreads her hands in front of her. "And here I am, trying desperately to keep my head."

"You don't know that you'd be killed."

"Do you remember the Lysium Hold? From twenty years ago?"

Vaguely, but I can't place it. I shrug, because I don't keep up with holder politics.

"The neighboring hold was Raderian Hold. Raderian decided that they wanted Lysium's land and attacked. Lysium Hold didn't have the force or the artifacts to defend against the bigger hold. The family was put to the sword, right down to the children. The personal staff were executed and many of the people lost their lands and businesses when Raderian attacked. They razed the buildings and annexed the hold as Raderian Secondary. The king fined Raderian Hold for being bad sports and that was it, because there was no one from Lysium Hold left to complain about what had happened."

"No one did *anything*?"

"What are they going to do? The family was dead, the people scattered. The king let the Raderian holders know that he wasn't happy, but he didn't act upon it otherwise because Raderian was now very strong and he wanted them as allies instead of enemies." She gives me a meaningful look through her spectacles, blinking owlishly at me. "I might not know a lot of things, but I know very well the dangers of my situation."

Brutal, but not surprising. The holders continue to have more and more power every year, it seems. "Maybe no one will find out for a while. Your secret is safe with me."

"Barnabus already knows I am here. He's the one I met at the inn." She idly picks a stray orange cat hair off her sleeve, ignoring the dozens adorning her skirts. "He came to threaten me. He's the one hiring guild teams to find artifacts at an accelerated pace so he can use them to take over my father's keep. He doesn't yet realize that there's nothing holding him from taking over except for a few grossly underpaid knights who serve my father out of loyalty."

"Your old fiancé—he's *here*?"

She nods. "Demanded that I marry him."

Everything in me clenches in anger. That fucking bastard, coming after my wife. Hot fury rushes through me and it takes everything I have not to flip a table—or go out the door to attack a lord holder. "You're already married," I grit. "To *me*."

"I noticed." Her tone is dry.

And there's another thing I don't understand. Aspeth has a noble bloodline. She could have approached any other holder's son and suggested an arrangement between them. "Why did you marry *me*, Aspeth?"

"Because I needed a chaperone—"

I shake my head. "No more lies. Why did you really marry *me*? When you should have married a holder's son?"

She pauses, her gaze fixed on her wrinkled, filthy skirts. She plucks a cat hair from a crease and then flicks it away, her expression melancholy. "All my life, I've been who my father expected me to be. I've been the dutiful holder's daughter. I've gone to endless parties and weddings. I've learned etiquette and sat up in my rooms, alone, when it wasn't becoming for me to go out and play with other children. I figured being obedient hasn't worked that well for me so far. I might as well be someone I want to be." She fixes her gaze on me, determined. "And I want to be part of the guild."

"Aspeth."

"And I want to be your wife. I want to do the Conquest Moon with you, just like I promised." Her cheeks flush pink. "Even if I married strategically, no one would care about me. They just want my title. When you look at me, I feel like you want *me* . . . even if you hate the fact that you do."

I groan, the hunger rising once more. *"Aspeth."*

"I know my timing is terrible and you think I'm manipulating you. I'm not. I just . . . I like it when you touch me. I like talking to you. I like talking to you more than anyone else in this world. And I want more of both." Her mouth teases up in a sly smile. "If I was truly manipulating you, I'd suck your cock."

She pauses.

"Though now that I mention it, I really do want to suck your cock. Just like those women in the alley did to those Taurians. Is that wrong?"

I groan, because her words are filthy and yet exactly what I need to hear. This thing between us, it's gone past a simple transaction. There's a strange attraction between us. I *like* her. I like her intelligence and her optimism. I like that she's utterly frank with what she wants. "I'm not one to be manipulated by my cock."

She bites her lip. "So that means I *can* suck it?"

I groan again, scrubbing a hand down my snout and then tugging at the ring in my nose. Of all the ways I'd imagined our conversation going, Aspeth confessing her lies and then asking to suck my cock anyhow was not an option I'd considered. It could absolutely be manipulation. She's good at hiding her feelings . . . and yet her cheeks are flushed, her breath escalated. Those things, she can't hide.

Aspeth gets to her feet. "Like I said, I know my timing is bloody awful. I know I should be thinking of ways to apologize to you and to show you my sincerity, but ever since the alley, I keep thinking about you touching me, and me touching you. I thought about how you put your mouth between my thighs and pleasured me, and when I saw the women in the alley, I realized I could do the same to you. And I see it whenever I close my eyes. It's a thing regular women do to their husbands, too, isn't it?"

"Aye," I say, voice ragged with need. She stands in front of me and I sink my hands into her soft, thick hair. It's tangled from her recent bath, with just a hint of lingering soap to her scent, but I like it. "You know you could do whatever you liked to me and I'd go along with it."

"I can?" Her expression brightens.

I nod.

She reaches for the ring in my nose and tugs my face down to hers, then plants a kiss on the end of my nose. "Thank you for trusting me."

I want to tell her that I don't. That I'm letting her use me because of the Conquest Moon . . . but it's not quite the truth. I want Aspeth. I want her nose kisses and her caresses. I want to bury my muzzle between her thighs and make her come. I want to feel her clenching around my cock, milking my knot with her sweet, tight cunt. I want to hear her laughter, too. I want to hear her talk about Old Prell for hours on end. I want to watch her dote on her ridiculous cat because I know she's got an incredibly soft heart that needs something to love.

I want to be one of the things she loves.

All of this was a mistake. I know that now. The gods push us in a direction, heedless of the consequences upon our lives, and the Conquest Moon is no different. I should have kept my distance, used her as needed, and moved on with my life. Now I'm too far in.

Now I'm picturing waking up every morning with Aspeth wrapped in my arms. I'm picturing her with more ridiculous cats, just so I can see her smile as she pets them. I'm picturing her with artifacts in her hands, her eyes shining with excitement.

I'm picturing her in my life, as my wife.

It's a life I can't have. Not with a holder's daughter.

I should turn and leave, but I know I won't. I know that even before she reaches for my cock, her hand eager and hesitant at the same time. She strokes the bulge of my shaft through my clothes, outlining it with her fingers. "I keep forgetting how big you are," she whispers. "I know Taurians are large, but I forget just how large until I touch you, and then my mouth goes dry."

Her hand slides lower, and she cups my heavy sac. She looks up at me, her gaze full of questions.

"What is it?" I stroke her cheek, fascinated by the arousal shining in them.

"This is a foolish question, but . . . I knew a lady who claimed she could take her husband's balls into her mouth and suck on them both at once. Yet . . ." She frowns and gives my balls the barest of squeezes. "I don't think it's possible. Not when I see this."

"Not all men are built the same."

"And Taurians bigger than most?" Her eyes are wide, guileless behind her spectacles.

She's killing me with her flattery. "We're built to scale."

"It's an impressive scale." She caresses my sac again, and it feels tight, full to bursting. "May I ask a favor?"

I stiffen, and in that moment, I realize I don't trust her as much as I want to. It's disappointing, because I don't know what she's going to ask for. "Mmm?"

"I wasn't wearing my spectacles before when I looked at you. Can I get a second look—a better one this time?"

Oh.

I'm an arse, assuming the worst. "Of course. Just one request."

"What's that?"

"Can we get the cat out of the room? I don't want him staring at me while I do filthy things to my wife."

Aspeth giggles. "Squeaker is a 'she' and she won't stare at anything, I promise. But yes, we can put her out of the room. I'll set her a plate of chicken in the kitchen, how's that?"

I nod, and she trails her hand down my chest as she heads out. Immediately, the fat orange cat waddles after her. I run a hand down my muzzle, trying to compose myself. My thoughts are jumping wildly, and all I know is that if she wants to fool around with my cock, I am absolutely going to let her. Part of me thinks I should leave her untouched, that she should be sent back to her father an innocent virgin.

But then I remember that's not what she wants, and her father is a fuckwit.

If Aspeth wants to fondle my cock, better mine than some spoiled lordling's. Better I educate her than someone who won't give two shits about her feelings or whether she's enjoying herself.

When she returns, she leans against the door, closing it behind her. Aspeth's eyes are big and dark behind the lenses, and she looks worried. "What's wrong?" I ask. "What now?"

"Do you think I'm ugly with them on? The spectacles?" There's a wariness on her face that tells me she's been insulted about them in the past.

"I think you are beautiful with or without them, but if you want to take them off so you can shove your nose up against my cock again, you are more than welcome." I gesture at my groin. "I certainly don't mind you taking a closer look."

Her smile returns, and she moves toward me. Her hands go to my chest and she gazes up at my expression, hesitating, and I wonder if she wants to kiss me. But then she presses her face to my chest, her hand sliding back down to my cock, and I forget everything but that squeezing hand exploring my length.

"Can I get you naked?" she asks.

"Of course." I strip my guild uniform off, layer by layer, while she steps back and watches. My waist belt jingles, along with my weapons belt. Then it's my jacket, my shirt, and pants.

"I guess a Taurian undressing is quicker than a human," she points out in a nervous, breathless voice. "No boots or socks."

"I'd look fucking stupid in socks."

Her giggling takes on a manic edge, and she presses her face to my chest again. She's nervous, I realize. I don't think she's ever taken the lead with a man—human or otherwise—before. I stroke her hair back from her face. She's still in her guild uniform, still dressed in all the layers the guild demands for proper attire. "Now doesn't have to be the time, Aspeth. We can do this later, when you're more comfortable."

She shakes her head, rubbing her nose against the thicker tuft of hair on my chest. Her fingers curl against my pectorals, and then she's gliding her mouth over my chest, exploring the lightly furred slabs of muscle with her lips.

I clutch her shoulders, because I feel like I need to put my hands on her somewhere. Anywhere. But I don't want to distract her, either. She wants to explore me, she gets to explore me. My cock throbs, freed from the confinements of my too-tight pants, and I suspect I'm going to start leaking pre-cum on the floor if this continues . . . and I don't fucking care. I'll leave a trail all over the floor of the entire dorm if it means Aspeth keeps touching me.

Her mouth trails over to my nipple and she kisses it, then pulls back, giggling to herself again. At first I don't realize what's so funny, but then she points at her spectacles—in rubbing her face against my chest, she's smeared the lenses. "Well, now I really can't see."

"Clean them off," I growl. "You deserve to look at everything."

She shivers, and then pulls the spectacles off, huffs a warm breath on each lens—a shockingly erotic gesture even for this horny bull—and wipes them with a corner of her blouse before demurely tucking it back in. Then she puts her spectacles on again and smiles up at me. "I'll have to be more careful."

"Or not." I wouldn't mind watching her breathe on them again, because it makes my sac tighten, imagining her doing the same to my skin.

Aspeth bites her lip and trails her hand along my chest to the thicker fur surrounding my cock. Her gaze slides down and she steps back, and then kneels before me to get a better look.

My hands clench into fists.

She tenses immediately at the sight of my hands, sending a worried look up to my face. "Is—is this okay? Me touching you?"

"You know it is. We're past that, Aspeth. You know I like it when you reach for me."

"I just want to make sure you're having fun, too." Her smile is small, uncertain, and I remind myself that she's a damned virgin. She's going to triple-check that everything is all right before venturing forth because she doesn't have the experience I do.

So I do my best to convince her. "Aspeth, you could tell me about Old Prell pottery for hours and I would be having an amazing time as long as you touch me." I run a finger around the shell of her ear. Even this is dainty compared to a Taurian's, and I'm fascinated by it. By everything, if I'm honest with myself. She isn't the first human woman I've been with, but she's the first one that's had such a *hold* on me. The first one I've ever obsessed over. The first one I can see myself being mated to long-term. I stroke that fascinating, rounded ear. "Just . . . touch me."

She bites her lip and runs her fingers along my cock as if it's a musical instrument to be played. "I've wanted to touch you for a while, actually."

"By all the gods, why haven't you, then?"

Her hand stills and she looks up at me. "Because you ran away from me after that night. In the alley."

I groan at my own stupidity. She's right. I have been avoiding her. Abandoning Aspeth didn't help my hunger; it just made it worse. And it let Magpie pull a stupid stunt that nearly got them into trouble. "I'm regretting it now."

"Me, too."

With that, she carefully strokes the pads of her fingers down my length again, and then feeds the tip of my cock into her mouth.

Her teeth brush against the sensitive head and I hiss out a warning. "No teeth. Be careful, little bird."

Aspeth immediately backs off. "I'm sorry."

I shake my head, stroking that soft, soft ear. "Don't apologize. You tell me what you like in bed, and I tell you what I like. It's what a married couple does."

Her cheeks flush and she looks up at me through her spectacles. A shy smile plays at her lips and then she reaches out and licks the head as if it's a treat. "Better?"

Just the sight of that is enough to make a Taurian's knees buckle. "Beautiful."

She licks the head of me again and then sucks on it, her plump lips taut, her tongue brushing against the underside of my cock head, and I've never felt anything so good. The breath huffs out of me and I resist the urge to stamp my hooves. "Just like that, pretty bird. Feed me into your mouth." She takes me deeper, and I run my knuckles along her cheek. "Do you taste me? That's my seed on the head of my cock. The more I drip, the more you taste, the more you know I like it."

Aspeth makes a muffled little moan, the sound of it vibrating around my cock. I'm probably coating her tongue in my taste, but she doesn't look upset. She looks . . . entranced.

"What do I taste like to you?" I ask her, curious. I've heard that some humans don't like to taste a Taurian's seed because it's different from a human's. Stronger, more musky . . . and there's more of it.

Her mouth slides off my cock, and my skin is shiny with her saliva. As if she hates to give me up for even a moment, she curls her fingers around the base of my cock and pulls the head in, rubbing it against her wet lips. Her eyes flutter closed, her expression one of fascination. "Like earth . . . and . . . and Taurian. Like all the things wild and dangerous underground. Exactly like I'd expect you to taste." Her tongue flicks out and samples me again. "Like strength."

"And do you like it?"

Her expression grows soft. "Oh, I do." Aspeth's gaze peeks up at me. "I like the feel of you on my tongue, too. The heat of you." She strokes a finger along one thick vein down my shaft. "You're so big. You could choke me if I tried to take all of you."

"Then just take what you can enjoy, little bird." If it's nothing but her face rubbing against my cock and her mouth tasting me, I don't fucking care. I just know I need this moment to go on and on, because the sight of Aspeth with my cock playing near her mouth is making me wild with hunger.

She moans, rubbing my cock against the lower part of her face, mindful of her spectacles, and I get a sudden filthy visual image of coming all over that pretty mouth and on her spectacles, too. Just covering her with my release and making it drip all down her face. Dirtying her. *Marking* her.

I growl with need. "Take me back into your mouth, Aspeth. Use your lips."

The tip of her tongue sneaks out again and she licks the divot in the head of my cock. "Will you tell me what to do? How to make you come?"

I manage a grunt. Part of me wants to grab her by her ears and fuck her face raw, but that's the Conquest Moon speaking through me. I know that she's a virgin. I know that this is her first time sucking a cock. I have to go slow and not scare her off. "Tap my thigh if it gets to be too much and we can stop, Aspeth. At any time, we can stop. You just let me know."

She nods, rubbing the head of my cock against her lips again. Her expression is one of bliss. "I like how you feel against my lips, Hawk. Is that strange? Your skin is just so soft and hot here, but everything underneath is so very hard. I could touch you all day."

Her words send another image flashing through my mind, of Aspeth lazily curled up in bed with me, her hair spilling over my chest as she just rubs my cock against her mouth for hours and hours. My hips jerk automatically, the urge to thrust overwhelming. She gasps in surprise when my cock butts up against her mouth, and then she takes me against her tongue, a soft little whimper in her throat.

"Use your lips," I pant, watching her with fascinated, hungry eyes. "Tighten them and work me, like I'm fucking your soft, wet mouth."

She rubs her tongue against the underside of my cock and takes me deeper, gazing up at me with worried eyes.

"You don't know how it works, sweetheart?" I don't know where the term of endearment comes from, just that it feels right in this moment. "How I'd fuck you?"

Her cheeks stain pink again and she makes a little noise of protest in her throat. Her mouth is stretched and wet around my cock, and she looks a bit like she's pinned down by my size, which shouldn't be nearly as sexy as it is. But watching her work her mouth around my length is fucking . . . magical.

"You want me to thrust into your mouth? Want me to take control?" I drag my fingers through her thick hair, knotting them in the soft tresses. When she nods eagerly, it's almost too much for me to take. I groan again, and I have to remind myself that she's a virgin. To go slow.

I manage a brief, sharp thrust, pushing deeper into her mouth.

She makes a startled sound, and then moans around my cock, her gaze hungry. As if she wants more. I thrust again, making my actions careful and slow this time, and she stretches her jaw to take me. I love it. I push deeper, and when her hands grip my thighs, I guide her head with my hand and begin thrusting, shuttling my cock into her supple, devouring mouth. Her lips are wet and gorgeous, stretched around my cock, and I can't stop staring at the sight of her taking me.

The need builds inside me, my sac tightening and drawing up as my release nears. I huff breaths through gritted teeth, trying to pace myself, to make this moment last, but there's no fucking way I'm going to be able to draw this out. Not with Aspeth's mouth rosy and taut around my shaft. Not with how slick her tongue is and how she rubs it against the underside of my cock. I jerk out of her mouth just before I erupt, breath heaving, and try to compose myself. "Wait—wait. Need a moment."

"What? Why?" She reaches for me again, and it takes every ounce of my control to pull my bobbing cock away from her hungry grasp. "I want you, Hawk. Please."

"Don't want to . . . surprise you . . . when I release. It . . . might be . . . a lot."

"But I came against your mouth," she protests. "I don't mind if you come inside mine."

"You sure that's what you want?" Even though I shouldn't, I take my hand and guide my cock back to her lips, just to watch them part eagerly for me. I drag the head against her tongue. "You want me to fill up your mouth? Coat your throat with my release?"

She nods, just a little, and opens wider, her trusting gaze fixed on me.

I pump into her mouth again—once, twice, and then I'm on the edge once more. It boils through my veins, threatening to erupt, and I suck in a deep breath. Her tongue rubs against the underside of my cock head and that's all it takes for me to lose control. I come with a ferocious groan, spilling inside her mouth.

Despite her intentions, Aspeth jerks and immediately draws back, and my seed spills down her lips and chin and splatters across the front of her guild uniform. She coughs, blinking, and swipes at the trails I've left behind.

It was too much for her. Too much for a first time. I know this, and I need to apologize because I gave in and did it anyhow. A million words bubble to the surface, but all I can do is squeeze my cock, milking my release and wheezing as another vicious round spurts out of me and splats onto her linen blouse. She tries to catch the last few drops as I shake them loose, her tongue darting out.

She looks wrecked, my poor human virgin. Her hair is in tangles. Her face is decorated with my release, her spectacles smeared once more, and a droplet of cum spattered on the lens. Her cheeks are flushed, and her blouse is sticking to her heaving breasts.

"I'm sorry, Hawk," she says after a moment. "I'll do better next time."

Better? I cup her jaw, wiping some of my seed away with my thumb, and force her to look at me. "Aspeth, you were incredible. If you were any better, you'd suck my soul out through my cock."

She giggles, just as breathless as I am. "I had fun. I like touching you. I like watching your responses."

By the bull god, this human is going to be the death of me. Her cheeks are stained pink, and it makes me think of when I'd had her spread before me and naked, because she'd flushed on her tits, too, and it had been the prettiest sight.

Well, I'm of a mind to see that again. I help her to her feet, and then haul her into my arms. She makes a squeal of surprise, and her sticky blouse rubs against my skin. "Wh-what are you doing?"

"Your turn." I toss her down onto the bed, loving the way her tits jiggle as she bounces. "I'm going to pleasure you."

She immediately sits up. "Oh, you don't have to."

"I know that." I climb over her. "I want to."

I pull open her blouse to see that her tits, barely covered by a thin chemise and heaving above her corset, are indeed flushed. I undo her pants and her belt, and then slide a hand inside. She's wet and slick, a sign that she truly did enjoy touching me, and her heat instantly seems to suck on my fingers. I push into her with two digits, watching her face. "How is that?"

"Full," she pants. "Very full."

"Bad full?" I use my thumb to graze against her clit, seeking the small bump through her folds.

When I find it, she jerks, her hands clinging to me. She shakes her head. "Not bad, no. Good. Really good."

"This is how it'll feel when I fuck you," I tell her, pumping my fingers in and out slowly. "Except my cock is much, much bigger."

Aspeth moans, clinging to me. Her hips move with my hand, as if she's increasing the friction, and I'm pleased. Gods, everything about her is so, so perfect.

It feels almost too perfect.

Suddenly I'm thinking about her story from earlier. How I'd gone from yelling at her for all of her lies to finger-fucking her because I want to see her come. Am I the one being fooled? Is this all an elaborate ruse on her end? I drive my fingers deeper, watching her response, and then hook them inside her, searching for the rough spot on her inner wall that will make her crazy with need.

Aspeth's legs jerk just as I find it, and she whimpers, holding tighter to me. "Hawk," she cries. "I . . . right there. Yes!"

"You like that?"

"Yes!" Her legs tremble, clasping tight around my hand as I drive into her.

"You wouldn't lie to me?"

She shakes her head in jerky little motions, even as her nails dig into my biceps. "Oh . . . oh . . ."

"And you're not a spy? Everything you told me earlier was the truth?"

Aspeth tightens. For a moment, I think she's coming, but then she jerks at my hand, trying to shove it out of her pants. "You . . . you . . . fuck you!" She shoves at my chest until my hand is free from her clothing, and then scrambles off the bed. "Th-that's not what this was about!"

I pretend casualness. "I had to ask. You do have to admit it seems a little too perfect. That all your secrets are found out and yet you somehow still want to suck my cock? Forgive me if I seem a little suspicious."

Aspeth clutches the sides of her blouse closed, her eyes suspiciously shiny and red under the magnified lenses of her spectacles. "I just . . . I just wanted to touch you. That's all. There's no ulterior motive."

"Then come here." I pat the bed, refusing to feel guilt. "I'll finish you off."

Her lip curls and she gives me her haughtiest look. "You are disgusting. Now I don't want you to touch me at all."

"Because I suspected you? Be fair, Aspeth. You've been lying this whole time."

"It was necessary." Her mouth flattens and she turns to one of her trunks, pulling out a fresh blouse. "I didn't enjoy it."

"But you did enjoy being Sparrow. Admit it. You've loved being here. Loved that no one knew who you were."

"Is that such a bad thing?" She doesn't turn to look at me, her voice soft. "Just wanting to be part of something greater? Wanting to live the life I've dreamed about?" Aspeth shakes her head and switches out her destroyed blouse for a new one. She buttons it in silence and then tucks it into her pants. "I'm going to check on Squeaker—"

"Wait," I say before she can go out the door. "A question."

"I'm not a spy."

"Not that question. A different one. What happens to us after all this?"

Aspeth turns toward me, mouth pulled into a frown. "What do you mean?"

"You get your artifacts for your hold, right? Then what? You head back there and pretend you never married a Taurian? Do you tell your father you married me? Do you give up on your dream of being in the guild?"

Aspeth blinks, considering, and then her shoulders slump. It's strange, but it feels as if my simple question has left her more defeated than anything else. "I haven't thought that far ahead, Hawk. Right now I'm just trying to stay alive. To fix things before they can no longer be fixed." A humorless laugh bubbles up inside her. "I'm just taking it day-to-day. One problem at a time. I'm sorry if that's not the right answer, but it's all I've got."

It's not the right answer, but it's one I understand. It's hard to think about the future when the present is an absolute gods-fucked mess. "It's fine. Go."

She disappears out into the hall and I flop onto my back, staring up at the ceiling.

I had to ask. I had to.

Still feels like I fucked up, though. Like I broke something fragile with my questions.

THIRTY

ASPETH

To MY CREDIT, I don't give in to the tears threatening to spill out of my eyes. I manage to keep it together, composed, even though my pussy is so sensitive I can feel my folds sliding against each other as I walk and sending tingling little waves of sensation through my body. My spectacles are smeary and I'm sure I'm a mess, but I don't care. I just need to get away from Hawk for a while.

His words hurt me. Painfully so. More than the words, the timing of it. To be so vulnerable to him and for him to look up at me with those intense eyes and demand to know if I'm a spy? I've never felt so angry and exposed . . . and used.

I hadn't had an ulterior motive in touching him, other than simply wanting to touch him. In being relieved that my secret was out. It felt like one less thing to worry about, and instead, it's going to be thrown in my face.

I can't even blame him. I'd probably be suspicious of me, too. I have lied. It's just . . . I wouldn't bring it up when my fingers were deep inside another person's private parts. That feels like a violation of an unspoken rule.

Sniffing back tears, I head for the kitchen. Squeaker will have finished eating, and if nothing else, I can hug my cat and feel sorry for myself for a while before heading back to bed. Hopefully when I return, Hawk will be asleep and I won't have to talk to him.

When I get to the kitchen, I'm surprised to see Gwenna. There's a candle on the far end of the table, providing a flickering light. Squeaker is sprawled on the near end, purring and content, while Gwenna rubs her fingers through the soft white fur on her abdomen. The cat's so fat she looks like a loaf of bread with legs, but I find that charming. "She's letting you pet her belly?" I ask, trying to keep my voice light. "She never lets me do that."

"I never go below the rib cage," Gwenna replies. "She doesn't mind that. Any lower and I'll get a claw dug into my arm." She continues to rub the cat and looks over at me. "What are you doing up?"

"What are *you* doing up?"

"Can't sleep."

That's an easy excuse. "Me, either."

"Yes, but you look like absolute hell," Gwenna points out. "I see you're wearing your spectacles again, too. And you've got something on them."

I do? I pull them off and to my horror, there's a splash of semen on the edge of one lens. Hastily, I rub it off with a corner of my blouse and move to sit next to my friend. "I have a headache and thought I'd wear them. It's been a long day."

"I'll fucking say." She watches me as I tidy my spectacles and then hook them over my nose. Once I do, she gives me a worried look. "I did something bad, Aspeth."

Oh no, what now? "What is it? What's wrong?"

Wordless, she takes something from her pocket and slides it across the table to me.

It's a ring. Encrusted with dirt and grime from centuries, but obviously a ring. There's a huge ruby cabochon in the center of an ornate setting, and around the setting are Prellian glyphs. Automatically, I lift it to my eyes and start to translate despite the low light.

For my wife. Proof that we are stronger together.

Sweet, but as I turn the ring over, I see etching on the inside of the thick band. I move closer to the candle, reading.

Your half of the power is the word. Say "tlanntra" when you wish to activate.

"It's an artifact," I whisper. "With a word of power."

"What's it do?"

"It doesn't say. I could research, but I don't have my tomes and I doubt they'd let me use the library openly." I turn the ring over in my hand and then look over at her. "Did you put this on?"

"Fuck no! I know better than that." She shakes her head violently. "I don't think you should, either."

"I'm not going to." I turn it over in my hands and note that all the writing is on one side, and the other side is perfectly smooth and flat . . . as if it was joined with something else.

Your half of the power . . .

After a moment, I realize just what it is, and a giddy flare of excitement surges through me. "It's a link-ring. Prellian couples would have them made to show the strength of an alliance. Each ring doesn't work properly on its own but together they're very powerful."

"Oh. Fancy."

I stare at her in shock, curling my fingers around the ring. Part of me wants to hand it back to her because it's hers, and part of me wants to steal it away because if I get both rings, this could be the answer Honori Hold needs. "Gwenna! How in all the gods' names did you get this?"

She offers me a weak smile. "I stole it from the dead guy."

"You *what?*"

Gwenna flinches and gets to her feet. Squeaker immediately rolls onto her stomach and trots away, likely heading back to my room. I remain seated, the ring pulsing warm with power, and Gwenna paces in the kitchen. She wrings her hands. "Every maid knows how to steal. Not that I would, of course. But it's helpful to know things sometimes. You pick up bits. You learn that when you're a maid, people know you're there but no one's really watching you. You're invisible in a strange sort of way and that makes it easy to lift things, especially when your employer doesn't pay you. You figure out a way to get paid anyhow."

I'm stunned. All I can say is "Oh."

She hastily raises her hands. "I've never stolen from you, Aspeth. Don't worry about that. But maids talk. We share tips and advice. And if some noble carelessly tosses something away, we grab it for ourselves. Your lot never misses it." Her arms cross over her chest, her posture defensive. "I know you think I'm the worst—"

"I don't, I swear I don't—"

"But you've always been good to me and made sure I was taken care of."

"Gwenna—"

She paces frantically back and forth. "And when I saw his bag and there was something shiny in it, my instincts kicked in." She grimaces. "I know it's wrong to steal but he's dead, right? And this could be a matter of life and death for you, so why not take it? But I guess this is the same as me stealing from the guild, and that's a bad thing. I probably should have left it, but I didn't, and I'll understand if you want to turn me over to Magpie or Hawk. Actually, if you have to turn me in, can we make it Magpie? I think she might be nicer than Hawk. Or she might not even say anything and trade it for a case of ale. I just . . . I don't want to go back to changing bedpans and getting tea trays, Aspeth. I want to do something with my life—"

"Gwenna." I set the ring down, get to my feet, and grab her by the shoulders before she can pace a hole into the floorboards. "I'm not going to say anything. Just . . . thank you. It's kind of you to think of me."

"You're my friend," she says, blinking at me. "You brought me with you when you could have left me behind and unemployed. You're helping me start a new life. Of course I'd look out for you."

Tears threaten again, because I'm so used to having to look out for everyone else at the hold that it feels strange to have someone watching over me. "You're my best friend, Gwenna."

She laughs, and sounds as tearful as I am. "I thought that was Squeaker."

"We won't tell her the truth."

"She's a cat. As long as she gets food, I don't think she much cares."

I bite back a hysterical giggle and look over at the ring on the table. It's a chance. It could be just what I need to save everyone. "Can I hug you?"

"Can I stop you?" she grumbles, but submits to my quick, happy squeeze.

I hold her tight, because she's truly proven herself to be the best of friends. When I release her, my gaze automatically is drawn back to the ring. "I wonder what it does."

"No idea, but it must have been important enough that someone was tomb robbing to get it, right? They said the body was old, and he wasn't wearing a guild uniform. Just some old, crappy armor. What else could it be but a tomb robber of some kind?"

She has a good point. It hadn't occurred to me that it would be a tomb robber. Those were common before the guild took over the ruins and established a stranglehold on the artifacts coming out of Old Prell. "Did you see another ring?"

"If he had both, do you think he'd have died there? Or do you think he was still looking for the mate to the ring when he got attacked by ratlings?"

"Or he didn't know what he had." I chew on my lip, thinking. "What if the guild has the other ring?"

"Then they'll be looking for this one."

She's right. They'll pull Drop Thirteen apart looking for a mate to another ring. The fact that they haven't yet tells me that they aren't aware of any artifacts in the area. Right now Magpie is just quarreling with them over sending us back because of paperwork. As far as I know, the guild still isn't interested in the drop itself. "We have to go back," I tell her. "Before they find anything. And we have to find the mate. If what these rings do together is powerful . . . it could help my father."

"I hate that we'd find something so amazing and it has to go to your father, who's just going to gamble it away."

I wince, because she's not wrong. Father is terrible with money. If he's not spending it on lavish trips to far-flung parties, he's spending it on his courtesan lover, Liatta. He couldn't care less about Honori, other than the fact that it is his and therefore it should always be his. "Once he knows Barnabus is angling for his lands, perhaps it'll wake him up. He thinks he's safe and that no one cares what he does. That because he's a holder he's automatically protected."

"He's an idiot," Gwenna replies tartly. "You must take after your mother."

I manage a small smile at that, because I can't remember my mother. I move back to the table and scoop up the ring, then hold it out to her. "You found it. You should keep it for now."

She puts her hands up, shaking her head. "No. I got it for you. You keep it. I don't know anything about Old Prell anyhow. It's safer with you than with me."

Maybe. I don't know. I examine the ring again, looking for any symbols I might have missed, and then tuck it into my neckline, lodging it between my corseted breasts. It feels like a pebble stuck in my clothing, but that's not a bad thing. I'll notice if it slips. I reach out and take her hand, squeezing it. "Thank you, Gwenna."

"I did it for you," she says, squeezing my hand back. "I didn't want something like that going to Barnabus. He's a prick."

"He is," I agree, my mind racing. "You think we can convince Magpie to take us back down to the drop? Tomorrow?"

She shrugs. "She's waiting for guild permission, right? It might be slow in coming, what with her drinking and all."

Gods, she's right. Magpie is a mess and everyone will know about it after what happened. I wince. Something tells me she's not going back anytime soon, and our Five can't go without a teacher.

As if she can read my mind, Gwenna asks, "What about Hawk?"

I think about Hawk. And his fingers. And his horrid questions. *Are you a spy?* "Hawk and I are not on speaking terms at the moment."

"Already? But we just got back."

"It's been a very fraught evening."

"Do you . . . want to talk about it?"

Do I? I consider this for a long moment, and then my shyness takes over. I can't imagine having to explain to Gwenna how Hawk had his fingers deep inside me, rubbing a spot in my body that made me want to fly apart—and then demanded to know if I was a spy. That I was feeling used because I'd sucked his cock just moments earlier and I thought we were in a better place than that. "Just trust me when I say if I approach him with a stolen ring, he won't help us. He'll probably turn us all over to the guild and get us sent home. He knows who I really am."

"He does? Shit." She paces back and forth, agitated. "So what do you want to do?"

"I don't know." I feel defeated. "Avoid him and hope he doesn't turn us in?" It doesn't seem like Hawk to turn me over, but he was also rather upset.

Gwenna grimaces. "He's definitely not much of a rule breaker. I don't suppose we know anyone in the guild who would be willing to help us?"

I stare at her. "You . . . you're kidding, right? *This* guild? The one that mocks us for being women? That thinks we shouldn't be allowed to go into the tunnels because we don't have penises? This same guild?"

"You're right. Stupid question."

Not stupid—we're just low on options. "Do you think Lark might know someone we can trust?"

"More than her *aunt*?"

Again with the impeccable logic. I purse my lips, pressing a hand to the ring in my dress. "I don't think we have a choice. We need to speak to Magpie and get her on our side. I know we stole from the guild but what if we offer her a cut?"

It's a risk, but what are our choices? The drop inside the walled-off area is completely controlled by the guild, with passes required and security at all times. Unless we bribe our way in, I don't see an option. And we don't have money.

There's another way to bribe, of course, but I don't even want to consider it. One single Taurian in my bed is enough trouble as it is. "Let's talk to the others in the morning first, see how they feel about helping us. Then we can approach Magpie."

I fish the ring out of my corset and hold it back out to her. "I feel bad keeping this when you found it."

Gwenna shakes her head. "You hold on to it."

"Are you sure?"

She pushes it away from her physically, her expression determined. "If I get caught with that thing, I'm a thief. If you get caught with it, you're a holder's daughter who's being mischievous. Do you see the difference?"

I do. I tuck it back into my clothes and hate that she's right.

THIRTY-ONE

ASPETH

2 Days Before the Conquest Moon

SLEEP WITH GWENNA that night, because I don't want to go back to Hawk's side. I don't sleep very well, though. I'm restless and worried, my thoughts focused on the ring I've looped around a ribbon and now wear about my neck.

She's right that I won't get into trouble for having an artifact. I'm a holder's daughter and his heir. If I run into any problems, I can wield that information like a cudgel and browbeat everyone into letting me slip out of trouble. I can insist that it's mine and take it back with me, but I'll also be sent back to Honori Hold on the first coach out of Vastwarren, never to return. The others won't have their Five and we'll all be sunk.

I can't let that happen.

I'm up before dawn, feeding Squeaker and rubbing her chin while I wait for Gwenna and the others to awaken. My uniform is a fresh one, and I'm starting to actually like the heavy, scratchy feel of the fabric against my skin. It reminds me that my old life is done, and this is my new one.

Plus the cat hair doesn't stick to it nearly as bad. I flick a tuft of loose hair off my fingers, wincing as it floats in the air. Sheesh.

Breakfast is a tense situation. We all meet in the kitchen and sit at the table, talking amongst our Five until Hawk stomps in, the clap of his hooves against the stone floor obnoxiously loud. Mereden flinches with each step and I force myself to remain stiffly straight, my posture unbending as his chair *scrreeeeeeches* against the stone and then he flings himself down into his seat at the head of the table. The nestmaid hands him a bowl of porridge and he angrily stirs it, glaring in my direction.

I ignore him.

"Where's Magpie?" he asks, flinging his spoon down. "Why isn't she with you?"

"She's sleeping in," Lark says. "Since nothing's getting done today."

"Is she drunk?" Hawk snarls, glaring at her.

Lark, bless her soul, glares back at him. "No, and it's fucking rude of you to even ask that. You're rather moon-touched at the moment, aren't you? Go jerk off or something."

I pay great attention to my food, the tension in the room palpable. I'm pretty sure that Hawk looks at me a few times, but I ignore him and he picks up his bowl, chugs his porridge, slams it down, and storms out of the room. A moment later, he thunders back in and points at Lark. "Tell Magpie I'm going to guild headquarters, and if she leaves again without notifying me, we're no longer partners. Understand?"

"Understood."

He stomps back out again . . . only to return one more time. This time, he leans over my chair, all menace and male fury. "And you . . . you're sleeping with me tonight. I don't want you running off every single time we argue. Got it?"

"Say please." My heart is racing like a rabbit's.

I expect him to blow up at me, to lose his temper and shout, because his hormones are all over the place. But he can't just order me around, not after avoiding me himself.

His nostrils flare and he leans in even closer. "Please."

I nod.

He gives one of those indignant, annoyed snorts that only a Taurian can, and then storms back out of the room again.

"Whew, the moon is hitting him hard," Lark says, her eyes wide with "Did you just see that?" amusement. "No wonder all the other Taurians are out of town or hitting the sex district."

"They're out of town?" Mereden asks, and Kipp tilts his head, equally inquisitive.

"Oh yeah. You guys don't know about the Conquest Moon?" Lark hoots. "Man, is it a story. If you ever see a Taurian with red eyes, get out of his way or you'll get your ass pounded into the ground."

"They fight?" Mereden asks again.

"No, I mean they'll fuck anything moving. Your ass pounded into the ground is . . . literally your ass . . . pounding . . . into the ground." Lark punctuates each word with a punch of her fist into her palm, oblivious to the way I'm trying to ignore her. "No orifice is safe—"

"We get the idea," Gwenna cuts in sharply. "Thank you."

"All I'm saying is that the Conquest Moon is probably striking him hard." She wiggles her brows at me. "That why you slept upstairs, Aspeth? Couldn't sleep for the thing poking you in the backside?"

I ignore that and spear a slice of ham with my knife, then nibble on it. "Where's your aunt this morning?"

"Drunk," Lark says.

Mereden gasps. "But you told Hawk—"

Lark shushes her, glancing at the door. "I know what I told him. But we really don't need them fighting when he's this close to the Conquest Moon. He's not going to be reasonable. Just ask Aspeth."

"He's not reasonable," I agree, and leave it at that. We need Magpie, drunk or not, and right now I'm going to take her side. If she's breaking rules already, what's a few more? I need the other half of the ring that's down below to save my neck.

Oh, and to save my father *and* the hold. But I'm vastly more interested in keeping myself alive, if I'm being honest. I'm not interested in being the heir or running things. Staying alive, though, that has my full interest.

"Look, it's fine," Lark says, getting up from the table and tossing her bowl onto the counter. The nestmaid currently cleaning the kitchen frowns at her, and Gwenna gives the woman a look of sympathy. "Until we get permission to go into the drop again, it's not like we can do anything. No one's going to be training because any teacher worth their coin is going to have their students combing through the ruins right now instead of learning lessons, because the guild is driven by money first, learning second."

She's right. In my hunger to join the guild to get to live my artifact-strewn fantasies, I always forget that the guild isn't nearly as interested in the history of Prell as they are in selling it. They're a guild of vultures, picking over the carcass of something long dead. "I suppose we could train ourselves."

Gwenna makes a face. "I am *not* going to run the obstacle course on my own for fun."

Kipp shakes his head, too.

"I could teach you some of the more common Prellian glyphs," I offer. "I read a delightful book about forgeries once that had sketches showing the great lengths that forgers will go to in order to pass off their items."

Lark makes a face. "Wow, that sounds really exciting . . . said no one ever." She shakes her head and pulls out a series of parchment envelopes, each one sealed with wax. "Or we could deliver these around the city."

"What are they?" I ask, taking one. The seal is that of a bird, but it's been stamped messily and a little difficult to determine *what* bird.

"Missives from my aunt demanding that we be allowed back into the drop. We're going to appeal to local authorities and the king's vizier to override the guild's decision." She hands them out to the rest of us.

My jaw drops. "The guild already made a decision?"

"No, but the answer is always the same. It's never in the favor of the Five. The guild steps in and lets their flunkies take over if there's even a sniff of treasure."

Gwenna glances over at me, uneasy. She takes an envelope and turns it over, running her finger over the seal. "So Magpie decided to write appeals already?"

"Oh, no, that was all me," Lark says. "I went into her room and borrowed her seal."

Kipp flicks the envelope away and slaps his tail on the table.

"Don't you sass me, lizard," Lark retorts.

"Lark!" Mereden scolds. "He's right to be upset at you. We can't go forging documents!"

"It's not a forgery if Aunt Magpie doesn't remember doing them or not." Her smile is bright. "And do you guys have a better solution? Because how things look right now, my aunt isn't going to be training much, Hawk's got blue balls until the god's Conquest Moon is out of his system, and guild rules won't let us go do anything fun without a chaperone. Unless you can materialize one, we're going to be practicing with our swords and running drills with rock-laden backpacks for the next season. With these two chuckleheads leading our team, we're not going to pass. We're going to end up as repeaters unless we're absolutely perfect, because we're women. And lizards." She nods at Kipp. "No offense."

He nods back.

Mereden picks up one of the envelopes. "I heard that the last time one of the nobles filed a special waiver for guild teams, someone found a really important horn. And that the team of students that found it got to bypass their test. They were allowed into the guild on the strength of that one find alone."

Now Gwenna's looking at me. "You know more about Old Prell than anyone else. Is that true?"

I rack my brain, thinking hard. A horn. A horn. A horn . . . ? "I can't think of any horns."

"A horn of water?" she asks, shrugging. "That's all I remember. My father was very impressed with it and talked about it for weeks. He bid on it but a sea lord to the south of us paid an astonishing fee for it."

"Oh!" I gasp as a memory floods in. "I remember now. The Conch of the Tides!"

Mereden snaps her fingers. "That's it!"

"What's the Conch of the Tides?" Gwenna asks. "Why is the tide so important?"

"The Conch of the Tides is ideal protection for a sea fortress," I point out. "It didn't even need a word of magic to activate it. If you blew on it, the tide would change. I recall that the holder who acquired it lives upon an island where his shoreline is only available at low tide. He's the safest holder alive, now."

"And why my father wanted it," Mereden agrees. "Our hold makes most of its income from low tide farming for shells and cockles because of the cove we're in. He was very disappointed." She eyes me speculatively. "You certainly know a lot about holders."

I exchange a look with Gwenna. It's time to come clean. I turn the envelope in my hands, running a finger along the edge. "I haven't been entirely truthful with all of you," I admit. "I'm not a merchant's daughter."

"I was wondering when you were going to speak up," Mereden says. "Honori Hold, right?"

THIRTY-TWO

ASPETH

MEREDEN HAS KNOWN the whole time.

I'm a little shocked, but I shouldn't be. Mereden is smart, and she sees everything that's going on. That she keeps her secrets without spilling them makes her all the wiser, because secrets are power. But as I confess the truth about how and why I'm here, Lark's jaw drops and continues to drop lower, and Kipp looks equally agitated. Once my story is told, I produce the ring from inside my corset and set it on the table, deciding to keep Gwenna's name out of it. "I managed to snatch this from down below."

"No, you didn't," Mereden continues. "I saw everything. If we're telling truths, tell all of them. We're all in this together."

"I took it," Gwenna says. "Aspeth's protecting me because she's a good person. Because she knows I'm worried. You two are noble, holder blood." She gestures at me and Mereden. "I'm a servant. Who do you think they'll come after if we're discovered?"

Mereden hesitates, and then nods.

"I didn't hear anything," Lark drawls. "Did you, Kipp?"

Kipp gives his head a quick shake. *Nothing.*

Gwenna manages a little smile. "Thank you."

Mereden reaches out to me, her hand palm up on the table. "I want you to know that your secrets are safe with me, Aspeth. There's nothing I want more than to join the guild. We need all five of us for that. And I won't say anything to my family, either, if you're worried. If I did, they'd probably attempt to take over your father's hold . . . and then send me promptly back to the Convent of Divine Silence." She makes a face. "My situation is slightly different from yours but no less awful."

"We're in this together," Lark declares, and slaps her hand down atop Mereden's.

Gwenna drops her hand onto theirs and I do the same. Kipp places his atop mine, small and sticky. His little touch feels like a big deal.

"Thank you," I tell them, and then feel the need to say more. "I know what we're doing is dangerous and illegal. . . . I just want an artifact that's enough for my father to protect the hold," I tell them. "If the ring will do it, that's all I need. Anything else can go to you guys. I know it's a lot to ask, and I wouldn't ask at all if my life wasn't on the line. No one's going to stop and ask me if I want to be my father's heir. They're just going to kill me, no questions asked."

"How do you know your father won't gamble it away?"

I don't. "I'll figure something out. Maybe I'll tell him it has a curse on it, and if it's sold or used for gambling, he'll be doomed."

"Tell him it has an ass-pox," Lark says.

Mereden gives her a strange look. "What is it with you and asses?"

Lark shrugs. "Asses are funny."

"Well," Gwenna says in her no-nonsense voice. She picks up one of the envelopes and holds it aloft. "Should we deliver these, then? The sooner we get things started, the better."

We head out to deliver the appeals, and I try not to think about the fact that Magpie has no idea of what we're doing in her name. Like Lark said, if she thinks she did them, it can work in our favor, too.

Lark has grown up in Vastwarren and knows her way around everything. She leads us to one manor house that looms high above the other houses in the area, a tall hedge separating him from his neighbors. The housekeeper takes the letter with a sniff, and something in me suspects it won't be looked at.

"That's why we have multiples," Lark replies cheerfully. "All we need is one person willing to override the guild."

The guild is so controlling, though, I don't see how. I'm about to protest this when Kipp races ahead of our party, down the street. His shell house bounces on his back as he trots away, and I look over at the others. "Where's he going?"

Mereden shrugs, and Gwenna does, too.

"Maybe he saw something suspicious?" Lark hurries after him, and I do the same, because it's not like Kipp to dart off without us. He's the responsible one.

We find him ahead in a market square, near a fountain. He's met up with another slitherskin, and as we approach, we can see them rubbing all over each other, their movements quick and frantic.

"Oh." Lark shrugs. "Give them a moment."

"What are they doing?" Mereden asks, shielding her eyes politely.

"It's nothing lewd," Lark explains, relaxing. Her gaze rests on Mereden for a moment, then flicks over to me. "It's how slitherskins got their names. They rub up against one another, and when they do, they transfer information. They can share memories through the touch of their skin and that's how their people communicate. That's why he's so fussy about being grabbed."

How fascinating. I've never seen it until now, and the sight of it is a little . . . slithery, all right. It looks downright obscene, but who am I to judge? I married a Taurian, and they have all kinds of strange customs, too.

Thinking of Hawk and his people's customs makes me think of the orgy in the alleyway and my face gets hot and flushed. I wish he wasn't such a prick.

I also wonder where he is right now. Probably storming the guild halls looking for someone to give him a job to get out of the house.

We stand by awkwardly a short distance away as the two slitherskins rub against each other with frantic, happy motions. Then they hug one last time and part, tails twining. Kipp trots over to us, a look of contentment on his small, lizardy face.

"Old friend?" Gwenna asks.

He shakes his head and then pauses. A flurry of gestures quickly follows as he tries to communicate with us, and it takes a few rounds but we finally figure it out. The slitherskin was a stranger, working for a traveling merchant. He saw Kipp in his uniform (now unbuttoned and open to the waist thanks to all the full-contact slithering) and wanted to tell him how proud he was of his fellow slitherskin.

I am first, Kipp gestures to us.

"You are?" I'm startled to hear this, but not entirely surprised. I haven't seen other slitherskins around and none of the guild's history books refer to slitherskins in any way. They barely reference Taurians, and Magpie is the only woman I know of who has joined.

Kipp lifts his chin, full of pride.

"Bunch of horrid men," Gwenna grumbles. "Don't like anyone who doesn't have the same equipment as them. The more I learn about this Royal Artifactual Guild, the less I like it."

"Which means it's all the more important that we join the guild," Mereden says. "These men need to realize that slitherskins—and women—are just as competent as they are."

Gwenna grunts.

I'm silent. So much is riding on this that the guilt is becoming overwhelming. I'm going to ruin everyone's chances if it's found out that I have the ring . . . or that I'm a noble. . . .

"That's why a Five is so important," Lark says, speaking up. She puts a hand on my shoulder and one on Mereden's, drawing us closer in the middle of the street. "The guild wants to emphasize teamwork so Fives work together, but doing this has made us more than a team. We're

friends. We have one another's backs. And we're going to join this fucking sausage party of a guild and turn it inside out."

We laugh at that, but I blink back tears again.

Before leaving home, I had no friends. Now I have four of them, and
it feels like I'm the richest person in all of Vastwarren.

ONCE THE LAST of the letters are delivered, we opt to head back to the
dorm and train ourselves. Kipp teaches Mereden and Lark some basic
stabbing moves with short swords, and I go over a few of the more common Prellian glyphs with Gwenna in the kitchen. I want her to be able
to recognize them to give her an advantage over some of the men in the
guild.

We're basically waiting and passing time until something happens.
Either Lark can approach her aunt and see if she'll help us with our plan,
or we'll get permission to go back down to the drop due to the appeals
we dropped off earlier today. Until then, all we can do is stay busy.

"The lovely thing about Prellian magic is that it's considered female,"
I tell Gwenna enthusiastically as I flick through a book I borrowed from
Hawk's small store of guild tomes. I pause on a rendering of a common
vase covered in glyphs and point it out. "So you're always going to see
the glyph for a female if there's magic referenced."

Her brows furrow. "What are you talking about?"

"When you reference magic, it's considered female," I explain, delighted to be able to talk about my favorite subject. "And it was Prellian
law that every object had to be labeled clearly with what it did for public
safety. They were really very advanced with law for their time. So every
object will have a statement of some sort as to what the magic is, and
since it's referencing magic, you can look for the egg symbol around this
particular glyph. The arrow over this figure means 'man,' but when it's
encased by an egg, it changes the symbol to 'woman.'"

"Is the arrow supposed to be a cock?" Gwenna asks.

Her blunt words make my face heat. Good gods, it seems I'm blushing all the time now. "No, of course not! It's an arrow, at least that's what
scholars believe. They think that it references back to the time when

men were hunters and would use arrows to feed and provide for their families."

"Looks like a cock to me," she says, and then adds, "I'm probably spending too much time around Lark."

"Probably." Though now it looks a bit like a cock to me, too.

The doors to the kitchen open and Hawk strides in. Gwenna and I immediately grow quiet, watching as he marches over to the water pitcher and pours himself a drink. He looks dusty and dirty, as if he's been in the tunnels, but I don't want to ask. The last thing I need is a more cranky Hawk jumping down my throat.

I'm sure I deserve some of the throat jumping but not all of it.

Hawk drinks his water, leaning against the counter, and I pretend to focus on the book in front of me instead of my very large Taurian husband, who might possibly hate me. He'll just finish his beverage, I think, and then we'll be alone again and ready to continue our lessons—

"Aspeth," Hawk says. "We need to talk."

I put on my best gracious-holder's-daughter smile. "We are in the midst of a lesson."

"Oh, it can wait," Gwenna blurts out, betraying me. She jumps to her feet and moves to stand behind my chair. She leans in and whispers in my ear, "Distract him and I'll check on the situation with Magpie."

And then with a brilliant smile, she leaves me alone with the moody Taurian.

I give him an impatient look. "You decided now is the best time to talk despite ordering me to sleep next to you tonight? It couldn't wait until then?"

"I didn't know if you were going to come to bed."

"Because you don't trust me, right?" I keep the words light and playful even as they cut.

He sighs heavily. "Because I wouldn't want to come to bed with me, either. Whatever frustration or anger you're feeling right now, I deserve it."

I run a finger down the front of the book, not looking him in the eye. I don't know what to say to that. It certainly wasn't what I expected to hear from him. "Was that an apology?"

"More of an explanation," he says. "Can we go talk in our room?"

Now I glance up at him, suspicious. Is this going to turn into another spy inquisition? But . . . Gwenna did tell me to distract him. Hells. I get to my feet, my chin held high. "If you're a boor, I'm going to leave again, fair warning."

"If I'm a boor to you, I'll absolutely expect it," he says, and moves to my side, putting a hand to the small of my back to lead me to our room.

Standing this close to Hawk always makes me feel slightly breathless. I'm a big woman—tall and strong and the opposite of dainty—but his hand on the small of my back makes me feel delicate. Like a thing to be protected. It's not something I'm used to—both the touch and the feeling of being something worth protecting—but I like it. And I hate that I like it, because it makes me feel vulnerable, like it can be used against me.

We head down the hall from the kitchen and into Hawk's private chamber. Squeaker is curled up on the window seat, spreading orange cat hair all over the cushions. She yawns when we enter and stretches in place but makes no effort to get up, and Hawk doesn't ask me to remove her. That means we're probably not going to get intimate.

I . . . can't decide if I'm disappointed or relieved.

He gestures that I can sit on the bed, and I move to sit on the edge, clasping my hands in my lap. I'm doing my best to remain composed, but being alone with him brings on floods of memories and scandalous thoughts, and it's hard to concentrate. Hawk paces at the far side of the room, his tail flicking back and forth, and I notice that the sleeves of his shirt are rolled up, revealing bulging muscles. He's discarded his guild jacket somewhere, too, and when he paces, I can see the fine, thick shape of his thighs and the rounded strength of his backside.

If he's trying to appeal to me by simply looking intense and delectable, he's doing an excellent job.

Hawk tugs on the ring that hangs from his broad nose. "Aspeth . . . I know I've behaved cruelly toward you."

That makes me pause. "Cruelly? I'd say you were an arse but I don't know if cruelty was involved."

"I've thrown things in your face that I shouldn't have." He shakes his head and paces some more. "I was furious that you were keeping secrets. That you didn't trust me. And of course, everything is amplified thanks to the Conquest Moon's rising—"

"Oh, come *on*, now. You can't blame everything on that."

He turns and gives me a sharp look. "You don't know what it feels like."

"I do not," I agree. "But I've also done my best to be accommodating for the Conquest Moon time, and you've lashed out at me in private moments. That's not the Conquest Moon. That's you being a shit."

His mouth tenses and he tugs on the ring on his nose again. "I know. I just . . ." More pacing. I wait for him to answer, because he seems to be conflicted. "I just . . . this should be transactional between us and it's not."

I tilt my head at him in surprise. Does he feel like I'm not holding up my end of the bargain? "It's not?"

A low growl escapes him, and then he storms across the room to my side. Hawk leans over the bed, caging me in place as he puts his hands on either side of me. "I *want* you. More than I should."

My lips part.

"No, that's not right." He shakes his head, his horns swiveling dangerously, and then lifts his face to meet my gaze again. "I want you more than a teacher should want his student. I want you more than I should for a marriage of convenience. And that's the part that fucking bothers me."

"It . . . does?" Why does that make my stupid heart flutter? He thinks I'm a spy, out trying to rob the guild of its riches or some nonsense.

"It does bother me," Hawk continues. He studies my face, his breath warming the air around us. "Because I think about you all the time. It's not just the Conquest Moon—I've felt its grip on me before. This is something else. If it was just the Conquest Moon, I wouldn't think about your smile. I wouldn't think about the way you laugh when you're trying to be polite, and how different it is from when you're truly amused. I wouldn't think about you and that stupid cat of yours and how you lavish affection on it when you come home and it makes me jealous."

My cheeks heat. He's jealous of Squeaker?

"I wouldn't be obsessed with the realization that I still owe you an orgasm from last night and how thinking about it has been distracting me all day long. I nearly fell off a drop earlier because I was thinking about the way your soft cunt clenched around my fingers, and how it's going to feel when I'm deep inside you for the first time."

"You were thinking about me today?" I'm breathless at the thought. Why do I *care*? Yet I do . . . terribly.

"Couldn't stop thinking about you." His hand trails up the inside of my thigh. "And how things left off last night. Figured I need to give you that orgasm or else it's going to continue to distract me."

I stop his hand before it can go up any farther. "Is this you apologizing for last night?"

His gaze meets mine. "Would you accept an apology from me?"

I swallow. "Maybe . . . depends on how good an apology it is."

Hawk gives me a slow, lazy smile. "Toe curling."

Oh gods. My pulse thumps a response right between my legs.

"I promised you I'd make you feel good," he murmurs, and leans in to nip the shell of my ear. He's incredibly gentle, and the feel of his teeth against my ear is more arousing than anything. "And I'm not holding up my end of the bargain. Moody or not, you being a holder's heiress or not, I need to be the husband you deserve." His hand stops on the inside of my thigh, his thumb rubbing against me through the fabric. "Can I make you come, wife?"

I bite back a moan. "If . . . I do . . . where does that leave us? You think I'm a spy."

Hawk pauses. "I know you're not. I'm angry that you didn't trust me. Hurt that you didn't. Probably more than a little pissed that I don't get to keep you after all is said and done. You're not a spy. I might not understand you or the way you work, Aspeth, but I know you're not a spy."

I suppose I should feel better at his confession, but it just reminds me that I'm in here with him to distract him away from what the others are doing . . . because we need Magpie and her loose interpretation of guild rules instead of Hawk's strict one.

"I'm just trying to stay alive," I tell him in a soft voice. "Everything I've done is toward that goal, because I really don't want to be killed over my father's poor choices."

"No one's going to touch you," he growls, and then he heaves me onto my back, my legs flying up. "No one except for me."

I suck in a breath as he rubs me through my pants. How is it that through layers of clothing, he knows exactly where to touch me and make it feel good? Whimpering, I squirm against his touch. "Hawk. Hawk."

"You want my fingers on your pussy?" He leans in close, continuing to rub me through the fabric even as he hovers over me, my smaller form swallowed up against his. "You want me to make you feel good?"

Nodding, I pull at the waist of my pants, fumbling with the belt until it's open and he can slide a hand inside. The moment he does, I cry out because it feels so incredible. His fingers are hot and callused against my softer skin and it shouldn't feel nearly as good as it does. But he pushes two fingers between my labia and rubs, framing my clit and teasing it from both sides. My legs draw up automatically and he pushes his chest against my knee, pushing me deeper into the mattress. The position spreads me wide for him, and the sensations only grow more intense.

"That's right, wife. I want your pussy to be wet around me all the time. I want you slick and aching the moment I walk into a room, because all you're going to think about when I'm around are the naughty things I'm going to do to you." He strokes deeper, pushing into my core and making me gasp with the way he stretches me. "I'm going to make everything so good for you, Aspeth. All you have to do is let me."

I moan again, clinging to the shoulders of his jerkin. "I'm your wife," I manage to pant out. "I vowed this to you. To be yours."

"You are mine, aren't you?" His words are a sultry whisper in my ear, his muzzle brushing against my skin even as his fingers pump deep inside me. I'm so wet I can hear squelching noises coming from my body with every thrust of his hand, but there's no energy in me to be embarrassed. Everything I am is focused on him touching me, on the pleasure of him making me come. "My pretty, sweet human wife. I shouldn't be nearly as possessive of you as I am, but I can't stop thinking about you, Aspeth. Can't stop thinking about how it's going to feel when I sink my knot into you. When I make you mine."

He drives into me with each word, leaving me whimpering.

"It's the bull god's hand on me," he whispers in my ear, his teeth grazing my skin. "The god's hand on my shoulder, telling me that you should be at my side, or under me. That's where I need to keep my wife. To fill her belly with my seed and have her give me many sons. To knot her and then play with her clit for hours while you squirm on my cock, trapped against me—"

Stars burst behind my eyes and I cry out, the climax hitting me like an avalanche. My legs curl up and he grunts with satisfaction, stroking his thumb against my clit even as his fingers work inside my body. He wrings the pleasure out for as long as possible, continuing to stroke and pet me until I'm shuddering and spent. I whimper when he pulls his fingers free of my body, again making a terribly wet noise, and watch as he licks them clean of my taste.

"So fucking good, Aspeth. I could plant my muzzle there between your legs for days and not come up." He looks down at me with such possessive lust that I swear I see a hint of red ringing his pupils.

It's that hint of red that alarms me, and I press the back of a hand to my brow. "I need a moment."

"Of course you do." He leans down and gently covers the tip of my nose with his mouth, so big that he nearly swallows the entire thing whole.

"What was that?" I ask, curious.

"A kiss." His voice sounds gruff, as if he feels a bit foolish at having to explain himself. "I want to be a good husband to you, even if this is just convenience. Even if we annul things after the Conquest Moon sails through. Until then, I want to be good to you."

I should leave it at that. I should acknowledge that it's sweet of him to say that . . . but . . . "Because now you know I'm a holder's daughter?"

Hawk goes still.

Immediately, I feel like an arse. Like I pushed too far.

"I suppose I deserved that," Hawk says, moving to get off me.

I reach up and caress his cheek—or at least what I think is his cheek—before he does. "Neither of us deserves any of this."

It's as close to an apology as I'll get. I'm still hurt from the spy comment.

He gazes down at me, and nips at my fingertips when I move them nearer to his mouth. "Is the trust between us gone, Aspeth?"

"Do we need to trust each other for the Conquest Moon?" I ask, keeping my voice light. It seems a safer thing to ask than *Did you ever truly trust me?*

"I suppose not."

But the moment is still ruined. And when he nuzzles my forehead and climbs off the bed, I let him go. He moves across the room and pours some water from a pitcher into a basin, washing up. I watch him, fixing my own clothing and torn between offering to touch him and wanting to check on Lark and the others. I'm aware he didn't come. Very aware. My body is throbbing and I can see the outline of his cock pressing against his pants, and part of me wants to sink to my knees in front of him and touch him again, because I enjoyed it. I loved touching him, loved the power it gave me over him. Loved watching him fall apart at my inexperienced caresses. It made me feel connected to him, and I want that again.

But we're too busy lashing out at each other, and it's going to get worse before it gets better.

Still, I can't stop myself as I move to his side. I slip my arms around his waist and press my cheek to his broad back, ignoring that I'm probably going to have to clean my spectacles again after all this face rubbing. "We'll get this figured out, you and I. I promise."

Hawk covers one of my hands with his bigger one. "I do want this to work between us, you know. Not just because of the Conquest Moon. I like you, Aspeth. I think you're smart and clever and driven. I've never met anyone like you. And I do want to try to make this work between us . . . however long we have together." He rubs his thumb over the back of my hand. "I'll stay close to the nest until the Moon's hand stops pressing on me. Stay close to you. We can spend more time together."

Oh no. This might be the absolutely wrong thing for our plans. "But the guild . . . you're one of the only Taurians left in the city . . . what if they need you?"

"Then they'll have to hire someone else." He half turns, pulling my hand to his mouth and kissing my knuckles. "I have a wife I have to prepare to take my knot."

I blush. Hearing that shouldn't be as thrilling as it is.

"And I should wash up," he says, and I could swear that red gleam is in his eyes again. "And then I'm happy to wash you, too."

"We need more water," I say brightly, detangling myself from his grasp and grabbing the pitcher. "I'll get it and return. Be right back!"

He reaches for me but I slink away before he can pull me into his arms again. I flash him a quick smile and hug the pitcher, practically running for the door. Squeaker follows behind me, no doubt traumatized after watching me get viciously (and delightfully) fingered on the bed.

I pump fresh water in the kitchen and look around for the others. I can't stay out for long or Hawk will come looking for me.

"Gwenna?" I whisper, pouring the water out of the pitcher and filling it slowly again just to waste time. "Lark? Mereden? Kipp? Someone?"

There's a scrambling sound and then Lark bursts into the kitchen. "Spoke with my aunt," she pants. "She's in. You keeping Hawk distracted?"

"Mostly?" I eye the pitcher, now full. "I'm about to head back in. We need to talk about plans because he's going to stay close for the next few days, until the Conquest Moon is over."

She groans. "That's a nightmare. Okay, I'll talk to my aunt again, figure something out. Did you hide the artifact?"

Shit. It's still on a ribbon around my neck. Hawk didn't notice it because he only shoved a hand in my pants, but if he wants to bathe after this, he's for sure going to see it and ask questions. I hastily slip it off and hand it to Lark. "Give it to Gwenna."

Lark races away again. "Talk more in the morning!"

If I don't collapse from stress first, sure.

THIRTY-THREE

ASPETH

1 Day Before the Conquest Moon

ALL THE REQUESTS were denied," Gwenna whispers to me over breakfast the next day.

Immediately my appetite curdles. "Already? But that's so fast!"

"Magpie has a bit of a reputation around town." She shrugs. "It was a long shot anyhow. I talked to Lark and she said that her aunt has connections. She knows someone who can make her a false pass and someone who can take us down the drop for the right price."

I stir my porridge, eyeing my husband from afar. He sits at the far end of the table from me, talking to the nestmaid, who's taking notes for food supplies for the week. We're on the cusp of the Conquest Moon and apparently it affects Taurians in all ways, including hunger. He needs additional foodstuffs, some of which will be prepared in advance and deposited into our room so we don't have to leave the bed during the moon time, a fact that makes me blush so hard my face feels scalding. Everyone is going to be extremely aware of what we'll be doing in that time frame.

It's no different from an arranged marriage, I remind myself, in which your husband would be keeping you in bed trying to get you with an heir as quickly as possible. Everyone knows you're having sex then, too.

"We're getting the counterfeit pass tonight," Gwenna murmurs, holding a mug of tea up near her mouth and cupping her hands around it to hide her face. "You're going to have to keep Hawk busy after dinner so he doesn't ask questions."

Oh. I nod, mind racing, as I try to figure out how one distracts a surly Taurian who's already distracted by sex. The obvious answer is right there, but I also don't want to rouse his suspicions. The last time I reached out to touch Hawk on my own, he called me a spy. I need him to instigate things. "I'll see what I can do."

I ponder this all day as we go through weapons drills, and we switch up our positions. Lark takes over shield-bashing everything, and truly, she's far more enthusiastic about it than I ever was. Gwenna takes over navigation, and that leaves me with either being the healer or the gearmaster.

"I kind of like being the healer," Mereden tells me shyly. "And I know a lot about tending to wounds thanks to my time at the convent."

"Then you should stay the healer," I agree, because I don't know anything about wounds. Gearmaster is a fairly simple position—I manage the supplies and ensure we don't run out . . . which isn't something you can practice at the dorm. I work with a shortened quarterstaff instead and try not to think about all the other things we could be doing. We're supposed to be learning more about artifacts and Old Prell itself. Magpie suggested we head to the guild's library earlier today, since it should be deserted (as everyone in training is currently in the tunnels except us).

Hawk said no.

Said he was in too bad of a mood to be around the rest of the guild. He's definitely been on the surly side of things, I think, as I glance over at him working with Kipp. The slitherskin bounces along the walls and flings himself off Lark's shield as the two of them counter Hawk's heavy, insistent blows with a club.

His temperament has gotten worse, as twice now, the guild has sent messengers today. Most of the Taurians are gone from the city, which means that the retrieval and assistance missions are all falling to him. He turns them away, too, but I can see his scowl growing deeper with every person who arrives at the door.

By the time we're done with lessons for the day, he's in an absolutely foul mood and the guild has sent a third messenger, only to be turned away. The others pile into the kitchen for snacks—and to escape his wrath—and I remain behind as he tidies up the training room. Gwenna told me to stick to his side today and I intend to do so.

I approach him delicately. "You know I don't mind if you want to help out with the guild—"

"I *said* I would spend time with you," he all but snarls.

I recoil.

Immediate remorse flashes over his face. He runs a hand down his muzzle, sighing heavily. "I'm sorry, Aspeth. It's not you. It's just . . . today. The guild. Magpie." He gestures at our surroundings.

"And the Conquest Moon?"

"Like a fist around my cock at all times," he admits. "And just as impossible to ignore." He runs both hands down his long face. "I'm going to be a beast to live with until this passes."

I want to make a joke about how as a woman, I know all about being cranky during certain times of the month. That I can relate to his foul temper being out of his control. But somehow, I don't think comparing my menstruation cycle to this will help cheer him any, touchy as he is. If he were a woman, I'd offer him sweets. But Taurians are fussy eaters and I don't even know if he likes sweets. Even so, feeding his mood isn't a bad idea.

"You know what you need?" I tell him, moving to his side and sliding my hands around his arm. "A nice, hearty meal out and away from everything."

That makes a smile quirk his hard mouth. "Are you offering to buy me dinner, Aspeth?"

"No, because I don't have two pennies to rub together." I grimace. "I spent all of my coin getting here. But it would be nice to go out for a bit, just the two of us. Get to catch our breath and not have five other people breathing down our necks."

It's the right thing to say. He pulls me close and nuzzles at my neck, sending shivers up my spine. "Change into regular clothes, hmm? I'll wash up and meet you at the front of the dorm in a few. I need to speak with Magpie."

I'm sure that's not going to help his mood, given that Magpie abandoned us early in the day because she had a "headache." I'm not sure if it's alcohol related or secret-plan related, but either way, it's bound to set Hawk off even more. But I nod and give him a saucy wink, watching as he leaves the room.

It feels wrong to lie to him, but once again, I'm back to not having a choice. I need the other half of that ring, and I absolutely can't let it fall into Barnabus's hands. I need to get my father some way to protect our people, and soon, because all the teams scouring the tunnels are bound to find something to help Barnabus wage war on my family's hold.

The moment he's gone, I race to Gwenna's quarters and knock on the door. She opens it a crack and then, after seeing it's me, lets me inside. The others are in there, except for Magpie. "I can't stay," I pant, because stairs are not part of our workout regimen. I rub the stays on my corset as my lungs heave against the confinement. "Taking Hawk out for supper at a tavern somewhere to keep him out of your hair."

"Good," Lark says. "We're meeting with Aunt Magpie and one of her friends later tonight to get the counterfeit pass. After that, we just have to wait until Hawk heads out again."

"I don't know if he's going to," I say. "He's intent on sticking close to me due to the moon tomorrow." Which is both flattering and frustrating.

"Aunt Magpie will figure it out." Lark is fully confident. "Just keep him occupied tonight while we work on this part of the plan."

I nod and then hesitate. "You guys won't go down without me, will you?"

"Never," Gwenna reassures me. "You're part of our Five."

I trust her. The one who has issues trusting is Hawk . . . and unfortunately, I'm going to give him even more of a reason not to trust me. I hate that, but I'm low on choices. I could ask him to help us, too. To ask him to break guild rules and help us steal from the guild right under their noses . . . but then I think about his hand and how he already owes the guild far too much as it is. I won't bring him down with me.

I know what he means when he says he struggles with caring too much.

I MEET MY husband at the door to the dorms a short time later, wearing a heavy dress of olive green with embroidered attached sleeves and a matching chemise that peeks out from artful gaps in all the fashionable spots. I always feel pretty in this dress, especially with a matching cloak over it, but I suspect it's ruined by my spectacles, which magnify my eyes and make me look owlish. Hawk looks pleased at the sight of me, though, and I twirl for his approval. "What do you think?"

"Luscious."

I'm both mortified and aroused. "You're not supposed to call me that."

"It's true. My mouth waters looking at you, because I know how juicy you are under all those skirts."

I move forward, pressing my fingers to his mouth to silence him, and all the while my breathing speeds up and need slides through my veins like liquid. "Hush. We're going out tonight to distract you, not rushing back to our quarters."

Much as I'd like to. I'm envisioning stripping him naked and rubbing his cock all over my face again, just because I liked the feel of his heated skin against mine, and how powerful and sexy it made me feel to touch him and give him pleasure, and how much it turned me on to do so.

But Gwenna, Lark, and the others need us out of their hair if they're going to pull this off, and the moment Hawk hears someone leave the dormitory, he'll be wondering what's going on.

So I run a hand down my husband's front. He's wearing the guild jerkin, fastened shut all the way to his throat, and his trousers are in guild colors as well. He's not wearing his sash denoting his rank, but that's the only difference I'm seeing. "I thought we were changing out of guild clothes for the day?"

"I realized that I didn't have anything else," he murmurs, leaning in and rubbing his muzzle against the side of my neck. "And that anyone who sees a Taurian in Vastwarren is going to know I work for the guild anyhow. Gods, you smell amazing."

His hand steals to the front of my bodice, skimming over one of my nipples through the fabric, and I bite back a moan. Luckily for me, my stomach growls in that moment, and that brings Hawk's amorousness to a halt.

"Hungry?"

"I could eat," I admit. I could also turn around and head back to our rooms and let him lick me all over, but the eating is part of the plan, and I need to focus on that.

Hawk pulls my cloak from the nearby hook and places it over my shoulders. "Come, then. I know a place. We'll have a nice meal, pretend the guild doesn't exist for a night, and then return later." His muzzle dips against my throat again, and he whispers, "And I'll undress you like I'm unwrapping a present."

By Lady Asteria, when they say Taurians grow amorous with the moon's advent, they mean it. We've barely decided upon dinner and I'm already flushed with heat and my pulse is throbbing between my thighs. Hawk isn't much of a conversationalist as we head out into Vastwarren, and I'm grateful for that. It allows me to compose myself as we walk, but when we near the King's Onion, I give him a sharp look.

"Not there," he reassures me. "It's just along the way. I promise I'm not starting anything, Aspeth. Tonight is just about dinner and spending time together."

I slide my hand into the crook of his arm again and nod.

True to his word, we stop at a tavern one street over. It's nearly deserted, with an elderly Taurian and his younger human wife behind the bar. The main tavern room is practically empty save for a few slitherskins near the fire, piled together with their houses stacked nearby. The

barkeep recognizes Hawk and makes him a huge bowl of lentil and vegetable soup with a half loaf of crusty bread, my portions only slightly
smaller. He puts the tray down at our table and then leans over, his gaze
on Hawk.

"I know it's a difficult time to be Taurian right now, son, but this is a
nice establishment. If you feel the need to take the edge off, head to the
alley. Understand?"

I should be mortified. Instead, it strikes me as funny, and I press my
fingers to my lips, doing my best not to giggle.

Hawk eyes me balefully as my shoulders shake. "You laugh," he murmurs as the tavern owner saunters away, "but some can't help themselves.
It's hard to serve a family a meal when there's a bull rutting into his hand
at the next table over."

That only makes me giggle harder. "I'm sorry," I wheeze. "I know it's
not funny. It's just . . . what if there are a lot of you who have the same
need at the same time? Do you all go to the alley together?"

"If we do, we don't make eye contact," he drawls, eyeing me. "And
thank you for that. My cock has sufficiently shriveled enough that I can
eat in peace."

I have to wipe the tears of laughter from my eyes. "I'm so sorry. I'm
just picturing you staring at one another and angrily jerking off because
your soup is getting cold and a stranger is standing too close."

"Can't be much of a stranger if I've got my cock in hand." But he
smiles at me as he says it. "Hope the food is all right with you. The old
Taurian's from my home village and his food reminds me of my mother's."

Oh. Hawk doesn't talk much of his home life, or his family. I'd love
to hear more. "This is lovely. It's nice just to get away from the guild life,
even if it's just for a few hours." I take a small bite of the food and try not
to wince. It tastes like, well, grass. I swallow and take another bite, because if this is what Hawk likes, I want to appreciate it as well. "I've
never had this sort of flavor before. You eat this back where you came
from?"

He's taking huge bites of the vegetable-laden soup, clearly loving it.
"The village I grew up in was nothing but Taurians. My parents were
farmers, so aye, we had a lot of dinners like this."

I take a bite of the crusty bread instead, because something tells me he's going to want to eat my share of soup, too. "Do you miss your family?"

Hawk shrugs. "They could write. They don't. I'm not part of their life anymore. So no, I don't miss them."

I ponder this as I take another bite of bread. "My mother died when I was very young and the only family I had was my father and my grandmother. My grandmother is a society sort and loves nothing more than a party. We've never seen eye to eye. She actually hates my spectacles and I was told not to wear them around her."

He huffs with annoyance. "So she'd rather you be blind than unfashionable? She's an idiot."

When he puts it that way, it does sound exceedingly stupid. "My father has been largely absent. I think he entertained the thought of another wife for a while, but nothing ever came to fruition, and he seemed content to have me be his heir and fool around with his mistress instead. We've never been close. I think I see him perhaps twice a year, despite the fact that we live in the same hold. Or rather, we *did*." I shrug. "So when you say you're not close to your family, I understand."

Hawk finishes his soup and I nudge mine toward him. He immediately takes it with a grateful smile and trades me the bread. "It's not that I'm lonely. The guild keeps me busy. I'm close to the other Taurians who work here in the city. I have Magpie."

"Mmm." I can't say much positive about Magpie. She's too erratic and absent.

"Once, she was a great mentor," he says, as if reading my sour thoughts. "I know she struggles now, but a decade ago she was clever and daring and no one could match her success rate. She seemed to know instinctively where to dig, and we'd come up with treasures more often than not."

"Did she use a dowsing rod then, too?" I tease.

"A dowsing rod?" His brow furrows. "Of course not. Those are fairy tales. A prank played on fledglings to keep them occupied."

"Just curious. I've heard, um, that some use them."

"Foolery." Hawk sounds cranky at the thought. "The best thing you can do is show your students the best places to dig, not to rely on sticks and magic. You look for places that would have lots of artifacts—old warehouses, or libraries. You look for merchant shops that specialized in the arts. And if you're really lucky, you'll stumble upon a wizard's shop. But just using a stick?" He makes a face. "That's a setup to fail."

He's not wrong. I just can't help but wonder if Magpie truly wanted us to fail or if she was lazy. There's no way she could have known about Gwenna's bloodline if even Gwenna had no idea. And we don't know that the dowsing rod actually led us to the ring. It could have been a fluke. Gwenna could have had shaky hands. Something.

"So may I ask you what your name was before you joined the guild? Who were you before you were Hawk? And what made you pick that name?"

He eyes me. "What, you think you can slide your soup over to me and suddenly I'll answer every question you ever had?"

I flutter my lashes at him, even though I probably look ridiculous through my spectacles. "Yes?"

The hard edges of his smile turn up just a little. "Maybe we order another round of soup and I can keep talking."

Grinning, I take another huge bite of bread, which truly is delicious for all that it's dry. I guess butter would be weird to minotaurs. "I think that sounds delightful."

THIRTY-FOUR

ASPETH

INNER IS FAR more fun than it should be. I know I'm supposed to be distracting Hawk and keeping him busy so the others can work on the counterfeit pass, but I've forgotten how enjoyable it can be to just talk to him. He's as obsessed with the guild as I am, but has a jaded, almost world-weary view of it while mine is more optimistic. He's sick of the politics, but still loves the joy of finding something new and exciting.

"Not that I get the chance to much anymore," he admits. "I'm too busy on rescue missions. It's like the guild isn't training anyone worth a damn any longer. I'm constantly being shuffled off to haul out some twit who didn't realize he was digging next to a support beam and collapsed an entire cave. Or some Five's gearmaster forgot to pack rations and now they're all too weak to make it back to the surface on their own." He shakes his head, making a face. "Who mucking forgets to pack food?"

It does sound idiotic.

Hawk eats three more servings of soup and I devour nearly a full loaf of bread, especially after the barkeep brings me a tiny pot of honey to dip the delicious bread in. We sip ale, too, but it's expensive and we don't want to drink Hawk's funds away.

He refuses to admit that he's afraid of spiders. Says I'm exaggerating.

He does mention that his name was Wallach before he became Hawk.

I try not to hold it against him.

He also mentions that he picked the name Hawk because it sounded fearsome . . . and it was easy to spell. "I'm not good with those little feather quill pens the guild uses," he says, turning his palms up. "My hands are too big. So the less I write out, the better."

"It's incredible timing you got the name when you did. I imagine there's always a 'Hawk' in the guild."

"There is, and timing has nothing to do with it." One side of his mouth draws up in a smile. "The old Hawk was getting ready to retire. I made sure I did him a few favors and hinted that I wanted the name when he was heading out. He decided to retire the same day I graduated to full artificer."

Clever. Clever and sneaky.

He tells me that someday he'd like to be a guild master, training his own recruits. "No Taurian's ever been a guild master before, though," he says with a shake of his head. "We're too valuable in our retrieval roles, I guess."

It makes me sad, because he'd be an excellent—if stern—teacher. I should know. He's done more to prepare us for the tunnels than Magpie has, but she gets all the credit.

Well, so to speak. I'm not sure she's bragging about us at the moment. So far all we've found is a dead body.

Okay, and a ring.

That we stole.

And I plan to steal a second one.

My thoughts turn in circles as I finish off the bread and I worry that the others aren't managing without me. Which is silly, but I still want to know what's going on. I feign a small yawn, smiling at Hawk, and then lick a droplet of honey from my thumb. "I must be tired after all of those weapons drills earlier."

"You need your sleep. When the Conquest Moon's upon me, I'm not going to let you have a moment's rest." His gaze is locked on my thumb, and he pushes his bowl aside. "Shall we head home?"

Even though he's not looking me in the eye, I feel scorched by the intensity of his gaze. I know he's thinking about sex. I know I certainly am. I flick my tongue over my thumb again and his tail slaps against the nearest chair so hard it sounds like a whip cracking.

Something inside me clenches with arousal, and I suspect if I dropped under the table right now, he'd let me. The thought fills me with heat, and while I'm a little appalled, I'm also titillated at the idea. "Are we . . . cutting through an alley?"

Is that me suggesting something lascivious? Absolutely.

This time, I absolutely see a hint of red gleaming in his eyes. "Aye."

I should be alarmed, but instead, I'm excited. "Then let's go."

He plunks down a coin with a meaningful slap onto the table and then rises to his feet. As he does, I get an absolutely obscene eyeful of the bulge in his pants, so thick and heavy that it's obvious to all what's going on. I glance around the near-empty tavern but luckily the barkeep is busy polishing a glass and the slitherskins aren't looking in our direction. There are a couple of humans near the hearth who smirk at us, and when Hawk growls low and terrifying, they quickly pay attention to their mugs again.

Hawk takes me by the hand and all but hauls me out after him. I'm breathless with excitement, and not entirely surprised when we stop by a familiar alley across from the brothel. There's no one outside of it except for a couple of sex workers looking for customers, but it doesn't matter. He pushes me up against the nearest shadowy wall and tugs on the front of my bodice, freeing one of my breasts from its corseted cage and holding it to his mouth, an offering. He sucks on the tip so fiercely it's a mixture of pleasure and pain, and I whimper, digging my hands into his clothing.

"Fuck. I've been staring at these pretty tits all night, watching them heave with every breath you take. How am I supposed to concentrate?" He flicks his thumb over my nipple and then lowers his head again, nipping and sucking on the sensitive tip. "Want to fuck you, Aspeth. Are you ready?"

That makes me pause. "You—do you mean *here*? In the alley? Or in general? Because I'd rather my first time not be in the streets—"

"Not here," he growls, and when he looks up at me, his eyes are gleaming red in the moonlight. "Home. Tonight. But I'm gonna make you come first."

And he mouths my nipple with such obscene dedication that all I can do is moan and cling to him. His tongue is big and broad, and it feels as if he's going to swallow my entire breast, but he only teases it, toying with my nipple until it's flushed and sensitive and every brush of his lips over my skin is making everything tingle.

He pulls up my skirts and fits me against his hips. "Wrap your legs around me."

I do, panting, and when he bucks his hips against mine, I realize he's freed his cock from his pants and the hard length of him is rubbing against my pussy underneath my layers of clothing.

"Where are your drawers?" he grits out, surprised when his cock slicks through the folds of my pussy.

"Not . . . wearing tonight," I manage, locking my arms around his neck. "We're not having sex here, right?"

"Just rubbing," he promises me. "Fuck, you feel so good." His cock glides through the wetness of my folds, dragging and striking against everything, and it feels as if I've caught on fire when the head of him slides against my clit. "I'm going to come on you, mark you with my seed. Your pussy is going to be soaked."

I gasp at what a filthy mental image it is. "Do it."

Hawk groans, thrusting against me, and then hot seed spills all over my skin even as he shudders over me. He comes, and it's a rich mess of slick heat that spurts over my thighs and pussy, coating my skin. I cling to him, watching his face as he climaxes, and it's fascinating how tightly wound he is . . . and then seeing him relax with a haze of pleasure. I scratch absently at the short, stubbly fur that covers his neck, the deep russet that almost matches his guild uniform.

He leans over me, nearly crushing me to the wall. "Too fast," he manages. "I should have lasted longer."

"I didn't mind." I squirm a little, because I'm wet and sticky down below my skirts and it's a strange feeling.

Hawk rubs his big head over the top of mine. "But you didn't come, did you? And after I promised I'd take good care of you."

His hand slips under my skirts, sliding into the wetness between my thighs. I whimper in surprise as his fingers drag through my labia, seeking my clit—and then I hiss because I'm so wet down there that his gentle, seeking fingers practically glide over my skin. He holds me close, murmuring sweet nonsense in my ear about how pretty I am and how much he likes it when I lose control, and all the while my thighs quiver and quake as he fingers me into bliss.

"That's better." He presses his muzzle to my sweaty brow in what must be a Taurian version of a forehead kiss, and then gently sets me onto my feet. I sway, knees weak, and he puts a supporting arm around my waist, even as he adjusts my skirts, smoothing them so they hang properly. Once that's done, he adjusts my bodice, tucking my shameless breast back into my chemise and then adjusting the entire thing so my clothing looks pristine . . . and hides the mess between my thighs.

I flush just thinking about it, because it's obscene and naughty and I'm enjoying being obscene and naughty with him far more than I should. "Well, now," I say, and take a tottering step forward. Sure enough, everything between my thighs is wet, wet, wet. I'm not going to be able to take a step without thinking about him and what we did. How he came this close to taking my virginity in a dirty alley across from a whorehouse.

It makes me pause. "Hawk? If we have sex tonight, you can make me pregnant, correct?"

He looks down at me, incredulous. "You're asking now?"

"Seems like a good time to ask."

"Aye, I can." His voice is terse, and I suspect this is just now occurring to him, too. "There are charms we can use but . . . I don't have any on hand. It usually falls to the woman to handle such things."

"When was I supposed to get a charm?" I ask him. "Before I came to Vastwarren and everyone would wonder who Lady Aspeth was fucking? Or after I got here, in between drills?"

Hawk grunts. "Excellent point. I'll get you one."

But that changes things. We were intending to head back to the dorm and have sex tonight. We're both ready, and we both want it. Except . . . "If we're going to have sex, shouldn't you get one before we do?"

He runs a hand down his face. "I'll get one first thing in the morning."

"So you and I . . . tomorrow, then?"

"Aye, tomorrow." He squeezes my hand. "We still have time before the Conquest Moon."

"How much time, exactly?"

He rubs the back of his neck with his other hand, expression awkward. "The morning?"

Oh goodness. Not much time at all. "And it has to be before then?"

He nods. "So I can be gentle. I don't trust myself once the hand of the god is fully upon me. Not with it being your first time and all."

I chew on my lip as we walk back to the guild dormitory in silence. I should be thinking about the Conquest Moon but instead, I find myself thinking about what happens afterward. I haven't allowed myself to think that far ahead, yet now I can't seem to stop. What does the future look like if I take the rings and head back to my family's hold?

What does the future look like if I stay Hawk's wife?

I've never really allowed myself to dream about what happens next. It's always been assumed that I would marry to keep the family bloodline going, and that it would be to someone who brings either wealth or artifacts to reinforce our claim upon Honori Hold. My parents were an arranged marriage, and their parents before them. I've never contemplated what I'd do if I wasn't tied to the hold and its obligation to its people.

But if I could . . .

I'd love to stay. Join the guild. Hunt for artifacts. More than that, I'd love to simply research and study the ones that the guild has. Immerse myself in the Old Prellian culture that I love as much as everyone else in the guild. Go cave diving at my husband's side.

Come home to him every night and curl up in his arms and talk about nothing more urgent than the day's findings (or lack thereof).

I suddenly want that so badly I ache. My eyes burn with unshed tears and I blink rapidly, holding tightly to Hawk's hand.

This is what happens when I allow myself to dream, so I won't think about it at all. It hurts too much.

We're quiet as we walk back to the guild dorm, both of us lost in thought. I keep my hand tucked in his, though, because I'm afraid of letting go. I think about Hawk's words, about how this is no longer convenient, no longer transactional, and he's right. I'm feeling entirely too much and I'm terrified of what this could mean.

As we head up the sloping street toward Magpie's nest, I see a light shining in the window. I check the front of my bodice again, immediately feeling as if I'm back in the alley with one breast hanging out. "Someone stayed up late."

"Never a good sign." Hawk gives my hand a squeeze and then releases it. "Let me talk to whoever it is. Keep quiet and stay behind me."

As a holder's daughter, I've never stayed quiet, much less hid behind a man. My back stiffens. "It's probably Gwenna."

"Or your ex finding out you've married and come to cause trouble."

My mouth snaps shut. He might be right. I tuck my cloak tight around my dress and let him take the lead.

Inside the dorm hall, there are two men seated on the bench, both in guild livery. One jumps up the moment we step through the doorway.

"The guild needs all Taurians in the city to report to the Everbelow," the first one says. "There's been a terrible accident."

THIRTY-FIVE

ASPETH

T HERE'S NO ACCIDENT," Magpie announces after Hawk sets off
with the guild messengers. She's got five packed bags on the table in
front of her, weapons laid out. "Or there was, but it was by design. Had to
say something to get him to head out."

"What are you talking about?" I ask, distinctly aware of the wetness
between my thighs. I want to go into our quarters and clean up and
change, but Magpie and the others seem determined to talk right now.
"What's the accident? Who was hurt?"

"No one should be hurt," Lark explains, casting a frustrated look toward her aunt. "We just knew that Hawk wasn't going to leave your side
for a regular retrieval. So we talked to the right people and they staged a
cave-in at a tunnel far away from Drop Thirteen."

"But no one was *hurt*," I emphasize. "Right?"

Lark looks over at Magpie.

Magpie shrugs.

I'm appalled. "So not only did we collapse a tunnel that might have
precious artifacts and historical findings, but there might have been
someone in there?"

"Do you want to do this or not?" Magpie demands. "Because if you
want to wait for Hawk to come back and try to explain that you're stealing from the guild to save your own neck, be my guest. I'm sure he'll
understand."

She says it in a way that makes it very clear that Hawk would not, in
fact, understand.

My heart sinks.

Gwenna moves to my side. "We talked this over with Magpie's

contact," she says, voice soothing and even as she pats my shoulder. "The tunnel we collapsed is a training tunnel, and no one's utilizing it at the moment because they're all in the regular tunnels."

"And Magpie's friend planted a team flag in the rubble so it'll look like someone was there, which means Hawk will be busy trying to dig them out, but it'll be discovered later that it was a clerical error and oops, no one was ever actually down there." Mereden offers me a wavering smile.

"It's a good plan," Magpie says, voice brusque. "Don't weasel out on me now."

I can't believe *this* is the grand plan. Collapse a tunnel? Sneak away in the dark while Hawk is off saving people? Things feel as if they're spinning out of control rapidly. "I thought we were supposed to get a counterfeit pass. Pretend like everything had been approved."

"My contact suggested this instead. Do you want to go down or not?" Magpie's impatience is evident. "The sooner we head into the Everbelow, the sooner we get back before Hawk suspects anything. He doesn't have to know about stolen rings or anything we find. In fact, it's best you don't tell him at all. The moment he knows you're a thief, he's going to turn you in to the guild and then we'll *all* be stripped of any rank and kicked out the door." She gestures at me. "And then your father still won't have anything to protect his hold."

"Right. Of course." The old anxiety returns, a tight ball of dread in my stomach. I'm out of choices. "It's just that the timing is rotten. I can't go. Tomorrow is the Conquest Moon."

Magpie shakes her head. "It's not a problem. We'll be back before dawn."

"How is that possible?" I think of the hours we walked last time just to get to our level. We know the area the ring will be in, but that doesn't mean we'll find it right away. There are no absolutes. "The timing—"

"I have a way to get us in and out quickly," Magpie says, her gaze sharp. "We can be down in the tunnels within the hour. If we don't have the ring before dawn, we'll come back and try again."

"It's cutting it too close," I protest, even as I'm filled with desperate yearning. Goddess, if this could work, it would fix all my problems. . . .

"We'll be back before dawn," Magpie repeats. "I swear it on Lark's life."

"Hey!" Lark cries.

"Now, are we doing this?" The guild master straightens, her shoulders going back. "Or is it all for nothing?"

Her words make my innards clench with anxiety. *All for nothing* echoes in my head. What if she's right? What if we can get there and back before dawn? Hawk will never know, and I'll be here for the Conquest Moon. It can all line up perfectly.

"Tell me how we're going to get down there," I insist. "Because the path takes hours to walk."

"An artifact. I can't tell you more without getting someone else in trouble."

Strangely enough, hearing that fills me with confidence. An artifact. Of course it's an artifact. That's how she's going to get us in and out quickly. Even though it's risky, I have to do this. I have to. Even if I hate it. Even if it makes me anxious about the timing. We know where the ring was found. We can locate the other, bring it back prior to morning, and return before Hawk suspects anything. "I promised Hawk I'd be here for the Conquest Moon," I say to Magpie. "No later than dawn."

"Dawn," she agrees. "I'm fine with that."

It's decided, then. Even so, I shift my weight on my heels and am aware once more that Hawk's seed is dripping down the inside of my thighs. "I have time to change, I hope?"

Magpie nods. "Quick, though. You're gearmaster for this particular excursion. I'll pack everything that you need but we have to be gone as soon as possible. Someone's meeting us at the tunnels to drop us in and we have to be there before he gets skittish."

Right. There's no time to waste.

OUR PACKS STRAPPED to our backs, weapons in hand, we file through the streets of Vastwarren in the darkness, heading for the fiercely guarded heart of the city—the entrance to the tunnels of the Everbelow. I've changed into my now-comfortably-familiar uniform and washed up after my interlude with Hawk, and my hair is bound into a tight bun at my nape, my spectacles cleaned of all fingerprints and smudges. My body aches with fatigue, but I'm not tired—my mind is racing.

I can do this. I can save my father's keep. Save the people there. Save my bloodline.

Save my own neck.

This time, instead of cutting through the impressive guild hall, we move along the wall that surrounds the drop zone. We meet a stranger there, lurking in the shadows behind a shop that touches the brick of the tall wall. He emerges from the darkness with a rope ladder, gesturing that we should hurry. "If you get caught, it's on you," he says, handing it over and then racing away once Magpie presses a coin into his hand. "Luck to you."

"Encouraging," Gwenna murmurs to me, but she always gets sassy when she's worried. Me, I just get an anxious knot in my gut that grows larger by the minute. "Hope you feel like climbing a rope in the middle of the night."

"Well, it was part of the obstacle course," I have to admit, watching as Magpie hooks it against the crenellation with skill. A moment later, Kipp scales the darn thing without pause. "They did try to train us."

"So they did, damn it." Gwenna makes a face and steps forward. "Fine, I'll go next. Let's get this over with."

Despite her griping, Gwenna clambers up the wall with little effort, and disappears onto the other side. Lark and Mereden each go up, both with a fair amount of skill, and I'm proud of them for how far they've come. A month ago we wouldn't have been able to manage. When it's my turn at the rope, I'm not nearly as adept as the others. I manage to get about halfway up before my arms get weak and I struggle. Magpie climbs up behind me and shoves on my backside, foisting me over the edge of the tall wall. There's another rope down the other side, and I manage to more or less tumble down this one without hurting myself.

It stings to know that I'm the least skilled of our Five, but when they pat me on the back and murmur encouraging things, I know they don't care. We're in this together.

Magpie gathers the rope and ushers us forward. "Come on," she whispers. "Mind your step and stick to the path. If you fall into a pit, I'm not coming after you." She points ahead. "Follow me to the drop."

We creep after her, and I'm at the back of the group. I can't help but feel that with the grounds deserted at night, it's like moving through a cemetery full of open graves. The wide-open pits yawn in the darkness, and I imagine losing my footing and stumbling into one, only to fall to my death in the ruins of Old Prell.

Quietly, I hook a finger into Gwenna's belt ahead of me. "Wish we'd roped ourselves together."

"There's something about this that seems off," she tells me. "It feels weird. Wrong."

I know what she means. Seeing the guild grounds deserted like this is strange. "Of course it feels wrong. We're sneaking in after dark to steal artifacts and lying to everyone." Poor Hawk is really going to hate me after this.

"Does Magpie seem a little manic to you?" she asks.

I glance ahead. It's true that Magpie is highly alert right now, her eyes bright with determination. Maybe she's eager to help us steal? Either that or she just wants this done quickly. "Perhaps we're just not used to seeing her sober."

Gwenna snorts. "That could be it, aye."

As we cut through the massive, deserted yard, a light flicks on and I see a man's face in the shadows. It isn't until we get closer that I see he's holding the same strange wand I saw previously. It's the man who was using the portal wand to transport rock. He's wrapped in a dark cloak and looks at Magpie nervously. "Is everyone here?"

"Yes. You know how to direct that thing to the drop?"

"Wait, we're not lowering ourselves down in the basket?" Lark asks, confused. "Whyever not?"

"Because I bribed the portal master, that's why." Magpie gives her an annoyed look. "Just shut your mouth and come stand next to me."

"But don't I need to tie in with my Five?"

"Isn't necessary," her aunt tells her, gesturing that Lark should come to her side again. "Come on."

"But—" Lark hesitates, glancing over at Kipp and Mereden, and then where I stand behind Gwenna. "I'm pretty sure the rules state—"

"The rules state a lot of things," Magpie snarls at her, "including that you shouldn't steal from the guild, but we're not paying attention to that part, are we?"

Lark jerks back in surprise, wounded by her aunt's tone. "Sorry. I was just asking."

"I don't think it's foolish to be cautious," I say, stepping forward. "And we've taught ourselves to tie together quickly. We can do so now."

"Fine. Whatever." Magpie gives a cross look to the portal master. "I hope you don't mind waiting on this nonsense."

He shrugs, uneasy. "You're paying me."

I don't like this. I don't like it because it makes me wonder how many others bribe their way into the Everbelow under the cover of night and steal from the guild. I don't like that I would normally condemn such deeds and instead I'm about to break the rules myself. I shove down all those unhappy feelings and rope myself in, passing it along to Gwenna quickly. She ties herself to me, and then we go down the line until we're all tied together and in position, Lark behind Kipp. Magpie watches us with annoyance, and then shakes her head. "Fine. Get ready to step through to the drop when he opens the portal."

We step through and immediately I can feel the cool shift of the air. The night was warm above but down below it's chilly and slightly damp. I hug my cloak closer and move toward the others so I don't jerk on the rope. The tunnel seems larger than before, which surprises me, but perhaps I misremembered it in my awe at being in Old Prell. Gwenna flicks on the lantern atop her staff—as she's navigator this time—and holds it aloft, looking around.

My heart flutters in my throat once more at the sight of the glory of the ancient city. Of the toppled columns and the broken cobblestones beneath our feet, and the lichen that grows over everything. What I wouldn't give to wander through all the tunnels and just drink it all in. Kipp pulls out his blade and eyes the tunnel behind us, taking a step forward and then patting his belt, frowning. He turns to Lark and then makes a gesture.

"Flags. Right. We forgot our flags," Lark says. "To mark our place."

"No flags tonight," Mereden points out, tugging the hood of her cloak over her tight curls. She has no cap over her head this evening, because we felt it would be too obvious if we ran into anyone else in the guild. "Just ask Magpie."

"The guild would have flags down here anyhow," I say, touching a series of glyphs carved into the wall. It looks familiar, but it's hard to tell for certain. "To ensure no one else digs in a spot that's under investigation. Are we sure this is the right place?"

"Hmm, let me check. Wait right here," Magpie says.

She turns and heads down the narrow tunnel, and then bends over. There's something glowing in her hand, and she draws a line across the tunnel floor with it, leaving an iridescent mark on the stone. "Sorry, Lark."

"Sorry for what?" Lark asks, pushing back to where her aunt is.

We move along after Lark, trained to walk together, and when she heads for the chalk line, she's immediately thrown backward, as if she's run into a wall. With a yelp, Lark stumbles, caught by Mereden and myself. I gasp in shock even as Lark struggles to her feet.

Magic.

Something's not right.

"What the fuck is that?" Lark demands, dusting off her jacket.

Magpie holds up the chalk from her spot on the other side of the line. "Magic, of course." She turns to the portal master. "You can send him down now."

I approach the chalk line, cautious. The closer I get to it, the more my hair stands up from my nape, the air humming around us. I poke the butt of my staff against the chalk line, only to have it jerk violently backward in my grasp.

"It's a spell," I tell the others.

"No shit," Magpie says. "And you the great scholar."

I ignore her, turning to the others. "The chalk must produce an entrapment spell. We can't break free without her rubbing the line out on her side."

Lark struggles out of Mereden's grasp and surges forward again. "What the fuck, Aunt Magpie?"

Magpie spreads her hands in mock apology. "I told you not to tie in with them, Lark darling. But you chose them over me. That's fine. I'll drink a bottle in your name." She turns her head as the portal shimmers and two new men come through.

I gasp, stunned, as Barnabus arrives to stand at Magpie's side, one of his soldiers close by him and holding a crossbow. "What's going on?"

Barnabus smirks at me. "I made your teacher a better offer, that's what's going on." He holds his hand out and Magpie drops the chalk into it. "Do you like my new toy?"

"If I say no, does it change anything?" I'm furious at him, of course, but my old training kicks in and I stiffen my back, putting on my bored-holder-lady expression, the one I wear at every social gathering. "You need to let us go."

"I don't *need* to do anything." Barnabus tosses the chalk between his hands, then lifts it into the air, admiring the carved handle that holds the delicate piece of chalk in place. "Though it is rather fortunate that one of my other teams located this just yesterday. It makes holding you captive far too easy."

"Is that what this is, then?" I ask, drawing myself up indignantly. "A hostage situation? Let the others go and you and I can figure out the problems between us."

Barnabus just rolls his eyes and flips the chalk (and holder) once more, unbothered by my demand.

Lark takes another step forward to the barrier, only for Kipp to pull her back again. "Why are you doing this, Aunt Magpie?" She's clearly heartbroken. "I don't understand!"

"How do you not understand?" Magpie snarls, her expression full of venom. She gestures at Barnabus. "He's paying me a great deal of coin, and I need security! The guild is going to remove my contract with them unless my team graduates this year, and I'll lose my commission. And we all know your Five won't pass the tests. There's no way."

Lark flinches. I just glare at our teacher. Former teacher. She's sold us out.

"Don't look at me like that." Magpie rolls her eyes. "At least with this lordling's money, I can drink myself to death without worrying about keeping a roof over my head."

"It's not all about you." I tell myself to be calm and collected, even as my hands curl into fists. "How can you betray Hawk like this?"

"I'm not betraying him! I'm looking out for me. The two have nothing to do with each other!" She focuses her angry gaze on me. "And you. You spoiled, foolish twit. Do you have any idea how hard I had to work to get my spot in the guild? Do you know how many years I suffered through bullshit before anyone took me seriously? You can't saunter in as some rich girl and expect the same treatment just because you'll suck a Taurian's cock. It takes more than that to be a damned guild master!"

I gasp at her words, stung. This is the person I idolized for so long? "I looked up to you!"

"Then that's your mistake," Magpie says. "All I've ever wanted was to get paid."

Barnabus clears his throat. "Are you ladies done jabbing at each other? Because I'd like to talk with my fiancée."

"I'm not your fiancée," I retort. "You can't force me to marry you."

"I know this, seeing as how you hooked yourself to the first male who glanced in your direction. A Taurian, Aspeth? Truly?" He looks revolted. "Was a human cock no longer big enough for you? Is that it? You have to go for something a little more titillating?"

"You're both horrid and disgusting. Hawk is worth ten of you." I flick my fingers at them. "Both of you together."

"Yes, well, you'll be pleased to know I'm no longer interested in marrying some bull-man's leavings." Barnabus pockets the chalk and its magical holder and pats his clothing, reassuring himself that it's in place. "In fact, you can stay married to him for all I care. I'm willing to let bygones be bygones . . . so long as you give me the artifact ring you found."

I go still, because of all the demands I thought he'd make, I'd somehow forgotten about the artifact ring. How is it that he's imprisoned us in the tunnel without stealing it for himself first? How is it that he hasn't figured out that I'm penniless and he doesn't need it to take over Honori? Or does he just think I'd steal willy-nilly from the guild? That might be the most insulting part of this, that he doesn't know me at all. "I don't know what you're talking about."

"The ring," he enunciates, his voice echoing off the narrow stone walls of the tunnel. "The one you found in the tunnel. Magpie told me all about it."

I shoot a dirty look at my teacher, and Lark makes another outraged noise. Magpie ignores both of us.

"I want the ring," Barnabus repeats again, pointing at the floor. "Take it off and kick it over here."

Something doesn't add up. "Why not come and take it, coward?"

He sneers at me. "I'm no fool. Your maid told Magpie all about the curse."

Curse? What is he talking about?

In that moment, Gwenna steps on my foot. "It's true," she says to me. "I told Magpie all about how it can't be transferred to another owner without permission once it's been worn. That the runes on it are quite clear about that."

Quick thinking, Gwenna. I could kiss her for being so smart. She anticipated trouble and lied to keep the artifact safe.

"Oh, you told them?" I pretend to be annoyed. "Well, it changes nothing. I still won't transfer the ring's power over to you, Barnabus. No matter how many times you ask."

He keeps smiling. "It's useless to you. We can make a bargain."

I'm sure we can, one that involves me selling out my family or my friends. Or both. "It's useless to you, too."

"Yes, but I have the means to get the other half." His smile grows broader. "I can have a team scouring every drop by morning, and you're stuck here in this tunnel. You might as well give up."

"You're right," I say neutrally. "Fine. You want the ring in exchange for letting us go?"

"I want the word of power, too."

"It's not a word, it's a gesture. Here, I'll show you." And I make the rudest, crudest gesture I can think of.

Lark snorts with laughter.

Barnabus's expression grows cold. "I see you choose to be a child about this." He shrugs. "Fine. We can pull it off your dead body in a few weeks once the unfortunate cave-in has been dug out."

Unfortunate cave-in—?

I eye the ceiling. It's close, but it looks solid.

When I look back at Barnabus, he takes the crossbow from his retainer. Too late, I see it has a strange, rounded end. I've only ever seen that in a war treatise of some kind, and they were always filled with some sort of explosive. . . .

Oh no.

The moment I realize it, Magpie ducks her head, racing away.

Lark flings her shield over us.

"Explosive!" she howls.

The rock walls of Old Prell move and shake above us, and then something hits my head. Everything goes black, and the tunnel collapses around us.

THIRTY-SIX

HAWK

SOMETHING ABOUT THIS is all wrong.

I can't quite shake the feeling of wrongness even as I continue to dig in Drop Twenty-Seven for hours on end. It's definitely collapsed in on itself—even now there's the occasional rumble of stone indicating movement in the rocks. Cave-ins happen all the time. It's a hazard of the job. I've dug out dozens in my time . . . but something isn't adding up and I can't quite figure out what.

It bothers me as I dig through rock, tossing boulders into the magic portal held open nearby by Master Siskin's partner. He's not as high ranked as Siskin, but Siskin shares his toys with his lover, and so Tern has been here at my side all night long, keeping the portal open so I can remove the rubble.

The thing that strikes me the oddest about this is that we're the only two here.

Cave-ins are always a threat when dealing with the cavernous ruins. Old Prell fell into the earth, and so it stands to reason that it would keep collapsing in on itself without much prompting. That's not the strange part. It's that no one else has arrived to assist. The other Taurians I normally work with on rescues are out of the city, of course, but someone else should be taking their place. There should be a handful of us here, trying to keep it together despite the moon's near rising.

If someone is in danger—buried under the rubble—shouldn't someone care enough to send more than just one tired Taurian down into the tunnels?

But perhaps they're just late in showing up. I continue in my rescue efforts, tossing great slabs of rock out of the way and rolling a boulder into the portal. I work until I'm sweating and covered in a fine layer of dust, and then pause to take a sip from my canteen. As I do, I glance over at my silent, yawning companion. "Where are the others?"

He blinks at me, sleepy. "What others?"

"The others coming to assist with the rescue."

"Oh." He ponders for a moment. "I don't know. There are usually more Taurians for a rescue, aren't there?"

"Usually," I agree. I wipe my brow and get back to work, but I can't shake the niggling feeling that something about this is off. After a while, I notice dawn light streaming in through the portal, and still no one has arrived to help. The rocks are getting larger, to the point that even a Taurian can't lift them, and the only other one here, Tern, isn't going to be much help, physically. I wipe my sweating face and fight the feeling of annoyance rising through me, because mistakes happen. Paperwork gets lost. "The rest of the rescue team still hasn't been diverted this way."

"It does seem so," Tern agrees. "Someone should be coming by to spell us."

I nod, eyeing the collapsed tunnel. I don't want to leave if someone is trapped in there, but at the same time, I can't dig out the entire thing on my own. "What team is assigned to this drop again?"

"Grosbeak's team," he says immediately, pulling out a parchment roster and eyeing it. "His Five fledglings."

A fledgling team. A nightmare scenario. "And no one is here to dig them out except us?" I take the roster from him and read down it carefully. Surely not everyone is deployed in the tunnels because of the lordling and his bounty? I'm used to being called in on rescue missions but not everyone goes into the ruins. Even so, I scan the list, looking for a team that might be working a nearby drop so they can come assist . . . and then I pause. "Grosbeak's Five are at Drop Seven. This is Drop Twenty-Seven."

"But—it's caved in? This is the right drop tunnel." Tern leans over my shoulder, looking at the roster, and points a dusty finger at the bottom of the page even as the portal sputters out behind him. "They're listed on here twice."

So they are. I skim the roster list, looking for anyone else who might have been assigned to this particular drop, but there's no one else. Just Grosbeak's Five, and they might not even be here. "Who exactly reported this tunnel collapse?"

Tern digs in his pocket for the message and holds it up to the lantern we have sitting on a nearby rock. "Ah. Here it is." He glances up at me. "The tunnel collapse was reported by Guild Master Magpie."

Magpie? What's she up to now?

And why does she want me out of the way?

ASPETH

I wake up to a small, sticky hand patting my face, and a throbbing pain above my ear.

Everything aches. I open my eyes, whimpering when it's just as dark with them open as it is with them closed. The tunnel collapsed on us. Magpie turned against us. Barnabus tried to kill us. Maybe he succeeded. Maybe I'm in the death god's entrance to hell.

The small, sticky hand pats my cheek again. "Kipp? Is that you?"

This time he gives me a little squeezing pinch on the cheek, like an old grandmother. I suppose that's him reassuring me. I flex a hand, and rocks clatter away from my fingers. Everything seems whole, if a little bruised. I think that's a good sign. I'm lying against something warm and soft.

I try to sit up, only to smack my forehead against rock. "Ow!"

Kipp pats my cheek again, and then I hear the sound of rummaging. There's the click of a striker, and then light flares. Kipp has a stub of a candle in his hand, and he holds it up.

It's worse than I thought.

The pocket we're in is surrounded by tumbled rock. The rocks themselves are oppressively close to my face, and if I sit upright, I'll be face-first into the rubble. I stretch an arm out and touch a toppled Prellian column, against which Lark's shield and Kipp's house and my quarter-staff have created a kind of triangle of protection for us. The top of Kipp's shell house is broken into a dozen pieces, but the little guy seems none the worse for wear. He holds the candle stub up to my face, peering, and I realize that my spectacles are broken.

For some reason, that makes me angrier than anything. Does Magpie realize how fucking hard it is to find spectacles that fit just right? Ugh. I pull them off and toss them aside, and as I do, I notice I'm lying atop another person.

Shit. Shit, shit, shit.

I scramble away as best I can—not easy considering that the room I have is less than the size of my clothing trunk—and try not to panic. Gwenna and Mereden are under Lark, who tried to protect them with her body. I roll Lark off of them and she groans, her clothing torn. We wake each person up as best we can. Gwenna has a bloody nose and Mereden is scratched up, her ankle swollen. Lark clutches her ribs but considering that we've just survived being buried in a cave-in, we're doing amazing. "Is everyone all right?" I manage, wiping at a strand of blood trickling down my cheek. "No one trapped under anything?"

"I'm trapped under a shit ton of rock with four other people," Lark jokes, and then winces, pressing a hand to her waist. "Oh, fuck, that hurts."

"Let's not think about the shit ton of rock, all right?" I offer. "Let's think about how we can get out of here."

"We can't," Gwenna states, holding a length of ripped sleeve under her nose to stem the bleeding. She hunkers down between myself and Mereden, and we're all crammed in here like matchsticks in a tinderbox. "If we move something, we could collapse the entire tunnel on us and die for sure."

"Well, we can't stay here." Already the rocks just overhead feel oppressive. I want to stretch my legs and stand upright, and the longer I can't do it, the more I feel the intense need to do so. I focus on Kipp and his tiny candle, already burning down to nothing. "Let's think. Where are our supply bags?"

"Buried," Mereden says in a small voice. "Just like us. I can examine everyone but I don't have anything to treat you with."

"It's fine. We're fine." I keep a bright smile on my face. "I'm good, but look over the others."

Mereden does a quick check, but there's nothing to be done for Gwenna's busted nose or Lark's ribs. They need a guild healer.

"I'm good," Lark says. "Had worse in a bar fight."

"I just want out," Gwenna moans.

"We're working on it." Gwenna whimpers with distress at my reassurance, and I reach over and grab her hand, holding it tightly. "Kipp. What else do you have in your house? Anything we can use for light?"

He scrambles up to his shell again and digs into the side, squirming his way under a broken piece and tossing out a few more bits. There's a bag full of stale cookies, a bundle of string, a handful of nuts, and one more tiny candle. We have no water to drink, very little food, and I'm trying hard not to think about how much rock could possibly be over us.

"Thank you," I tell Kipp, and hand the cookies to Mereden and Gwenna, because they're both looking shaky. "You two eat these."

I expect Lark to complain, but she doesn't. Even clutching her ribs, she seems more settled than both Gwenna and Mereden, who look like they might fall apart at any moment.

I keep talking in order to seem like I have everything under control. "I think with the nuts and a bit of ripped fabric, we might be able to make a candle that will burn longer. In Prell, they used nut oil in their candles and that's why it left greasy smears on a lot of the paint in the ruins—well, it isn't important. The important thing is that we're not going to run out of light, all right? We'll figure something out."

Lark nods. "Once I catch my breath I can try to see if any of the rocks are loose."

"No, you stay where you are. Kipp, are there any cracks in the rocks that you can squeeze through?" I shift my weight, nearly hitting my head on the oppressively low ceiling again. "If so, see if you can figure out the best way out. If not, just let me know. We've got options."

"Options?" Gwenna lets out a hysterical bark of laughter. "What fucking options do we have? Die fast or die slow?"

"No," I say firmly. "First of all, if we can't find a solution out of the . . . rubble, then we wait here." I don't use the words *cave-in* or *buried alive* even though it's the first thing that comes to mind. Since Gwenna is still panicky, I decide to go further with my lies. "There was a team about thirty years ago that lived in the tunnels for a month before they were rescued. They ate moss and drank trickles of water that came in through the rock. We'll be fine. People survive in the ruins all the time. We can wait for rescue."

It's not true, of course. I'm certain teams are rescued from dire cave-ins regularly but after a certain amount of time passes, it's generally assumed that all are lost. I've read plenty of dramatic stories about such tragedies but I keep that to myself.

Kipp nods and points at the rocks, then heads into the jumble, squeezing between a few precariously perched stones even as the stub of the candle flickers and wavers. The rope around him slithers, and Lark hastily unties it from her waist, wincing the entire time. He's a hero, Kipp. When we get out of here, I'm making sure that everyone knows how amazing he is. He's kept his cool all this time, and I need to do the same. So I take the flickering stub of the candle and light the taller one. "Everyone untie and give Kipp some slack to explore. Gwenna?"

"Yes?" Her voice sounds shaky even as she unties the rope at her waist.

"Do you think you can dowse for us if Kipp isn't successful?"

She makes another hysterical sound in her throat. "Dowse for what?"

"For whatever tugs you," I say, keeping my tone even and soothing. "If you can dowse for a way out, that's perfect. If not, just dowse for an artifact and we'll see where that takes us. We're just considering our options."

"Options. Right. Okay." She sniffs and another line of blood drips from her nose. "Shit."

"You're all right. We're all a mess right now." I reach over and give her hand a squeeze.

The rope at my waist jumps. I've been so busy coaching the others that I've forgotten to untie myself. "Sorry Kipp," I call out. "Hang on!"

It jerks out of my hands and snags against the rocks. Pebbles rain down on us. Gwenna screams and holds on to me, and just then, the entire ceiling overhead seems to shift and groan.

Oh, Lady Asteria, we're going to die. "Under the shield," I call out. "Everyone, try to get your head under the shield—"

The largest of rocks sinks inward, tumbling down, and I scream, waiting for the rest of Old Prell to collapse over us. Instead, Kipp bounces down and brushes dust and pebbles out of my hair, and I look up into a yawning cavern of darkness.

We're out.

Sort of.

THIRTY-SEVEN

HAWK

The Conquest Moon

OUTSIDE, I CAN see the rounded body of the Conquest Moon looming in the early dawn skies. The hand of the god will be fully upon me tonight. There's no more time to waste. I need to find Aspeth and prepare her for our mating. There's still time for me to get a charm for her, still time to find a cream to ease my way into her tight, virginal body. . . .

But when I find Magpie seated in the dormitory kitchen, sharing drinks with a well-dressed stranger, all logic vanishes. I think of the frustrating night I just spent digging in a tunnel, and for some mucking reason, it looks like she's celebrating.

Something's wrong.

"Who the fuck is this?" I demand as I storm in. "Why are you drinking again?"

She stares at me in open-mouthed surprise. "What are you doing back so early?"

A hot, hostile anger comes over me. "Early, am I? Exactly who am I supposed to be digging out, Magpie?"

"How would I know?"

She feigns ignorance, but it only makes me angrier. I recognize the full-throttle anger churning in my gut, but I'm helpless to stop it. I storm over to my quarters, but Squeaker is waiting there by her empty bowl. She howls at the sight of me, plaintive, and circles around her empty food dish. There's no sign of Aspeth.

I return to the kitchen, where Magpie is fighting back a smirk. "Where are the others? Where is my wife?"

"Your wife," the man sneers. "Your marriage has been annulled, bull-man. Not that it should have happened in the first place."

Red floods my vision. "Aspeth wouldn't do that."

"She's not here, though, is she?" He sounds so very confident.

"And where is she?" I demand again.

"Left," Magpie says, slurring her words. No surprise, she's had too much to drink once more. "Poor little lady left town and went back to Daddy's hold."

It's a lie.

They're mucking lying to me.

Aspeth is infuriating and spoiled and hardheaded, but she's no deal-breaker. I think of last night in the alley, and how she'd looked up at me with such heated eyes. How she'd reached for me.

None of that was a lie . . . was it?

I think of Aspeth's soft expression as she gazed up at me. How she'd let me eat her soup as we talked. The nights we'd lain awake in bed while she petted her cat and told me about her excitement over joining the guild.

Her cat.

Squeaker's bowl was empty, the cat indignant. Aspeth would never abandon her cat. Aspeth would never let it skip a meal.

I eye Magpie and the oddly triumphant stranger, and then I move forward. I grab Magpie by her brown master's jacket and haul her to her feet.

"Wh–what? What are you doing?"

"I'm bringing you both to the Royal Artifactual Guild," I announce. "You can tell Rooster what you've done to your fledglings."

THIRTY-EIGHT

ASPETH

BARNABUS'S STUPID CHALK has saved us.

We climb carefully from the rubble, retrieving our packs as we do. On the other side of the chalk line, the cavern is destroyed, the rocks blocking the tunnels so large it would take ten Taurians to budge them. On this side of the chalk line, there's nothing but a cascade of slightly larger rocks, most of them moved with just a bit of shoving. Most of the cave-in seems to have occurred on the other side of the chalk line, with its invisible shield protecting us even as it prevents us from leaving.

Once we're free of the rocks, I suck in a deep breath and try not to think about all the rock still pressing on us from overhead. Of how nothing but a narrow tunnel is between us and death. I'm going to have nightmares about rocks and cave-ins at some point, but for now, I'm forcing myself to think of other things. "All right, ladies and lizard. Let's get our packs on and rope together again. Kipp, you take sword, Lark, you're our shield, and Mer, you're our healer. Gwenna, are you good with navigating?"

"What do you mean?" she asks, giving me a tired, blank look in the flickering candlelight. Our lantern was smashed in the collapse, and we're still down to only a candle for light, but at least we're not buried. "We should just sit and wait."

"That was the plan before," I announce. "Now the plan is that we're going to find our own way out."

"Why can't we just wait for someone to come and get us?" Mereden looks up from wrapping her ankle with strips of gauzy bandages. "It's almost Hawk's Conquest Moon time, right? He's going to come looking for you."

I flinch at her words. It is the time of the Conquest Moon, true. And the one thing that has been impressed upon me is that once it arrives, Hawk won't have control. Even now, he might not be sensible. He might be in bed with a stranger even as I rot in the Everbelow. My heart aches at the thought. "We can't assume. We can't assume anything. Not with Magpie and Barnabus working together. How do we know that she didn't tell someone we left the city?"

"But the drop—"

"Is an unlucky one," Lark points out. "No one's going to sign up for Thirteen unless everything else is taken. It could be weeks before it gets out of the guild's paperwork piles anyhow. It might take the investigation team a while to get to it, and we don't know what my aunt is telling them."

"Or Barnabus. He's kind of shitty," Gwenna adds. She looks over at me. "No offense."

"None taken. He *is* kind of shitty." I put my hands on my hips, and a shooting pain jolts up my arm. I must have tweaked it in the cave-in. Doesn't matter. I move my hand from my hip and gesture at our surroundings. "For all we know, they've been planning things for a while. This is Drop Thirteen again, right? Even though they wanted the other half of the ring, they dropped us here. The way I see it, they either want to collect the paired rings from our dead bodies, or they dumped us here because it's easiest for their lies. They can pretend ignorance, say that we acted without Magpie's permission and crept down here."

"Never mind that she was all in," Lark mutters.

"Never mind that," I agree. "We have to assume no one is coming for us. So what's the best thing we can do?"

"Find another artifact," Mereden replies, voice wavering. "Hopefully one that leads us out of here and somewhere safe."

Exactly. "And the best time to get started is now." I glance around the mess of the cavern. "So what do we have here that we can use as a dowsing rod?"

We dig around in our packs to cobble together a reasonable substitute. The one Gwenna had is busted in three places, and it doesn't seem to react when she holds it. We end up finding a triangular-shaped piece of Kipp's broken house and hack at it until it vaguely forms a Y-shape. Kipp winces when Gwenna picks it up, his expression one of longing. I want to comfort him, but I don't even know where slitherskins get their houses from in order to replace his. We'll figure it out after we're free, I decide. For now, we've got to tackle our immediate problems.

"Here," Gwenna tells me, taking me aside. She pulls a ribbon from over her head and holds the ring out to me. "You might as well take this. It's yours anyhow."

I manage a small smile, clasping my hand around it. The ring has been covered in a crude leather pouch with a stylized lizard drawn upon it. Gwenna said she disguised it so people would think it was a slitherskin good luck charm. I tuck the small leather bag under my breast and relace my corset.

To think, days ago the ring brought me so much relief. Today, it's just another problem I have to solve on top of the mounting pile of problems. "So much trouble. I hope it's worth it."

"Don't beat yourself up," she tells me.

"How can I not? I've risked everyone's lives." I gesture at the wreckage around us. "If we make it back alive, the guild will have our heads."

"We knew the risks, Aspeth," Gwenna says, her expression serious. "We know you're not doing this for your gambler father. You're doing it for everyone who lives at Honori Hold and has no idea that he's putting their lives in danger. You're doing it for the cook, and the stable boy, and my mother, who still works at the hold. You're doing it for them and you're doing it to protect yourself. This isn't a bad thing, Aspeth. I know it's stealing, but you're stealing for a good cause. It's not a bad thing to try to help people other than yourself. Isn't that why the guild started? They wanted to bring magical objects to people to help them with their day-to-day lives."

She makes it sound so noble. I'm truly just trying to stay alive . . . and

selfishly, to keep my father alive because I don't want to be the one running the hold.

We rejoin the others, and Kipp gives us a pained look at the piece of
his house in Gwenna's hands. At Kipp's expression, she gives him a sol-
emn nod. "I'll take good care of it, I promise, and then it's yours again."

Kipp nods, tapping his chest in what looks like an encouraging gesture.

Gwenna holds the rod out and waits.

We wait, too.

After a long moment, she lowers it. "I . . . I don't feel anything."

"Maybe close your eyes and concentrate?" Mereden asks.

"Right." Gwenna closes her eyes, focusing, and the "dowsing rod" in
her hand jumps to life. It points deeper into the tunnels in the opposite
direction of the cave-in.

"It's working," I breathe. "Keep your eyes closed."

"Oh, sure, easy for you to say," Gwenna mutters, but she does as I
suggest. "Someone lead me around, please." I move to one side and Lark
to the other.

"Of course it's pointing deeper into the tunnel," Lark says. "There's
nowhere else to go."

"If you have a better idea, now is the time," I say.

Kipp just gives us all an exasperated look.

"Fine. I'm shutting up." Lark hands Mereden her staff. "Let's go. You
need help walking?"

"I'm all right." Mereden leans heavily on the staff but manages to
limp along, favoring her ankle. I stay at Gwenna's side, the others clus-
tering as close as the rope lead will allow. We move together down the
rough-hewn cave, progressing in a slow but steady fashion.

Then, as luck would have it, the candle sputters out.

I curse. Mereden whimpers.

Gwenna pauses in place, her eyes still tightly closed. "What is it?
What's going on?"

"We're in the dark," I explain. "Candle went out."

"Can I open my mucking eyes now?"

"Not yet! Don't lose the trail," I tell her. "Let me see if I can make
another light somehow."

Kipp touches my leg, and when I automatically glance down, I notice that the front of my corset is glowing with a soft red light. I fumble in the front of my chemise, digging out the ring. It's fallen out of the leather pouch, and the moment it clears my clothing, reddish light spills all down the cavern, casting ominous shadows.

"I don't know if that's better or worse," Mereden says.

"Worse," Lark chimes in. "Definitely worse."

I hold the ring aloft and eye the tunnels. They look like they're washed in blood, but there's light, at least. "Hush," I tell them. "It beats stumbling around in the darkness."

"Does it?" Lark asks. "Does it really?"

I ignore her and tie the ring and its ribbon to the top of my staff and hold it aloft, letting it light up the immediate area. "Let's keep going. Gwenna is onto something."

Gwenna continues to shuffle ahead with slow steps, the divining rod jumping in her hands. Her eyes are still tightly closed. "I don't want to lose the trail." She wanders ahead, moving at a snail's pace. "You guys are with me, right?"

"We're right here."

The tunnel twists and turns, then finally splits. Gwenna jerks to the right, letting the divining rod lead her, and we continue at her side, while the ruins of Old Prell spread out around us.

The rod immediately jerks in her grasp and turns once more, and Gwenna leads us down another tunnel. It abruptly opens up into a large chamber where the ceiling soars higher overhead, propped up by more of the fluting columns that the Prellians were so fond of. Ruins are collapsed along the walls, tumbling amidst the rocks, and water drips down from above. "This looks like an old temple," Lark points out, her voice echoing. "Were we here before?"

I shake my head, because I'd remember something like this. We must be deeper into the drop than before, or we've gone another way.

The divining rod continues to guide us past the front of the temple, and pauses near the stairs. I swing the strange red light toward the stairs, and see what looks like a lump of fabric of some kind.

Oh no.

"Please tell me we need to go up the stairs," Lark whispers.

"Wait here," I tell her, and step forward, because my stomach is in knots, and I'm pretty sure that's not a lump of fabric. Not with my luck.

"We can't wait here," she points out, touching my arm. "We're roped together, remember?"

I keep forgetting. Kipp steps forward, drawing his weapon, and he seems dainty and fragile without the rounded shell of his house on his back. We creep forward as a cluster, and all the while Gwenna's pointer continues to direct us right toward the pile of rags, which is taking on a larger, more solid shape the closer we get.

Leaning the light in as we approach, I don't know if I'm the first one to see the guild insignia on his shoulder, but I suck in a breath, and then a moment later, the others do, too.

"That's not good," Gwenna says in a trembling voice. "Can I look now?"

"You might as well," I say. "I don't know if you're pointing out artifacts, but you found something, all right."

Her eyes open and she blinks rapidly, adjusting to the strange red light. "What did I find?"

"A dead guy," Lark says. "Your second one. You *sure* you're dowsing for artifacts?"

THIRTY-NINE

ASPETH

THE DEAD MAN is a guild man, evident by the uniform he's wearing that matches ours. He's also recently dead, evident from the spreading stain of blood under his clothing. He's face down, and no one wants to turn him over.

"I thought your aunt said no one in the guild was going to be hurt by the cave-in," Gwenna says to Lark, panicked.

"I thought so, too!" Lark looks just as worried. "Do you think our plan got him killed?"

The thought makes me queasy. Even so, something's not adding up. "Unless they knifed him first, he wouldn't be bleeding like that from a cave-in. Plus there's no fallen rocks around here." I gesture at the dead guy. "We should turn him over and see how he died. Just in case."

"I'm not doing it!" Lark backs away a step.

Mereden rolls her eyes. "I'm the healer. I'll do it. Maybe he needs healing. Or something." She rolls her shoulders and then takes a deep breath.

Then she moves forward and squats next to the dead man, the reddish light casting lurid shadows over everything.

"He's not breathing." She looks up. "I'm going to turn him over. If you're squeamish, look away."

To our credit, no one looks away. Mereden grabs him by the shoulder and hefts his weight over to the side, rolling him onto his back.

I suck in a breath as his face is revealed. Not because I know him, but because it looks like he's been chewed on. His nose is almost gone, and the rest of him looks equally unpleasant. His uniform is torn and there's blood on everything.

Mereden sits back on her heels, eyeing the dead man. "This wasn't a cave-in."

"Not unless the rocks got hungry," Lark agrees. Kipp just shakes his head sadly.

"Ratlings, then," I tell them. They're the reason everyone carries weapons when excavating, but somehow it's never occurred to me until now that we might run into them. Everything has been so quiet in the tunnels themselves, and we haven't seen anything larger than a spider.

To be fair, the spiders *were* rather large.

But now the shadows take on a more ominous look. "What do you think he was doing down here alone?" I ask, clutching my staff a little closer to me. "Where's his Five?"

Mereden gets to her feet, dusting off her clothes. "You heard what Magpie said. They were going to close down this particular drop until the guild decided what to do with it. Maybe the guild sent him down to guard things."

"Alone?" Gwenna asks, skeptical.

"Almost all of the Taurians are out of the city," I point out. "They must have sent a repeater here to keep an eye on the drop, assuming there was no danger."

Mereden shakes her head. "Horrible." She leans over the dead man and crosses his arms over his chest in dedication to Asteria, so the goddess will look out for him in Romus's hells. Then she pauses. "Artifact?"

"What?" I blink at her, not following.

"He's supposed to have an artifact, right?" Mereden turns to Gwenna. "That's what we were dowsing for, yes? Should we check his pockets? It feels wrong."

"What, because he's dead?" Lark counters. "What do you think we're doing down here? We're robbing the dead constantly. That's what the guild *does*."

She's right, I finally admit to myself. We are tomb robbing in a sense, because those who died when the city fell are still here. Even so, it's different when someone's centuries dead versus a death from a few hours ago . . . isn't it? We must all be thinking the same because no one moves forward to check him.

With a huff, Kipp moves to the dead man and runs his small hands over the body, feeling his pockets and checking under his clothing. After a thorough investigation, he looks at us and shakes his head. Nothing.

"Maybe I'm dowsing wrong," Gwenna frets. "It's not as if we were educated on the proper way it works."

"I don't think it's supposed to work," I point out. "I think she gave us that to waste our time."

"Well, it's wasting our time if he's got no artifacts," Gwenna says. "All he's doing is giving us more things to worry over."

I move forward and check the body again, trying not to cringe at how strange the dead man feels under my grasp. It's a bit like clay—room-temperature clay—and if I think about it too hard, I'm going to be sick. But I check his pockets and under his guild uniform again, looking for trinkets or jewelry. His boots are plain, and there's nothing hidden in the soles. After I run my fingers along the curve of his ear looking for an earring, I sit back on my haunches. "Well, unless he swallowed the artifact, he doesn't have one. Is it possible that the dowsing rod is picking up the dead instead?"

"Who would possibly want to dowse for a dead man?" Gwenna makes a face.

"Someone who misplaced a body?" I get to my feet, brushing at my skirts. "I don't think we should stay here. If it's ratlings that chewed off his face—"

"What else would it be?" Lark interrupts.

I ignore that, because I don't know. "—then this area isn't safe. They could be here even now, watching us and waiting for us to let down our guard. Gwenna, your dowsing is leading us somewhere, at least. I propose we keep dowsing and see what we find."

She doesn't like that idea. "What if it keeps leading us to more dead guys?"

"Then we've got bigger problems." I move to pick up my staff again. "Let's get into formation once more, just like we've been taught. Sword and shield at the front, navigator in the center. Mereden and I will make up the back."

I wait for someone to argue, to point out that I'm not a leader. That I'm married to a teacher but not in charge myself. No one does, though. They just nod and we position ourselves.

When we're in place, with Kipp and Lark at the front of our group, Gwenna turns and gives me an uneasy look. "You're sure you want me to do this again? What if we're messing with something we don't understand? What if we're pissing off some sort of ancient magic that lives down here?"

She has a point, but I've never been the type to be overly worried about the gods. "We're not doing this to be cruel. We can make a big apology donation to the church once we're out of here."

"With what money?" Lark sputters. "I'm broke."

"We'll find something. That's a problem for the future." I nod at Gwenna, where she holds the makeshift dowsing rod. "Are you all right with doing this again?"

"Do I have a choice?"

"Do you want to stay here and wait for the ratlings to return?"

She sighs heavily and closes her eyes, holding the dowsing rod out in front of her again. "Please lead us to an artifact this time."

The thing practically jumps in her grasp. It immediately turns her, veering toward the wall, where the tunnel has been collapsed over time. There's no path there, no way forward, nothing but piles of rubble in front of us.

Kipp glances back at me and sheathes his blade, pulling out a tiny pickaxe instead.

I nod. "Looks like we're digging for a while."

WE PICK AT the rocks, loosening them, and roll the larger ones aside. As we do, a pattern starts to emerge, and I realize we've encountered a stone wall of some kind. It pains me to destroy it, but if getting to the other side will somehow get us out of here, we have no choice. Still, it looks as if Gwenna has pointed us in the right direction once more, a fact that elates me and unnerves Gwenna.

One of the stone bricks crumbles under Kipp's pickaxe, and open air appears with a puff of dust. It's dark inside, and as we push the crumbling rocks away, the entrance grows larger and larger. We've tapped into an antechamber of some kind.

Gwenna surges forward, the rod practically demanding that she go through the broken wall. "Should we go forward?" she asks, turning to me, and practically fights the stick in her hands. "Aspeth?"

I nod, grabbing my pack. I'd set it down nearby so I could dig. "Let's see where it takes us."

"If it takes us to a graveyard, I'm holding you personally responsible," she tells me.

"There were no Prellian graveyards. They buried their dead in an antechamber attached to the family's home so the spirits of the ancestors could be close and watch over them." I lean the staff over the hole, looking inside.

"That's horrifying," Mereden says, settling her pack on her shoulders.

I thought it was kind of sweet, but I guess it could be unpleasant, too. I swing the light from my staff forward, the red bleeding into darkness. "It doesn't look like a graveyard anyhow. It could be a shop of some kind." I turn to the slitherskin. "Lead the way, Kipp."

He nods, pickaxe moving to his belt and changing it out for his small sword once more. We move forward as a group, stepping into the hole and through to the other side. There's more rubble here, with part of the ceiling of the old building collapsed, and dust drifts down from above. Mereden waves a hand in the air, trying to clear it, and my heart thumps with excitement.

It's a ruin of Old Prell. Judging by the dust that's filtering in, we're probably the first ones to see this. I swing my staff toward the wall, where a mural of a family is made out of chips of tile. The family offers bowls of fruit to the gods, their depictions crude and stylized in the Prellian fashion.

It's incredible.

"Where are we?" Lark asks. "What is this building? What are these racks?"

"Racks?" I ask, turning my light source toward her. Sure enough, on the other side, there are fallen racks on the ground, and what look like niches carved out from the stone. They repeat in a regular fashion and the floor is covered in some sort of dark stain, along with coils of hammered metal on the floor. "Gwenna, try pointing the rod toward the floor and see if you pick up anything."

She lowers herself, her eyes still closed tight, and turns the rod in a half circle before shaking her head. "It's pulling me past. There's nothing here it wants."

"But it looks like a tomb," Lark points out.

"What?!" Gwenna's voice takes on a sharp edge. "Aspeth?"

"It's not a tomb," I say, trying to soothe her. I put a hand on her shoulder, because I can't imagine how terrifying this is with her eyes closed. "Like I said, the Prellians didn't make tombs like we do."

"It's a wine cellar," Mereden blurts suddenly. "This is where they kept their wine."

"How do you know?"

"My father has a similar cellar."

"So where's all the wine?" Lark demands. "If this is a wine cellar."

"The wood rotted away," Mereden says, nudging some of the metal hoops on the floor. "All it left behind are the cooping." She glances over at me. "My father is *really* into wine."

It makes sense. I nod. "I think you're right. And wherever Gwenna is leading us, it isn't here, so we keep going."

"So we're in a wine cellar," Lark says as Kipp pushes farther into the darkness. "Does that mean there's a wine store above us?"

"Or someone's estate. My father keeps his barrels in the cellar of our hold and he checks them daily." Mereden picks her way forward, the rope tugging at my waist as she moves. "There's bound to be a door somewhere."

The room is full of rubble that has to be climbed over, along with piles of dirt, leaves, and twigs (of all things). We guide poor Gwenna, grasping her arm. I thought it would be more impressive to find intact ruins, but this place is so full of rotted garbage that it's impossible to tell what we're climbing over mixed in with the rocks and debris. The darkness doesn't help, either.

Then Kipp points into the shadows at the far end of the massive chamber.

"There's a door," Lark calls out.

At the same time, Mereden shrieks and points in the opposite direction. "I just saw eyes!"

We all turn to where Mereden is pointing, and then I see them, too. Eyes, glowing red in the darkness. Something hisses and brushes past my skirts, and I bite back a scream, swinging my staff.

Ratlings.

"Friends, I think we've stumbled into a nest," Mereden whispers.

FORTY

ASPETH

T O THE DOOR," Lark barks out, pushing in front of me with her shield at hand. "You all go to the door and get it open. Kipp and I will protect you."

"We're roped together," Mereden cries. "We have to stay together!"

"I'm opening my eyes," Gwenna warns.

That makes me panic. We're so close to finding whatever it is it's pointing us to. "But the dowsing—"

"Fuck the dowsing," she says, fumbling for her sword. "It's no good if we're dead!"

A ratling jumps toward us from out of the shadows, and I shriek, batting at it with my staff. The light in the room wobbles wildly, causing the others to yell out. "Sorry!" I blurt. "It's on my weapon!"

"We need it to see!"

The ratlings swarm toward us. They're smaller than I thought they would be, each one about a head shorter than Kipp, who comes to my thigh. But there are so many of them, and they're aggressive. I can absolutely see why we need weapons training, now that we've run into the horrid little monsters. I try to keep my staff upright, flicking the butt of it at any ratling that gets near and kicking at them. Mereden has a shortened staff like I do, but she swings it fitfully, not connecting with anything. They circle around us in the midden heap that is the ruin, and Lark swings the shield outward, trying to bash anything that comes close.

"Door," I croak out when one tries to climb my skirts. "We need to go through the door."

"Hold the light steady," Lark barks out at me. "Get the door open if you can. We'll hold them off."

"I've got your back," Gwenna says, moving to stand behind me. "Do what you can, Aspeth."

Me? I'm supposed to open the door? But I can't use my weapon, so I suppose it does fall to me. I don't argue, just rush forward up the three steps to the massive square door that fills the archway. It's classic Prellian architecture and normally I would love to admire it except for the fact that it's made of some sort of tarnished metal and has a ring and a weird contraption for the door lock made of swivels and golden stems encrusted with jewels. I've never seen its like before, and I fumble with it for too long before making a sound of frustration and pulling my knife free from my hip holster and jamming it into the works. I think I've just broken a priceless mechanism of some kind but I can't find it in me to care.

I wedge it into the lock and tug on the door. It holds fast, and I scream in frustration.

Gwenna cries out as a ratling flings itself at her, and she jerks backward, the rest of us pressed together on the stairs falling together. "Kick it back!" Lark cries. "Kick all of them back!"

"Door!" Mereden pants. "Open the door!"

I jerk on the door again. "I'm trying! I'm trying!"

"Try harder!"

I groan in frustration, pulling on the door with all my might. It doesn't budge. Frustrated, I slam my hands on the heavy doors.

They fall open. Inward.

Oh.

"Inside!" I yell at the others, grabbing Gwenna by the waist and hauling her with me. We tumble inward, and the ratlings surge after us. Kipp stabs one, the creature screeching and thrashing on the floor as another grabs the wounded one and drags it backward. The others jump on it, attacking and biting it, and Lark shield-bashes another, then kicks it down the steps. The other ratlings chase it—looking for easy pickings—and we slam the door shut.

It immediately shakes, the force of several ratling bodies flinging themselves against the door.

"Barricade," I pant. "We need to barricade."

Mereden immediately shoves her staff through the metal handles of the door, preventing them from pushing it open. I nod agreement, wrapping my belt around the handles to double the effect.

"That'll stop them for a while," Lark says, catching her breath. She's still clutching her ribs, which is worrisome, but there's nothing we can do about it right now. "We need to find a better place to hide out."

"Where are we anyway?" Gwenna asks, wiping her brow. "Is this another wine cellar?"

I cast my light around, and my bad wrist sends a wave of pain up my arm. I ignore it, because there's nothing to be done. This room isn't a mess like the other one. It's a smaller chamber with a low ceiling and looks like it's been carved directly from stone. There's a stone couch at the far end of the room, and several more short ones carved into the walls, all of them littered with long-rotted debris. I move toward the one at the back of the strange chamber and touch the decaying flowers across the bench. They turn to dust, and I wipe it away. As I do, I see the glyphs written across the slab and groan.

"What?" Gwenna asks, turning to me in a panic. "What now?"

"Remember how Lark said we'd landed in a graveyard?" I ask, tired. "And I said no, the Prellians buried their dead in their houses because they wanted them close by?"

"NO," Gwenna cries, realization dawning on her. Kipp slumps, his hand on his snout.

I nod. "We found the crypt."

The others sag with defeat. I know how they feel. It's like we're being hit with bad luck over and over again. The door shakes and rattles once more, and everyone looks uneasy. Lark and Kipp untie their rope leads, and I don't blame them. I untie mine, too. We're not going anywhere.

"We need to reinforce the door," I point out. "I don't think there's another way out of here, but at least they can't get in."

"Yet," Lark adds.

"All right, all right, enough sunshine from you," Gwenna tells her. She holds the piece of shell back out to Kipp. "You can have this back. It's caused enough trouble for us so far."

He cradles it to his chest lovingly, stroking the hard, jagged edges.

The door jerks again.

"Reinforcements?" Mereden asks in a small voice.

"What can we use?" Gwenna looks around, frustrated. "I don't see any furniture and this is the one place there are no fallen rocks."

I hate myself even as I brush the dust off the bier at the end of the small crypt. "This has a stone lid. We can use it."

We all pause, considering.

"Ugh," Gwenna says after a moment.

"I know. I want to smack myself for even suggesting it, but I think whoever is in there would understand." I want to wring my hands but my wrist feels like loose shards of glass. "It feels wrong, but to me it's more wrong to let those things in."

"Even more wrong than wrong if we let them kill us," Mereden says. "I vote we grab it."

"Let's just do it and we'll apologize to the dead later," Gwenna says.

We five move to the side of the stone bier. The sides are high, the sarcophagus deep. The lid looks thin, barely two knuckles wide, but the weight feels near impossible. It takes all of us heaving and struggling to even lift it just enough to tilt it off to one corner. From there, we slide it to the floor and then continue to slide it over to the door. Once we lean the stone against the double doors, I collapse against it, exhausted.

Nothing's coming in through this, that's for damn sure.

"I could sleep for a week," Lark says dramatically, flopping her pack down beside me.

"Even with all these dead bodies around?" Mereden asks.

"Even with."

"Not me. I'm going to have nightmares about Magpie and Barnabus and rats," Gwenna states as she slides down to the floor across from us. Kipp nods, still petting his shell fragment.

"Magpie and Barnabus *and* rats? Aren't they all the same thing?" Mereden jokes. We groan, and she smiles with fatigue, looking over at Lark. "Sorry."

Lark waves a hand. "She's dead to me after this."

It's easy to say such things when you're in a bad place and hurting, but something tells me that Lark will have a harder time detangling herself from her aunt's influence, especially if Magpie remains our teacher. Just the thought makes me want to burst into hysterical laughter. To think I'd counted myself lucky—lucky!—that the famous Magpie was going to be teaching us.

I should have run for the hills.

Gwenna comes to sit next to me. "You all right, Aspeth?"

Her kind words make me shrug. I genuinely don't know if I am or not. Of all of us, I'd thought I had the most to gain or lose—but it's all the same when you're about to die, isn't it? The door shakes again, but it's clear nothing is coming through, not with the heavy slab parked against it and us leaning on it. The ratlings aren't leaving.

Well, neither are we. There's nowhere for our Five to go.

But Gwenna wants a better answer than a shrug. I can tell by her expression. "Just thinking about Hawk. If he finds us, he's going to be really, really mad."

"At us or at Magpie?"

"Both." I imagine his furious expression, his eyes narrowed and his nostrils flared, and instead of making me worry, I feel a bolt of longing so intense it hurts. I miss him. I wish he were here. Hells, I wish I were at his side instead of down here in the catacombs.

I've failed in my end of the bargain, too. I'd promised him I'd be his wife and partner through the Conquest Moon's grasp and instead ran away into the Everbelow only to get trapped. He won't have anyone for his Conquest Moon. He'll think I've betrayed him, that I haven't held up my part of our deal.

Poor Hawk will have to rely on sex workers. I picture him in the alley, women crawling all over him and begging for him to touch them, and something deep inside me dies.

I don't want anyone to touch him but me. He's mine.

It's just another thing I've ruined. Another person's life I'm casually destroying.

Strangely enough, it hurts more than everything else. Perhaps it's because I've had time to get used to the idea that I'd be hunted like an animal if I didn't get artifacts to save my father's hold. I've bedded down with that realization for months now. But the loss of Hawk is new, and it aches. I'd allowed myself to hope for something more.

That maybe after all the dust had settled, he'd still want to share a bed with me, still want to talk to me late into the night, just telling me about his day. . . .

"Hawk will understand," Gwenna says, interrupting my melancholy thoughts.

I don't think he will. Even now he's probably bending some woman over in an alley while we wait for ratlings or starvation. "He's not coming for us. It's the Conquest Moon. He's going to be . . . occupied for the next several days."

And cursing my name the entire time.

"And there are no other Taurians in the city right now. Not any guild ones." Lark leans against the slab heavily. "We're in for a long wait."

"But you do think someone will come?" Mereden asks.

"Oh, I do. They're bound to come after the ring." She waves a hand at the ring tied to the top of my staff, the red glow continuing to pour forth. "It could take a long time for them to find it—and us—though."

Kipp gets to his feet. He dusts off his tail, licks his eyeball, and then looks around the chamber. He moves to the far corner of the crypt and we watch him from our spot by the door, and when he pokes and prods at the walls, I finally speak up. "What are you doing, Kipp?"

He turns and gestures. It takes me a moment to realize he's indicating that he's looking for a way out.

I sit up. "This room is sealed. It has to be, or else the ratlings would be coming in. They've probably had a nest in that room for ages."

Kipp slumps, nodding. Then he shakes himself off and goes back to his prodding. To him, it doesn't matter. He's still going to look for a way out. He's not going to give up.

I'm filled with intense affection for the slitherskin. "He's right," I say. "We can't just give up. We should try to find a way out. I don't want to die here." I think of the tomb robber we'd found in the drop just a short time ago and hope that's not our fate. To come so close to success and yet die on the way.

The doors surge again, and Gwenna gets to her feet. "Two of you keep leaning against this at all times. We can take turns searching the room."

I get up, ignoring the throb of my bad wrist. "Mereden, why don't you come sit with Lark?" They're both the worst injured, though Lark would probably deny it. "I'll help Gwenna and Kipp look around."

They settle in against the slab, and Mereden's face looks tightly drawn in the shadows. Her curly hair is covered in pale dust, which I know she has to hate. She's particular about her hair.

"Hey," Lark tells her softly.

"What?" Mereden looks over at her, her expression weary.

"I need to get something off my chest just in case we don't get out of here."

Mereden sits up, her focus on Lark. "What?"

Lark leans in and gives Mereden the lightest, sweetest kiss on the lips. "That."

"Oh." Mereden touches her mouth, but she's smiling.

They make me ache with how cute they are. I bite back a smile of my own as they link their fingers, and I wonder about Hawk. Does he miss me right now? Or is he furious at me for disappearing right before the Conquest Moon after I'd promised him?

I wanted to keep that promise so badly, too.

With a miserable sigh, I shake out my now-torn skirts and stretch my legs, eyeing the crypt. Everything is awash in crimson shadows, making it seem far more ominous than it truly is. It's just a crypt of Old Prell, I remind myself. Where they honored the dead. Gwenna walks briskly to the far end of the crypt and leans over the open sarcophagus, and then turns back to me, her expression stunned.

Oh gods, what now?

"Aspeth? You need to see this."

FORTY-ONE

ASPETH

I MOVE TO GWENNA'S side, my heart hammering with dread at what she's found. Kipp crawls up to the corner of the sarcophagus, peering in, and I can hear Lark and Mereden stirring from their position by the door. My thoughts race as I try to figure out what it might be. More ratlings? The corpse of a fae? But no, they're all gone. They left this land when the god Milus was destroyed by the other gods. Maybe it's a spider. Maybe it's a whole nest of spiders.

But when I get to the side of the sarcophagus and peer in, the sight inside is strangely calming. It's a woman, a thousand years dead, her hands clasped over her heart in a benediction to Lady Asteria of the Skies. Her skin has withered tight against her skeleton, her long hair spread out about her in a decaying tangle. Her head is covered with a faded fabric and circlet, and her dress is of the same faded blue that must have been vivid and beautiful once. Her expression is serene, as if she's finding the afterlife as calm and enjoyable as promised, a hint of a smile on her tight, narrow lips. Preserving lichen coats the inside walls of the sarcophagus and is dusted over her corpse.

"She's beautiful," I say, and to me she is. She's slept here, undisturbed, for over a thousand years. Longer, because she would have been buried before Old Prell fell into the earth. "The blue of her dress is called Asterian blue, and they wore it in funeral rites so Asteria would smile upon them—"

Gwenna nudges me. "Save the history lesson. Look at her hands."

I look. I don't see it at first, because I'm too busy noticing all the wrong things, like the embroidery on the cuffs and the fact that her belt is crusted with jewels and her shoes probably are, too. She has bracelets on each wrist, and each one has glyphs on it, and I want to pull one off and interpret it even though that seems a terrible thing to do—

—and then I notice the ring.

Her hands are folded over her heart, one under the other. The one hidden underneath is wearing a ring, and the ring glows with a faint reddish light. It's the same shade as the rest of the light, which is why I didn't notice it at first.

I suck in a breath.

"Is that the same ring?" Gwenna asks. "The match to the one we have?"

"It could be."

But I know it is. I just know.

"Who do you think she was?"

"Someone important. She was buried with her jewelry instead of it being passed down to the family, which means they had plenty of wealth. Her dress is one of nobility, too." The inside of the sarcophagus has more glyphs along the edge, and I run a finger over them, deciphering as I go. "'My beloved wife. My other half. We will be together in Asteria's paradise. Wait for me.'" I touch the final symbol. "This is probably their family name, but it's unpronounceable in our language."

"How beautiful," Gwenna breathes. "He must have really loved her."

I eye the little smile of the dead woman and stupidly, foolishly, think of Hawk again. If we'd had time, would he have loved me like this woman was loved? I'm an idiot for even thinking about it right now, but I can't help it.

"May I see?" Mereden asks, getting to her feet and keeping her weight off her ankle.

Gwenna and I exchange places with Lark and Mereden, and as I lean against the slab, I run my fingers over the glyphs on it. I know they say the same thing.

> Beloved wife.
> Other half.
> Wait for me.

Lark sits on the edge of the sarcophagus and gazes down at the woman. Then she glances over at me. "You should take the ring, Aspeth."

Her suggestion feels like blasphemy. "I can't. It's hers." I glance over at my staff. "I should return the other to her. We don't know where her husband's body is, or if it's even here. At least we can reunite them that way."

"She's dead," Lark says, ever practical. "She has no use for two rings, much less one. You should take them and save your father's hold. I'm sure the dead would understand."

But the very idea feels wrong to me. Whenever I've thought about the guild, I've had such a romantic view of it. Of dashing through tunnels and uncovering artifacts just lying about, waiting to be retrieved. Now I know the reality. There are spiders the size of plates. There are ratlings and cave-ins and guild politics.

And the dead have faces. And we're robbing them.

I shake my head. "I don't think I can."

"Now is not the time to grow a conscience, Aspeth," Gwenna says, worried. "You said these rings were powerful. That you needed them. They're here. We're here. Might as well take them."

Take them. Become a grave robber.

Because that's what the guild is, right? It's got a fancy name, but it's just a bunch of people looting corpses. The thought hurts me down to my soul. Is this what I've idolized? Glamorized? Dreamed of all my life? I want to learn about Old Prell and the magics they used every single day. I don't want to strip the dead of their possessions. I don't know if I can do one without the other.

Mereden's voice rings out clear in the crypt. "My father would take the rings."

I sit up, looking over at her.

Her expression is calm but full of sympathy. "I understand how you feel, Aspeth. But my father would take the rings. He would break every finger from this corpse to take the rings. He would tear every bit of jewelry from her and not feel a bit of remorse. So would anyone else in the guild." She gestures at the sarcophagus. "You can put the ring with her and close the lid. And it will probably stay closed for a few more days, until someone comes to find us. And then they'll loot this place, because that's what the guild does. They'll end up sold separately or together to some rival of your father's and then where will you be?"

She's right. I hate that she's right.

"You can put them back and have a clear conscience and let Barnabus conquer your lands," Mereden continues in that practical voice of hers. "He'll put your family to the blade and Honori will become Chatworth Secondary, because there's already a Chatworth Hold. You can leave all of this for someone else, or you can take the rings and keep them together as they were intended to be." Her voice grows soft. "You can honor the people they came from."

"How do I do that?" I ask, aching.

"Name your kids after them," Lark suggests.

"I can't pronounce their names!"

"You'd better mucking practice," Lark replies, but there's a gentle note in her brusque words. "Make sure their names live on. Make sure their love lives on. What greater way to honor them?"

To my horror, I'm crying. I'm crying because I can be morally right and dead, or I can do something I know is wrong and save a father I don't even like and people who don't care about me. I cry because all I wanted was to save myself and have an adventure, and now I've doomed my friends at my side, and the Taurian I'm falling for is going to hate me.

So I cry.

And I take the rings. Because at the end of it all, I still want to live.

I inwardly thank her for the rings and commit her unusual name to memory. Andhrbrhnth. His name—Mhrfnswth. I'll remember them.

Then I put the rings together, holding them aloft, and the inscription glows.

To create the impenetrable mist wall about your domain,
wear both rings upon one finger and recite the word of power.

An endless mist wall about Honori Hold.

It's exactly what my father needs.

FORTY-TWO

HAWK

MINE.

   Find Aspeth. Knot her. Claim her.

Fill her belly with your seed.

The thoughts echo and repeat inside my foggy mind. I'd had the presence of mind to grab both Magpie and Barnabus before they could escape and bound them together before hauling them down to the guild, but the Conquest Moon has now risen and I can barely think. I'm dimly aware that I'm still at the guild hall. Still listening to the order question both Barnabus and Magpie, and all the while, the hand of the god tightens upon my cock, my knot throbbing.

Mine.

Mine.

Mine.

I don't have to look at the sky to know that the Conquest Moon is blazing across the heavens. I can feel it in every beat of my pulse.

Mine.

Mine.

Mine.

I move through a fog of red haze, my cock hard and throbbing. It's intolerable right now, but by tonight, I'll be insensible. I have things to do before I completely lose myself. I try to focus. I head to the nearest room and take myself in hand, imagining Aspeth's creamy breasts spilling from her bodice. I come hard, milking my knot as best I can, but it rises just as quickly once more, leaving me unsatisfied.

Fuck. This is going to be a long day.

I grab a curtain and rip it from its moorings, using it to clean off the mess I've made. Normal-thinking Hawk would be horrified. Conquest

Moon–crazed Hawk doesn't give a fuck. I tuck my sensitive cock into my pants and make my way back to the guild magistrate's office, where Magpie and Barnabus are being questioned separately.

Find her.

Knot her.

Fill her with your seed.

Mine. Mine. Mine.

Rooster appears in the fog and I snarl at him. He backs up a step, but remains close. "It appears that Drop Thirteen has been collapsed."

"She told you that?" *Mine. Mine. Mine.*

Find Aspeth.

Get her squirming on your knot.

"No. But we've done a cursory check of the drops and Thirteen looks as if it's been tampered with. We had a man stationed there and he hasn't reported back. This is terrible. Just terrible." He peers at me. "Are your eyes . . . red?"

Mine. Mine.

Aspeth. Where is Aspeth?

Aspeth's cunt clenching around my knot. Aspeth panting and rocking against me. The scent of her in my nose.

Find her.

Knot her.

". . . going?"

The word barely penetrates the haze. I look up and I'm outside. Not sure how I got there. Not sure why Rooster's following me. Bad idea to follow a Taurian on the edge of rut.

"Hawk?" he demands again. "Where are you going?"

Where am I going? I consider for a moment, but one word beats inside my head over and over again. *Mine. Mine. Mine.*

Mine.

I push past the humans. "Find Aspeth . . . Drop Thirteen."

"It's not safe. Wait until we can send a rescue team. . . ." He continues on, chattering, but I barely hear him. ". . . file an emergency order . . . no Taurians . . . patience . . ."

Mine.

Mine.

Mine.

"Not waiting," I grit out. "I'll find her." They say a Taurian with the god's hand upon him can pick up the smell of his female from a thousand *yents*. We'll see if that's true. Even now I'm sniffing the air, trying to find her scent.

". . . you . . . sent a missive to Lord Honori . . . in danger . . . coup . . . his daughter is here . . ." Rooster continues rambling, walking at my side even as I stride toward the drop zone. "Wait up," he calls. "Hawk—"

I turn. Grab him by his collar. Lift him into the air. Red hazes my vision. Red is everywhere. My pulse is in my ears.

Mine.

Mine.

"Are you trying to stop me from finding my wife?"

His eyes widen and his fear smells acrid on the air. First time I've ever smelled fear. Huh. "N-no. Of course not."

I pull him closer to me, his nose practically pressed to mine. "You see . . . Conquest Moon . . . in the sky?"

He blinks. Nods.

"You know what that means?" When he nods again, I set him down as carefully as I can, because I still need a job. "I'm finding my wife."

Mine.

Mine.

"Your wife is in trouble with the guild," Rooster continues, oblivious to the danger he's in. "If Magpie's side of things is correct, she was stealing."

Mine.

Mine.

"That can't go unpunished—"

I'm barely aware that I'm lunging at him. He dodges, fast for a squat little turd like him, and I snarl in frustration.

Rooster puts his hands up. "You're not yourself right now, Hawk. We can put you with a nice sex worker, get you taken care of—"

"Wife," I growl. "Finding my wife."

And I turn toward the drop center once more. I don't have a pass. I don't have flags to demarcate where I'm going. No one stops me, though. They get out of my mucking way and avoid me. Good.

I'm barely aware of finding the drop. Of pushing past guards and climbing into the basket to be lowered. Of snarling at the drop attendant until he lowers the basket with just me instead of a Five.

The red haze in my vision grows thicker. My cock is painful in how tight it is, how much the knot around the base of my shaft aches. I'm barely aware of digging into the rubble that covers the tunnels into Drop Thirteen.

Barely aware of flinging aside a boulder as if it weighs nothing.

Mine.

Mine.

She's in there, and she's mine.

I don't know how long I dig. The red haze covers everything. I should take my cock out, jerk off again, try to cool the heat that seems to have lodged itself directly into my groin . . . but Aspeth is here. Somewhere. I can scent the faint tang of her on the air.

I want *my wife* on my knot. Nothing else will satisfy.

I'm only vaguely aware that there's a team behind me, keeping its distance. I sometimes hear them mutter, but it doesn't stop me in my mission. They're staying away from me, as they should. A moonstruck Taurian is a dangerous creature, and if I don't find my wife by the time the Conquest Moon crosses the smaller moon, I'm going to turn and fuck one of them. I won't be able to wait any longer. I'll lose control of myself.

I'm barely in control now.

I break through the rocks and then I rush forward down the empty tunnel. Then another. And another. The scent of Aspeth is old here, but lingering, and a primeval sound escapes me.

"Wait," someone calls from far behind.

I ignore him. My mate is close. My mate is here.

Mine.

Mine.

Dimly, I'm aware of charging through a broken wall into a ratling nest. The others call out a warning but I grab the ratlings as they try to swarm me, snapping necks and tossing them aside as if they're nothing.

Nothing is going to keep me from my mate.

Nothing at all.

I shove aside a larger ratling, and then the scent of Aspeth hits me, hard and fast. This one has a piece of fabric from her skirt, and when I lift it to smell it, there's a strand of orange cat hair stuck to the fabric.

I bellow my fury even as the hand of the god claims me.

FORTY-THREE

ASPETH

D ID YOU HEAR that?"

I rouse from sleep, my body aching something fierce. I'm hungry, too, but we're trying to save our rations because we don't know how long we'll be here. The red light from the first ring continues to glow atop my staff, and the second is secured around my neck via a lace broken off from one of my boots.

Lark is sitting upright, her attention focused on the stone walls. Everyone else is asleep, with Mereden and Gwenna lying against the slab and Kipp curled up in Gwenna's lap, clutching the last piece of his house in his arms.

"Hear what?" I murmur, keeping my voice down so I don't wake the others.

She looks over at me. "I thought I heard something."

"Ratlings?"

She considers for a moment, then shakes her head. "No. It sounded different. Like a shout of some kind, but it was far away."

I sit up, too, and cock my head, listening. I don't hear anything at all, not even the ratlings. They stopped flinging themselves against the door some time ago, and we went to sleep with one person on guard. I'd taken the first shift, and passed it over to Lark when I got too sleepy. It feels as if I've barely closed my eyes, and I rub them again. "Maybe it's the stone settling."

Lark doesn't look convinced. "Maybe."

I settle back down on the hard stone floor, barely cushioned by my cloak, when there's a muffled bellow, followed by an angry thump.

And then another.

We both jerk upright.

"You think someone's come to rescue us?" she whispers, eyes wide.

"ASPETH!"

Hawk's roar is muffled by the thick stone walls, but I know his voice. He sounds desperate and unhinged.

I've never been so happy to hear anyone. "It's Hawk!" I jump to my feet, shaking Gwenna, Kipp, and Mereden awake as Lark grabs her weapons. "They've come for us!"

"If it's Hawk, he might be with Magpie," Lark warns, pulling her sword from its sheath. "They might be here to arrest us."

"Isn't that better than dying down here?" Gwenna asks.

There's another furious bellow and someone says something on the other side of the door. Hawk roars with what sounds like Taurian rage.

My heart skips in my throat with delight. I want to weep tears of happiness, because we're not going to be trapped in this tomb for weeks, waiting to die. He's come for me. Arrest or not, we can figure things out once we're on the surface and not hemmed in by ratlings.

Oh gods, the ratlings! They'll swarm him.

I step over Mereden and Gwenna, perching on the edge of the slab, and then bang my fist on the door. "There are ratlings!" I call out. "Be careful!"

My response? Another incoherent roar.

"Stand back!" someone says, voice so distant I barely hear it. "He's coming through! We can't stop him!"

I look over at the others and then the door lurches, another mighty roar shaking the interior. I could swear that dust filters down from above, the sounds Hawk is making are so loud. "Should we move the slab?" I ask, fretting. "I don't want it to break—"

Something big and heavy slams against the double doors, and the slab jerks and then topples onto the floor, breaking cleanly in half. I let out a sound of dismay, only for Hawk to bellow in fury again, and the doors groaning once more with the force of his weight being flung against them. He throws himself against them again and I wince, because that has to hurt.

"Hawk?" I call out.

He snarls something, but I can't make it out. It sounded a bit like "Mine" but that doesn't make sense. I pick up my staff and my bag, and when he flings himself against the doors again, the leather belt stretches and breaks and Mereden's staff snaps like a twig. The doors are thrown open.

Hawk storms inside, shoulders heaving. His clothing is torn, his chest is sweaty, and a trickle of blood runs down one bicep. He's covered in dust, but the most startling thing is his eyes.

They're a bright, vicious red. He's gone wild.

The Conquest Moon is fully upon him.

FORTY-FOUR

ASPETH

I STEP FORWARD, MY pulse skittering with a mixture of arousal and unease. "Hawk?"

"Mine," he snarls again, and thunders toward me, his hooves incredibly loud on the stone floor. He grabs me and pulls me against him, and I bite back a sob of relief at the sight of him. We're rescued.

"Thank the gods you're here," I whisper.

His hands roam over me, and then he grabs my arse and drags me against him. His cock is rock-hard, the heat coming off of him absurd. He grinds me against the bulge at his crotch and makes a guttural sound.

And then he tears my overskirt off.

The Conquest Moon. Of course. It's upon him, and he's warned me over and over again that he won't be himself when the god's hand is upon him. That he'll be mindless with lust. He didn't come after me because he was worried about me. He came after me to fuck me.

And the others are standing around, gaping.

Hawk hauls me tighter against him, grinding me against his shaft, and he makes another sound, one of pure bestial need.

"It's the Conquest Moon," I cry out, even as he claws at the waist of my pants, desperate to get inside them. I look over at Lark. "He's not himself. You need to get out of here."

"This way," calls someone else. "Over here! We've got the ratlings under control."

Lark hefts her shield and heads out the doors. The group rushes out, Gwenna and the others fleeing the chamber that's kept us safe for the last while. I remain locked in Hawk's arms, and I don't think I could get free if I tried. He's all over me, clinging and ripping at my clothing as if it offends him.

"Leave the Taurian behind," the guild soldier calls. "He's gone mad."

Hawk rubs his snout against my head, drinking in my scent, even as he squeezes my backside so tightly that I squeak.

"He's not mad," I call back. "He's just in rut."

"Regardless, leave him behind. We'll shut him in until it's safe for him to come out. You can return with us and we'll lock him in."

Leave him *behind*? Leave him trapped in the crypt by himself when he needs me the most? That's the cruelest of things to suggest.

Hawk's hands are roaming over my body, squeezing and touching everything. If he were in his right mind, he'd be full of apologies, because though Hawk is many things, he's always considerate. But he's not himself right now. He warned me, and warned me again. His big hand finds the front of my top and tears my chemise down, exposing my breast to his roaming hand, and I hastily fling my cloak over both of us as his mouth closes on my nipple.

I make a whimpery noise despite myself.

"Aspeth?" Lark has her weapons out, and she steps toward me. The others are behind her, ready to confront Hawk to save me from him.

I shake my head, clinging to him even as he sucks on my nipple, hard, under the cloak. "You . . . you all should go. Lock us in. Bar the door. Leave food. Come back . . . when the Conquest Moon is gone." It's hard to speak with his mouth being so distracting, and his fingers are driving between my legs, rubbing me through my pants.

"Are you sure?" Lark hesitates, about to reenter the crypt.

Hawk lifts his head from my breast and growls, low and menacing. I push his head down, back to my breast, and meet Lark's gaze. I nod at her and mouth, "Go." I've heard stories of the brutal rampages that Taurians in rut will go into, and it makes the ratlings seem tame.

I promised Hawk I'd be with him, and I mean it.

"Aspeth—"

"Get out of here," I yell, even as his fingers tear a hole in my pants. "Lock us in!"

Gwenna surges back into the room, and for a moment I think she's going to try to stop me. Instead, she tosses down her bag of supplies and then grabs the doors, shutting them behind her. I hear scraping and a bit of discussion on the other side as they try to figure out the best way to seal the doors, and—

—and then Hawk is pushing a finger into my channel and I suck in a breath, because I'm dry and his finger feels huge and invasive.

"Wait," I tell him, squirming against his hand. "Wait."

He growls, this time directed at me.

"Hawk," I say, keeping my voice even. I have to stay focused, and hope that my calm bleeds over into him. I grab one of his horns and angle his head back, forcing him to look me in the eye. He thrusts his finger into me again, his features full of mindless hunger as his red gaze meets my determined one. "I'm here."

"Mine," he growls.

"Yours," I agree. I squirm atop the finger that pushes deep inside me. "I'm here with you. I'm going to be with you every moment of the Conquest Moon's passing. But I need to be prepared so it doesn't hurt, understand?"

"Aspeth," he rasps. "Mine."

This isn't going as I'd like. Time for bigger moves, then. I grab him by the face and kiss his nose. It's broad and dry, and when he huffs like a charging bull, he huffs right in my face. If he can't be in his own head enough to prepare my body, I need to take control. Maybe I can make him come at least once just to get the edge off. If nothing else, if I can get his cock wet with his dripping seed, maybe that will ease the way enough. "Hawk." I make my tone as sultry and seductive as I can. "I want to put your cock in my mouth."

"Aspeth."

I can't tell if he's hearing what I'm saying or if he's completely lost. "Aspeth's mouth," I say in a flirty voice, and lick his nose. "Your cock. My tongue."

He groans, dropping me to the floor.

I'll take that as a good sign. I slither out of his clinging grasp—not as easy as it sounds—and clamp my thighs together. He's cored a hole right between the thighs of my pants and ripped my skirt. The buttons on my shirt have popped off. I need to get rid of the rest of my clothing before he leaves me nothing to wear at all.

So I make a tease out of it. I undo my cloak, twirling away when Hawk reaches for me again. He snarls angrily, lunging for me, his red eyes wild. I'm baiting him, but I can't help it. I need a breath or two to strip down. "I'm yours," I remind him. "You want me naked, don't you?"

"Naked," he replies thickly, and strokes his hand over his cock.

"Naked," I agree. I shimmy as I kick my boots off and slither out of my pants, hoping they survive the next few days. Once my socks are gone, I give my arse a little wiggle and he reaches for me again. He grabs me, pulling me close, and buries his face against my neck even as he reaches for my pussy.

"You want my mouth on your cock, don't you?" I ask, even as I hastily pull the remnants of my blouse and corset off. There's not much left to salvage, and my thin chemise is in tatters. The sight of my clothing seems to frustrate him, and before he can destroy more, I hide it behind me. If he keeps this up, I'll be left without a top, but then his mouth is on my breasts again and I forget everything else.

He's ravenous with need.

Hawk's mouth roams over my skin, and then he focuses on my nipple, sucking on it as if his life depends on it. His other hand strays between my thighs again, and I wait for him to tease my clit, to prep my body. He doesn't, though—just goes straight for thrusting again—and I work my way free from his grasp again. "No," I tell him when he tries to drag me back.

"*MINE—*"

"Yours," I agree. "But you don't want to hurt me, right? I need to get used to this. All of this." And I cup his cock boldly.

It's a mistake. He immediately hisses as if in pain, recoiling.

Oh. His knot.

I feel it, like a swollen ring radiating heat around his groin.

I've been thinking so hard about myself that I've forgotten that this isn't fun for him. My poor, honorable Hawk. I run a hand down his chest and pet him, trying to soothe. "New tactic," I whisper. "Wanna watch me get myself off?"

He groans, his gaze locked on me, and I'm going to take that as an affirmative.

All right, I've never performed this for another, but now seems like a great time to start. The last time I touched Hawk's cock, it didn't feel as . . . swollen is it did just now, so I can only assume that his knot is adding all kinds of terrible pressure and me mouthing things wouldn't help. I need to prepare myself for this or it's going to be a very long Conquest Moon.

I spread a discarded cloak on the floor of the crypt like a blanket and then sit down upon it. Every moment feels like a moment in which I'm waiting for Hawk to pounce on me, but as long as he's still got his pants on, I can take things a little slower. I suspect that when the pants come off, so will the last of his control, and it's probably a good idea that I'm not pleasuring him with my mouth.

I . . . I don't know what I'd do if he pushed his knot into my mouth. Choke to death on his cock, I suppose. I bite back a hysterical giggle at the visual image and spread my thighs apart.

"Mine," Hawk rumbles, reaching for me as he kneels on the floor to watch.

"Not yet." I bat his hand away, living dangerously, and ignore his angry snarl. "I'm preparing myself."

He reaches for me again, and then pauses when I brush over my clit.

His wild red eyes focus there, and he watches as I strum my fingers over my body, trying to entice it into arousal. I'm nervous, not only at Hawk's aggressiveness, but at the fact that this is the first time I've done something like this at all.

He tried to prepare me, though. If I hadn't run off last night, determined to get the other half of the ring, we'd have had sex this morning. We'd probably still be in bed, and none of this would have happened. It's too late to fret about such things now, and it's certainly not going to help me come. So I lie back and try to picture things that I find arousing. Things like . . . Hawk's broad shoulders. The way he rubs his muzzle over my neck, as if he can't get enough of my scent.

When he rubs his muzzle over the curve of my hip, I moan.

"Aspeth," he groans, and then he pushes my thighs apart with big, strong hands. "Mine."

"Yours," I breathe, even as I trace circles around my clit. I watch as he dips his head between my legs, his thick tongue snaking out and licking my entire cleft all at once. My toes curl and he clamps his hands around my thighs, holding them open as he pushes his tongue inside me. It feels enormous, but wet and hot and so strangely good. I whimper again, and touch myself faster, determined to climax at least once before we get down to business.

He works his tongue furiously in and out of me, thrusting with it in an imitation of mating, and it teases my very insides. I've never felt anything like it before, and combined with my frantic rubbing of my clit, I can feel the orgasm building inside me. "Please," I whisper, arching my hips. "Oh, please."

Hawk thrusts his tongue into me again, lapping at my core. It makes a wet squelching sound, and then he grunts with pleasure. *"Slick."*

"Slick?" I echo, dazed.

He pulls away briefly, glancing up at me with those wild red eyes. His fingers brush through my folds and then sink into me with another indecently wet sound. He makes it happen again, and again, and I'm mortified at how wet I am and how more of it just seems to keep coming. "Slick," he says again. "All mine."

Oh. Right. Because my body is responding to his. Because his scent is all over me and my pussy is deciding now is the time to gush like a waterfall. I'd be embarrassed but Hawk loves it, loves every wet slurp his fingers make as he eases into me again.

My fingers slip down to my clit once more, teasing it.

He pushes my hand aside and closes his mouth over my clit, sucking on it as he watches me with bright red eyes. His fingers move in and out of me with wet sucking noises, like my body is licking him back—

I come, my legs jerking and a cry escaping my throat. It rips through me with all the force of a storm, so intense that my back arches off the cloak even as Hawk continues to suck and suck and *suck* upon me.

I wait for the climax to ebb, even as Hawk continues to work his mouth over me. When he doesn't lift his head, I realize he has no intention of doing so, and another small climax bursts through me, my legs curling up even as he shoves them down and continues to suck on my now-oversensitized clit with near-brutal intensity.

Oh gods. There's no distracting him away. I push at his head, only for him to ignore me and continue to lap and suck at my clit, sending quivers through my body. I shove at him again. "Hawk, let me breathe."

He only holds my thighs tighter, the suction around my clit growing more intense by the moment. How many climaxes is he going to give me before he stops? Ten? Twenty? The thought makes me clench, both with excitement and a little bit of worry.

"Hawk," I insist again, and then shove at his face. How do I distract him? How do I get him to notice me? To lift his head? An idea hits and I moan loudly, then cry out, "Oh, *Wallach*."

He stills over me. My nerves prickle, and I immediately worry I've made a mistake. Does he even realize that's his name? Who he was before he was Hawk?

"Mine," he growls again, crawling over my prone body. "*My* wife."

"Yes, yours," I agree, cupping his face in my hands as he settles his weight over my body. "I just wanted to get your attention because—"

I break off in a squeak of surprise as he rubs his cock against the entrance to my body. Oh, okay, we're doing this now. He pushes into me, and I make another whining noise, my hands sliding to his shoulders and clinging as he continues to push into me with what feels like entirely too much cock. It's not painful, but it doesn't feel incredible, either. It's an uncomfortable sensation, of being stretched in places I've never been stretched before. I gasp and pant for air, feeling as if I'm being hollowed out from inside.

He eventually stops pushing forward and I tremble, holding on to him as he gazes down at me. I know he's lost to the Conquest Moon's hold on him, but truthfully, he's being quite gentle for someone abandoned to a rutting frenzy. I reach up and stroke his cheek to reassure him. "I'm here, Hawk. I'm here with you. Just like I promised."

I love you.

The words float to the top of my mind but I don't say them. It seems wrong to in this moment, when he might not even remember they're said. When he's crushing me under his weight and his cock is trying to reach my navel from the inside.

He groans, pressing his muzzle against the side of my face, and his hips jerk. He thrusts into me, and I suck in a breath, because that feels . . . different. Different than just having his enormous penis hanging out inside me, forcing my innards to make room for him.

Hawk thrusts into me again, and my breath stutters. All right, that definitely feels good. "Better," I whisper. "Oh, so much better. I think I like that."

If he can understand me, he doesn't show it. He grips me by the hips and continues to pound into me, his movements slow and steady and sure. I relax, because this whole "rutting" thing isn't so bad. My pussy is a little achy, but overall I'm enjoying this. I love the strange way he feels over me. How big he is and how small and dainty he makes me feel. I never thought I'd care if I was tiny or helpless, but under him, I like the sensation of being smaller and lost against his larger strength.

He moves quicker, his shuttling hips picking up speed. His breath accelerates, too, and he's starting to push into me with such force that our hips slap together, and my pussy makes a wet, squelching sound. He leans over me and drives deep, his hips working, and I gasp as he lifts one of my legs, locking it around his hips. It changes the angle of his thrusting, and everything feels intense. My pussy clenches around him, tightening as another orgasm crawls through my veins, and I wheeze as every muscle in my lower body locks up in response, the climax making my back taut.

Hawk grunts, and then moves faster, hunching over me. I'm dimly aware of his presence, of his pounding, merciless cock, as the pleasure of release washes over me. I'm so glad I agreed to do this. So glad that Hawk is mine. So . . .

He pushes deeper into my body, and something enormous hammers at the entrance to my channel.

My eyes fly open, and I tense. "H-Hawk?"

He grunts again, lost in the moment, and pushes harder. When that unyielding, too-large bit pushes against my body once more, I realize that he hasn't knotted me yet. That there's even more to fit inside.

Oh gods. I suck in a breath. Now I see the issue. He pushes against me, and when my body doesn't give, he makes a frustrated, bestial sound. He lifts his hand to his mouth, his long, thick tongue snaking out, and licks his fingers. Then his hand moves between our bodies, quicker than I can process what he's doing, and he rubs my clit with it.

I cry out at how good it feels, new pleasure surging through my body. More slick comes from me, the wet noises between us growing even louder.

As I do, he thrusts forward sharply, and then he's inside my slicked, well-juiced body. Sort of. He pushes and pushes, wedging his knot into my wet heat, and I bite my lip. All the while, his hand works on my clit, and it's the oddest mixture of pleasure and discomfort I've ever felt. It's too much, his knot. I can't take it all. He continues to press into me, and I feel as if my body is going to shatter around him, that I'm too tight. That I can't take any more. I clamp on to his surging body tightly, unable to do more than hold on as he knots me.

He fills me so full that I can't bear it, and all of me quakes and trembles. With another animalistic growl, he pushes deep again, and it's like something *gives* inside me. We both gasp, and then Hawk is the one shuddering, his big body shivering as his release boils out of him. I wait, and then it's like something wet spills inside me. I squirm at the sensation, and he makes a low gasping sound and it sets off another round. Over and over, I feel him bathing my insides with his release, and just when I think he's done, he lets out another jet and groans once more.

And I'm helpless to do anything but take it. Take all of it. The exquisite pleasure of the orgasms have disappeared, and everything feels tight and achy and uncomfortable. Even Hawk's pleasant, heavy weight over me feels like a bit too much. I bite my lip, because this is part of what he warned me about—that he'd knot me and we'd be stuck together, bodies locked, until he releases me.

I just didn't ask how long it would take.

I really should have, I chide myself, even as I shift underneath him, trying to get comfortable. How long are we going to be together like this? Hours? Days?

I remain quiet, playing with the short hair that covers his shoulders as I wait for him to find himself.

Hawk eventually groans, lifting his head. ". . . Aspeth?"

"I'm here." My voice is small, and I wriggle my hips, trying to find a better position. There isn't one. I still feel like an overfilled waterskin. "Are you all right?"

He pants, as if he's been running up a mountain. "Just . . . trying to stay in my head . . . difficult." Hawk's big body shifts, and then he surges into me again, almost involuntarily. "Knot . . . Conquest Moon . . ."

"I know." I stroke the short, fuzzy fur on his cheek, a wave of foolish affection moving over me. "You're all right. I'm here with you."

The god's grip on him must be less intense while his knot deflates. He runs his muzzle over my shoulder, then my ear. "Where are we? Did I . . . hurt you? Are you . . . all right?"

"I'm fine." More or less. I'm alive. I'm knotted, and my husband is here with me. He sounds full of remorse and I don't want him stressing over anything. "You were very gentle."

He snorts, and I swear, it makes his cock jump inside me. "That doesn't sound like a Taurian in rut."

"You were enthusiastic, then. But it wasn't so bad." I pause. "Also we're in a crypt, which is slightly creepy, and there might be ghosts watching us."

He lifts his head, and as he does, I can see that the crazed look in his gaze is somewhat lessened, but not by much. "So we are. You haven't seen any spiders, have you?"

Laughter bubbles up inside me, and giggling just makes the tight connection between our bodies that much more sensitive. I shift under him, smiling. "We were a bit too busy being attacked by ratlings to check for spiders, alas. But we've been here for a while—most of a day, I think—and no sign of spiders."

Some of the tension in his shoulders eases. "Good. The last thing I need is a spider biting my balls while they're aching like this."

I smother another giggle.

"Where are the others?" he asks.

"They beat a hasty retreat when you freed my breast and started licking it."

"Smart." His hand moves to my breast, teasing the nipple. "They are quite lovely tits, though."

I bite back a moan, because it's evident that even though Hawk is himself at the moment, he's still not sated.

"I could make you come," he murmurs, stroking my nipple with slow, thoughtful motions. "I could make you come over and over again while you're locked against me. While you're helpless and pinned against my knot. I love that thought. In fact, I'm going to do that . . . but after you tell me everything that's been going on. Spare no detail."

"It's a bit of a long story."

"Neither you nor I are going anywhere for a while, little bird."

I rather like that he calls me his little bird. It doesn't sound like he hates me. So I tell him about the ring we found. The ring that even now is painting everything with a continual red glow. I remind him of my father's artifact issues and how I need to save him. I don't tell him that Gwenna was the one that initially stole the ring—I put that on my shoulders. And I tell him about how it was my idea to come down here and talked the others into coming with me. "I blackmailed them," I tell him. "They're blameless."

"You're full of shit," he tells me, an amused smile curling his mouth. "Blackmailed them with what?" He continues to stroke my nipple, sending flickers of desire through my tightly knotted body.

I'd anticipated a few things about Hawk's rut, but I hadn't anticipated this—the constant staring into each other's faces while we wait for his knot to go down. The intimacy of this moment, with his body so deep into mine. The connection between us. It's changing everything, and I feel vulnerable and yet so very seen, too.

"All right, perhaps I didn't blackmail them. But it was my idea and I don't want them to suffer for it." I tell him then about Magpie, and how she'd suggested that she knew people and she'd come with us . . . and then finding out she was working with Barnabus when he showed up.

Hawk doesn't seem surprised by that part. "I found her with him. They were celebrating. Said you'd left. I knew they'd done something and I lost my shit. I might have had them arrested." He pauses, thinking. "I might have also punched Barnabus in the face, but my memory is hazy. I can blame it all on the Conquest Moon."

"Arresting them?" I shake my head, frowning. "What's arresting them going to do? That's a slap on the wrist. The guild—"

"Won't do much, aye. At least not to Barnabus. Just like they won't do much to you. They can't ruin their relationships with the holders. But the rest of us can get caught in the cross fire."

My heart aches. "I'm not going to let anything happen to you."

He just gives me a wry smile, as if he doesn't quite believe me. "You couldn't have waited for me to come home? Asked me for help instead of Magpie?"

"You're too honorable. You wouldn't help."

"You think I'd rather sit around with my horn up my arse? Watch you get sent home and put in danger?"

"First of all, I don't know how you could put your horn up your own arse without some pretty thorough twisting. Second of all, I don't know. I've been so used to taking everything on, to expecting no one to help me. I'm sorry I didn't come to you."

"You should have. I'm your husband. It's my job to protect you."

"You're my husband in name only, remember?"

"That's not what it feels like." He rocks his hips, and I suck in a breath, because it does, indeed, feel like we're far more than just two strangers in a marriage of convenience. Today has changed everything.

No, I realize. It changed long ago. I've just not acknowledged it until now. I've lost my heart somewhere along the way to this huge, fierce Taurian who hates spiders.

FORTY-FIVE

ASPETH

JUST LIKE WE had in bed at home, we talk of nothing and everything. With Hawk's help I bind up my injured wrist so it has some support. Hawk caresses me idly while I tell him about our caved-in adventures, and then we separate, his spent cock pulling free from my body. Oh. It feels strange to not have him inside me, stretching me past comfort into something that's bliss. I sit up and look around for something I can use as a chamber pot, since my stomach still feels incredibly full of his release.

In the end, I empty a bag and designate a corner, humiliated that we don't even have the privacy for this. I remember my ladies talking about things one does after sex—always pee afterward, and hop to get rid of his leavings. I do both while Hawk politely ignores me, and I'm mortified at the absolute flood that leaves my body. Taurians sure do have a lot of seed.

I clean myself up, cheeks burning, with a dampened scrap of fabric torn from my sleeve. The pack Gwenna tossed has several canteens, much to my relief, and I don't feel terrible using a few spoonfuls to clean up.

Once I feel a bit more like myself, I pull on a short chemise I had in my bag. Well, now, that wasn't quite the ordeal everyone made it out to be. I turn to Hawk, the satchel of foodstuffs in my arms. "Would you like a snack—"

He rips the bag from my grip and grabs me by the waist. I yelp in surprise—though he isn't hurting me—and Hawk tugs me against his groin. It's rock-hard once more, and when I look up, the red is back in his gaze, stronger than ever.

Poor Hawk . . . that wasn't much of a break from the madness.

He grabs my chemise at the collar and I stop his hand before he can tear. "If you rip this, I won't have anything to wear!"

He snarls at me, all red eyes and hunger, and I slither out of his grasp, going underneath his clutching arms. The chemise is loose and falls off the moment I do, and I collapse on the floor, naked once more.

Hawk is over me in a heartbeat.

He presses me to the rumpled cloak that's serving as a blanket and shoves me forward. In the next moment, he pulls my hips into the air and spreads my thighs while I'm on hands and knees. That's all the warning I get before he's pumping into me again, his strokes quick and decisive and so full of hunger that it takes my breath away.

My body is still stretched and slick from before, and he's able to knot me in less time, and then he's coming, quaking over me as his release takes control. That time was fast and furious, and while it didn't give me multiple orgasms like before, I don't mind. The feel of Hawk over me and inside me is erotic all on its own, and I ache for him because he's clearly lost right now.

I'm glad it's me with him and not a stranger.

He collapses over me, pressing me into the floor, and I shift, twitching and full, trying to get comfortable underneath him. After a few minutes pass, Hawk rubs his face against the back of my head, further tangling my wrecked hair. "Mmm. Aspeth."

"I'm here." I pat the hand that reaches for me. "Here and fine."

"I didn't make you come that time, did I? I feel like it was fast."

"Fast but not rough. It's fine." I love that he's still inquiring about me, as if I'm just as important as his endless hunger.

"'Fine' is not acceptable." He strokes his hand down my soft belly, moving between my thighs. "And the nice thing about you being knotted is that you can't squirm away while I touch you." He deftly strokes my clit, and the combination of his cock filling me and the sensitive nerves being strummed makes me whine loudly. "And oh, how I love to touch you."

He pins me to the floor and works my clit until I come three times in a row, all the while whispering filthy words into my ear. When his cock eases free from my body again, I know there won't be much time between rounds of rutting, but this time I'm prepared. I do my business quickly, tidy up, drink some water—

—and then he's reaching for me again, lost in the rutting madness.

Now I see why the Taurians speak of the Conquest Moon with both love and dread.

On and on, the cycle continues. Hours pass.

Maybe entire afternoons.

I can't tell if it's day or night in the crypt. Time runs together— sometimes between bouts of rutting, we'll doze, locked together, only for me to wake up to Hawk fucking me again. We have sex over and over, until everything below the waist for me is tender and sore, and my pussy feels permanently sticky. Everything in the crypt seems to be covered in a layer of sweat and Taurian leavings, and I'm both embarrassed that we've defiled this place and a little proud. We're together.

And after this, I feel closer to him than ever.

FORTY-SIX

ASPETH

Post–Conquest Moon

HAWK RUBS MY hip, drawing little circles into my skin. "I think it's slowing down," he murmurs, sounding as exhausted as I am. "I don't feel as if my skull's about to burst any longer."

I smile idly, too tired to move from my spot tucked at his side. Our bodies are joined, his cock still knotted inside me, and I ache. My legs ache. My back aches. My pussy certainly aches. But I still feel good. "Has it been several days? I can't tell."

"We're low on food and water and this place is a mess. I think so."

His hand slides to my pussy and I tense, because even that area feels achy. But he only takes some of the wetness of our mingled juices and drags his fingers through them, then paints my skin as if marking me. "Thank you again."

"Thank you" feels . . . strange to hear in this moment. I want to hear words of love, not thanks. "It was our agreement," I say, trying to keep the vague hurt out of my tone. "I always said I'd do this with you."

"Aye, you did." He leans in and rubs his long, broad nose against my temple. "Where are your spectacles? Did I break them?"

"They shattered in the cave-in." I'm trying not to fret over that because spectacles are expensive, and I don't have any coin left. I've got bigger issues to deal with than broken spectacles. "I'll manage."

He tuts. "We'll get you new ones. I know a Taurian in the city who can put something together for you. We'll just need to wait for him to come back from the plains."

He sounds so casual, and that makes my heart ache, especially after that tepid "thank you." "You make it seem like we have a future together," I say, tone cheery.

Hawk stills against me. "After all this, you doubt me?"

I immediately feel like an arse. I turn my head, gazing at him. "No, I'm just feeling needy and lost. I . . . I don't know what's going to happen with me, Hawk. I'm a holder's heir who just got caught stealing from the guild."

He pulls me tightly against him, hugging me from behind. "I'll be at your side, no matter what happens, as long as you want me there."

I wrap my arms around him. "Don't leave me. Never leave me."

"As long as you want me there," he repeats, making it a promise. He rubs his muzzle against my hair again. "But we both know a lady holder shouldn't be married to a Taurian."

I know that. I'm trying not to think about that. "I never wanted to be a lady holder anyhow," I force myself to say lightly. "So they'll just have to cope."

He chuckles, nipping my ear. His hips surge against mine, and I realize that the Conquest Moon is upon him again. I hold him tight, and his hand steals to my breast, teasing the nipple and sending tired pleasure skittering through my body.

IT FEELS LIKE eternity has passed when Hawk wakes me from a nap and his eyes are bright gold and not the red that tinted them with every moment of our time in the crypt.

It's time to go.

I ache and I'm filthy and I want a real night's sleep, but I'm still not ready to go. I don't want to face the world outside. Not after what we've shared in here. I dress with stiff fingers and try to pull my hair into some semblance of modesty, but I stink of sweat and sex and more sweat and more sex. I'm a wreck, and I'm trying not to think about all the things that I've forced out of my mind for the last several days.

"Do you think Squeaker is all right?" I ask, worried. "Do you think the nestmaid fed her? Changed her litter? Petted her?"

"I'm positive," Hawk reassures me, pulling on his clothes. "Magpie might be self-serving but no one's going to take their revenge on a cat."

I hope he's right. That Gwenna is back—or aware of the situation—and she'll look after Squeaker for me. My poor cat. No one's been there to pet her and snuggle her for days. She must be feeling so abandoned. I hate that aspect of guild life—staying away from home for days on end. My cat won't understand.

Then again, I'm probably going to be booted from the guild, so what does it matter?

I fasten my blouse, wincing at how the buttons have been ripped out by Hawk's rampaging hands. He was in such a rush—and I was so full of my own plans—that we forgot the most basic need: birth control. There's no sense in stressing over it now, though. What's done is done, and if I have a Taurian's child, I suppose my father won't oppose my marriage nearly as strongly, will he?

As if he can sense the despairing turn my thoughts are taking, Hawk moves to my side. He takes my hand in his and kisses my knuckles. "Aspeth. I can hear you thinking."

I sigh.

"Whatever comes next, we do it together. Remember?" He kisses my knuckles again. "I love you, little bird."

I blink up at him in wonder. It's the first time he's told me that he cares for me. "I love you, too, Hawk. My husband."

He smiles down at me, my hand tucked against his muzzle, and for a moment, I'm truly content.

But then it's time to go. We gather our things and tidy up the crypt. I should be repulsed that we've spent the last several days amidst the dead, but it feels like they were watching out for us. That somewhere in the Underworld, the lady with the unpronounceable name and her husband know that I want to keep their rings together, and that if it were up to me, their crypt would remain otherwise untouched. But the guild is the guild, and if there's a hint of magic to be found, it'll be torn apart.

At its core, the Royal Artifactual Guild is a guild of tomb robbers. And I don't know if I have the heart for it. Maybe I never have.

Maybe I was never meant to be Sparrow after all.

FORTY-SEVEN

ASPETH

THE MOMENT WE step out of the Everbelow, I'm immediately arrested. Even Hawk's protests can't save me, and I'm politely but firmly dragged to the guild jail.

I didn't even know the guild had a jail. But apparently there's a tower with small, uncomfortable rooms that are guarded by more guild employees—repeaters. Mine has a small window that looks out upon the city, far too high up for me to jump out and try to escape. There's a narrow cot along the wall and a small stool and a bucket to serve as a chamber pot.

Not unexpected.

I crawl into bed and sleep for what feels like days. When I wake up, there are three trays of food, untouched, sitting by the door. I'm ravenous and eat everything, and then collapse back into bed again. I wake up when someone brings me more food and water, but this time I use the water to clean up. Once I'm reasonably tidy—as reasonably as one can be in a jail cell—I sit on the stool and look out the window.

They've confiscated my rings, the rings I fought so hard for in order to save my father's keep.

I knew they would, but the realization still depresses me. All of that work, all of the striving, and I still have nothing to show for it. Barnabus could be conquering my father's keep even now. Hawk had mentioned he turned both Barnabus and Magpie over to the guild, but the fact that I'm imprisoned tells me whose side they've taken.

So I stare out the window and mope.

There's nothing else to do, after all. Worrying about my cat, or my Five, or my husband or my father or my people or my own neck won't help things, so I admire the clouds and watch people scuttle along the streets below and imagine stories for them.

Someone brings me food and water twice a day. I ask for a book to read—even if it's just guild pamphlets about the proper binding of documentation, just something—and they ignore me. I sleep a lot, too, because when it's dark outside, even the window provides no entertainment.

I wonder if Hawk is relieved that I'm gone, now that his rut is over. I wonder if he still feels the same.

I wonder if they're sending him into the tunnels even now to pick clean the crypt we spent so much time in.

I wonder what stories Barnabus and Magpie are telling about me. I'm sure they're painting me as the villain of the tale. In a way, it does look bad, and without me there to explain properly the reasons behind my theft, I seem spoiled and greedy. No one is going to take my side, especially if they don't hear my half of the tale.

Time passes. Eighteen days in agonizing slowness. There is no boredom quite like sitting and staring out a window, waiting for your fate. At times, I just want them to get on with it. To sentence me and be done.

Or perhaps I've already been judged and this is the punishment? Death by boredom?

On the morning of the nineteenth day, the door to my small room opens. I jump to my feet, hoping against hope that it's Hawk. That he's come to free me. That love shines in his eyes and I haven't been forgotten.

I'm a little disappointed when Lark, Kipp, Mereden, and Gwenna come through. But only a little. Then I squeal with happiness and fling myself forward, hugging each one of them. "What are you guys doing here?"

"Gods, you smell," Lark says after she hugs me. She fans her face, grimacing. "Don't they bathe you up here?"

"No luxury baths for prisoners, I'm afraid," I tease, not hurt by her words. Lark has always been the first to say exactly what she's thinking. And I'm positive I do smell. I've been washing myself with bits of extra water to keep the grime off my skin, but my hair is filthy and I'm wearing the same tattered clothing I wore prior to the cave-in, and there's been no washing for them. A terrible thought occurs to me. "Have you all been arrested, too?"

Mereden shakes her head. "No, we're to be tried together as a Five. That's why we're here. We're meeting before the guild masters shortly."

We are? Oh gods. I touch my messy hair and torn clothing and grimace. "Someone help me clean up?"

Kipp slithers free of his house—a new one, I see, with the piece of old shell affixed to the back with leather stitching through a few purposeful holes—and holds out a comb. A moment later, he pulls a fresh chemise from his shell and a bundled guild coat.

"You are a wonder," I tell him, and he gives me a lizard-like wink. I think.

They help me get ready, with Gwenna braiding my wrecked hair into a tight bun at the base of my neck. The new jacket fits a little tight but it's clean and I don't feel like a gutter-goblin at least. I straighten and put on my best lord-holder's-daughter demeanor. If nothing else, I did what I did out of duty. No holder would find me guilty. They would understand.

We're marched down the tower stairs and across the great, sweeping halls of the guild's network of buildings. Everyone seems to be in their best livery, and the halls are crawling with people. It's strange to see, though I don't let my confusion show on my face. When another guild master rushes by with his sash heavy and clinking with pins, Mereden links her arm with mine and leans in, as if we're two ladies on a jaunt instead of a prisoner and her co-conspirator. "The king is here."

I lose my composure and jerk to stare at her. "What? He is?"

She nods, her expression serene. "Guild law apparently states that a dispute with holder nobility requires a royal decision."

Gods. This is worse than I thought.

"Courage," Mereden tells me, and gives my arm a squeeze. "I've sent a letter to my father stating that if we're all kicked out of the guild, I will insist you go with me to the Convent of Divine Silence. No one will touch you on holy ground."

I manage a weak smile. So I won't die instantly. I'll just die slowly at the convent. Lovely. But I appreciate that Mereden is trying to save me. I just don't know what I'll do without Hawk. At some point in all of this, he's become more important than the guild. More important than anything.

And Magpie is his boss. Ugh.

We're led into what looks like a courtroom, with several benches along the walls. Instead of the judge's seat, there's a large throne, and upon it sits a middle-aged blob in colorful clothing. I squint to see that the king is balding and has a sour expression on his face. Goody. He wears a thin circlet over his brow and his sleeves are encrusted with jewels, showing both fashion and wealth. His heavy necklace has three thick medallions upon it, and something tells me that if I could see more than blobs, they'd probably have Prellian runes on them.

I've only met the king once or twice in my life, but the look on his face doesn't bode well.

Our Five are shuffled to a bench at the corner of the room, with guards on both sides. Lark and Mereden sit together on one side of me, with Gwenna and Kipp on my other side. I can't help but notice that Lark's and Mereden's pinky fingers are locked together as they sit. I'm glad they've got each other.

I keep squinting as I glance around the room, looking for familiar faces. Across from us, Magpie sits on one bench wearing her guild regalia, and a bench ahead of her, Barnabus sits with his retainers, his clothing as colorful as the king's. Today he's got three feathers in his stupid hat. I squint on past him and look for a dark reddish face and horns. Hawk is near the door, close to another Taurian. The Taurians must be returning to the city, then.

"Are all present?" The king demands when the room settles.

Rooster steps forward, wearing his guild sashes and awards as well. For all his short, squatty height, his sash is so decorated that it trails on the ground after him, tinkling with metal. Perhaps he was once a very successful tunnel diver before he found a love of bureaucracy. He approaches the king's throne and bows deeply, then nods. "All accused are present, Your Majesty."

"Good." He gazes around the room, and I could swear his attention locks onto me briefly before he pulls out a scroll he has in his lap. "I have read the charges against Lord Barnabus Chatworth of Chatworth Hold, Magpie of the Royal Artifactual Guild, and Lady Aspeth Honori of Honori Hold. I have conferred with my advisors and with the guild leaders and have come to a decision upon all three parties. Magpie of the Royal Artifactual Guild, please stand."

I can't believe what I'm hearing. A decision has already been made? But no one's talked to me or asked me anything. Panicked, I clutch Gwenna's hand, but hers feels sweaty and trembles in my grip. If no one spoke on my behalf, how can they possibly make a decision for me? How—

Magpie stands. "I am here, Your Majesty."

"Do you abide by the king's ruling?" Rooster focuses his gaze on her.

The question is a formality only. Everyone knows that you don't cross the king. That's the quickest way to make an enemy for the entire guild.

"Of course I do," Magpie says, and I can't tell if she's sober or not. I do notice that no one is seated upon her bench with her in support, not even Hawk. I hope that's a good sign.

"Magpie of the Royal Artifactual Guild, you have been accused of conspiracy to overthrow Honori Hold and of conspiring to withhold artifacts from the guild. I find you guilty on both charges."

The king reads from his scroll in a bored voice, and I suck in a breath. She's guilty.

"You will be stripped of your rank as guild master and all such benefits have been revoked. You will no longer be able to teach classes and receive a tithe from students. Such monies will be diverted to the guild's coffers. Furthermore, you have been stripped of guild status entirely. You will now be referred to by your given name, Mary Turner, and are ineligible to return to guild employment. Please surrender your sash and jacket."

I squint hard, but I can't see Magpie's reaction. Being stripped of her guild honors isn't unexpected, but it means that possibly someone believes my side of things. I clutch Mereden's hand tightly, and Gwenna grips my other one.

Magpie moves forward and slaps her guild sash down onto Rooster's hand. She shrugs off her jacket and pushes it into his grip, too, and then spits at his feet.

"That was a long time coming," Rooster says in a bland voice. "You've been a piss-poor guild master for years now. You have until tonight to clear out your rooms in your nest."

She scowls at him and says nothing.

"Dismissed," the king says with a flick of his hand.

Magpie—Mary—gives a jerky nod and then slams out of the room, pushing past everyone in guild uniform.

"Lord Barnabus Chatworth," the king says, "you are accused of conspiracy to overthrow Honori Hold."

I don't dare breathe as Barnabus gets to his feet. "It is a misunderstanding, Your Majesty," he says in an unctuous voice. "Lady Aspeth is paranoid and seeking revenge after I spurned her."

The nerve! I clamp my jaw shut to keep from yelling out about his lies.

The king holds a hand up. "You have left a paper trail of your intentions with the guild, I'm afraid. The time for claiming innocence is long past. I find you guilty of conspiring to take over a hold, though whether or not it is Honori Hold is questionable. The Chatworth Hold must donate no less than eight artifacts of the guild's choosing, four major and four minor. These artifacts will be split between the guild and the throne as penance for your crimes."

That . . . that's it?

That's a slap on the wrist.

It'll hurt Barnabus's family in their trove, of course, but considering that he just had a bunch of artifacts dug up, I'm not thrilled. They'll easily acquire comparable artifacts again, and I love how the king was sure to specify that the artifacts are going to go to the guild and to him. Nothing for my poor family's hold, which was on the verge of being wiped out.

Even so, I know this is how the game is played. The king is always careful with the holder families, because he doesn't want them rising up against him. He's also careful with the guild for the same reason. It's all a game of power, and Magpie is nobody to him, whereas Barnabus might be an ally in the future. Hence, the slap on the wrist.

It's ironic that if Barnabus had succeeded in taking over my father's keep, we'd have been murdered and there would be no repercussions because there would be no family left to protest to the king. But caught in the act? Caught in the act, you pay the price.

Barnabus isn't happy with the king's ruling, though. "Your Majesty," he protests, "this has all been a misunderstanding. I've never tried to take over Honori Hold. To do so would be foolishness, as I'm to marry into the family."

"The lady is already married," a familiar voice calls out, and Hawk strides forward. My heart flutters and I clutch my friends' hands tightly as the big Taurian approaches the king. Even though I'm squinting, he looks amazing. Handsome. Powerful. Strong. "Aspeth is my wife."

Swoon.

Barnabus flicks a dismissive look over at Hawk. "A marriage in secret to a Taurian commoner doesn't count."

"The lady is married to a guild master," Rooster corrects, "and a highly respected one. Do not disparage him."

I gasp. Guild master? When . . . ?

Sure enough, Hawk's sash is the bright, vivacious red of the guild masters, and sprinkled with many pins. They must have seen his brilliance and finally given him the rank he deserved all along. He should have been the master all this time instead of Magpie. Elated, I sniff back tears of joy. If nothing else, Hawk will be fine. He will teach students to succeed and then he'll make enough from their tithes that he'll be able to pay back his hand. More than anything, he'll get the respect from the guild that he deserves.

"Silence, all of you," the king says in a bored voice. He raises a hand in the air, waiting for the courtroom to quiet. When it does, he eyes Barnabus. "You have heard my verdict. Do you have a problem with it?"

Barnabus's expression grows sulky. "I just—"

"Do you have a problem with it?" the king repeats, his tone flat.

"Of course not, Your Majesty." He bows and backs away. "Chatworth Hold will comply with your decision. I will inform my father's men at once so they can prepare the treasury."

And I'd be willing to bet that his father won't be thrilled.

"Let us continue," the king says. "Bring up Magpie's students."

Hands linked, we get to our feet. Kipp leads the way as we head to stand in front of the king. I keep my chin up, because I don't want to look guilty. I know what I did. I accept responsibility for it.

"Magpie's students, you have been accused of attempting to steal from the guild. You—"

"It was me," I blurt out, stepping forward. "I was the one behind everything. The others are innocent."

"No, Aspeth—" Lark protests. Gwenna takes my hand and Mereden steps forward to my side, Kipp next to her.

The king sighs heavily and then raises his hand, silencing us. "Let me speak, or it's going to go badly for you."

Chastised, I duck my head. Can't piss off the king or we're just going to make things worse.

"I have been told that while Aspeth was the mastermind, she could not possibly work on her own. Seeing you now, I agree."

Ouch.

"Therefore, I find the Five of Magpie's students guilty of attempted theft and breaking guild law. Guild law states that you should be expelled from the guild entirely."

My heart sinks. I've doomed the others.

"I've also been told that in the crypt you found, multiple Greater Artifacts have been discovered. And that the discovery of a Greater Artifact automatically gives a student full membership into the guild."

I ache all over again, because I have mixed emotions. Part of me is devastated that the crypt has been robbed of its treasures, but at the same time, I'm grateful that something was found to help our cause. I'm just as bad as any other tomb robber. Does this mean that we're safe?

"I can't let the two cancel each other out," the king continues. "Because then you would be left with no punishment at all. So my punishment is thus: You will be rejected from this year's schooling. You will be repeaters, or you can leave. Should you wish to stay and repeat your lessons, you will work for the guild in whatever capacity any rejected students provide work to the guild, and then you will be allowed to enroll again next year. I don't approve of your actions, but your teacher was Magpie. A corrupted pool poisons all that drink from it. Next year, when you rejoin the guild as students again, keep this in mind and stay out of trouble, hmm?"

I'm crushed to hear his answer. No more school for us. We're to work for the guild and try again next year. I've caused the others so much trouble, and again, it was all for nothing.

"Lady Aspeth Honori, I would speak to you in private," the king says. He gets to his feet and flicks his hand again. "The rest of you are dismissed."

Uneasy, I look at the others. Mereden has tears in her eyes, and Gwenna is stoic. Lark looks as if she wants to punch something, and Kipp licks his eyeball over and over again, a nervous tic. I squeeze Gwenna's hand and let it go, then turn to the others. "We'll meet up after this and talk. I'm so sorry."

"There's nothing to be sorry over," Lark tells me.

"We knew what we were getting into" is all Gwenna says. "Now, go mind the king."

She's got a fear of nobility and their reprisals, I remember. I nod and follow after the king, his guards moving to flank me. I don't know what he has to say in private, but I'm sure it's nothing that's going to make me happy. If he was exonerating me, he'd do so in front of everyone.

And there's no reason to exonerate me, truly. I *am* guilty.

FORTY-EIGHT

ASPETH

THE GUARDS LEAD me down the hall to a room with a large, rounded door. A guard stands outside, and when I go in, there are two more of the king's honor guard there, crowded in behind a heavy, ornate wood desk. On one wall, there's a shelf full of artifacts, and on another, rows of old books. Behind the desk is a large painted portrait of Rooster in all his guild regalia, and I suspect this is his office. I don't know if it's ironic or amusing that he's got a huge portrait of himself in his office, but it fits what I know of him.

"Shut the door behind us," the king tells his guards, walking a few steps ahead of me. He pauses behind the desk, pulling off his gloves, and then thumps into the seat. I carefully stand across from him until he waves in my direction, indicating I should sit, too.

Once I've perched on a chair, he eyes me.

"Explain to me the reasoning as to why a sheltered holder's daughter would go to Vastwarren by herself and join the Royal Artifactual Guild. I'm trying to piece it together in my head and it seems a ridiculous choice." He indicates I should speak. "So make me understand."

"My father has gambled away our ancestral artifacts," I say, uneasy. I hate telling that to someone in power like the king, but I'm also aware he could try to confiscate my father's holding at any time regardless. "We're exposed and helpless without any sort of magic to aid us in protection of our people. Our hold is also penniless. There are no funds to replace anything. So I thought I would join the guild and get replacement artifacts for my father."

"By stealing them?"

"No, I was going to do it the right way, the honorable way. Have it taken out of my guild tithe, no matter how many years it takes. Repair our defenses quietly. But Lord Barnabus arrived and started paying for guild teams to hunt artifacts so he could go to war, and I knew where he was planning to attack. I had to do something."

He nods thoughtfully, leaning back. "It seems to me that you could have prevented all of this by marrying someone, Lady Aspeth. Like, say, Lord Barnabus. I'm told there was a broken engagement?"

I nod. "He said unpleasant things about me to someone and I overheard it. He was marrying me for my position."

"Then it seems to me that the best revenge would have been to marry him." The king gives me a polite smile. "Let him pay for artifacts for his new home."

"I didn't trust him to do so," I say bluntly. Fury builds inside me, but how can I expect the king to understand? He's a man, born to privilege. Of course he'd suggest that I marry Barnabus. "I expected to find myself having an 'accident' once he determined there were no artifacts in the Honori treasury. Then he would have both the hold and a rich new bride, and my father and I would be dead."

"An extreme scenario. You think he would plan such a thing?"

"I believe it to be true."

The king taps his fingertips together. "As much as I hate to admit it, Lady Aspeth, your suspicions match mine. I've been watching the Chatworth family for some time and nothing he's done this day surprises me. He's a holder's son, though, so you understand why I cannot punish him more harshly than I have . . . just as I cannot punish you properly. You both deserve to go to prison and yet here I am with my hands tied."

I say nothing, my hands clasped politely in my lap. Something about the king's choice of words and his too-affable expression tell me that he's very angry about the entire scenario.

"I'm tempted to just marry you to Barnabus as was the original plan and send you home, but I would also hate to be responsible for your untimely death, should it happen."

"And I am already married," I say lightly, trying to smile.

"Yes, to a Taurian. Tell me, was that willingly?"

I nod. "It was my suggestion. I'm quite happy in the union."

"And do you expect this guild Taurian to run your father's hold as his heir?" When I shake my head mutely, he arches a brow. "But marrying him is considered a disgrace, and now, as far as you know, your father has no suitable heir. What were you thinking?"

"I was thinking that I would like to stay alive, Your Majesty. I took the problems one at a time. I still haven't solved that one yet."

He huffs a laugh. "Nor have I. I am going to have to think on it for some time today." The king sets his hand on the table and drums it, his many rings winking. I recognize at least two of them as Prellian. "Which brings me to the current issue of the artifact you stole. The two joined rings. The mist-wall artifacts. You recall them?"

I hold my breath, trying to remain neutral. "Yes, your Majesty."

"As stolen Greater Artifacts, they have been returned to the guild and thus sold to a holder."

"I . . . see."

I should have expected it. I *did* expect it.

Even so, hearing such a thing breaks something inside me. All of that work for nothing. All of the danger, the betrayals, the cave-in, the ratlings, the crypt . . . it was all for nothing. Tears slide down my face, even though I do my best to keep my composure. I clench my hands tightly in my lap to keep from outright sobbing in the king's face, but the silent tears escape no matter how hard I try.

"You understand you left me no choice. I couldn't very well just hand them over to you after you stole them." The look he gives me is admonishing.

"Of course not." Defeat crushes me. There's no hope left.

Honori Hold is lost.

"The guild wished to press charges, but I've managed to soothe them. I've handled the artifacts in question and I have removed your name from their rolls. You have been removed from the guild, with no option to re-enroll."

Removed from the guild.

Permanently.

Is it considered a knife to the heart if your heart is already stomped into the floor? "I understand, Your Majesty."

"I don't know that you do," he snaps. "You cannot imagine the sheer number of meetings I've had to soothe ruffled feathers over this and prevent war. You had better appreciate what I've done for you."

"I do," I say dully. "Thank you, Your Majesty."

No guild. Ever. A small part of me thinks I was never cut out for it. That I'd rather sit by a cozy fire with a book and read about Old Prell than cave dive into the ruins. But now I can't help my father acquire more artifacts. I can't help Honori Hold, and once word gets out that our home is defenseless, other families will come sniffing around, trying to accomplish what Barnabus did not.

There's a knock at the door.

"Good," the king says, a hint of a smile on his face. "The lord holder is here to pick up the artifact rings I've sold to him."

Is this part of my punishment? I wonder as the guard goes to the door. That I have to watch the handoff of all my hopes and dreams?

The door opens and a bearded nobleman steps in, dressed in fur-trimmed robes and wearing a feathered cap.

My . . . father?

FORTY-NINE

ASPETH

THE KING'S PLAN is brilliant," my father says over dinner. "You're lucky he stepped in to fix things after you botched them, Aspeth darling. What a ridiculous plan you had."

I poke at my stew. After the king dismissed us—and sold my father the artifacts I worked so hard to retrieve—we've regrouped for an evening meal. Or rather, we're supposed to be eating, but I don't have much of an appetite. I can't get over that my father's here. I can't get over that the king was toying with me, when he'd already made plans with Father. He just wanted to see my responses. It sits sourly in my belly, just like the oniony stew. My father didn't want to stay on guild property, as he feels they spy on holders. So I find myself at the King's Onion again. The same barmaid is slinging drinks, a sympathetic look on her face when I arrive with my dour, unpleasant father. Father sniffs in distaste at the look of the place, but his attitude changes once I tell him that they have an artifact from the king himself. Artifacts always impress everyone. The stew tastes heavily of onions and meat, and it smells delicious. My stomach, however, is far too tense for me to take more than a bite.

Father has no such issues. He has a bowl of stew in front of him, his second one, and he sips froth from his beer, his manners impeccable despite the sheer amount of food he can put away. Hawk eats just as much as my father, I realize, but Hawk eats nothing save vegetables and grains. My father, however, just likes to eat. And drink. And gamble. He spoons a chunk of meat and shakes his head at me. "Well?"

I glance up, feeling like a chastised child. "I'm sorry?"

"What were you thinking, daughter?"

Ah, yes. I was thinking that someone had to do something to save Honori Hold, but of course I can't say that to my father. He'll reach across this table and slap my mouth, and no one will stop him because he's a holder. I toy with a chunk of carrot in my stew idly. "I thought I could help."

"It's lucky for you that we have Liatta to thank," he grumbles, glancing up. "Ah. Here she comes now."

The fair Liatta. I've never been in the same room as her, because mistresses and daughters don't mix. We're kept in very careful circles, and I'm supposed to pretend like I don't know that my father has a mistress at court. That Liatta is so beautiful she's slept with the king himself, and that she's been my father's paramour for a long while. I've never met her, but the woman who glides through the crowd of tables fits my expectations.

She's beautiful, of course. Well dressed. And from the look in her eyes, sharp. I suppose you need to be all those things to survive at court, and Liatta thrives there. Her brocade dress is sumptuous, her neckline deep enough to show the swells of her breasts just above her tightly cinched corset, and she wears a fashionable little ruff around her neck in lieu of jewelry. Her hair is pulled into multiple knots atop her head, each one covered in a ruby-studded golden net. Her dark eyes are crafty as she flicks her bracelet-encrusted arm, indicating her servant should pull out her seat. The woman attending her does so, brushing off the wooden chair with a napkin and then wiping the table before Liatta sits down gracefully. She has to be at least ten years older than me, but you wouldn't know it just from looking at her. Liatta makes me feel old and frumpy, with my dirty hair and a freshly cleaned (but extremely plain) dress that Gwenna brought when she'd heard I was going to be released.

"Lady Aspeth," Liatta says in a rich, careful voice. "It's lovely to finally meet you."

Is it? Because it feels awkward to me. I smile, but I genuinely don't know what to do. Society says that I should ignore her, because she's a courtesan. But then again, society also says I shouldn't marry a Taurian. "My father tells me I should thank you," I blurt, parroting his words. That seems safe. "Have you spoken to the king on my behalf?"

Liatta chuckles. "Not quite." She nudges her servant, and the woman trots off to get her food and drink. "A great deal has been happening while you have been awaiting your trial."

I'm puzzled, and I glance to my father.

"Your new husband, the Taurian . . ." Father pauses and gives me another disapproving look, as if he can't let a moment pass without reminding me that he's not happy about Hawk. "He sent a crow with a letter. Said you were in Vastwarren and needed the protection of the family name."

My eyebrows go up. "He said that?"

Liatta shakes her head. "His missive was incoherent, actually. It was full of rambling about marriage and the guild and danger and magpies."

"Ah." He must have been totally lost in the Conquest Moon's thrall, and yet he still knew to contact my father so Lord Honori could throw his weight around. "And after you received that, you contacted the king?"

They exchange a look. "We happened to be at court already, and I suggested to your father that we needed to reestablish business with the guild anyhow."

So it wasn't about me. Yet something about all of this isn't making sense. "But there's no money—"

Liatta clears her throat. Father just takes another bite of bread and chews, stubbornly avoiding eye contact with me.

I blink at the two of them, wondering what it is I'm missing.

"The queen is pregnant with her second child," Liatta says delicately after a long pause. "They are hoping this one is a son."

I wait for a further explanation, because I'm still not following. I take a bite of stew.

My father finally speaks up, seeing my confusion. "Liatta needs to leave court. So I married her."

I choke on the stew, spewing it into my napkin. "You *what?*"

It's commonly accepted that a nobleman will have relations with a courtesan, but marrying one . . . ? Marrying one is about as likely as, well, a noble marrying a Taurian. Still, my father has always been such a stickler for propriety. He's been seeing Liatta for a decade now and has never mentioned marrying her.

"I married her," Father retorts angrily. "You're one to talk."

"I'm not talking." I cough. "I'm just surprised."

"The queen doesn't wish to see me at court any longer." Liatta gives me a polite smile as I drink some water to soothe my throat. "The king and I had a liaison once, and she feels threatened. I understand that it's in my best interests to retire to the countryside, so the king offered me a dowry."

I nod, sipping more water. The queen must really want beautiful Liatta gone if he's throwing money at her to make it happen.

My father speaks again. "So I married her and had our son legitimized."

I spew water this time. *"You have a son?"*

Liatta's expression is carefully blank, but my father's is defensive. "Yes, we do. His name is Garoth and the king is his godfather."

"Oh" is all I manage to choke out.

"He's seven," Liatta says.

Oh.

My father has had another child for seven years and no one told me? Everyone at court must have known. The king must have known . . . which means he was truly just testing me.

"Garoth is the heir now that he's legitimate," Father says, and focuses a scowl upon me. "Which is a good thing, because your behavior has been shameless. What were you thinking, Aspeth?"

Again with the "what were you thinking." I drink more water, trying to keep it down this time, and eye Liatta. Her expression is careful, and she doesn't touch the stew or wine that her maid sets down in front of her. She's watching me. Waiting to see how I'm going to take the news that I've been deposed from my position as heir.

I suppose I should be angry. Furious. Hurt.

I'm relieved. So damn relieved I want to laugh aloud. Liatta has schemed at court for years and now she's neatly tangled my father. She will be Lady Honori and her son will be Honori's heir. He can't be any worse than my father is, so I don't have a problem with it. I can stay in Vastwarren . . . or I can leave.

My future is finally mine.

"I see," I say carefully. "My congratulations to young Garoth. But I must recommend again, Father, that you acquire more artifacts. I know you said the king sold you my rings—"

"The rings you stole, you mean," Father corrects with a stern glare. "Such a bad look, Aspeth. I taught you better than that."

"—but one set of rings is not going to protect the entire hold," I continue, ignoring him. "More has to be done. The knights have to be paid. The guild has no Honori team. Crops—"

Liatta holds up a beringed hand. "I understand your concerns," she says, stopping me. "It is a conversation I had with your father prior to our marriage. I am not handing over my fortune simply for him to toss it away. I am in charge now." Her expression hardens ever so slightly. "I will control Honori's funds. And I've established a team with the guild so we can repair our defenses. It will be expensive, but necessary."

Father frowns at his new wife. "I really don't think—"

She turns to him and freezes him with a look. "I'm in charge of the finances, Corin." Her voice is firm but sweet. "You'll recall we've discussed this extensively. You'll have an allowance."

I smother the laughter that threatens to rise from me. I suspect Honori Hold is in excellent hands. Liatta has maneuvered her way about court for so long that she's going to know just how to handle my father. She's not going to let him bankrupt the hold and then leave her son with a mess. She's going to rule with an iron fist. She's going to put my father on an *allowance.*

I almost want to be there to see it. Almost.

FIFTY

HAWK

MY WIFE HAS been gone for too long.

I know it's just for dinner with her father so she can explain her motives. I've met the man, and a more pompous and careless fool I've never seen. He's like every holder lord I've met, concerned with his own comforts over the needs of his people. His court lady should keep him in check, though. I've met her type before and she hasn't worked this hard to let him piss away everything she's gained. I'm not worried they'll insist Aspeth return to Honori Hold. The new wife won't want Aspeth around to object to how she runs things.

Mostly, I just want to grab Aspeth and hold her tight against my chest. It's been a long, eventful day—a long, eventful month, actually—and we haven't had a chance to have a conversation since we left the crypt. I've been embroiled in guild bullshit all day and all night, working with Rooster to move Magpie's master ranking over to me, establishing my guild contracts, ensuring that Magpie will have a stipend of some kind no matter what happens, fighting for her students to be given another chance, and then because I'm Taurian, pushing for others of my kind to be given more weight with the guild. Osprey, Raptor, and so many others work too hard to get overlooked permanently. I haven't gotten as far as I want, but with me as a guild master, I'm hoping that it will pave the way for others.

That's for the future, though. For the present, I want to know what Aspeth's plans are.

I want to know what's going to happen between us.

I want to know what the king said.

I hate having to wait to even talk to my wife. That the guards outside the inn have made it very clear I'm not allowed in to see her until she leaves her father's table. So I stand outside, in my full guild master regalia, and I wait, arms crossed.

I can be just as bullheaded as any noble. I'm making it clear to them that I'm not leaving without my wife. Bad enough that she's been sent off with her father without anyone letting me know. I've already filled Rooster's ears on what I think of that.

"They're holders," he'd explained as if that answered everything. "They don't answer to me."

I don't care if he's right. I'm still pissed about it.

So I wait. And when one of the guards sends a message inside, I half expect to be escorted from the premises despite all my trappings. Instead, they open the door to the inn and let me through. My wife is on her feet, and she dutifully kisses the cheek of her father, an elder balding man with a thick gut and ridiculous pointy shoes that mean he cares more for fashion than for common sense. He gives me a dismissive look—which I ignore—and then heads out with a pretty woman on his arm. Aspeth remains a few steps behind, her gaze on me.

"Wife," I say when she gets close enough, a wealth of meaning in my tone.

She doesn't seem to notice my choice of words. Her hands smooth down her plain dress and she leans toward me, her voice low. "You should have joined us for dinner. Perhaps then he wouldn't have lectured me as if I were a foolish child."

I want to tell her that I tried to join them for dinner, but it's just as well. People have been lecturing me for days now on taking advantage of a noblewoman. Of my shameful morals in daring to marry a holder's daughter while being Taurian. I can miss out on hearing it (again) from her father. "I'm here now."

Aspeth squints up at me, and then touches the bright red sash across my coat, studded with golden pins. "And you look very fine, too. Red suits you."

"You approve, then?" I offer her my arm.

She takes it, gazing up at me as we exit the inn. "Why wouldn't I approve? If anyone deserves it, it's you. I've seen how much you do for the guild."

Things are different now, though. She's seen it through the eyes of a student, a hopeful who dreams of joining the guild. Someone who put everything on the line to join and has now been banned from it entirely. I know Rooster's decision and I hate it, but the king supported it. I know Aspeth must be crushed inside. She had her reasons for joining—to save her father's hold—but I also know that she's dreamed of and studied the ruins of Old Prell so extensively that it's been more than just a recent plan. No one loves Old Prell half as much as Aspeth Honori, and now it's been taken from her.

And it makes me feel helpless, because I don't know what to do about it. If you need brute force, I'm the one. If you need an expert on the maze of tunnels beneath Vastwarren, I'm the bull you need. Taurians have a keen sense of smell and an innate ability to always know where we are going. That's why we're perfect in the Everbelow. I can handle that, just like I can handle teaching students how to become part of the guild.

What I can't handle is the thought of my wife's crushing disappointment. I don't know what to say that will make it better.

So I'm silent as we walk through the sloping, cobbled streets of Vastwarren. It's dark, with flickering lamps lighting the streets. Someone's horse snorts nearby, and I neatly move Aspeth out of the way of a particularly muddy patch on the street, but other than that, we walk in silence.

"My father has a new heir," Aspeth finally says, her fingers playing on my sleeve as we walk.

"Ah." Dark God's five hells, what am I supposed to say to that? Not only has she lost the guild, but she's lost her inheritance? This is just getting worse with every step.

"I'm sorry it's not us. I hate to disappoint you."

She's thinking about me? I turn to look down at her, surprised. "I haven't given it a single thought, Aspeth."

Now she's the one who looks surprised. "No? Most people marry a holder's daughter because they want power. They dream of what they can do with the hold in their control."

"I didn't know you were a holder's daughter when I married you, remember? All I was thinking about was how uncomfortable the upcoming Conquest Moon was going to be if I didn't have a partner. And if I recall correctly, you propositioned me." I shake my head. "It's never been about your hold." When she simply nods, her expression distant, I try to change the subject. "Besides, I'll be busy here."

"Because you're a guild master." She reaches out and touches my chest, and the sash proudly displayed across it. It's not something I'd normally wear around the city, because I hate pretentiousness, but Aspeth seems to like the sight of it on me. If she touches my chest one more time, I'm tempted to find the nearest alley and fling her up against a wall with her skirts over her head.

Hells, I'm tempted to do that anyhow.

"Are you happy?" she asks me, her voice soft.

I consider this. Am I? It's something I both wanted and assumed I would never have. "I am. It gives me more of a voice. It lets me pave the way for other Taurians. It lets me train fledglings the way I think they should be trained . . . and I'll make coin if they graduate. So aye, I'm happy." I flex my hand, the magicked one. "And I got Rooster to waive my debt for this."

Her eyes go wide. "You did?"

"Aye. He can't very well take it away from a guild master, can he? That wouldn't look right. I used his love of bureaucracy against him. Told him it's a far better show of his leadership to have strong, competent masters who are loyal and wield the artifacts that they teach about . . . that, and I'd put in a good word with the Taurians when it comes time to reelect the head guild master."

Aspeth grins up at me, but then her expression fades. "Have you seen Magpie since she left the courtroom?" she asks. "Was she very upset?"

I don't know if she's avoiding a hard conversation with me or if there's simply too much to cover, but I'm surprised she asks about Magpie. After all, the woman tried to get her killed. "I have not. Rooster dealt with her prior to today. For all her courtroom dramatics, she knew she was in danger of losing her position simply from the drinking and how many classes she's had fail in the past few years." I pause. "She actually told Rooster he needed to promote me, though. That if she was giving up her spot, it should be given to me."

"She's right."

I sigh. "It's just always complicated with Magpie. She does something unforgivable, and then turns around and tries to make it better. I can't look past that she tried to have you killed, though." I shake my head. "She's destroyed any friendship we might have had." I pull Aspeth a little closer to me.

"And the others? Gwenna? Lark? Kipp? Mereden? Were they devastated at failing?" Her tone is careful, but I know just how much her Five means to her.

"They're drinking away their sorrows," I tell her. "They've joined the repeater ranks. It's not a bad thing, though. They'll get more guild experience, and after hearing what was found in the crypt, I think more teachers will be eager to pull them in. . . ." I wonder if the next part will hurt her feelings, but decide to say it anyway. "I've let them know I would be happy to teach them again."

"I'm glad. You're an excellent teacher and they deserve the best."

I wait for her to say more, but Aspeth falls silent again. We make it to Magpie's nest—my nest, now, I suppose—and pause in front of the door. The lights are out, and no one is inside except a big orange shape in the window. Aspeth makes a choked little sound of happiness at the sight of her cat, and I suddenly get tired of dancing around the topic I really want to ask about. "What about you?"

She looks up at me, her eyes dark and glossy in the moonlight. "What do you mean?"

"I know what the king decided. What are you going to do now?"

The pain on her face is obvious, and I ache that she's had her dream torn away from her. If I could give it back to her, I would, and I hate how helpless it makes me feel to realize that no amount of work, no amount of sweat equity I put in, can bring back Aspeth's most cherished dream.

I can't fix this for her, and it mucking kills me.

"I don't know," Aspeth confesses. There's a fragile expression on her face. She's completely lost. "I tried not to think beyond my goal—protecting the hold. That was my entire purpose. But now there's a new heir and Liatta's money and I'm not needed or even wanted at Honori. The guild doesn't want me, either. I . . . don't know what to do with myself."

"You could stay married to me." I feel like a fool blurting it out. She probably doesn't want anything to do with me now. Aspeth could do so much better than a nobody like me. She deserves wealth. Stability. A home of her own. I have none of these things, my life tied to the guild.

But I would love the fuck out of her every day.

She looks up at me with an expression of pure surprise. "You still want me?"

Everything that's been happening must have truly beat upon her self-esteem if she questions this. I thought I'd made it quite clear how I felt the two dozen times I knotted her in the span of a few days, but perhaps she needs to be told again. "Woman, I'm obsessed with you. I think I'd lose my mind if you left."

"But it was supposed to be a marriage of convenience," she tells me, stepping a bit closer. "So you could chaperone me."

"It's still convenient for me. It will likely be convenient for me in fifty years, when I'm old and gray and my horns are pitted. It will be convenient for me until the end of time, Aspeth. Do you understand? I need you. I want you with me. And I know it might be hard for you to stay, but . . . I would love if you tried." My voice grows suspiciously hoarse. "Please."

She gazes up at me, quiet.

Then, with an undignified squeal, my aristocratic holder wife flings herself into my arms. She jumps and I automatically wrap myself around her, even as her legs go around my waist. "I love you," she tells me over and over, peppering my long nose with kisses. "I love you, Hawk. Are you sure?"

"More than sure. You belong with me." I hold her tightly in my arms, my heart light. "You're my wife. My love. My everything."

She slides her arms around my neck and kisses the side of my face. "Let's go inside. I want to be with you."

Five hells, I want that, too. But I hesitate, because I need to be certain. "I just don't want you to have regrets, Aspeth. I know you can do better than me—"

She tugs lightly on my nose ring. "You hush. I wanted someone who loved me for me. Someone who doesn't care if I talk about Old Prellian glyphs for hours. I don't care if you have no money." She laughs, the sound bright. "I don't, either! I'm not even the heir anymore! I'm . . . free." She says the word in a dazed voice, as if not quite believing it, and then laughs again. "I can do as I like." She gives me a sly look. "I can do *who* I like."

"So you can." I open the door to the dormitory and carry my wife in. The flags and banners still show Magpie's symbol, but that will all be changed over the next few days, along with the master's quarters. For now, I'm content to be in the room at the front of the dorm, where I've always been.

The moment I open the door, the big orange beast launches itself off the windowsill with a yowl.

"Squeaker!" Aspeth cries with delight. "You're all right!" She slides out of my grip and runs to her beloved pet, scooping the fat cat into her arms and hugging it tight. She presses enthusiastic kisses to the cat's head just like she did to me, and ignores the fur flying around her. "I was so worried about you."

"Gwenna helped me," I say, feeling a little foolish. "She made sure your cat was taken care of. And contrary to what it might look like, I did brush her." I wave a hand in the air, swatting at some of the orange fluff drifting past. "It doesn't do any good."

Aspeth chuckles. "I know. She's the woolliest cat ever, but that just makes her special." She squeezes the cat again, and I feel like I'm interrupting their moment as she scratches the thing's head and purring fills the room.

"She slept with me every night," I grumble, watching as my wife sits on the bed with her cat. "Right on your pillow. I woke up with a mouthful of fur every morning."

"That's how you know Squeaker approves of you," Aspeth says happily, and presses another elated kiss atop the cat's head. "She likes you just as much as I do."

"I know you love her, so I made sure she was safe. I wouldn't let anyone touch her."

Aspeth bows her head over the cat, and then she looks up at me. Tears streak down her face again, and I feel like an arse for making her cry. "I know you wouldn't. You're the best of men."

"I'm not a man. I'm a Taurian."

She gives a watery giggle and sets the cat down on the bed. "Even better." She crosses to my side, and her clothes are covered in drifting cat hair, but I don't care. She gazes up at me, her eyes full of emotion, and then slides a hand under the sash across my chest. "My Taurian."

"Yours," I agree. "Since the moment I laid eyes upon you."

And then I lean in and press my muzzle to her mouth.

It's . . . vaguely a kiss. Taurian mouths don't match up with human ones, and it feels awkward even as I try it. But I still want to try. I lift my head and gaze down at Aspeth. She looks wonderstruck, touching her mouth. "Did you just kiss me?"

"I must have done it wrong if you have to ask."

She shakes her head. "It was wonderful."

I cup the back of her neck and tilt her face up to mine once more. "My sweet Aspeth," I murmur, pressing a second kiss on the tip of her nose. It feels just as awkward as the first, but she makes a happy sigh, and so I continue, kissing her cheek and then her brow. "My lovely, precious wife."

Her expression grows dreamy, and her hands roam over my coat. "Shall I distract the cat with food from the kitchen so I can be alone with my husband?"

"I like that idea."

Aspeth gives me a sweet smile and scoops her cat up again, burying her face against its neck as she carries it across the dormitory. I pull off my sash and coat, stripping off some of the many layers of full guild regalia. I'm most comfortable in just a shirt and breeches, but I suppose that will be changing now that I'm a guild master. Ah well.

She returns a while later, her arms empty and her clothes changed, her hair wet from a bath. Aspeth immediately crosses the room to me, a sly smile on her face. "I decided to wash up and borrowed one of the fledgling uniforms. Getting started without me?"

"Just taking a few things off." I pull her into my arms and rub my nose against the curve of her neck. It's half-hidden by the high collar of her uniform, and I want to tear the damn thing from her body. "How I've missed your scent."

"I've missed you, too. Everything about you." Her hands roam over my shirt, as if she wants to touch me everywhere all at once. "Can I undress you?"

I nod, and then she pulls my clothing off, piece by piece, until I stand before her in nothing but my skin. She makes a pleased sound, moving forward and pressing her mouth to my chest, even as her hand slides to my cock. Aspeth curls her fingers around my length, teasing it, and then glances up at me. "No knot?"

"Not for another five years."

"It'll be strange without it," she confesses.

"I'll make it good for you. You won't be disappointed."

"Never disappointed," she says, voice achingly sweet, and strokes my cock again. Her fingers dance over the tip, and when a bead of pre-cum appears, she draws circles on my skin with it. "How far we've come in just two months, you and I."

"Yes. Now you're no longer asking me why I'm dripping."

She buries her face against my chest, her shoulders shaking with laughter. "Cruel of you to toss that in my face."

"I thought it was charming. I think I fell in love with you in that moment."

"Well, you had a funny way of showing it. I thought you hated me for the longest time."

Never. "Just fighting my feelings. I'm not good with them."

Aspeth smiles up at me, and she's the most beautiful thing I've ever seen, Taurian or human or fae or anything else. Nothing can compare to my wife's teasing smile. I want to crush her against me and hold her tight and never let her go. "I still haven't yelled at you for your stunt in the tunnels."

"Tomorrow," she tells me, her hand tightening around my cock. She gives me a pump with her fist, one that makes my breath catch. "Tomorrow we think about the rest of the world. Tonight I just want it to be us."

I like that idea.

FIFTY-ONE

HAWK

I REACH OVER AND tug the shirt over her head and then untie the laces of her corset, grumbling at how many layers women wear. All the while she pets and toys with my cock. It seems to take forever to get her undressed, but once her clothes are pooling at her feet, there's nothing but soft, dimpled flesh in front of my eyes and I want to feast on her forever.

I cup one heavy breast, pleased that it's large enough to fill my hand. Her nipple puckers and I stroke it even as I rub my muzzle against her face and neck. Her hand continues to tease my cock, but it doesn't take long for me to get as hard as a rock. I know from my hazy memories of our time in the crypt that Aspeth is responsive, but she needs to be petted a bit first. So I haul her over to the bed, set her down on the mattress, and lie down next to her. I use one hand to play with her gorgeous breasts while I finger her cunt until she's slick with arousal.

She makes these sweet, gaspy noises when I touch her that set my body on fire with need, and I stand up to move between her parted thighs, murmuring encouragement as I fit my cock to her entrance. She's hot and wet and clutches at my cock like a glove, and when I rock over her, she moans and wraps her legs around my waist.

"I like the knot," she pants between my thrusts, her tits bouncing as I fuck her, "but this is nicer." Her hand strays down my arm, and she digs her nails into my muscles, her back arching. "Oh gods, you feel huge even now."

Such flattery.

I make love to my wife, my strokes leisurely and deep as I claim her, and when Aspeth comes, she quakes around my cock and holds tightly to me, her orgasm a thing of beauty as she falls apart in my arms. Then it's my turn, and I slide my thumb over her clit, making sure she feels every stroke as I pound into her. Her cunt clenches around me a second time as I come, and then stars dance before my eyes, my hooves slamming on the wood floor as I grind deep inside her, shooting my release.

Aspeth runs her fingers over my pectorals while I come back to myself. "We never had birth control. In the crypt. Or now."

It's something I thought about, days after, while Aspeth sat in prison and waited for the king to arrive in Vastwarren. I reach for the table next to the bed and pull out the drawer, producing a bead on a leather thong. "You can wear this."

She sits up—or tries to, except I've got her pinned, her hips locked to mine. "Is that a Prellian pause-bead?"

"Aye. You've seen them?"

"Heard of them. The books were very reticent to discuss anything that affected female anatomy. How does it work?"

"As long as you wear this, even if you're pregnant now, nothing in your womb will advance in time until you take it off. We'll handle the whole children thing when you're ready."

Aspeth pauses. "What if I'm never ready?"

"Then you can wear that to your grave." I nuzzle another kiss against her jaw. "I just want you to be happy, Aspeth. I've never demanded children from you. Never would."

"I know. I just . . . I'm not ready yet. I think I would like children but not now. Not with everything so uncertain." She slips the bead over her head. "Maybe in a year?"

"Whatever you decide," I say, and I mean it. "You—"

There's an urgent knock at the front door.

We both groan. Aspeth skitters out from under me, grabbing a robe and wrapping it around her body. "Are you expecting someone?"

I shake my head. "Perhaps one of the others forgot something? They've been moved into the repeater barracks." Her expression clouds, and I know she's thinking of them and the trouble she's caused. I squeeze her hand, because it wasn't as if she forced anyone to do anything. They are her friends and chose to help her. They have a chance to enter the guild again next season. "Don't blame yourself."

"I can't help it—"

The knock at the door occurs again, louder and more insistent, and I growl in frustration. If it's Magpie, I'm going to march her to the nearest jail. I shove pants on while Aspeth cleans up, and I head out to the main entrance, my hooves stomping and expressing my irritation loudly to all. When Aspeth appears in the doorway to the bedroom with the robe tight around her body, I move to the front door and fling it open.

A guild scholar is there, his hand raised as if he means to knock a third time. He shrinks back at the sight of an angry Taurian looming in the doorway, uncertainty on his face. He holds a box in his arms and clutches it tightly even as he steps back. "I was told Lady Aspeth was here?"

"*My wife* is tired. Guild business can wait." It can wait forever, as far as I'm concerned. They've made her miserable enough. "Come back tomorrow. Or next week. Or next month."

Aspeth pushes past me, squinting. Then a look of surprise crosses her face at our visitor. "Archivist Kestrel? Is something wrong?"

He brightens at the sight of Aspeth. "Lady, pleased to meet you again. Nothing is wrong. Well, not yet. There is a matter of some urgency and I thought to ask you something. You can read Prellian, yes?"

She glances up at me and then gives a tiny nod. "Old better than new, of course. New Prellian is region-dependent and we don't have great examples of some of the more far-flung regions. . . ." Aspeth trails off as he opens the box in front of her, revealing it like he would some sort of offering. "Oh. A sistral?"

The archivist nods eagerly. "You know of them?"

Aspeth pulls the thing carefully out of the box. "Just that they were musical instruments. So few of them have been found intact and I'm told the only two enchanted ones are in Lord Besral's care." She holds it reverently, squinting in the flickering light, and then makes a frustrated sound. "Come inside."

The little man hurries inside, carefully giving me as much space as he can. If I wasn't in the process of going to bed with my wife, I'd be amused. As it is, I'm cranky and feeling protective. "Aspeth has had a long day," I warn him. "This had better be quick."

"This is an instrument scheduled to ship out to Lord Besral tomorrow, actually," Archivist Kestrel says, trotting after Aspeth as she strides toward the nest's communications desk. "That's why I'm here tonight. I need a second opinion on the inscription, and my colleagues and I cannot agree. I know Lady Aspeth is supposed to be an expert with reading glyphs, and so here I am."

I grunt, still annoyed. Aspeth's no longer part of the guild—they made that quite clear. If he harasses her even a little, he's going to find my hoof in his arse.

But my wife digs around in a drawer, looking for a magnifying glass and carefully holding what looks like a hand-sized harp on a stick—the sistral—in her other hand. After she finds the glass, she makes another frustrated noise at the shadows. "It's too dark in here."

Sighing, I pull an unlit candle from its wall sconce and bring it to the desk, then light it and set it in a holder. "Better?"

"Yes, thank you, love." She peers down at the sistral with the magnifying glass, and I try not to preen at being called "love" in front of another. Ridiculous. I'm not some green lad in love for the first time, and yet my ears twitch and I catch myself beaming at my wife as she works.

Because she's *mine*.

"Oh dear," she says after a moment.

"What? What is it?" the archivist asks.

Aspeth straightens and turns to him, biting her lip. "I'm sorry, did you say that you're shipping this out to Lord Besral in the morning?" When he nods, she winces. "I'm sorry to tell you, but I believe this is a fake."

"A fake?" He sputters, though the sound isn't all that convincing, and my hackles go up. "What do you mean?"

"Do you see this glyph?" She pulls the magnifying glass out and holds it over the sistral's handle, pointing at a tiny triangular shape with her pinky finger. "It's the correct glyph, but the proper usage would have it after the descriptor, not before. . . ."

She trails off as Archivist Kestrel begins to chuckle, clasping his hands in delight. Her gaze flicks to me.

"It's a fake," Kestrel hoots with delight. "You are quite correct!"

"You seem rather excited about that," Aspeth says, expression careful. "Lord Besral—"

Kestrel waves a hand in the air. "It's not being shipped out. I was lying. I just wanted to test you one last time before I was certain." He looks absolutely thrilled. "It is indeed a fake and I should know; I created it for training purposes."

Aspeth's gaze slides to me again. "I don't understand. Why bring it here now? It's almost midnight."

I shrug, because I'm puzzled as well.

"Because I have to offer first!" The archivist reaches for Aspeth, and when I growl low, recoils again. He clasps his hands in front of him once more. "I want you to join us. We are not part of the guild officially, but we are employed by them. We take each uncovered artifact and record it and its purpose, and we study the ones that are mysteries. We look for ways to fix the broken ones, and work with the lord holders when they wish to acquire a magical artifact. We write treatises upon the artifacts in our care and train the guild's fledglings on how to properly spot a fake. I cannot think of anyone who would be better for archiving than you, Lady Aspeth."

Aspeth's eyes grow wide as he speaks. She looks at me again, excitement on her face, and then back at the archivist. "But . . . I've been forbidden . . . the guild . . ."

"You have been forbidden to join the guild, yes. No one said anything about the archivists. We are the ones who find ourselves not quite right for guild work, the ones who would rather study all day long instead of climbing through tunnels. We work in the guild hall and in the libraries, doing recordkeeping instead of excavating. As for the guild . . . Rooster himself recommended I come here this evening to speak my piece before others arrive."

Rooster did? I shouldn't be surprised. Even though he's overfond of politics, he always looks out for the guild, and the archivist is right—Aspeth would be an amazing archivist.

"It sounds like a dream," Aspeth breathes, and then pauses. "Wait, you said others are going to arrive? What others?"

Archivist Kestrel shakes his hands in the air with excitement. "Why, *all* the others, dear lady! Ever since that day in the artifact training room, word of your skills and knowledge has spread around Vastwarren. Every black-market merchant is going to be looking for ways to pay you to assist them, and every forger is going to want you. That's why I had to come here in the middle of the night. I had to get here before you agree to work for any of them. I would love to work alongside you, lady. I truly mean that."

Her lips part, and Aspeth's soft expression is gorgeous to see. It makes me ache, because now I want this for her. "I . . . I would stay here with Hawk, yes? I'm not going to leave my husband's side."

"Of course. It's a short walk from here to the archives. You will sleep in his bed every night, unlike a guild explorer." Then he colors red, as if he realizes what he's just said. "I mean . . ."

"She knows what you mean," I say dryly. "Well, Aspeth?"

Her eyes wide, she nods. "Yes, of course. I would love to."

"Splendid!" The archivist races forward and hugs Aspeth, then skitters away again. "I'm sorry! That wasn't well done of me! I'm just excited! You should see the things we have in the archives that are waiting to be deciphered and recorded. There are so many who can't read Old Prellian quite as well as me and I don't trust their interpretations, and I could truly use another set of hands and—" He gives a full-body shiver. "This is so very exciting!" He bounces toward the door, then pauses and scrambles back toward the desk. "Could I retrieve the sistral . . . ? It's the best fake I have."

"Oh, of course." She helps him box it back up.

When he clutches the box again, he beams at her once more. "I will return in the morning with the official guild contracts. You won't accept anyone else, will you? I'll insist that your salary be the equivalent of any man's."

"I won't disappoint you," she promises him.

"Then I will return at dawn!"

With that, the excitable archivist races back out into the night, leaving me amused and Aspeth dazed.

"Congratulations, little bird," I say to my wife. "It's not quite guild work but—"

"It's better," she blurts out, pressing her hands to her mouth. "Oh, I don't mean that. It's just . . . I think I'm vastly more suited for studying and analyzing than sleeping in tunnels and prying rings off the dead. I've felt so very guilty about everything in the crypt, Hawk. I don't think I could do it, even if I wanted to."

"Well, now it's decided. You'll work in the archives by day and come home to my bed every night," I tease.

She lets out another girlish squeal and then flings herself into my arms again. "Oh, Hawk! This is wonderful! I shall need new spectacles! Two pairs, at least! And more books! And—"

Her giddy delight fills me with joy. "And save it for the morning, sweetheart. There's time enough. For now, you need to relax. It's been a long day."

"The longest," she agrees, sagging against me. Then she pauses. "Do you suppose his name really is Kestrel? Is he like Lark and named after a bird?"

I snort. "No, the archivists take bird names as well." I lift her chin and kiss her on the mouth, and I think I'm getting better at this with practice. "You can be Sparrow after all."

"Your Sparrow!" she cries triumphantly. Then she pauses. "Don't hawks hunt sparrows?"

"They devour them."

Heat flares in her gaze. "Sounds lovely."

"It does, doesn't it?" And I lock the door behind me, then carry my wife back to our quarters. The future will have a lot of changes—there's an archivist to be inducted into her work, and a guild master who's going to need fledglings. There are repeaters—Gwenna, Kipp, and the others—to get settled.

There's a Taurian ring ceremony that needs to happen.

But all of that can wait until the morning.

Tonight—and every night thereafter—Sparrow is mine.

AUTHOR'S NOTE

ONE OF THE number one things we get asked as authors is "Where do you get your ideas?" And I usually reply "Everywhere," but I realize that's not a good answer. I've joked that my ideas are a sticky ball of trash (if you've ever played *Katamari Damacy*, you know what I'm talking about) and the ball keeps rolling around picking up random bits until it becomes a story. As I worked on *Bull Moon Rising*, I made a list of the major influences that made this story pull together for me. I thought I'd discuss them here. Enjoy!

Before we begin, I should explain that every story spends a little time on the back burner of my imagination before it becomes ready to write. This is where the ball of trash is quietly rolling around in the far reaches of my mind, trying to pick up enough bits to become a story.

One of the major bits for this particular story is the Royal Geographical Society. My brain goes down the rabbit hole on certain topics and I read nonfiction obsessively about the subject until I can figure out how to use it in a book. For a while, it was historical shipwrecks (which showed up in *Sworn to the Shadow God*) and then it was the Trojan War (which flavored a lot of *Bound to the Shadow Prince*). This book's rabbit hole was the Royal Geographical Society—a club of sorts that, during the Victorian era, was devoted entirely to exploring and mapping the world as they saw it. Like most societies and clubs, it had all kinds of backbiting and hierarchies, and of course female explorers were rarely welcome. I thought Isabella Bird (note the bird) was particularly inspiring. It might have been a boys' club, but Isabella Bird ignored that and did her own thing. She became a member—the first female member elected—and wrote books of her experiences. I knew I wanted to write a story about a similar sort of club and what it would be like as a woman explorer of the time. Add this to the rolling ball of trash.

A while later, I watched an archaeological documentary called *Secrets of the Saqqara Tomb*. This was such a great documentary about ancient Egypt. In it, they had teams of excavators that would get to work on the Saqqara plain—literally anywhere on the plain—and they would uncover something. Someone could be eating a sandwich on the side of a hill and would kick at the dirt and boom, an artifact. Another person could drag a spade over the sand and boom, a sarcophagus. Now, while this is an exaggeration to a certain extent (and probably for the film, too), I was fascinated at the thought of this entire buried civilization being . . . not so buried? Like, do people show up on weekends and just dig stuff out? Can anyone show up to Saqqara with a shovel and pail and hope to find something? I'm sure there are answers for those questions, but I preferred to let my mind noodle with this—so into the trash ball it went.

All of these background items really started to coalesce into a story as I played more video games during the pandemic. It's no secret I have a love for a good farming sim, and *Stardew Valley*, *My Time at Portia*, *Rune Factory*, and the like feed my exploration need without my having to leave home. Most of these games have some sort of "cavern" component where you go in and uncover minerals and gems, and the occasional artifact.

What if there was an old civilization that was readily explorable and full of all kinds of life-changing artifacts? What if a guild had a stranglehold on who gets to explore and who doesn't? What if that guild is a total boys' club? How would my heroine handle joining them?

Vastwarren and the seeds of the Royal Artifactual Guild were born. I wanted my heroine to be this sheltered, rose-colored glasses sort who doesn't realize that women aren't supposed to want to join. And because I'm me, and I love monster heroes, I thought about what kind of hero would be best to pair with this world and how he would relate to the heroine. Immediately I knew that he would be a Minotaur, because who else is better in an underground maze of tunnels than a Minotaur? Obviously! The bird imagery and fledglings and bird names were inspired by

Isabella Bird, because I love a really random throwback, and Magpie being the only woman in the guild was also inspired by her.

(Side note: I don't know anything about Isabella Bird's drinking habits. Magpie being an alcoholic was of my own making.)

I had to do more thinking about what sort of world would be so focused on artifacts dug up from an ancient civilization, so I placed my story in a world with feudal-society callbacks. Each hold is a small kingdom unto itself, answering only to the overall king. This causes all kinds of issues when it comes to the guild and how they deal with the holders and Aspeth herself. Holders are considered untouchable, so what do you do when one is in your midst and keeps fucking up? It was fun to find out. I also wanted their world to be one familiar with magic, but not so familiar that magical artifacts wouldn't be prized. I wanted there to be more than humans running amok—there are actually five races but not all are around at the time of the story. I wanted things to truly feel like Vastwarren had this big, heavy history behind it and Aspeth and Hawk are only experiencing a small slice.

A few other items made their way into the story that I wanted to explore—tomb robbing, for example. One of the earliest "archaeologists" was an ancient Egyptian man named Khaemweset who was a son of Ramses II. At the time that Khaemweset was alive (he was born in approximately 1285 BC), tomb robbing was already very much a thing. Egyptian monuments were being destroyed and tomb robbers would set in quickly post-burial. Khaemweset was big on exploring and preserving the ancient tombs and temples of the Egyptian people. Which sounds bananas to us because he was ancient Egyptian, but when he was born, the pyramids were already about 1,300 years old. I liked the idea of the later end of the empire excavating the *earlier* end of the empire. Just another tidbit for the trash pile!

Another tidbit is the field that Aspeth and Gwenna pass at the beginning of the book. This was inspired by my childhood visit to the Crater of Diamonds State Park in Arkansas, which is not a crater as much as it is a dirt field. You can show up and dig, and if you find a diamond, it's yours! But literally . . . you are digging in a muddy field. People have found diamonds, though! They *are* there. The Crater of Diamonds also sees thousands and thousands of tourists annually, because who doesn't love the idea of digging out a priceless object that will change your life?

Kipp was originally not going to be a large part of the book, but I kinda fell in love with the competent little guy. He was also originally going to have a talking role—like there would be a big reveal at the end that he could talk after all and just didn't *want* to—but I rather liked Kipp's unique way of communicating. Also remaining silent until the end seemed like a dick move, and that felt very un-Kipp to me. Giving him a different method of communicating was a good way to remind myself—and my characters—that everyone brings different strengths.

I have to say that while I loved writing this story, one of my favorite things to write in was Squeaker, Aspeth's fat and very spoiled cat. Squeaker is derived from my big orange goof who passed away in 2022. She was a cat that loved to sprawl on a chest to sleep, never mind that she was fifteen hefty pounds. She loved a bowl of chicken, she loved to be carried like a baby, and she would "talk" to you with meows that were practically commentary. Squeaker also shed like nothing I'd ever seen before. It did not matter how often you brushed her; the moment you petted her, hair would be flying in the air. You learned to love bringing tufts of orange hair with you everywhere, because they'd show up no matter how much you tried to avoid them. She was also lazy, and messy, and had so much personality you couldn't help but love her. I miss her every single day and adding her to this story allowed me to spend a little more time with her. If she seems ridiculous, I assure you she was, but she was also the best. 😄

So that is a bit of how this story came to be. I hope you enjoyed the peek behind the curtain, and when you ask your favorite author how a particular story came to be, don't be surprised if they vomit a lot of random nonsense at you. I swear it's coming from somewhere!

—*Ruby, October 2023*

ACKNOWLEDGMENTS

ACKNOWLEDGMENTS ARE SOME of the trickiest pages to write, because there is always that feeling that you're going to leave someone off, no matter how many people you mention. Here is my attempt at thanking everyone who had some part in things that I am aware of.

My husband, who patiently lets me gripe about the decomposition rate of dead bodies and keeps me on an even keel. Even if I wake up cranky, you're doing whatever you can to improve my mood. You're the best man I know, you always make me laugh, and I love that we have our own goofy language after twenty years together. Thank you for being my person.

My assistant, Emily Prebich, who holds down the fort when I disappear for days on end because of deadlines.

Kati Wilde, who knows more about what I've got going on than I do. I would be lost without you, both as helper and as friend. You really are an angel. A talented, sexy angel with fantastic hair.

My novel-writing friends, who let me bitch in email about the various stages of my book and how it's frustrating me that day: Lana Ferguson, Michele Mills, Celia Kyle, Kati Wilde (again), Lea Robinson, Ginny Sterling, Lissanne Jones, and Finley Fenn.

The Berkley team—you made this happen! Cindy, thank you for being as excited about this book as I am. Picture me right now making a heart shape with my hands. Your title is so much better than mine. Angela Kim and Elizabeth Vinson, who answered all my emails promptly and probably did a whole heck of a lot more behind the scenes. The art team, who put together this absolutely gorgeous package that blows my mind: Kelly Wagner for the cover art, lilithsaur for the endpaper art, and

Rita Frangie Batour for pulling it all together and blinging it up. Y'all nailed it. The colors! The edges! I'm just so in love.

Christine Masters for the incredible copyedit. You are the soul of patience. Fabi Van Arsdell (production manager) for the behind-the-scenes work, and Katy Riegel (interior design) for making the innards as beautiful as the, er, outers. Michelle Kasper (production editor) for the fantastic and thorough job you always do. I'm terrified of how sharp your mind is and also you need a raise. Thank you for the incredible job you did! Thank you also to marketer Jessica Mangicaro and publicists Stephanie Felty and Tina Joell, who worked behind the scenes to make this book happen.

My agency team, Holly Root, Alyssa Maltese, and Heather Shapiro. Y'all are on it. Your hair is spectacular, and your brows are perfection. Workwise, I would be a puddle of anxiety without all of you. Thank you for always being in my corner and making me feel like we've got it all under control, even when things might be on fire.

If I missed thanking you, please consider yourself thanked right here. Just write your name in and know that it was always meant to be there.

Thank you, _____. You're a shining star (with great hair, too).

—*Ruby*

Keep reading for an excerpt from the first book in *USA Today*

bestselling author Ruby Dixon's alien romance series

ICE PLANET BARBARIANS

Available now from Berkley Romance!

GEORGIE

Up until yesterday, I, Georgie Carruthers, never believed in aliens. Oh, sure, there were all kinds of possibilities out there in the universe, but if someone would have told me that little green men were hanging around Earth in flying saucers, just waiting to abduct people? I would have told them they were crazy.

But that was yesterday.

Today? Today's a very different sort of story.

I suppose it all started last night. It was pretty ordinary, overall. I came home after a long day of working the drive-thru teller window at the bank, nuked a Lean Cuisine, ate it while watching TV, and dozed off on the couch before stumbling to bed. Not exactly the life of the party, but hey. It was a Tuesday, and Tuesdays were all work, no play. I went to sleep, and from there, shit got weird.

My dreams were messed up. Not the usual losing teeth or naked in front of the class dreams. These were far more sinister. Dreams of loss and abandonment. Dreams of pain and cold white rooms. Dreams of walking in a tunnel and seeing an oncoming train. In that dream, I tried to lift my hand to shield me from the light.

Except when I went to raise my hand, I couldn't.

That had woken me up from my slumber. I squinted into the tiny light someone was shining in my eyes. Someone was . . . shining something in my eyes? I blinked, trying to focus, and realized that I wasn't dreaming at all. I wasn't home, either. I was . . . somewhere new.

Then the light clicked off and a bird chirped. I squinted, my eyes adjusting to the darkness, and I found myself surrounded by . . . things. Things with long black eyes and big heads and skinny pale arms. Little green men.

I'd screamed. I'd screamed bloody murder, actually.

One of the aliens tilted its head at me, and the bird chirping sound happened again, even though his mouth didn't move. Something hot and dry wrapped over my mouth, choking me, and a noxious scent filled my nostrils. Oh shit. Was I going to die? Frantically, I worked my jaw, trying to breathe even as the world got dark around me.

Then, I went back to sleep, dreaming of work. I always dreamed of work when I was stressed. For hours on end, angry banking clients yelled at me as I kept trying to tear open packs of twenties that wouldn't seem to come open. I'd try to count out change only to get distracted. Work dreams are the worst, usually, but this one was a relief. No trains. No aliens. Just banking. I could deal with banking.

And that brings me to . . . here.

I'm awake. Awake and not entirely sure where I am. My eyes slide open, and I gaze around me. It smells like I'm in a sewer, I can feel a wall behind me, and my body hurts all freaking over. My head feels blurry and slow, like all of me hasn't quite woken up yet. My limbs feel heavy. Drugged, I realize. Someone's drugged me.

Not someone. Some*thing*.

My breath quickens as a mental image of the dark-eyed aliens returns, and I look for them. Wherever I'm at, I'm alone.

Thank God.

I squint in the low light, trying to make out my surroundings. It seems to be a large, dark room. Faint orange light is emitted from small running tubes in the ceiling about twenty feet above. The walls themselves are black, and if I didn't know better, I'd say this looks like a cargo bay from some weird science fiction movie. On the wall opposite me, I count six large six-foot metal tubes lined up against the wall like lockers. Orange and green lights run up and down the sides of the tubes in a variety of squiggles and dots that might be some sort of alien writing. On the far wall, there's an oblong oval door. I can't get to the door, though, because I'm behind a metal grid of some kind.

And there's a god-awful smell. Actually, it's not just one smell, it's several of them. It's like a piss-shit-vomit-sweat cocktail, and it makes me gag. I try to cover my mouth with my hand, but my arm is slow to respond and all I manage to do is flail a little. Ugh.

I swing my drugged, heavy head, looking around the room. Actually, I'm not alone, now that I look around. There are others piled onto this side of the grid, bodies curled up and asleep. In the low light, I count seven, maybe eight forms about my size, huddled together like puppies. Seeing as how we're all on this side of the metal grid, I'm starting to suspect I'm in a jail cell of some kind.

Or a cage.

I guess if I have to be in a cage, it could be worse. There's room enough to stand, though not much more than that. At least there are no aliens in here with me. I want to panic, but I'm too out of it. This is like going to the dentist's office and getting a dose of laughing gas. I'm having a hard time focusing on anything.

My bare upper arm aches, and I sluggishly rub my fingers on it. There are several raised bumps on my arm that weren't there before, and I rub it harder, feeling something hard under the skin. What the fuck? I try to peer at it in the dark, but I can't see anything. Images of the aliens and the light shining in my eyes, the nightmares, the terror—it all rises, and I panic. A whimper escapes in my throat.

A hand touches my other arm. "Don't scream," a girl whispers.

I roll my too-heavy head until I can look over at her. She's about my age, but blonde and thinner than me. Her hair's long and dirty, her eyes big in her lean face. She glances around the room, and then puts a finger to her lips in case I didn't understand her earlier warning.

Silence. Okay. Okay. I choke the cry rising in my throat and try to remain calm. I nod. Don't scream. Don't scream. I can keep my shit together. I *can*.

"You all right?"

"Yeaaah . . ." I slur, my mouth unable to form words. And . . . I drool all over myself. Lovely. I lift one of my heavy hands to swipe at my mouth. "Thorry—"

"You're okay," she says before I can panic again. Her voice is pitched low so as to not wake up the others. "We're all a bit hungover when we wake up. They drug everyone when they arrive. It'll wear off in a bit. I'm Liz."

"Georgie," I tell her, taking time to sound out my name properly. I rub my arm and point at it, at the strange bumps. "Whattth going on?"

"Well," Liz says, "you were abducted by aliens. But I guess that one was obvious, right?"